Rosie Goodwin has worked in social services and as a foster carer for many years. She has three children, and lives in Nuneaton with her husband, Trevor, and their foster children. This is her second novel.

Praise for *No One's Girl*

'A beautifully woven tale of tangled lives . . . An author able to balance emotions, especially love, with skill and wise involvement'
Coventry Evening Telegraph

'Brilliant, a real tissue box tale, heartrending'
Daily Echo, Bournemouth

'One to make you laugh and cry'
Our Time, Cambridge

'A lovely story of two women finding their way in life – very enjoyable . . . It's a real page-turner'
Yours

Praise for *The Bad Apple*

'Goodwin is a fabulous writer and surely has a bright future. She reels the reader in surprisingly quickly and her style involves lots of twists and turns that are in no way predictable'
Worcester Evening News

'A promising and well-drawn debut'
Lancashire Evening Post

'A story of adversity and survival'
Huddersfield Daily Examiner

'A good tearjerker . . . compelling'
Reading Evening Post

Also by Rosie Goodwin

The Bad Apple

NO ONE'S GIRL

ROSIE GOODWIN

headline

First published in Great Britain in 2005
by HEADLINE BOOK PUBLISHING

First published in paperback in Great Britain in 2006
by HEADLINE BOOK PUBLISHING

A HEADLINE paperback

3

ISBN 978 0 7553 2098 1

Typeset in Monotype Calisto by Palimpsest Book Production Limited,
Polmont, Stirlingshire

Printed and bound in Great Britain by
CPI Group (UK) Ltd, Croydon, CR0 4YY

Headline's policy is to use papers that are natural, renewable
and recyclable products and made from wood grown in sustainable
forests. The logging and manufacturing processes are expected to
conform to the environmental regulations of the country of origin.

HEADLINE PUBLISHING GROUP
A division of Hodder Headline
338 Euston Road
London NW1 3BH

www.headline.co.uk
www.hodderheadline.com

For Jane.
Best friends are angels
who lift us when our own wings have trouble remembering
how to fly; the siblings God forgot to give us.

Acknowledgements

First of all, a huge thank-you to Pete Yeomans, my personal Computer Technician! Many a day or night he's rushed round to my house when something's gone wrong and got me out of trouble. You're much appreciated, Pete!

Also, a big thank you to Peter Lee, Nuneaton's historian, whom I can always rely on when doing research for a book.

Special acknowledgements to:
My husband Trevor, who supplies me with inspiration and endless cups of tea.

My wonderful children. Donna, who graduated earlier this year and fulfilled her dream of becoming a nurse, and Sarah, Christian and Aaron. I am so proud of you all. Also Steve, Jason and Rachel, their partners.

A special mention for Nikki, my lovely granddaughter, almost a little lady now. And Daniel (fusspot), and little Charlotte (Charlie Bear!). You are all so very special to me . . .

Mum and Dad.

My sisters and brother, Elaine, Christopher and Debbie.

Kerry, Janette, Heather, Shay and Kyran.

Betty and the Babes, Lena, Kate, Lesley, Anne and Nancy, always at the end of the phone to offer support, encouragement and most of all their friendship.

The wonderful team at Headline – Flora, Helena, Nicola, Jane, Joan and Alice to name but a few . . .

And of course, Philip Patterson, my brilliant agent.

Desma, and my friends in the Social Services Department who helped with research for this novel.

And last but very far from least to all readers who took the trouble to get in touch to tell me how much they had enjoyed my debut novel, *The Bad Apple*. It meant the world to me.

Author's Note

Henry Street

Henry Street Children's Home was built in 1912 at a cost of £1,470 to house 40 children. Many of those initially placed there were the children of widowed mothers who had been forced to live in the nearby workhouse.

The girls helped out with household duties around the home, whilst the boys ran errands and worked in the workhouse gardens, which gave them a chance to see their mothers.

When I was a child, my mum would tell me stories of how, on each Christmas Eve, she would go with my gran and many other local people to deliver presents for the children who lived there, and I remember feeling very sad for the poor souls who couldn't share Christmas with their families.

By the time I had grown up, Henry Street Children's Home had closed and become our local Social Services Department, and when I became a Placement Support Worker for our town, I shared an office there.

The inside of the building is just as I described it in the book, although, of course, the dormitories had been converted into offices and the boot room had become the interview room. Typical of buildings of its time, it had long corridors, high ceilings and huge sash-cord windows.

Some members of staff claimed that at times they had heard children crying. On many occasions after running an evening course, I would find myself alone there and my imagination would run riot. It was very eerie at night and sometimes I imagined I too could hear the sound of children's laughter and crying as I hastily locked up and switched off the lights, not that I ever hung around long enough to be sure!

The Department has recently moved to newer premises and Henry Street is now boarded up and empty. The corridors that once rang with the sound of children's laughter and tears are silent now . . . or are they?

Rumour has it that soon it is to be knocked down for flats to be built in its place. It will be a sad day for many of the people who lived and worked there.

The end of an era . . .

Prologue

'*Jane, be careful, sweetheart. You know what a bruiser Billy is – he'll have you over if you ain't careful.*'

Jane turned to flash a smile at her mother as she romped with her pet dog in the soft pile of autumn leaves. Up here, high on the hill, was her favourite place. From here she could see for miles across the rolling Warwickshire countryside, and she liked to pretend that this was the top of the world. But today was an even more special day, for it was her fifth birthday. 'Will the icin' on me cake be dry yet, Mam?' She giggled as Billy ran rings around her.

Joan Reynolds smiled. The gentle smile that Jane had come to know and love, the smile that could make everything right with the world.

'*Soon, my darling,*' *the red-haired woman said.* '*We'll have to be off shortly though, else your Aunty Lil will be there before us. You won't want to miss your own birthday tea, will you?*'

Jane's emerald-green eyes turned to the canal as she searched for a sight of her aunt's brightly coloured narrow boat, Firefly. *Aunty Lil was lovely too, but not as lovely as her mam, of course. No one was as lovely as her mam.*

3

Jane struggled out of the deep pile of leaves, laughing as they flew in all directions, and ran into her mother's outstretched arms, breathing in the special smell of her. No one smelled quite as nice as her mam. It was a mixture of soap and lavender, that for Jane represented everything that was clean and good.

'Will Aunty Lil bring me a present?' she asked.

Joan cuddled her daughter's small sturdy frame against her. 'I should certainly think so. She's never missed yet.'

'But what if she's too far away to get here?' Jane frowned as the frightening possibility suddenly occurred to her.

Her mother told her reassuringly, 'Wild horses wouldn't keep her away, not even if she were in Timbuctoo.'

Contented, Jane's eyes turned back to the farm far below. 'Why do the animals always shrink when we come up here, Mammy?' she asked innocently.

Her mother's chuckle hung on the air before she replied, 'It's magic, Jane.'

The child nodded, never doubting her word for a second. 'Will you read me a story out of me new book tonight?'

Instantly the woman nodded, setting her red hair dancing on her slim shoulders. 'Of course I will. Which one shall we read first – Cinderella?'

'Ooh, yes please.' Jane's eyes stretched with anticipation as she thought of the beautiful pictures of fairy princesses and handsome princes. They were all in the new book waiting for her on the kitchen table, in the small farmhouse below them.

'An' can I put the candles on me cake when we get home if the icin's dry?'

'Of course you can, all five of them. But you mustn't push them into the cake too far, mind.' Joan stroked little Jane's silky

curls, but then the child was up and chasing after Billy again, too excited to keep still.

She could see her father in a field adjoining the farm and just for a second the smile slid from her face. Her father wasn't as kind as her mam. Sometimes he shouted at her for getting in the way. 'But still,' she told herself, 'I won't have bad thoughts today,' and soon she was happily rolling around on the damp earth with Billy.

'Jane! Get up. You'll need to be changed again at this rate. Look at the state of you,' her mother called indulgently. 'You look like you've been pulled through a hedge backwards. I think you an' Billy have got more leaves stuck to the pair of you than has fallen from the trees. Come on, let's be getting home so we can put the finishing touches to your cake, eh?'

The woman stood up and held out her hand, and instantly Jane ran to her, her green eyes sparkling with excitement, her auburn curls shining in the sunlight. Life was good.

Chapter One

Canalside Farm, 1 October 1959

A cold wet nose nuzzling at her hand jolted Jane Reynolds's thoughts sharply back to the present. She looked down expecting to see Billy, but instead a large collie dog stared up at her from soulful brown eyes.

'Hello, boy. Where did you come from then, eh?' She fondled his silky ears as her eyes scanned the hillside for a sight of his owner, but at first glance it appeared that she was alone.

A whistle from a nearby copse made the dog prick up his ears, and as a young couple walked from the shelter of the trees, he suddenly lost all interest in his newfound friend, and was gone like the wind towards them. Jane saw the young woman bend to stroke him, then take the young man's hand, and together the couple once again disappeared into the copse with the dog close at their heels.

Jane turned her attention back to the panoramic view spread out before her. In the far distance, farmers appeared as small as ants as they drove their tractors in neat symmetrical lines up and down the russet and gold fields, turning the earth to darkest brown in their wake as they ploughed. Closer to, cars and lorries ran in straight lines along the old Roman Road, now known as the A5, and nearer still, the canal cut through the landscape, sparkling in the weak autumn sunshine.

Nestling against the banks of the canal beyond a small copse below her was Canalside Farm, her home since childhood. It was small by comparison to most farmhouses and Jane had always considered it to be more of a cottage. She loved every brick of the old dwelling. However, today the sight of it brought her no joy. It was a house of secrets.

Today she felt no joy in anything, for it was her thirty-seventh birthday. She was aware that to most people a birthday was something to celebrate, but to her it was just another day that emphasised the passing of time, and her utter sense of loneliness.

Today for the first time she had noticed that her vivid red hair, which had always been her most striking feature, was fading. It mattered little. Apart from herself there was no one else to care.

Tears stung at the back of her eyes as she stared down at her muddy Wellington boots and the old coat with its string belt that she wore for working around the farm. This was the extent of her wardrobe. There were no fashionable clothes for Jane Reynolds, just bare necessities.

Life was passing her by. This year, there would be no birthday presents, no party. Only a solitary card from Lil – she never forgot. Aunty Lil was the only person she had to care about now, but Lil hadn't visited the farm for months, and even when she did call by, Jane's father soon drove her away. Jane shuddered as she thought of him, and a feeling of despair settled around her like a cloak.

Her beloved mother had died many years ago. Instinctively, Jane glanced around, half hoping to see her mam as she had in her mind only minutes before. But there was nothing, save for the wind that whistled through the leafless branches. She pulled herself to her feet, aware that she was becoming lost in self-pity. Her father would soon be home from delivering the produce they grew on the farm and, birthday or not, there would be hell to pay if his meal wasn't ready. Brushing the loose grass from her old coat she set off sure-footedly down the steep incline.

'This liver's far too chewy – but then yer never were any good at cookin' liver. Yer know the sayin' – when it's brown it's cooked, when it's black it's buggered. Here, put the stuff in the bin where it belongs. I'll need a new set o' teeth if I attempt to tackle that.' Disgruntled, her father pushed the meal across the table.

Sighing, Jane lifted it and carried it to the pigswill bin. 'Well, it *has* been in the oven for the past two hours, Dad,' she pointed out in her own defence, and he frowned at her as he took his pipe from the shelf and began to stuff it with tobacco.

'Less o' yer lip, me gel – else you'll feel the back o' me hand. I called in at the Malt Shovel as it happens as I passed through Hartshill on me way home, though why

I should have to explain me movements to you is beyond me.'

'You don't have to explain, Dad. All I was sayin' is, if you'd been home on time the liver wouldn't have been a bit tough.'

'A bit tough? Huh! That's an understatement if ever I heard one. Tough as old boots is more like it. Even the pigs will have a job to get their teeth round that. I don't know – you're about as much use as an umbrella in a snowstorm. Still, we already know that, don't we? An' what's that card?' He stabbed his pipe towards the solitary birthday card on the mantelshelf.

Jane bit back the hasty retort that hovered on her lips before answering him. 'In case you'd forgotten, it's my birthday. The card is from Lil.'

'I might have known *she'd* have to stick her nose in. Wasting good money on cards. Still, that's just about what you'd expect from the likes of her. Floating up an' down the cut, week in, week out. A hard day's work would kill her, an' that no-good bloke of hers were no better,' he grumbled, as he dropped heavily into the chair at the side of the fire.

Jane could see that he'd had more than a few pints, so she bent her head across the deep stone sink of steaming water and began to wash the supper pots. Alfred Reynolds turned his attention to the newspaper that was folded on the arm of the chair ready for him. She held her breath, waiting for the tirade that was sure to follow. She didn't have to wait long, for soon he flung the paper away from him in disgust. It was the same every night and she sometimes wondered why he bothered to read the papers at all.

'Makes yer wonder what this bloody country's comin' to,' he muttered, as he stared into the flames that were licking up the sooty chimney. 'First they puts a woman on the throne, which is a surefire recipe fer disaster, if you ask me. An' then there's the bloody countryside bein' eaten up wi' housing estates springin' up everywhere yer look. Not to mention them so-called bloody tower blocks o' flats they've just built in Liverpool. I dare say they'll be goin' up around here next. I know there are plans for some in Coventry. It ain't natural, is it? I mean – to live wi' yer head in the clouds like that. An' to go on the roads now is to take your life in yer own hands. There's bloody traffic everywhere. Back in my day, yer considered yerself lucky if you had a bike, let alone a motor car.'

Jane dried her hands on a rough towel that was hanging on a hook at the side of the sink. 'I think it's called progress, Dad,' she dared to say.

He snorted with derision. 'Progress – is that what it is? Well, yer can keep yer bloody progress as far as I'm concerned. That's *your* trouble. Never gone short of nowt, you ain't. You open yer mouth an' expect to get what yer want – like the bloody bathroom yer insisted on having! Huh! There were nowt wrong wi' the tin bath hanging on the wall outside so far as *I* were concerned. It were allus good enough fer me – but no, you had to have a bathroom, didn't yer? An' yer give me no bloody peace till yer got it! It cost an arm and a leg to have installed. No doubt you'll be asking for one o' them newfangled television sets next.'

'No, I won't,' Jane denied quickly. 'But I still think an inside bathroom was a good investment. I mean, well . . . it was a bit embarrassing having to bath in front of the fire after a certain age.' She broke out in a sweat as she thought back to how terrified she had been when she had insisted on the installation of a new bathroom, but she hadn't been able to bear the old routine any longer.

'Rubbish. You ain't got nothing as I ain't seen a million times before. I reckon yer just like to come up wi' ideas fer me to spend me money on. That's the trouble wi' you women – want, want, want. Yer mother were no better.'

Jane snatched her coat from the back of the door and struggled into it as her father watched her from hooded eyes. She stared back at him, taking in the heavy jowls and the ruddy complexion that was the trademark of farmers from spending so many hours outdoors. Jane suspected that her father's complexion was also partly due to the amount of whisky he consumed, but wisely kept her opinion to herself.

Now as she walked towards the door, he growled, 'Where the bloody hell do yer think you're going?'

'To get the hens into the chicken-runs. The fox has had four this week to my knowledge. You'll be having to pay a visit to the cattle-market an' buy some more at this rate.'

'Right! I'll get me gun out later then an' see if I can't

12

shoot the bugger. Wily old sod, he'll soon find he's met his match in me. No doubt he'll be back now he's got a taste for 'em, an' it'll be all the worse fer him when he comes.'

Jane had no doubt about it, and as she let herself into the yard she sighed. Her father was not an easy man to live with, but she was used to his ways now and had learned to keep out of his road as much as she could. Even so there were times when her life seemed almost pointless, as it did today. Sometimes the terrible thoughts she had about him made her tremble with guilt. She imagined him dead in bed, dead in a field, dead at the bottom of the stairs. The thoughts would creep up on her when she least expected them and bring the colour flooding into her cheeks.

She stared up at the half-moon suspended in the black velvet sky, praying that Alfred would have drunk himself to sleep well before she had to return to the cottage.

That same night, a mile or so away in the respectable Nuneaton suburb of Chapel End, a small girl called Alice also felt afraid of her father.

'*Are you in bed?*'

Scampering away from the window, five-year-old Alice Lawrence scrambled into bed and hastily pulled the covers up to under her chin. Seconds later, the door inched open and her father's head appeared. His face creased into a frown as she stared back at him sound-lessly.

13

'*Good.* Makes a change for you to be doing what you're told for once.'

The child held her breath and prayed that he would leave. Her prayer went unanswered as Robert Lawrence strode into the room and scowled at the drawings that were littered about the bedroom floor.

'*What's all this mess?*'

She gulped deep in her thoat before whispering, 'Th . . . they're drawings that I . . . I did at school.'

'What? You call *these* drawings?' Robert Lawrence snatched one up from the floor, sneered at it then screwed it into a ball and threw it into the wastepaper basket. 'Looks more like a load of scribbles to me. But then I suppose I shouldn't expect any better from you. You're s . . . s . . . s . . . simple-minded, you are, with your blasted non-stop stuttering. Christ, it gets on my nerves. I wonder sometimes if I did right, pushing for you to go to a proper school. You might have been better off with the rest of the loonies at a special school.'

Alice wasn't sure what the difference was between a proper school and a special one, but was too afraid to ask. Tears pricked at the back of her eyes as she brushed a stray red curl from her forehead and looked fearfully up at him. She had hoped that her father would be pleased with her drawings. Her teacher had told her that they were very good, but then her father never seemed to like anything she did, although she tried so hard to please him.

He bent to retrieve the rest of the drawings and flung them into the bin to join the other one.

'Now,' he said, as he turned his attention back to her, 'just make sure that you clear up this room in the morning. It's no wonder I can never keep a cleaner or a nanny, with you so damn untidy and clumsy all the time. I don't want to find a single thing out of place the next time I come in here. Do you hear me?'

'Y . . . yes.' Alice's eyes were huge in her small face as she nodded her head.

'Right. I have a lot of papers to mark tonight so I don't want to hear another peep out of you. Is that *quite* clear?'

Again Alice's head bobbed in agreement.

He gazed at her scornfully before switching off the light, plunging the room into darkness, then turning on his heel and slamming the door resoundingly behind him.

Only then did Alice allow herself to breathe easily. She listened to his footsteps on the stairs and waited until she heard the lounge door close behind him. When all was quiet she slowly sat up in bed and her eyes returned to the bedroom window. The light from the moon was casting a pool of silver light onto the floor and she gazed at it in wonder. After a time she slid from the bed and silently crossed the floor to stare at the half-moon suspended amongst a star-lit sky. It was so pretty that it almost took her breath away. After a time her eyes moved to the shadows beneath the trees at the bottom of the garden.

Her nanny Mrs Skeggs had told her that fairies lived there, and that if she was very good, one night she might see them. She never had, but that didn't really surprise

Alice. She *wasn't* good. Her father told her every single day how bad she was, so how was she supposed to see them?

Thoughts of Mrs Skeggs, who had just stopped coming one day, brought a lump to her throat. Mrs Skeggs was just one of the many nannies her father had employed to look after her, but she had been different from all the others. Mrs Skeggs would sit Alice on her lap and cuddle her and tell her stories. The little girl hugged herself tightly as she remembered how wonderful it had felt. None of the other nannies had ever cuddled her or kissed her. They had just told her to be quiet, but Mrs Skeggs played with her and sometimes even took her to the shop and bought her sweets, just like a mummy would. She wondered when the nanny would be coming back, but was too afraid to ask her father.

A solitary tear slid down her cheek as Alice imagined how nice it would have been if she could have had a mummy like other little girls did. She had never realised what she had missed until she had started school and watched the other children's mummies kiss them at the gate.

She had asked Mrs Skeggs once why she didn't have a mummy and the nanny had gently explained that her mummy was in a place called heaven that was up in the sky. Alice had never seen her there, although she stared at the sky every single night after she had looked for the fairies.

'At least you have a daddy,' Mrs Skeggs had told her brightly, but Alice wasn't so sure that this was a good thing.

Her father had never kissed or cuddled her either, for that matter, or played with her. But of course, that was her own fault. Even at the tender age of five she knew that she didn't deserve to be loved because she was bad *and* she had a stutter, which made her father angry. He, on the other hand, was clever, because he was a teacher at the school for the bigger children next to Nathaniel Newton Infant School, which she attended.

She squinted into the shadows at the bottom of the garden again, willing a fairy to appear, but after a time her eyes moved back to the moon. Mrs Skeggs had said there was a Man in the Moon who smiled down on her, and Alice believed it. She believed everything that Mrs Skeggs told her because the nanny was so kind.

Her hand moved to her arm where a bruise was just appearing. She wished she wasn't so clumsy, then her father *might* start to love her. She hadn't meant to spill her drink all across the nice clean tablecloth – it was just that he made her nervous when he shouted at her.

Sighing, the little girl crept back to her bed and crawled beneath the blankets. Tomorrow she would try harder to be good.

Chapter Two

'*What?* You want *me* to take over the deliveries?' Jane stared incredulously at her father as a bubble of excitement formed in her stomach.

'That's what I said, ain't it?' grumbled Alf Reynolds. 'Or are yer deaf as well as daft? This arthritis in me knee is gettin' worse an' it won't hurt fer yer to get out an' earn yer keep. I didn't pay fer yer to take yer drivin' test fer nowt, yer know. What's more, if things don't improve yer might have to take over the two market days, an' all. All that standin' about all day on the stall in bad weather ain't helping me at all. Mind you, it'll mean you alterin' yer attitude if you're to be servin' customers. You're a right surly bugger just lately. In fact, come to think of it, you ain't never been no different. God knows, there's enough jobs to do about this place an' if it's me here doin' 'em they might get done right fer a change.'

Jane almost choked. She worked hard every single day from dawn until dusk, but she said nothing, afraid that he might change his mind. She had been longing for a chance to get away from the farm for years, and this was a golden opportunity.

'So, reckon yer can manage it or what then?' he

barked, pulling her thoughts sharply back to what he was saying.

She nodded, trying not to appear too eager. 'Course I can do it, Dad. Just make me a list of what needs delivering an' where, an' you can consider the job done.'

He wiped his nose on the sleeve of his coat. 'Huh! That remains to be seen. So far as I'm concerned, the proof o' the puddin' is in the eatin'. For now though yer can pop up into the village an' get me a bottle o' whisky – purely fer medicinal purposes, o' course. This here knee is giving me gyp today, I don't mind tellin' yer.'

He dropped a ten-shilling note on the table and sank down into the fireside chair, rubbing dramatically at the offending knee, and as Jane thrust her arms into her coat she watched him from the corner of her eye. Once upon a time she supposed that her father must have been quite a handsome man, but now his stomach bulged beneath his ill-fitting clothes and his hair, which had receded on top, gave him the appearance of a coarse and impious monk.

The man's hands and fingernails were caked with ingrained grime, and as Jane's eyes settled on them she realised with a little start that she couldn't even remember the last time he had bathed.

She was almost at the door when his voice made her pause. 'Jane!'

She turned back, her spirits sinking. 'What?'

His lips curled back in an evil grin from his tobacco-stained teeth. 'Don't let the fact that you'll be doin' the deliveries give yer any ideas about leavin', will yer? Your place is here. But then I don't need to tell yer that, do I? If you walk away from this place you'll have nothin', not a penny to yer name. An' besides . . . there's nobody would want yer now – is there?'

Jane turned blindly back to the door. She had to get away before she said something that she might regret. Snatching up the van keys, she took the ten-shilling note he had tossed onto the table and let herself out into the cold crisp air.

The old van that was parked next to the disused stable started first time and Jane steered it out of the farm drive into Apple Pie Lane. Once she had reached the top of the steep hill she paused to stare at the market town of Nuneaton spread out before her in the distance, its lights twinkling in the darkness. After enjoying the sight for some moments she turned the van towards Hartshill, the small village on the outskirts of which they lived. For the first time in years she had something to look forward to! She thought of the places she would soon be visiting when she delivered the produce. Alf Reynolds had a regular list of the people he supplied, but up until now he had never seen fit to show it to her. Pulling up outside the small shop on the end of Oldbury Road, Jane allowed herself a few minutes to think of what it would be like to have a break from the farm. She knew that one of the regular places on the list was the children's home in Henry Street in Nuneaton, and she found herself looking forward to going there.

A young woman walked by, her high heels clicking on the pavement. Her hair was piled high on her head in the latest back-combed fashion and Jane struggled to remember what it was called. 'Beehive' – that was it – and she was wearing one of the new shift dresses that were becoming so popular. A transistor radio dangled from her hand and as she passed, the haunting strains of The Four Aces singing 'Three Coins in the Fountain' hung on the air.

Jane grinned in the darkness. Fashions had changed so quickly during the last few years that she could barely keep up with them. Not that clothes were high on her list of priorities. Still, it was nice to see the young ones enjoying themselves.

It came to her with a little jolt that they would soon be entering a new decade. The 1960s. Time was passing her by at an incredible pace. She was thirty-seven years old with nothing to show for her life. Suddenly the happy feelings were gone as with heavy tread she climbed from the van and made her way into the village shop.

On a cold morning in December, as she prepared for her first outing, Jane heard her father say for the fourth or fifth time: 'So – are yer quite sure as yer know where yer goin'?'

'Yes, Dad. We've gone through the list a dozen times or more.'

The young woman kept her voice light, terrified that even now, Alf might change his mind and prevent her from doing the deliveries at the very last minute. She slammed the back door of the van shut and hurried around to the driver's seat with him close on her heels.

'Shouldn't take yer more than three hours at the very most.' His voice became louder as she started the engine and put the van into gear. 'An' don't forget – yer collects the money off 'em there an' then. I'll have no debtors, me.'

'Yes, Dad.' She began to reverse out of the yard, and only when she was finally driving along Apple Pie Lane did she allow herself to relax. This was it, three whole hours of freedom. There were four deliveries to make at local shops and then lastly an order for Henry Street Children's Home. Whistling a few bars from 'Three Coins in the Fountain' she glanced in her mirror and drove on.

One Saturday morning some months later, Jane entered the kitchen to find her father having a full-scale tantrum.

'No bloody wood chopped again!' he bellowed. 'What the hell have yer been doin' all day, gel? Sittin' on yer fat idle arse?'

Jane gritted her teeth at the insult. She'd been so busy that this was the first time she had entered the kitchen since early morning. Her day had begun with the feeding of all the animals, not to mention her father. She had then spent the rest of the day tending the vegetable plots that gave them their living, but it would be no use telling him that, so instead she said quietly, 'Just let me get these vegetables prepared for your dinner an' I'll go out an' get some wood chopped.'

'Huh! Don't bleedin' bother. I'll go an' do it meself. At least then I'll know the job's been done right. Things would have been different if yer mother had given me a son instead of a good-fer-nothin' gel, but the useless sod couldn't even do that.' Struggling from the chair, he pulled up his braces, which were dangling around his knees, and snatching his coat from the back of the chair he pulled it across his string vest before storming from the room, leaving in his wake a waft of foul-smelling breath that made her stomach turn.

Jane bent wearily over the task at hand, but inside she was seething with rage. Even now, after all these years, she hated her father for the way he spoke of her mother. Not that she would have dared to voice her opinions.

She had become a dab hand at doing the deliveries by now and had also taken over the markets – but things were not working out quite as she had hoped. Her father still expected her to do the same amount of work on the farm as she had before, and so now she rose with the dawn and rarely saw her bed before late at night, by which time she was so exhausted that she could scarcely crawl into it.

She watched him now as he made his way to the woodpile from the kitchen window and thought what a cruel man he was. She rarely allowed herself to acknowledge that fact, since she had discovered long ago that hating him did no good. However, today she was so tired that she found herself really loathing him. She watched the axe rise and fall, glinting in the last of the sun's rays, and unbidden, a memory sprang to mind. Her red, chafed hands became still as she drifted away into the past.

14 May 1928

*'Mammy! Mammy!' As the child's screams rang through the
house, the woman at the sink quickly dried her hands and
hurried towards the door. She was only halfway across the
kitchen when it was thrown open so violently that it danced on
its hinges and the coals on the fire crackled and spat. Jane flung
herself into her mother's outstretched arms and as the woman
held the trembling child to her she asked soothingly, 'What is
it, sweetheart?'*

*The child was so distressed that for a time she was unable
to answer, but eventually she stuttered, 'D . . . Daddy c . . .
cut the chicken's head off an' it ran round the yard. There was
b . . . blood an' . . .' Her sobs increased and she was unable to
go on, as the woman gently stroked her hair.*

*'Shush, darling.' She would have said more but then once
more the door was flung open and Jane's father appeared with
the unfortunate bird dangling from his hand. Blood dripped
onto the freshly scrubbed floor from the place where its head
should have been as Jane buried her face in her mother's skirts
in a fresh torrent of sobs.*

*The woman glared at him. 'Did you have to do that in front
of Jane, Alfred?' Her eyes flashed her displeasure but he only
grinned.*

*'For Christ's sake, woman. This is a bleedin' farm, not an
animal sanctuary. She has to know that the livestock is here
fer a reason sooner or later. What do yer want me to do, wrap
the spoiled little bugger in cottonwool? She'll be no good to
neither man nor beast, the way you ruin her.'*

As the woman detected the amusement in his tone she lost her temper. She knew that she would pay for it later, but for now she was too angry to worry about the repercussions. 'You did it on purpose to upset her, didn't you, you cruel bastard?'

A look passed between her parents that set Jane shivering again. She had never heard her mother stand up to her father as she was doing now, and the way he was glaring back at her was frightening.

'Get her upstairs out o'the way right now, else she might see sommat else as yer don't want her to.' Jane was terrified as she saw that his eyes were glittering dangerously.

Gently her mother nudged her towards the stairs door, but Jane clung to her skirts, aware that the woman was now trembling almost as much as she was.

'I want to stay with you, Mammy,' she sobbed, but her mother dragged her carefully into the hall.

'I want you to be a good girl now, Jane. Go upstairs an' don't come down again until I tell you to.'

Something about the tone of her mother's voice made Jane pause and wait outside. Within seconds, the sound of her father's raised voice reached her through the thick wooden door and although she couldn't hear what he was saying, the little girl knew that he was very angry. She stood there, unsure what to do, but then suddenly she heard her mother scream and the sound of something overturning. Terrified, she fled up the stairs as fast as her little legs would take her. Once there she dropped onto her bed and hid her head under a pillow, and there she stayed for the rest of the day.

* * *

'So, is my bloody dinner on the go yet, or what then?'

The paring knife that she was holding loosely in her hand clattered into the sink as Jane turned to stare at her father, who was struggling with a basketful of logs towards the hearth. A sick feeling rose in her throat, threatening to choke her, but she remained outwardly calm as she lifted the pan of vegetables and carried it towards the cooker. 'It won't be long now,' she informed him coldly.

There was the sound of a car drawing up outside, followed by a knock at the door. When Jane went to answer it, she found a young, heavily pregnant woman standing on the doorstep.

'Hello.' The young woman flashed her a friendly smile. 'I was wondering, could I have half-a-dozen eggs, please? I'm sorry to call so late.'

'S'all right,' Jane muttered sullenly as she shuffled away, leaving the door swinging open. She crossed to the table and quickly placed six eggs into one of the cartons that she kept ready. Closing the lid, she went back and thrust them at the woman, who dropped some money into her hand.

'Thank you, good evening.' The caller flashed her another smile and turned back to the waiting car, her flared skirt swinging in the breeze.

Jane's eyes noted the way the pretty blue blouse with the Peter Pan collar strained across the girl's heavily swollen breasts and abdomen. There was a young man waiting in the car for her and he smiled at his wife affectionately before pulling out of the yard. He was a handsome young man with hair heavily Brylcreemed into the

27

latest fashionable quiff, and in her mind, Jane likened him to Marlon Brando.

A wave of envy washed over her. They were young and obviously in love, with a family and their whole lives to look forward to, whereas she . . .

'Well – are yer going to stand there all night lettin' the cold in, or what?' her father nagged. 'I tell yer, the way yer talk to people, it's a wonder as we ever sell owt at all.'

Snatching her coat from the back of the door, Jane let herself into the yard, unable to bear to look at him a moment longer. She made her way into the field adjoining the cottage where the two latest additions to the farm were tethered. They were goats, whom Jane had affectionately named Tilly and Moses. As she approached them they strained at their tethers and nuzzled into her sides as she offered them the treats she had hidden in the deep pockets of her old coat. The sun was sinking on the horizon and darkness was casting its cloak across the landscape. The familiar feeling of lone-liness closed in on her as she stroked their wiry heads. 'Hello, you two. Had a good day, have you?'

Intent on the treats she had brought them, they ceased their affectionate nuzzling. Jane found herself thinking of the children's home she now regularly delivered to, and some of the children who stayed there. There was one little girl to whom she was particularly drawn, and she smiled as she thought of her. Her name was Susan and Jane found her highly amusing. She was a tough little character, or at least she pretended to be, but Jane could see right through the hard exterior she presented to the world, to the lonely child within. Perhaps because there was an answering loneliness in her? She thought how nice it would have been to have a child of her own, someone to love and cherish. Once upon a time, a lifetime ago, she had dreamed of having her own home and a family, like the young couple who had just called by for the eggs – but who would want her now? She stared off into the distance, wishing that her life could be different, but knowing in her heart that it never would be. What was done was done. The time for dreams was past.

Chapter Three

'Will you *please* stop that silly wailing? How many times do I have to tell you that Mrs Skeggs *won't* be coming back!'

'B . . . but *why* w . . . won't she? Is it because I've been n . . . naughty?'

Robert Lawrence sighed with annoyance as he stared down at Alice, who was sitting at the kitchen table. He supposed that he would have to tell her the truth.

'If you *must* know, it's because she's dead!'

When Alice stared at him blankly he ran a hand distractedly through his hair. It had been a real shock when the woman had died, just like that. When she'd caught a dose of flu, he'd never expected her diabetes to cause fatal complications. It was damned inconvenient, as was everything to do with this brat. It meant that he would have to start looking for a new nanny-cum-housekeeper again, and as he had discovered to his cost over the years, good ones were few and far between. At least Mrs Skeggs had been reliable. Now on top of all his other worries, he was confronted with a near-hysterical child.

'Dead means . . .' He struggled to find a way of

explaining to Alice so that she would understand. 'Dead means that Mrs Skeggs has gone to heaven,' he said finally.

Alice sniffed. 'Mrs Skeggs said that my mummy was in heaven,' she told him innocently.

Her father sneered. 'I rather doubt that,' he muttered.

Alice was completely confused now. 'So – c . . . can Mrs Skeggs come b . . . back from heaven?'

'Of course she can't!' he snapped. What little patience he had with her was fast ebbing away.

When she began to cry he stabbed his finger towards the stairs. 'Go and get into your pyjamas and put yourself to bed. I really can't be doing with this sort of performance tonight.'

Alice almost fell off the chair in her haste to do as she was told. When her father used *that* tone of voice she knew that it was wise to get out of his way.

Once she was changed, she crossed to her bedroom window as usual and stared up at the sky. A full moon was shining, and just as Mrs Skeggs had told her, the Man in the Moon seemed to be smiling down at her. But tonight there was no answering smile from Alice. Tears began to run down her cheeks and drip onto her pyjama top as she thought of Mrs Skeggs, and she dashed them away with the back of her hand. Everything had seemed better in the few brief months that Mrs Skeggs had been caring for her, but her father had said that she would not be coming back and the thought of never seeing her again was unbearable.

Mrs Skeggs had been the one good thing in her life

and now she suddenly felt completely alone. There would be no more cuddles. No one to tell her stories and play with her. From now on there would just be her and her father again.

Alice crossed to her bed and climbed under the blankets and there she curled herself into a tight little ball and sobbed as if her heart would break.

Jane lay in the old brass bed and stared at the ceiling, wondering why she couldn't hear her father pottering about in the kitchen downstairs. Lately, he seemed to spend half of his life in an alcoholic stupor, leaving most of the work to her, but he rarely lay in bed in the morning.

She looked towards the faded curtains hanging at the window. The first streaks of dawn were painting the sky in shades of red and pink and it looked set to be a fine day. This was just as well, for it would mean that she'd have a good day at the market. It never ceased to amaze her, the way the weather could influence people's lives. Should it be raining, far fewer shoppers would invade the marketplace, and Jane's takings would be down. That would then induce her father's anger when she arrived home. Still, she consoled herself – at least she had her delivery to the children's home to look forward to, whatever the weather.

In a slightly better frame of mind now, she swung her legs out of the warm bed and shuddered as her bare feet came into contact with the cold wooden floorboards. April could sometimes be very chilly. Shrugging into an old candlewick dressing gown that had been washed so many times its original colour was now lost, she cautiously crossed to the bedroom door and inched it open. Only silence greeted her as she crept along the narrow landing and down the stairs. When she entered the kitchen it was deserted as she had thought it would be, so quickly she took up the bellows and blew some life back into the fire before throwing some cobbles of coal and logs onto it. When she was sure that they were burning she filled the kettle at the sink and while she was waiting for it to boil she hurried upstairs and hastily dressed, pausing on the landing to listen at her father's bedroom door.

There was nothing, not even the sound of him snoring, so she stole back to the warmth of the kitchen, enjoying the few precious moments alone. The back of the van was piled high with produce that she had packed ready for market the night before, and soon it would be time for her to leave. She allowed herself a leisurely breakfast as she waited for her father to put in an appearance. Settling at the table she poured a second cup of tea and soon became engrossed in the daily newspaper that was one of the very few luxuries Alfred Reynolds allowed them. She was heartened to read that the new Coventry Cathedral was about to be opened to the public. It had taken six whole years to build, and Jane promised herself that if she were able to get some time off, she would visit it. There were many places of interest in Warwickshire that Jane would have loved to have seen, some of them no more than a stone's throw away from her, such as Arbury Hall, which was on the outskirts of Stockingford.

It was an old Edwardian stately home that was steeped in history, and yet Jane had never managed to visit it, for her father always found her something to do whenever she suggested going there.

Glancing at the clock she was shocked to see that it was now almost 6 a.m. and there was still no sign of him. She would have to go soon or she would be late setting up the market stall. Chewing on her lip, she wondered what she should do. Eventually she put the kettle back on to boil, deciding that perhaps she should take him a cup of tea in bed before she left. At least that might put him in a good humour.

She shuddered at the thought of going into Alfred's room. It smelled of his unwashed body and dirty socks, but then if she didn't wake him before she left, she would be in trouble when she got home, and this seemed the lesser of the two evils.

Having prepared a tray, she reluctantly climbed the stairs, pausing outside his door to tap on it as she balanced the tray precariously with the other hand. There was no reply so she tapped again and waited. After the third knock she placed the tray on the floor and inched the door open. She gagged as the rancid smell of the room struck her full force, then cautiously she whispered into the inky darkness, 'Dad, it's time to get up. Can you hear me?' Again there was only silence, although as her eyes adjusted to the light she could see the mound of his shape in the bed. Her heart began to pound as she stepped into the room.

Crossing to the curtains she opened them just enough

to allow a little light to flood in before tentatively approaching the bed.

'Dad, I have to be goin' now else I'll be late settin' the stall up. Can you hear me?' Nothing, save the sweet song of a bird in the garden outside as it heralded the start of a new day.

'Dad—' She reached out and gently shook his arm and it was then that his hand suddenly snaked from beneath the covers and grasped her wrist. His bloodshot eyes blinked up at her as she started in shock and stared at the empty whisky bottle at the side of the bed.

'I ain't feelin' so good, Jane. Why don't yer get in an' keep yer old dad warm fer a bit, eh?'

A shudder of revulsion ran through her and she struggled to free herself from his grasp. 'Get off me,' she panicked. 'I've told you, if I don't go now I'll be late settin' up.'

'Won't hurt fer one day.'

She managed to free herself and started to back towards the door, but he was already swinging his hairy legs from the bed, and she saw that he was very drunk. He must have been drinking until the early hours. She reached the landing as he tottered across the room towards her.

'Come on, lass. Be nice to me, eh?' His voice had taken on a wheedling note that made vomit rise in her throat.

'I . . . I've got to go.' Panic made her stumble across the tray she had left on the landing as she turned to run towards the stairs. Then the hairs on the back of her

36

neck stood to attention as his dirty hand again grabbed at her coat.

She tried to shake him off but he had a firm grip and he clung on as she inched along the narrow landing.

'Get back to me room *now*.' The wheedling tone was gone and now he was threatening.

With all her strength she pushed him, and losing his grip he fell back heavily against the wall. Cursing, he lunged for her again, but she was already clattering away down the stairs, intent on escaping him. With a muttered oath he dragged himself back to his feet as Jane cast a terrified glance across her shoulder. And then everything seemed to happen in slow motion, for as he lurched unsteadily towards the top of the stairs his foot suddenly caught in the loose carpet and it was as though he launched himself into the air. Jane's breath caught in her throat as he appeared to hover like a bird, his arms flailing wildly, then he was banging down the stairs as the scream that had been building in her, rent the air. He landed with a sickening thud at her feet, his head at an unnatural angle, and lay very still.

For long seconds that seemed like a lifetime she stood as if cast in stone before she breathed, 'Dad, Dad . . . can you hear me?'

When there was no response she began to tremble uncontrollably. She took a step closer, noting the way his eyes gazed unseeing up at her. His mouth was hanging slackly open, but still she could not bring herself to touch him.

Realisation hit her. *He was dead*. Her father was dead.

37

She had pictured this scene in her mind a million times. Tears washed her pale cheeks, but they were not tears of regret or even guilt. They were tears of joy, for now Alfred Reynolds could never hurt her again. Her prayers had finally been answered.

The following days at the cottage took on a nightmare quality for Jane. Knowing that her father was lying in his coffin in the front room filled her with terror. She could feel his presence so tangibly that he might almost have still been alive. And so it was that when the door opened and Lil strolled into the room like a burst of sunshine on the day before the funeral, Jane heaved a sigh of relief. Although Lil was her late mother's sister, and therefore her aunt, they had done away with the formal title many years ago when Jane reached her teens. But still she looked forward to her visits, for over the years she had come to look on Lil as her guardian angel. She was a scrawny little woman, with a passion for brightly coloured clothes. It didn't matter to Lil if they were gaudy: 'the brighter the better' was her motto. Her soft, silver-grey hair was cut short, although it was still thick, with a tendency to curl. Jane had never known her exact age, but she must be getting on because she had once glimpsed a pension book in her open bag.

'Oh, Lil!' Jane had never been one to show her emotions, but now she flung herself into the older woman's arms and began to sob out the whole sorry story of her father's death.

Lil listened and stroked her hair, then pressing Jane

into a chair she made them both a hot drink and took her niece's hands gently in her own.

Lil was a small woman but she had a big heart, and as she looked at Jane, all the love she felt for her shone in her eyes.

'I can't pretend I'm sorry to see the back of him,' she admitted truthfully. 'An' I'd be a hypocrite to say otherwise. But what I can say is, thank God I chose this time to call in. I've been down at the canal basin in Birmingham for a few weeks an' for some reason I suddenly had the urge to come an' see you.'

She smoothed her richly coloured skirts around her bony knees as she sipped at the drink she had just made. Jane looked pale and drawn, but from where Lil was standing once the shock of what had happened had worn off, her niece would be a thousand times better off without him.

'Where is he now?'

Jane shuddered as she nodded towards the front room where her father lay in his coffin on the table that was rarely used.

Lil nodded and taking a deep breath, she rose and without a word made for the front room. Once inside she closed the door quietly. The coffin lid was nailed down as Jane had requested, yet even so Lil could sense the man's presence, just as her niece had.

'May you rot in hell, Alfred George Reynolds,' she cursed as she stared down on the smooth polished surface. Then, turning on her heel, she left the room and returned to Jane.

She found her standing at the window gazing down the garden to where Lil's narrow boat *Firefly* bobbed on the water. Laying her head against Jane's broad shoulder, she whispered, 'The worst is over now, love. After tomorrow you'll be able to put your life into some sort of order.'

Jane absent-mindedly kissed Lil's grey hair and nodded, but deep inside she too felt dead. It was too late for her to have any other sort of life than the one she had known. She was destined to be lonely forever: her father had seen to that. It was a sobering thought.

The small congregation stood at the side of the open grave in the peaceful churchyard of the Holy Trinity Church in Hartshill, as the vicar solemnly intoned the words of the funeral service – hackneyed, words that said nothing of the cruelty of the man who was being buried. Only Jane and Lil were present, plus a handful of villagers who had come as a mark of respect for the daughter, and a few more who were there out of idle curiosity. Jane felt strangely detached from it all, and the vicar's words seemed to be coming from a long way away. Her eyes kept wandering to the adjacent tomb, where her beloved mother lay. She had deliberately asked the vicar to bury her father in a separate plot. Every now and again, Lil had to dig her in the ribs with her skinny elbow to bring her thoughts back to the present.

When the vicar eventually held a small wooden box full of earth out to her, Jane stared at it numbly. Suddenly realising what was expected of her, she flushed and, grabbing up a clump, threw the baked dirt into the grave. It landed with a dull thud and instantly scattered and turned to dust as it hit the coffin lid below.

Jane stifled the urge to laugh. It seemed strange that on such a beautiful May day anyone could be being buried. Her father would never feel the sunshine on his arms again. Never feel the wind in his hair or the rain on his face. Strange, but fitting as far as she was concerned. The man who was being buried had deserved nothing better.

Now the rest of her life lay before her, such as it was, for what had he left her as a legacy? Nothing but a rundown old farm and a solitary existence to look forward to – she felt that she was too old to expect anything more now. He had ensured that.

And then at last it was over and she was shaking the vicar's hand as he looked at her sympathetically and offered the usual condolences. As he turned and walked away, already intent on the rest of his day, Jane watched his vestments flap about his legs in the warm May breeze. Lil, who was standing at her side, seemed nervous and ill-at-ease, but Jane supposed that was to be expected. Lil had never made a secret of the fact that there was no love lost between her and Alfred Reynolds. But then no one liked funerals.

'Jane . . . there's something I should tell you – something as I should have had the courage to tell you years ago. Ever since your mam died I've been promisin' meself that I would, but somehow I never seemed to find the right time. Now, though . . . Well, now is as good a time as any. You see . . .'

Lil was interrupted from going any further when a stooped old woman from the village approached Jane and smiled at her sadly.

'God bless you, me love,' she said kindly. 'You were a good gel to stay with your dad all them years, so you were. It ain't often you see a father an' daughter so devoted nowadays. It were tragic, the way he went. Still, accidents happen. Life has to go on.'

She turned away and it was all Jane could do to stop herself from laughing aloud. If only she knew – if only everyone knew what her life had really been like. For the first time tears stung her eyes, and Lil, taking them for grief, squeezed her arm reassuringly.

Jane shook her off roughly. 'What were you saying?'

Lil gulped deep in her throat – the moment was gone. 'It'll keep, love.'

Jane stared at her. Lil was all she had left in the world now, but she didn't need her. She didn't need anyone any more. She had learned a bitter lesson long ago, following the death of her mother. To love someone was to let yourself in for a load of heartache, and she would never love again. This was her solemn vow as she walked away from her parents' final resting-place.

Chapter Four

The child crept down the sloping lawn, pausing as a scudding black cloud blocked out the light of the moon. She stared fearfully up at the sky, but thankfully within seconds the moon reappeared and she continued on her way. A startled chicken clucked noisily as she trod on its tail feathers. She gazed back at the curtained windows of the cottage behind her, but they remained drawn, so she crept on, shivering as the drizzling rain moulded her thin nightshirt to her body. Her dressing gown and her slippers had long since become soaked through. Alice Lawrence was now seven years old, and that night, when her father had found her staring out of the window and yelled at her to get back into bed, she had fled from him. Lost and scared, she was looking for somewhere safe to hide.

At the bottom of the garden a barge was moored in the black water; perhaps there was a space on the boat where she could shelter for the night? She moved on towards it. The water looked very deep and cold and she wondered briefly what would happen to her if she should fall in. The rain was making the grass on the canal bank slippery. She might drown. But, she decided, even that was better than having to go home to her father. It appeared that the only way to get aboard the barge was to jump, so taking a deep breath she launched herself into the air.

She hung terrifyingly for a brief second between the canal bank and the barge, but then her shin connected painfully with the side of the boat and she fell onto the deck. She heard her nightdress tear and was aware of something warm and sticky trickling down her leg. She lay there for a moment trying to get her breath back then cautiously ran her hand down her calf; this made her wince with pain. Peering around the small deck she cocked her ears listening for any sound that might indicate someone was aboard. Finally, certain that she was alone, she crawled on hands and knees towards the cabin door and tried it. It was locked, so she dragged herself into the shelter of a little wooden overhang and sat waiting for her heart to slow down.

The hoot of a lonely owl in a nearby tree pierced the silence and she shuddered in fear, pushing her wet red hair from her eyes. The boat rocked gently on the lapping water and despite the fact that she was cold and frightened, the soothing motion gradually calmed her. She drew her knees tight into her chest, and as the tears dried on her cheeks, she fell into an uneasy, exhausted doze.

Yawning, Jane stretched and dragged herself out of the comfortable fireside chair. Lil, whose knitting needles were making a furious clicking sound, smiled across at her.

'I'd best get out and shut the chickens into their runs else that damn fox will be having a feast at my expense again,' Jane explained.

It was so good to have the older woman's company. Apart from Lil she rarely saw anyone, except for the two days a week when she still ran a market stall in Nuneaton town, and when she made her deliveries. Sometimes it annoyed her that Lil obstinately refused to move in with her permanently. Following her father's death she had managed to convince herself for a time that she needed no one. But she had soon come to realise that Lil might be the only company she would ever have. She could understand her aunt's reasons for staying away when her father was alive: he and Lil had never seen eye-to-eye or even tried to. But Alfred had been dead for almost two years now and still Lil preferred to sail up and down the canal on her barge, with an energy that would have done justice to a woman half her age.

'It's me home, an' there ain't nothin' to match the leafy green Warwickshire countryside when yer sailin' through it. Heart o' the Midlands, so it is . . . But who knows, per'aps one day I'll drop anchor,' she would say, every time Jane brought the subject up. But Jane knew it was unlikely.

Now as Lil looked towards the rain that was lashing at the windows she shuddered. 'Rather you than me, love. It's fit fer neither man nor beast out there tonight.' Laying her knitting down she hurried to fetch Jane's coat from the back of the door and held it for her as her niece pushed her arms in.

'I shan't be long,' Jane promised and, calling Holly, her little white Westie, to heel, she stepped out into the bitter night.

Lil crossed to the sink and filled the kettle with water, which she placed to boil on the old hob. Glancing around the kitchen she sighed. Although it was nearly two years since Alf's death, the room remained unchanged. Now that she came to think of it, the whole farm remained unchanged. The only difference was the fact that she could now visit Jane whenever she liked, which she did on a far more regular basis. There again it suited her, too. Her beloved Wilf had been dead for over five years and somehow the canal and the life they had led had lost some of its appeal now that she was on her own. Shaking her head at the unfairness of it all, Lil hurried away to get the cups ready for their bedtime drink.

'Right, you lot – let's be havin' you.' Jane picked her way across the wet grass and herded the chickens towards a run that was built along one side of the lawn, cursing as one particular chicken evaded her efforts to shoo it inside.

'Come on now, you stupid little thing, else you'll make a tasty supper for the fox – an' it'll serve you right an' all.'

Jane frantically flapped her hands at the chicken as Holly danced around her feet.

'Holly, stop it, you daft thing. Ain't I got enough to handle with these here hens, without you startin'?' Jane's voice was impatient, but the dog ignored her and continued to bark before scampering off down the sloping lawn.

Jane fastened the door on the chicken run and cursing under her breath, she followed her pet. 'Give over, will you? That racket's enough to waken the dead. You'll have the whole bloody village out of their beds at this rate. What's so interestin' anyway?'

Coming to a halt on the canal bank she found Holly standing with her legs apart yapping at Lil's boat. She leaned forward and peered into the shadows but saw nothing. 'See, you daft mutt, there's nothin' there. I reckon you'd yap at your own shadow. Now come on, let's get inside an' get out of this drizzle before we both catch our death of cold.'

She turned and was just about to make her way back to the cottage when a resounding crash behind her made her stop dead in her tracks. Her heart began to beat a wild tattoo. 'All right then . . . I know you're on there,' she called out, 'so whoever you are, show yourself now else I'll set the dog on you.'

When only silence greeted her, Jane's heart began to settle back into a steadier rhythm. Must have been the wind blowing a bucket over, or a water rat or something, she assured herself, when a movement on the boat caught her eye. She inched closer and peered into the shadows, then swung herself onto the boat and started to walk cautiously along the deck.

'I know you're there, so you may as well come out,' she warned again. By now she was almost adjacent with the doors to the cabin and as her eyes grew accustomed to the inky blackness she saw what appeared to be a child crouching in the shadows. Her eyes opened wide in surprise.

'Good God above. What have we here then? What's a little 'un like you doin' out an' about all alone at this time of night, eh?'

Alice stared up at her from tear-drenched eyes and for a second it was hard to tell who was the more shocked of the two of them.

Jane shook her head in disbelief, then leaning towards the child she held her hand out to her. The child slapped it away, stifling a sob.

Jane stood back up and scratched her head, bewildered. 'Look, little 'un, you can't stay here all night – you'll freeze to death. Why don't you come into the cottage with me, an' then we'll see what's to be done, eh?'

Alice sniffed loudly, and stubbornly shook her head, so seeing no alternative, Jane leaned forward and lifted her, protesting loudly, into her arms. She seemed to weigh little more than a feather.

'I ain't goin' to hurt you,' she promised the squirming child, then cautiously she swung her leg over the side of the barge and clambered clumsily back up the canal bank.

When she kicked the back door open and deposited the child on the red-tiled floor of the kitchen, Lil, who was in the process of banking down the fire, stared at her incredulously.

'By the saints! What have we here then?' she gasped.

Striding past her, Jane grabbed a towel off a hook at

the side of a deep stone sink before hurrying back to the child. 'Here.' She thrust it towards her, but Alice ignored it and simply hung her head.

Lil snatched the towel back from Jane and approached Alice, and before the child could protest she began to rub at her hair.

'What in heaven's name is a little 'un like this doin' abroad all by herself at this time o' night? It ain't safe to be wanderin' around, not like it were in my day, not with all these 'ere bloody Mods an' Rockers rampagin' about. Jane, go an' fetch a jumper or somethin' as the child can slip on. She's soaked to the skin.'

'But Lil, my clothes will bury her,' Jane protested.

'So, we'll turn the sleeves up then! Just go an' get one an' do as yer told for once. We ain't plannin' on a fashion show, yer know.'

Lil began to peel the wet night things from the child's shivering body, frowning as she saw the bruises that they had concealed, but she made no comment. Instead she tried to rub some warmth into the child's blue fingers and toes until seconds later, Jane returned and passed her a Winceyette adult-sized nightie and an old jumper.

'There, that's better, ain't it?' Lil said kindly as she slipped the faded blue woolly across Alice's head and pulled a pair of thick socks over the frozen little feet. 'Now you come an' sit by the fire an' I'll get yer a nice warm drink.'

Jane followed her to the sink and once they were out of earshot she hissed, 'What the hell are we goin' to do with her?'

49

'Well, from where I'm standin' I reckon the first thing as we should do is get somethin' warm inside her. I'll be shocked if the poor little scrap ain't already caught her death o' cold. Then when she's calmed down a bit we'll try an' find out where she's from.'

Lil carried a hot drink to the child, who was staring into the fire, seemingly oblivious to their presence, and sinking to her knees she looked into her vacant eyes.

'All right then, pet. What's yer name, eh?' Her question met with no response, so she tried again. 'If you'd just tell us yer name or where yer live, we could get in touch with yer mam an' dad. They must be goin' out o' their heads wi' worry lookin' for yer.'

Alice's head suddenly snapped up and her startling green eyes flashed. 'I . . . I h . . . haven't got a m . . . mum. And my d . . . dad won't care where I am. I'm not going back to him. N . . . not ever!'

Over her head Jane and Lil exchanged a worried glance, and this time it was Jane who addressed the child.

'Why don't you want to go back to your dad?' she asked softly.

The child's eyes when she raised them to hers were full of pain. 'My d . . . dad doesn't want m . . . me. He says I'm b . . . bad.'

'I'm sure that ain't true,' Jane reassured her gently.

Alice stared back at her, her eyes bleak. 'It *is* t . . . true,' she whispered, and Jane and Lil had to lean towards her to hear what she was saying.

'I killed my m . . . mum,' she finished, then she stared into the fire as a horrified silence settled on the room.

Chapter Five

'Lord love us, what a night. Who would have thought it, eh? I ain't slept a wink, not since the coppers left. I reckon as yer could do the shoppin' in the bags under me eyes.'

As Jane looked across the table at her aunt she grinned. They were seated in the kitchen, enjoying the first cup of tea of the day, and she, like Lil, had hardly slept at all.

'I wonder where they'll take the poor little mite?' she mused, as she stirred another spoonful of sugar into her tea.

Lil sadly shook her head. 'Your guess is as good as mine. Some children's home, no doubt, till they find out who she is an' where she came from. I just hope as they have more luck gettin' it out of her than we did. Yer know, I'm really glad it was you as found her an' not me. I reckon if I'd got on that boat an' seen them big green eyes starin' at me out o' the dark, me old ticker would have conked out there an' then.'

'I doubt it,' Jane said fondly. 'You're as tough as old boots, you are. It would take more than a shock like that to finish you off. I'm just glad that you were here to help me deal with it, that's all.' She meant every word she said and shuddered to think of how she would have handled the situation had she been alone.

Looking away from Lil, the little runaway she had found on the boat the night before returned to her mind, and again she pictured those amazing green eyes, and her startling red hair. The child's hair had been the first thing that struck Jane. It was a lovely rich shade of red, which had reminded Jane of her own hair when she had been young. Jane had always prided herself on being fiercely independent. Because her mother had died when she was very young, she'd had to learn to be. But although she would never have admitted it, there was something about the child that had touched her deeply. Perhaps it was because she had recognised an inner loneliness in her that matched her own? She wasn't sure what it was, but she hoped that things would turn out well for the child.

'I wonder what the little girl meant when she said she'd killed her mam?' Lil's voice jolted her thoughts back to the present.

Jane shrugged. 'I ain't got no idea – an' to be honest I think we'd be better to put it from our minds now. The way I see it, we've done our bit by handin' her over to the authorities. What becomes of her now is none of our business, is it? An' anyway – I can't sit here jawin' all day. I've animals as need seein' to, so I'd best get to it. What are you plannin' for today anyway?'

'Well, I thought as I might head down to Tamworth and anchor up there for a bit,' Lil replied.

Jane sighed. 'You've only been here two days, Lil. Do you have to rush away so soon?'

Lil looked at her with a wealth of affection shining in her eyes. 'You should know me by now, pet. I ain't never been one fer stayin' in one place fer too long. My Wilf allus reckoned as I'd got a bit o' the water gypsy in me. I wish I could have been more like yer mam, feet firmly on the ground, God rest her soul. But that's the way of it. As different as chalk from cheese we were, even when we was nippers – in looks as well as in natures. Our mam always reckoned as I were the black sheep o' the family. It fair neat broke her heart it did, when I upped an' run off to live wi' my Wilf on the cut. "It's livin' in sin," she said, "an' it won't last." But she was wrong, weren't she? 'Cos I don't mind admittin' in front o' God Himself that I worshipped the ground my Wilf walked on till the day he died an' I never had a single regret. We didn't need to be conventional an' get wed. To our minds, marriage was just a bit o' paper. All we needed was each other.'

Jane glanced at her sympathetically, sensing the grief that her aunt's words betrayed. But Jane had never been good at expressing her feelings, and unable to come up with any words of comfort she began to heave herself up from the table. Lil pulled her thoughts sharply back to the present and eyed her niece's pale face with concern. 'Yer know, pet, yer should get yerself out an' about a bit more. It ain't natural fer a young woman like you to keep herself so much to herself.'

Jane laughed. 'I'm comin' up for forty, Lil. I'd hardly

say that were young. An' anyway, who am I supposed to go out an' about *with*? I mean, look at me. I ain't hardly what you'd call a fashion-plate, am I? Who's goin' to want me?'

'No doubt there'd be loads as would if you'd give 'em a chance,' Lil disagreed, but Jane just grinned.

'Holly!' She called the white Westie, who was dozing in front of the fire, to her feet and unhooked a dirty brown coat from the back of the door. Securing the waist with a stout length of string, she then slipped her feet into black Wellington boots.

Lil sighed with frustration. Jane never seemed to care what she looked like; it had always been that way. But if she had only made an effort, she could have been reasonably attractive. She watched her walk to the door, and when it closed behind her she dropped her wrinkled face into her hands.

'May God forgive me for the wrong I've done that poor girl,' she whispered to the empty room, then rising slowly she let herself out of the back door of the cottage and pottered away down the lawn to *Firefly*, cursing herself for the coward that she was.

Jane took a great gulp of the fresh morning air and instantly her head began to clear. It was a cold crisp morning, and as always she experienced a little rush of pleasure as she looked around her. The farm that she had been brought up on was unchanged since her childhood, lacking many of the labour-saving devices that most modern homes boasted. But that was how she liked it. The farm amounted to little more than a smallholding now, for since her father's death she had sold off most of the land adjoining it and just kept on a couple of acres. She had no regrets; the land she had kept was more than enough for her to manage on her own, and furnished her with enough space to grow the fruit and vegetables that provided her with a steady income. Twice a week she ran a stall in the marketplace in Nuneaton town centre, selling her home-grown produce and fresh eggs. But apart from that she prided herself on keeping herself very much to herself.

Now she headed for a dilapidated old barn that served many purposes. It was a garage for her rusty old van. It was also a store for the animals' foodstuffs, and a place where she could house the goats should it become too cold in their field. She bent to stroke her faithful Westie's head. She had come across Holly at an animal rescue centre soon after her father's death and had fallen in love with her sad brown eyes. It was a love affair that had flourished and grown, and now the two of them were inseparable.

'Shall we go an' see to Tilly an' Moses first then, gel? We have to look after our little mum-to-be, don't we?'

Holly wagged her tail furiously as if she understood every word her mistress said, and when Jane had filled a large bucket with the goats' food, she trotted content-edly at her mistress's heels as she headed for the goats' field.

The goats watched her approach, taking no notice of the little dog at all, and when she was abreast of them,

Jane called out. 'So, how are we doin' this crisp cold mornin' then, Tilly?' She dropped to her knees and ran her hands expertly across the goat's swollen stomach. Smiling with satisfaction she patted her affectionately. 'Ah, you won't be too long now, gel. I dare say as you'll be glad when it's all over, won't you?'

Rising, she poured the food into a metal trough that ran along the side of the hedge, and once it was full she called Holly to heel and began to hunt for fresh-laid eggs. The chickens had a habit of laying them in the hedgerows and within ten minutes her pockets were full. Next she headed for the gap in the hedge that separated the goats' field from the farmyard and walked towards the pigsty that stood in the far corner.

Two enormous pigs grunted a greeting.

'Mornin', Samson, mornin', Delilah. Are you ready for your snap then?'

She lifted a large bucket of pigswill she had prepared the night before and entered the sty to tip it into their trough. The second that it was done they lost all interest in her and turned their attention to their breakfast.

Jane yawned. 'I reckon as I could do with a bit of breakfast inside me meself,' she told Holly. 'Come on, gel, let's go an' get some bacon on the go, eh?'

The kitchen was deserted when she entered, so she lifted down a large iron frying pan and placed it on the old-fashioned range. The bacon was sizzling nicely when Lil reappeared and she sniffed at the air appreciatively.

'Cor, that smells like a bit o' good stuff,' she grinned and without being asked she began to lay the table.

Just before they sat down to their meal, Lil switched the old wireless on and the sound of The Beatles filled the room.

'Lord love us, what a din. "Love Me Do" – what sort of a bloody title is that for a song, I ask you?' Jane grumbled.

Lil chuckled as she loaded a fat juicy sausage onto her fork. 'The trouble wi' you, me gel, is you ain't with it.' Her foot was tapping in time to the music. 'Personally I never thought as anyone could sing like Billy Fury, but I have to admit to likin' these lads. I reckon as they'll go far.'

Jane raised her eyes to the rafters and, highly amused, Lil grinned. They had almost finished their meal before the topic of the child Jane had found the night before was raised again.

'Do you reckon the little 'un will be back wi' her dad by now?' Lil asked thoughtfully.

Jane sniffed, not willing to admit that she too was concerned for the child. 'I wouldn't know, an' to tell the truth, I ain't that much bothered. As I said earlier, it ain't none of our business an' I certainly ain't goin' to lose no sleep frettin' about her.'

Exasperated, the older woman said, 'Don't come that wi' me, gel. This is Lil – remember? You might like to make out as you've got a swingin' brick fer a heart to everybody else, but I happen to know different.'

Jane flushed and dropped her eyes, and for the sake of peace, Lil changed the subject.

It was well after dinnertime before Lil finally left, and Jane stood on the canal bank to wave her off.

'Now are you quite sure as you've got everythin' you need?' She asked.

'Yer must have asked me that a dozen times already,' Lil said patiently, 'so again I'll tell yer, yes I have.'

Jane frowned as she pulled her baggy coat more tightly about her. There was a bitterly cold wind blowing, and choppy canal water the colour of sludge slapped at the side of the boat as she stared off into the distance.

'You must be mad takin' off in this weather,' she muttered disapprovingly. 'I wouldn't be surprised if there weren't a frost tonight. You could wake up in the mornin' an find the cut covered in ice.'

'It wouldn't be the first time, but I don't think there's much chance o' that. It's not cold enough for snow an' ice just yet,' Lil answered, then she started the narrow boat's engine and smiled with satisfaction as it throbbed into life.

She raised her hand in a final cheery greeting and Jane waved back as her aunt steered away from the canal bank.

Jane stood there and watched until *Firefly* was out of sight before turning sadly back to the cottage. To everyone who knew her, apart from Lil, it had appeared that she and her father had lived in harmony until his death, although even Lil could have had no idea what Jane's life had really been like. She was considered by the village people to have been the perfect daughter. But Jane knew that if they ever found out the truth, they

would look at her very differently. Aching, familiar loneliness closed around her as slowly she made her way
back up the sloping lawn.

Chapter Six

'So just what the hell are we supposed to do now then, eh?' The tall, dark-haired policeman shook his head in bewilderment as he climbed into the Panda car that was parked on the driveway of the house in Chapel End.

His colleague sighed. 'I ain't got the foggiest idea. I don't mind tellin' you, in all me years in the Force I ain't never come up against a situation like this.'

They had just been to inform Mr Robert Lawrence, who had reported his small daughter missing earlier that night, that she had been found safe and well. But they had not received the response they had expected – far from it, in fact.

'That bloke must have a heart made of stone,' the first policeman said quietly. 'I mean, most people would be goin' out of their heads with worry if a little one went missin'. I know I bloody well would if it were one of mine – but him! How can he turn round and say, cool as a cucumber, that he don't want her back? She's his own flesh an' blood, for God's sake. An' it can't be money worries, can it? Not lookin' at the house – it's like a little mansion inside. Another thing – where was the child's mother? Funny, ain't it? That she weren't about, I mean.'

The policeman who was sitting at the steering wheel nodded in agreement. 'There ain't much more that we can do at the moment. We'd best get back down the station an' then leave them to handle it. No doubt they'll call in the Welfare Department.'

'I suppose you're right!' The first policeman lifted the radio. 'Come on, I'll radio ahead to tell them what's happened and then we'll slip down there an' see what's to be done.'

His colleague started the car and within minutes they had reversed off the drive and were on their way.

'What the hell do you mean – her dad doesn't want her back? What does he expect us to do with her then?' The Desk Sergeant stared at the two officers as if they had taken leave of their senses, as they shuffled from foot to foot uncomfortably.

'Don't ask me, Sarge,' the taller of the two said. 'We're just tellin' you what he said. There was no shiftin' him. He was quite adamant, in fact. The only thing I can suggest is you get in touch with the Welfare Office an' get them to send someone out to try and reason with him.'

'I suppose you're right,' the Desk Sergeant admitted reluctantly. 'Meantime, I've got the poor little soul in the office through there.' He nodded across his shoulder. 'I could hardly lock her in a cell, could I? Why don't you two go through an' keep her company while I phone the out-of-hours' Children's Officer.'

'Right you are, Sarge.' The two men filed past him

and disappeared through a door as the harassed Sergeant lifted the phone.

When the two policemen entered the room where Alice was waiting, her eyes almost popped out of her head with fear. Her father had always told her that if she continued to be bad, a policeman would come and take her away and she would be locked up for ever. Now, Alice was convinced that that day had finally come and it was all her own fault for running away.

Yet when they approached her and bent to her level their eyes were kind and their voices soft.

'Don't cry,' the older of the two said gently, and fumbling in his pocket he produced a chocolate bar as if by magic. He held it out to Alice but she was too afraid to take it so he put it down on the huge desk beside her, within her reach. Taking off his helmet he winked at her as he looked over his shoulder at his colleague.

'How about if my mate here were to go off to the canteen an' get us all a nice drink, eh? An' while he's gone I could perhaps tell you a story?'

Slightly reassured, Alice nodded and knuckled the tears from her eyes as he squeezed onto the seat next to her.

It was almost three hours later when the door swung open and a well-built, grey-haired woman with piercing blue eyes approached the desk.

Sergeant Fitzgerald looked up from a report he was writing. 'Can I help you?'

She nodded solemnly. 'I'm Angela Wilson, the Duty Children's Officer. I am here regarding Alice Lawrence, the child who went missing earlier this evening. I believe you have Alice here?'

The Desk Sergeant nodded quickly, relieved that she had come. 'Yes, we have. It was me who spoke to you earlier. She's in there fast asleep in the chair, poor little mite. Have you managed to speak to her father?'

'Oh yes. I've just spent nearly two hours with him, not that it did a scrap of good.' She ran her hand wearily across her eyes as the policeman frowned.

'What – you mean that he's still saying he doesn't want her back?'

'Not only does he not want her back, he wants her to be put up for adoption. I must have every single item of clothing the child possesses in the back of my car. He'd packed everything she owned by the time I got there. It's almost as if he can't get rid of her quickly enough.'

The man's face registered his horror as he stared back at her. 'So what will happen to her now then?'

Angela Wilson shrugged. 'Well, obviously I shall have to make some alternative arrangements for her. I'm hoping that they'll have a bed at Henry Street Children's Home available while we decide what we're going to do with her. Would it be possible for me to use your phone so that I can speak to the housemother there?'

'Of course.' He lifted the flap on the desk to allow her through and she followed him into a room where Alice was curled up in a chair fast asleep.

'She's a lovely child, ain't she?' the policeman whispered, as Angela stared at her sadly. 'Do you reckon her father will have a change of heart?'

She shook her head. 'Not a chance. There's a lot more to this than meets the eye, unfortunately. From what he told me, it's been coming for a long time. But now if you don't mind I'll start on the phone calls I need to make. I may have to pop round to Henry Street to put them in the picture. Will it be all right to leave Alice here with you for a little longer?'

Sergeant Fitzgerald motioned to a phone on a desk in the corner of the room. 'Take as long as you need,' he told her obligingly. 'It would be a shame to disturb her anyway. The poor little soul looks worn out.'

It was another hour before Angela finally drove round to Henry Street. Julia, the housemother at the children's home, had a large pot of tea ready and waiting for her in her office, and she smiled at her sympathetically as Angela stifled a yawn. The first cold fingers of dawn were just lighting the sky and the Duty Officer looked totally worn out. It had been a very long night.

'So – this is a bad state of affairs, isn't it?' Julia kept one eye on Angela as she poured the tea.

Angela nodded wearily. 'You can say that again. I don't think I've ever dealt with a situation like this before, and just between you and me I hope I never have to again. I went out to the child's father thinking that I would be able to resolve the situation, but believe me, I think there's very little chance of that now.' She sipped gratefully at the tea and began to repeat the sorry story that Robert Lawrence had related to her.

'Alice's father is an English teacher at Hartshill School and he has a lovely home in Chapel End. Apparently he and his wife had a wonderful marriage. There was only one thing missing – a child. They had tests done earlier on in their marriage that showed the problem lay with him, so at her insistence he underwent hospital treatment. Unfortunately, the couple still remained childless until the wife, Mary, was forty-three years old – when she suddenly informed him that she was pregnant. It seems that Robert had long since given up hoping for a family, but after the initial shock had worn off, he was pleased about the baby. She was ecstatic, apparently – he admitted that it had always been her that wanted children more than him. At one stage in their marriage, it had become almost an obsession with her, but then as the years went by and nothing happened, she settled into what he described as a dull acceptance of the situation.' Angela paused to take a bite of a ginger nut biscuit, and Julia refilled her cup.

'Anyway, she got to about six months and her health started to deteriorate. She developed blood-pressure problems and on top of that she became diabetic. Her age for a first baby was against her as well, and according to Robert, she started to get very depressed. At first he put her mood swings down to her condition. The hospital wanted to admit her at this stage and keep her in for bedrest until after the delivery, but she refused to go, saying that she wanted to get the nursery perfect for when the new baby came home. So, another month went by and one night he came home to find her sobbing. When he asked her what was wrong, she eventually broke down and admitted that the child she was carrying wasn't his.'

Julia gave a little gasp and the two women exchanged a look of compassion. It wasn't the first time this had happened in a family, and it certainly wouldn't be the last.

'Needless to say he was devastated and they had a flaming row,' Julia went on. 'She told him that she'd had an affair with a man at the office where she worked, purely to try and get pregnant before she was too old. She swore that she had no feelings for the man, but Robert was in no mood to talk about it and ended up storming out of the house. When he went home some hours later after he'd cooled down, he found her lying in a pool of blood on the bathroom floor. He phoned an ambulance, but by the time they got Mary to the hospital, her blood pressure was so dangerously high that they had to perform an emergency Caesarean. Sadly, complications arose during the birth and Mary died, leaving him with a child that he felt he could never love.'

Angela got up and paced the room for a minute or two. She turned to face Julia. 'And so there you have it. Unfortunately, over the years things have gone from bad to worse and tonight's episode, her running off like that, made up his mind. I offered him various kinds of support, everything that I could think of, but he's quite adamant that he doesn't want her back. The fact that she has certain learning difficulties is hard for him to come to terms with, being a teacher himself. He wants to put her up for adoption and I don't think there is anything we can do to change his mind. In fact, he's already applied for a teaching post in Leeds and informed me that as soon as he's sold his house he'll be moving up there. So that, I think, is the end of that.'

'Oh dear.' Julia's brow creased with concern. 'It's a good job there's a place available here then, isn't it? Where's Alice now?'

'Still down at the police station. I'm going to drive over to pick up a colleague shortly and then we'll go and bring Alice here. I'd like to get her dressed first though. At the moment she's wearing a nightdress and a jumper that the lady who found her lent her. I don't want her to come like that or the other children will be more curious than ever.'

'You're not wrong there,' Julia admitted. 'Children can be cruel and it sounds like the poor little mite has enough on her plate as it is without having to be a figure of fun.'

Angela rose and extended her hand. 'Right then, I'd better go and fetch her. No point in delaying it any longer than we need to. Thanks for the tea.'

As Julia escorted her to the door she smiled reassuringly at the other woman. 'I'll be waiting – and don't worry. I'll do all I can for her whilst she's here.'

'I know you will,' Angela said, but underneath she was thinking, *Will it be enough?* After all, how could any child ever get over a rejection like the one Alice was about to face, even with all the kindness in the world?

Chapter Seven

'Here we are then, lovey. I'll just get your case out of the boot and then we'll go inside to meet Julia, shall we? I'm sure that you'll like her!'

Janet Taylor, Angela's colleague, was in the back of the car with Alice and as Angela Wilson heaved her ample frame out of the driver's seat and hurried around to the back of the car, she smiled and squeezed her hand reassuringly.

Alice stared out of the window at the bleak façade of the children's home. It looked cold and impersonal and very, very big.

'You'll like it here,' Janet told her, but Alice ignored her. Soon Angela reappeared and Alice felt herself being lifted bodily out of the passenger seat and stood on the concrete. Her heart began to thump wildly, and when the big woman grasped her hand, it was all Alice could do to stop herself from snatching it away.

Janet appeared at the other side of her, and she was led into the home. They passed through a heavy wooden door, and when it banged to behind them, echoing hollowly in the long corridor, Alice jumped. She noticed immediately that the inside of the home was almost as bleak as the outside. There were no pretty pictures on the walls here like there were at home. No soft rugs on the floor, only tiles, and she listened as her shiny patent-leather shoes made a tap, tap, tapping noise as the women whisked her along. All of the doors leading off the corridor were painted a dull cream colour. At last Angela paused outside one, and knocked on it.

'Come in!' A voice carried to them from the other side and Angela led her into a room with a very high ceiling.

'Ah, hello there. You must be Alice.' A lady with pretty brown hair and a nice smile rose from behind a desk and came to greet her. 'We've been expecting you, my dear. Welcome to Henry Street Children's Home. I hope you'll be very happy here with us. I'm Julia Tuffin, the house-mother, and you'll be seeing rather a lot of me.'

The little girl stared back at her from huge, bewildered eyes, and Julia felt a pang of sympathy.

'She's feeling a little nervous,' Angela explained.

Julia nodded. 'Well, that's understandable, but don't worry, Alice – you'll soon get used to us all. At the moment, most of the other children are at school. You'll get to meet them all tonight. In the meantime, I'll ask Susan Cotton to show you around and keep you company. Susan has lived here for a long time. You're going to be sharing a room with her. She's off school today with a sore throat, or at least she says she's got a sore throat, but just between you and me, I think she's pretending.'

She winked at Alice conspiratorially, but the friendly gesture met with a blank stare.

Undeterred, Julia went on, 'Right then, I'll just give Susan a shout and you can go and get settled into your room. Angela and I have lots of paperwork to do, but later on we'll talk again. Will that be all right?'

Alice nodded, as Julia walked to the door. 'Susan!' Her raised voice echoed along the corridor, and in seconds Alice heard someone mumbling as they stamped across the tiles.

'*Now* what do yer want?' A girl with a mop of mousy-coloured hair and a liberal sprinkling of freckles across her nose appeared at the door.

'Susan, this is Alice. She'll be sharing your room with you, as I told you earlier. I wondered if perhaps you could take her upstairs and help her to get settled in whilst I get all the paperwork out of the way?'

Susan sighed heavily. 'Cor blimey, there's no flippin' peace fer the wicked. I'm about done in, I am. It would have been easier at school. Come on, kid, follow me.'

When Alice made no move to join her, the older girl raised her eyes to the heavens in exasperation. 'Come on, I ain't got all day, yer know.'

Tentatively Alice took a step towards her, as with comparative ease for her skinny frame, Susan swung her suitcase off the floor.

'I'll get Glen to carry that up for you,' Julia offered.

Susan glared at her disdainfully. 'Ain't no need for that – I ain't a weaklin', yer know.'

Ignoring the amused twinkle in Julia's eye, she grasped Alice's hand firmly, then without so much as another word or a backward glance, she yanked the new girl out

71

of the room. They turned right and walked a little way until they came to a tall staircase.

'This way,' Susan informed her shortly, as they began to climb. 'Our bedroom's at the top o' the stairs on the right. Only here we don't call 'em bedrooms. We call 'em *dormitories*. Mine, or should I say ours, is number four an' we're lucky 'cos there's only two beds in this one. Some of 'em 'ave four in.'

Breathless, they reached the top of the stairs. Alice found herself on a small landing with an identical staircase to the one they had just climbed leading away down the opposite side.

'That's the boys' staircase,' Susan explained as she placed the heavy suitcase down for a minute. 'An' that door there leads to the lads' dormitories. We girls ain't allowed past there an' they shouldn't come through here. But sometimes they do.' She chuckled as, leaning towards Alice, she lowered her voice. 'One o' the older girls as lives here an' one o' the older lads is courtin'. I caught 'em snoggin' on the landin' the other day. I made 'em promise to slip me a bit extra on pocket-money day, else I'll tell on 'em to Moanin' Maggie. That's what we call Margaret – she works here an' all. But actually she's all right really. Most of 'em are if you know how to butter 'em up. 'Cept fer Nora, o' course – an' you'll get to meet her later, more's the pity.'

She dragged Alice to a door further along the landing. 'This is it, kid.'

She threw the door open and nudged Alice before her into the room.

The bewildered girl looked around her as Susan threw her suitcase onto a neatly made bed. It was covered in a beige candlewick bedspread. At one side of the bed stood a heavy wooden wardrobe and on the other side was a matching chest of drawers. Directly opposite was Susan's bed, with an identical wardrobe and chest of drawers at either side. A huge old sash-cord window took up almost the entire end wall, and faded pink curtains hung limply at either side of it. The floor was covered in drab linoleum, and the walls were painted in the same dull cream as the doors. In a far corner, a cracked white sink leaned drunkenly against the wall. Alice thought that she had never seen such a horrid room, and suddenly the lump that had been growing in her throat all morning, swelled and threatened to choke her. Big fat tears glistened on her lashes as Susan stared at her, horrified.

'Hey, come on, kid. Don't yer dare turn cry-babby on me. It ain't that bad here. In fact, once you've got used to it, it's all right.' Curious now, she looked Alice up and down. 'How old are yer, anyway?'

Alice gulped. 'I . . . I'm s . . . seven.'

'Bloody hell, yer just a babby then. I'm nearly ten – been here five years, I have, ever since me mam died. Has your mam died?'

'Y . . . yes, a l . . . long t . . . time ago.'

'So where's yer dad then?'

'He's g . . . going a . . . way.'

'Snap, so has mine. At least I imagine he did. Pissed off an' left me mam when she were havin' me, he did.

73

Mind you, it's never much bothered me. It's like they say – what you've never had yer never miss, do yer?'

Alice hung her head as Susan unlatched the suitcase purposefully.

'Come on then, I'll help yer get this lot unpacked, then I'll show yer round a bit. Not that there's that much to see, mind.'

She began to fling underwear and woollies haphazardly into the drawers and then she hung Alice's dresses none too tidily in the wardrobe.

'Some o' this gear must have cost a fortune,' she commented. 'Is yer dad rich, or what?'

Alice shrugged, not quite sure what rich meant. 'H . . . he's a t . . . teacher,' she stuttered.

Susan nodded. 'Ah well, that explains all the posh clobber then.'

Finally she threw Alice's pyjamas across the foot of the bed and stood back to survey her handiwork.

'There yer go, all done and dusted. An' not a bad job, even if I do say so meself.'

She turned her attention back to Alice, and helped her as she shrugged her arms out of her warm coat. Susan took it off her and then that too was flung into the bottom of the wardrobe.

'Right, come on. I'll show yer round now – but don't expect too much. Like I said, there ain't that much to see really. It's just so as you'll know yer way about, like.'

Alice dutifully followed her back along the landing.

'This is the girls' bathroom.' Susan swung back a heavy door and the hinges creaked loudly in protest.

Alice looked inside. A big white bath on heavy metal feet stood against one wall. On the other wall was a toilet and an impossibly high ceramic sink. Every wall was covered in white tiles, many of which were cracked, and Alice thought that it looked very cold, although she didn't dare to say so.

'I reckon as you'll need a hop-up to reach that sink,' Susan teased her. 'But don't worry, there's some showers further along. Trouble is, the water's allus freezin'.' Again she trotted off with Alice close on her heels. She paused at another door. 'The showers are in there. An' that door over there is the bedroom that the night staff sleep in.'

She led her back down the staircase and into an enormous room. Easy chairs formed a circle around a large square television set in a far corner, and in the opposite corner was a dilapidated snooker table. The felt was ripped and it leaned at an odd angle.

'The lads use that mostly,' Susan told her. Alice nodded solemnly.

'There are some books on that bookcase over there, look. Not very good ones, mind yer. An' them boxes over there is full of toys an' games, though half the games have got bits missin'. We always get people turnin' up out o' the blue at Christmas bringin' us presents, but most of 'em is a load o' rubbish. I reckon as everybody thinks we're all babbies as live here. Still, I suppose it's the thought that counts at the end o' the day, ain't it? Come on, I'll show yer the kitchen an' the boot room next.'

The tour continued and Alice's head began to spin.

There were so many rooms and so much to remember that she was sure she would get lost the second that Susan left her side. By teatime she was completely exhausted and couldn't eat a single thing.

Julia and another lady that Alice had noticed when she arrived went off duty at six o'clock. Julia promised her on her way out that she would speak to her in the morning, and as they left, two other women, one dark-haired and one fair, replaced them.

'Watch her,' Susan whispered to Alice, as she prodded her in the ribs with her elbow and nodded at the dark-haired one. 'She's a stickler fer the rulebook, she is. "Nasty Nora" we call her. Wi' most of the staff yer can get away wi' murder if yer know how to get round 'em, but her – phew! You have to mind yer p's and q's when she's about. The only time I've ever seen her be nice is to babbies. But we don't get too many of them come here, an' when they do they find homes quick as a flash. The other one is Margaret an' she's nice. Lets yer get away wi' murder she does, so most o' the kids here like her.'

Alice watched as the two women hung up their coats. The fair-haired one called Margaret was pretty, with kind eyes that twinkled when she smiled at you. The dark-haired one looked slightly younger but Alice noticed that her eyes were sad and she wondered why.

When they both began to walk towards her, Alice's heart missed a beat.

'Hello there. Julia told us that we had a new girl here. You must be Alice,' Margaret smiled.

76

Alice nodded but kept her mouth firmly clamped shut.

'I hope you'll be very happy here,' Margaret told her kindly. 'And I hope that our Susan is looking after you?'

Alice's head again bobbed in agreement, and sensing her distress, Margaret's face softened with sympathy. 'If there's anything at all that you find you need, don't hesitate to ask either myself or Nora.' She smiled encouragingly, then both women turned and disappeared into an office that led off the main hall.

'See what I mean about Nora?' Susan muttered as soon as the women were out of earshot. 'She's mean, that one is.'

'She l . . . looks sad,' Alice stuttered.

Susan threw back her head and laughed aloud. 'Yer won't say that when yer get to know her, not when you've felt the length of her tongue.'

Alice noted that Nora hadn't said so much as a single word to her and her terror increased. By now she was feeling so lonely and completely out of place that she just wanted to go home and hide beneath the covers on her own little bed. But she knew that could never happen now. She was bad, her father had always told her so, and now she would never see him again. The thought was frightening, for although at times she had feared him, he was the only constant person she had ever had in her short life, and now that he was gone she had no one. From now on she would have to share a room with Susan and she would never see her own bedroom again.

She had been an object of curiosity ever since the rest of the children had arrived back at the home from school, and now she just wanted to be left alone. It was almost a relief when Susan finally led her back to their room at bedtime. Some of the older children were still downstairs in the day room playing Elvis Presley records on an old portable record-player, and she felt their eyes on her as she hurried along behind Susan. She washed herself at the cracked sink in the corner of the bedroom, aware of Susan looking at her bruises as she pulled her pyjamas on, but thankfully the older girl made no comment and soon Alice clambered into bed. The cold cotton sheets made her shiver, and at long last, the tears that had been threatening all day welled in her eyes and spilled unchecked down her cheeks. She heard Susan turn off the lights and climb into her own bed.

'Ah well, I suppose if I've got to share a room I'm lucky to have dropped on a quiet 'un. You've hardly said two words all day. Are yer allus this quiet?'

There was no answer. Susan glanced across at Alice's bed and in the dim light that struggled through the thin curtains she saw her slight frame trembling beneath the bedclothes. She realised that Alice was crying, and chewed on her lip, wondering what she should do. Alice's silent tears progressed to harsh wracking sobs, and eventually, unable to ignore it any longer, Susan swung her legs out of bed and padded across the cold lino. Tentatively she placed her hand on Alice's shoulder.

'Come on, kid. Give over – you'll have me at it in a minute if yer don't pipe down.' She felt tears sting her own eyes as she remembered back to her first night at the home, and how lonely she had felt. She guessed that Alice must be feeling the same now.

Hastily coming to a decision, she peeled back the thin blankets and self-consciously climbed in beside her. Then roughly she pulled Alice's skinny little body into her arms and cradled her against her own, bony chest. 'Calm down now,' she urged. 'I'll stay with yer till yer get to sleep. Things won't look half so bad in the mornin', you'll see. But don't yer dare tell none o' the others, mind. They'll think as I'm goin' soft.'

Alice's arm snaked around her waist and very slowly the harsh sobs subsided until at last, exhausted, she sank into an uneasy sleep.

'I'll just give her another minute or two to make sure as she's properly gone off, an' then I'll get back to me own bed,' Susan muttered to herself. But she was so warm and comfortable that soon she too was fast asleep, so Alice spent her first night at the home wrapped in the older girl's arms.

Chapter Eight

Downstairs in the office Nora Fitton pulled Alice's file towards her and began to read. She liked to know as much as she could about the children who came to stay at the home. The report was very brief at the moment. It seemed that as yet, there was very little known about the reasons for her being put into care. But even so, as she read the report, the colour drained from her face and she found it hard to breathe as a name leaped off the page at her. *Robert Lawrence.* Her heart began to thump wildly as memories that had lain just below the surface for many years resurfaced. She read on, her eyes hungrily scanning the pages. The child was seven years old and the family home was in Chapel End. Her late mother's name had been Mary. It was just too much of a coincidence. It had to be *her* Robert, and Alice was the child that had ruined her life.

Scalding tears pricked her eyes and she angrily knuckled them away. She hardened her heart and after a time a bitter smile played around her lips. So – the child Alice was Robert's daughter, eh? She stared again at the girl's address and the forwarding address on the file for her father in Leeds. Snatching up a scrap of paper, she hastily scribbled it down and pushed it into the pocket of her skirt. At last it was time for revenge.

The next morning, a Saturday, Alice awoke with a start. On the landing, doors were banging, and she could hear people laughing and shouting. For a moment she lay still, totally disorientated, and then slowly the happenings of the day before came back to her. Her cheeks felt stiff and sore, where the tears had dried on them. Cautiously she turned her head to look into Susan's sleeping face. Afraid to disturb her, she lay perfectly still, until at last Susan stirred. She yawned and stretched her legs down the bed, then her eyes slowly opened and as she saw Alice solemnly surveying her she flushed with embarrassment.

'Oh Christ, I must have fell asleep an' bin in wi' yer all bloody night.' Pulling her arm from underneath Alice, she clambered clumsily out of the bed. 'Come on, shake a leg an' get yerself dressed. Cook allus does us a fry-up on a Saturday mornin'.' She shuffled away and began to pull on the clothes that lay in an untidy heap on the floor at the side of her bed.

Alice did as she was told, and once she was dressed, Susan tugged a brush none too gently through her hair.

'There then, you'll do. I don't know, I feel as if I'm yer bloody mother. I'll have to watch it else the others will be takin' the rip out o' me. Now, come on. I ain't prepared to miss me fry-up fer you nor nobody else.'

Obediently Alice followed her, and soon they were seated in the dining room. Plates piled with sausage, bacon, eggs and tomatoes were placed in front of them.

Susan lifted her knife and fork and licked her lips in anticipation. 'Cor, this is just what the doctor ordered. This place might not be the Ritz but yer can't fault the fodder.' Alice was temporarily forgotten, as with an appetite that would have done credit to someone twice her size, Susan tucked into her breakfast.

Alice made a valiant attempt to eat, but all the curious eyes on her made her hands tremble.

One boy who was sitting directly opposite her was paying her particular attention. 'What's your name then, Carrot-top?' he grinned.

Alice watched fascinated as he shovelled food into his mouth at an alarming rate. 'A . . . Al . . . Alice.'

He collapsed across the table in a fit of giggles as Susan glared at him. 'Leave her alone, Steven Mann, else I'll clock yer one.'

'Ooh, hark at Susie. Gone all soft, have you?'

'No, I ain't. I just think as yer should pick on somebody yer own size fer a change, that's all.'

'Huh, I'm sure as little Carrot-top here can stick up for herself.'

The interchange was stopped from going any further when a member of staff appeared in the doorway.

'Cotton, Mann – enough now, the pair of you! Please try and behave like human beings – at least whilst you're at the dining table.'

Susan raised her eyebrows at Alice, and Steven scowled. Alice's appetite had completely disappeared and she stared miserably at her plate. Once Susan had cleared her own she glanced hungrily at Alice's. 'Don't yer want that?'

When the little girl shook her head, Susan instantly stabbed a sausage.

'Ah well, waste not want not, that's what I say. I'll polish it off fer yer.'

In minutes Alice's plate was cleaned too and Susan sat back and patted her bloated stomach contentedly. 'Ah, that's better. Ready for anythin' now, I am.'

When she stood up, Alice almost tripped in her haste to follow her newfound friend into the corridor, causing Steven to smirk with amusement.

'Look kid, you'll have to entertain yerself fer a bit now,' Susan told her, and Alice's face fell.

'I usually go for a wander off down to the library on a Saturday. Why don't yer go out into the garden fer a while? Glen's got it really nice out there. He's the odd-job man; he talks a bit posh, like, but he's a good sort really. It's just across the playground at the back, through the gate.'

Alice nodded miserably as she watched Susan walk away. Then slowly she slipped out of the side door. Anything was preferable to finding herself alone with Steven. The playground, which was little more than a square covered in tarmac, was deserted and she was almost at the gate when a voice halted her.

'Hello there. You must be Alice.'

She started and looked in the direction of the voice. A tall man with dark hair, greying at the temples, and twinkling grey eyes was smiling at her.

As he approached her he held out his hand. 'I'm Glen. I do all the odd jobs about the place. Was I right in thinking that you're Alice, then?'

'Y . . . y . . . yes.'

'Ah, well then, Alice, we'd better start as we mean to go on.' He winked at her and delving into his overall pocket, produced a boiled sweet with a flourish. Bending, he put it into her hand and was rewarded with a glimmer of a smile.

'Were you just going to have a look at the garden?' She nodded.

'Right, I'd better open the gate for you then. It can be a bit stiff.' He walked ahead of her and swung the wrought-iron gate back on its hinges. 'There you are, madam. I'm afraid it's not the best time of year for the garden. Most of the flowers are over now. But it was a picture in the summer, even if I do say so myself.'

She stepped past him and looked around. It was nowhere as big as the garden she had back at home. In one corner of the lawn was a bench, and at the side of that was a slide and a swing with a rusty frame. All at once a wave of homesickness swept over her. He watched as her eyes filled with tears then bending to her level he patted her shoulder. 'Don't cry, Alice, you'll be all right.'

She heard the kindness in his voice and slowly reached out and took his hand. She liked this man, although she had only just met him. The feeling was mutual.

'I . . . I'm seven.'

'*Really!*' He made a big show of being amazed. 'Well, I never. You being such a big brave girl I thought you must have been seven for ages.'

She blinked rapidly and a little smile hovered around her lips. 'I . . . was seven two weeks ago.'

'Well now, you be sure and let me know exactly when it was. I'll have to see if I can't manage a little present and a nice birthday card.'

He rose slowly, strangely reluctant to loose her hand. 'Come on, little one, I'm afraid I've got a list of jobs as long as your arm to do. But I'll tell you what. It's too cold for you to be standing about out here so I'll take you into the kitchen first and we'll see if Cook can find you a nice biscuit and a drink. How would you like that?'

She nodded and together they walked back into the home, he matching his steps to hers. She was formally introduced to Cook, who was a large pleasant lady, and soon found herself seated at the most enormous table she had ever seen, sipping warm tea and dunking biscuits. It was while she was there that one of the older girls she had seen at breakfast stuck her head around the kitchen door.

'Are you Alice Lawrence?'

Alice nodded.

'Good. Julia wants you in her office.'

Alice paled, wondering what she had done wrong. But obediently she slithered off the stool and followed the girl along the corridor. When they came to the office door the girl stopped and pointed.

'Julia's in there.' She paused to wipe her nose on the sleeve of her cardigan as she stared at Alice curiously. 'You don't say much, do you?'

'N . . . n . . . n . . . no.' Alice was so afraid that her stutter was even worse than normal.

The girl giggled cruelly. 'Blimey, it's no wonder, is it? With a stammer like that I'd keep me trap shut an' all.'

She swaggered off, chuckling to herself, and Alice saw Steven Mann come out of the boot room to join her. She was aware of them pointing at her and tittering, as colour flooded into her cheeks. Hastily, she tapped at the office door, and it was immediately opened.

Julia looked down at her. 'Ah Alice, come on in. I thought we'd have a little talk. I'm afraid I didn't get much time yesterday, but seeing as most of the others are out, we may as well have a chat now, while it's quiet.'

Alice followed her into the room and Julia closed the door behind them. Alice thought that the housemother was looking very pretty in a flared skirt that was cinched in tight at the waist with a broad belt, but she said nothing.

'There, that's better.' Julia noticed her frightened eyes and, smiling reassuringly, she motioned towards a chair. 'Come on, don't look so worried – sit yourself down.'

Alice hoisted herself onto a hard-backed chair as Julia looked at her. 'So how did you sleep then?' The question was asked kindly.

'A . . . a . . . all right, th . . . th . . . thank you.'

Julia nodded encouragingly. 'Well, all I really wanted you for, dear, was to explain a little bit about what's going to be happening. I can't tell you too much at present because to be honest, I don't know myself. But for the time being at least you'll be staying here. We'll make sure that you get to school, although it may not be the one you've been attending, and we'll be having lots of meetings to decide what's best for your future. You'll soon get used to our routine, I'm sure. It's fairly easy-going here and we try to make it as homely as we can. You'll soon get to know your way about – mealtimes, bedtimes, et cetera. Is our Susan looking after you?'

Alice bobbed her head.

'Good. I thought she would. Susan is a bit of a rough diamond, but at heart she's not a bad kid.'

Alice had no idea at all what a rough diamond was, so she said nothing.

'Now, my dear, unless there's anything you want to ask me, I won't keep you. If ever I'm not here and you need anything, ask Margaret – she's my deputy. On the odd occasions when neither Margaret nor I are here, you can go to Nora instead. There will always be someone here to help. I'm afraid Saturdays and Sundays can be pretty hectic, as you'll discover. They're visiting days, but there are lots of books and toys in the day room so just help yourself, and if you should have any problems come and see me.'

Relieved, Alice slid off the chair and disappeared through the door without a word. Julia sighed. At present Alice was the youngest child in the home, and Julia had an idea that things were not going to be easy for her.

When Alice emerged from the office, Steven Mann and the girl who had fetched her from the kitchen were waiting to confront her. They sauntered up to her, and as Alice hovered uncertainly, Steven suddenly grabbed her elbow and hauled her into the boot room. She found herself pressed up against one of the deep stone sinks that ran in a row along the length of one wall. She stared up at him petrified, but too defiant to cry.

The older girl rammed a finger viciously into her ribs, causing her to gasp. 'Come on then, Carrot-top, say somethin' for us. I want Steven to hear you stutter.'

Alice glared up at her but remained stubbornly silent as the girl's face twisted in a sneer. 'Well, come on then – *say* something.'

Again Alice ignored her as the girl glanced at Steven over her shoulder. 'See – I told you, didn't I? She's thick, a brick short of a load if you ask me.'

He laughingly agreed. 'I reckon you're right there. She won't last here for five minutes. She'll soon get the stuffin' knocked out of her.'

The girl stood beside him and shoulder-to-shoulder they stared at her. But Alice never flinched although her rib was throbbing painfully where the girl had jabbed her. The girl drew a packet of Woodbines out of her pocket and lit one with a match, which she struck on the bare brick walls. Then casually she sauntered over to the metal shoe-racks that covered almost the whole of the opposite wall.

'See this?' She waved the cigarette at Alice. 'All us older ones come in here for a crafty fag. You snitch on us an' you're dead.'

Laughing, Steven snatched it from her hand and took a long drag then he knelt to Alice's level and blew evil-smelling smoke into her face. 'She won't say *nothing*, Lisa. If she does, she'll be sorry.' He narrowed his eyes menacingly at Alice. 'Are you goin' to keep your mouth shut?'

She nodded vigorously.

'Good. Well – get your arse away then. When me and Lisa have finished this fag we're goin' to have a snog, an' I don't particularly want an audience.'

Lisa giggled, smoothing her swinging skirt across the many layers of net petticoats beneath it. Cautiously Alice edged towards the door then she flew along the corridor and clattered up the uncarpeted wooden staircase. She didn't pause until she reached her own room, and once inside she slammed the door behind her. At last, the tears she had valiantly held back came in huge, rasping sobs that shook her small frame. She wished that Susan were here but she had no idea at all what time she would be back. One thing she *was* sure of – there was no way she would venture outside of the room again until Susan was back. Instead she curled up on her bed and sucked her thumb.

Susan returned just before lunchtime. Staring at Alice, who was still coiled in a tight ball, she frowned. 'What's up, kid? No one's been givin' yer grief, have they?'

Alice shook her head, but Susan was not convinced. Tossing her library books onto her bed she nodded towards the door. 'Well, come on, then. We'd better get down else we'll miss dinner.'

Alice looked at her solemnly. 'I . . . I'm n . . . not h—'

'You're not hungry.' Susan finished the sentence for her, and Alice nodded, wondering how the other girl could be either, after the enormous breakfast she had shovelled away.

Susan hovered, uncertain what to do. Eventually she shrugged. 'Suit yerself then. If yer change yer mind, just come down to the dinin' room. But don't be too long makin' yer mind up about it else you'll be too late anyway.'

When Alice heard the door close behind her she pulled her knees together into her chest. Then she lay wrapped in misery, not caring if she never ate again. After a time she slipped into an uneasy doze and was awoken some time later by another dig in the ribs. But this time it was a gentle one. As her eyes blinked open she saw Susan standing over her.

'Here, kid.' She held out a parcel, crudely wrapped in a paper serviette.

As Alice opened it, two cheese sandwiches spilled onto the crumpled bedspread. She smiled tremulously. 'Th . . . th . . . thanks.'

Susan waved her hand. 'Don't thank me. Just eat 'em. Yer look like yer could do with 'em – yer as skinny as a rake. I reckon if we stood yer sideways, we could lose yer down a gap in the pavement.'

Alice bit into the bread, and although she hadn't felt hungry she ate the sandwiches in minutes and wiped the crumbs from around her mouth.

'That's more like it.' Susan nodded her approval. 'Now come on, get a flannel round yer face an' brush yer hair, an we'll go downstairs. I think me aunty might be comin' to see me today. You'll like me aunty, she's nice. I go an' stay overnight with her sometimes. She's got six kids of her own, otherwise she'd have me to live with her, I know she would.'

Alice heard the regret in her voice as she padded to the sink. She wet the flannel under the tap and wiped her tearstained face. Then she tugged the brush through her hair. She felt a little better and managed to raise a smile, as together they went downstairs.

The day room seemed to be bulging with people. Extra chairs had been carried in and little groups of visitors and children were dotted here and there.

As Susan's eyes scanned the room they immediately dulled with disappointment. 'She ain't here yet. Come on, we'll go out into the car park to wait fer her. You can't hear yerself think in here.'

She slouched along the corridor, her shoulders stooped, and once they were outside she kicked at a stone viciously with the toe of her scuffed shoe.

Glen was just entering the outbuilding and he waved at them.

'Have yer met Glen yet?'

Alice nodded.

'He's all right, Glen is. Kind.' Susan grinned. 'He's got me out o' more scrapes than a little, he has. If ever I ain't about and yer need some help, go to him.'

Alice nodded solemnly and together they sat down on the cold concrete, their backs against the wall to wait. The afternoon stretched away but still there was no sign of Susan's Aunt Betty. By the time the visitors had begun to leave Alice had grown stiff from sitting still.

'Aw well, it don't look like she could make it after all. She won't come now.' Susan tried to mask the disappointment in her voice. 'Come on, little 'un, we may as well go in an' see what's on the telly.'

Standing up, she hauled Alice to her feet, and they were just about to go back into the building when a large old Bedford van rattled into the car park. Instantly Susan brightened. 'It's Banana Jane. Now leave her to me. She can be a bit frosty at times but I know how to handle her. If we play us cards right we might wangle a bit o' fruit out of her. That's why I calls her Banana Jane.'

Alice gazed at Susan admiringly – it seemed that she knew how to handle everybody. Almost forgetting Alice, she ran to the van. The driver's door opened and a strangely dressed lady stepped out.

'Hello there, Susan. How are you, me gel?' The woman smiled awkwardly at Susan before her eyes came to rest on Alice. Instantly the colour drained from her face as she recognised the child she had thought she would never see again.

Unaware of her surprise, Susan pulled Alice forward. 'This is Alice. She only came yesterday. She's sharin' my bedroom an' I'm lookin' out fer her.'

Alice and Jane surveyed each other cautiously, until eventually Jane remarked, 'To tell you the truth, Susan, I reckon as me an' Alice have met before, ain't we?'

Alice recognised the lady as the one who had found her on the boat the night she ran away. She stared at her from guarded eyes, but was saved from having to answer, because just then Glen appeared and began to help the woman to unload the van.

'You've met our new addition then, have you?' he asked, nodding towards Alice.

Jane looked decidedly uncomfortable. 'That I have, an' Susan here tells me as she's lookin' out for her.'

'Yes. She's a good girl, is Susan.'

Susan's pigeon chest swelled with pride at the praise, and for now the disappointment of her aunt's missed visit was forgotten. She stood to one side holding Alice's hand as Glen and Jane carried the boxes through to the kitchen. Then she winked at Alice.

'Stand tight, Banana Jane's like Glen. She's a bit strange but a good sort all the same. Most o' the kids here are a bit wary of her. The staff reckon as she's somethin' called "centric". Well, somethin' like that anyway, but I bet you any money, before she leaves she'll slip us a bit o' fruit. Seems like she's in a good mood today.'

A small group of children were assembling behind them, and by the time Jane reappeared for the last time, they were all hovering expectantly.

Hands on her hips she looked at them solemnly. 'I suppose you'll all be lookin' for a treat, eh?' Her face broke into a rare smile, displaying a surprisingly nice set of straight white teeth. 'Come on then, let's see what we can find.' Apart from her own seasonal, home-produced fruit and vegetables, she also bought more exotic fruit wholesale at the fruit market, and included it in her deliveries.

She dragged a box to the rear end of the van and

tapped her chin thoughtfully. Hmm . . . what have we got?' She looked at Susan and Alice. 'You two, come on, I reckon you were first in the queue. So it's only fair if you have first pick.'

Susan stared into the box eagerly, and greedily scooped up a big orange.

'An' what would you like?' Jane asked Alice as the child gazed into the box.

'A . . . a . . . b . . . ba . . .'

'She means she wants a banana,' Susan grinned.

'Right you are, a banana it shall be.' Jane self-consciously pushed the largest banana in the bunch into Alice's hand and the child's mouth worked.

'Th . . . th . . . Th . . .'

'She says thank you,' Susan told Jane, and was rewarded with a grin as Jane methodically worked through the little group until everyone had a treat. They began to drift away and Glen stood aside with Susan and Alice as Jane climbed into the driver's seat.

'I'll see you all next Wednesday then.' Raising her hand in a final salute, she erratically reversed off the playground.

Once she was out on the road again, Jane Reynolds chewed on her lip and the smile slid from her face. The police had told her when they returned her clothes that Alice had been identified and was being returned to her father. So what was she doing at the children's home? Why hadn't he come to claim her?

The more she thought of the pale little face, the more irritated she became, and the more frustrated.

What business of mine is it anyway? she asked herself, and the answer came back. *None – none at all!*

Eventually she turned her thoughts to the jobs that were waiting to be done at Canalside Farm. But in the back of her mind the haunting little face remained.

Chapter Nine

'Hello, there! Are you busy then, gel?'

Startled, Jane swung around from her task of cleaning out the pigsty to see Lil beaming over the wall at her.

'Well, don't look so surprised to see me,' her aunt chuckled. 'Yer know well enough by now that I have a habit o' turnin' up like a bad penny.'

'You're right enough there, Lil,' Jane joked. 'I reckon you're tryin' to catch me out doin' somethin' as I shouldn't be.'

'Huh, I gave up hopin' for that years ago.' Lil looked around her as she spoke and pulled her multi-coloured cardigan more tightly around her thin frame 'So how much longer are you goin' to be doin' that?' She screwed up her nose as a waft of pig manure hit it.

Jane grinned. 'Only about another ten minutes or so. While I finish off, you can go an' put the kettle on. I'll be in then an' we'll have a natter.'

'Right you are, luv. I don't need tellin' twice – it's enough to cut a body in two out here.'

Jane watched as Lil picked her way through the puddles in the farmyard, her gaudy skirts flying around her legs, then she continued with the unenviable task of mucking out the pigs. It was some twenty minutes later when she joined Lil in the kitchen, by which time the fire was roaring up the chimney and the kettle was singing on the range.

'Ah, so you're here at last. I was beginnin' to think as you'd got lost. I wouldn't mash the tea till yer got in, fer fear of it stewin', but it won't be a minute now. Everythin's ready. You sit yourself down by the fire an' take the chill off.'

Bustling across to a large brown teapot, she poured in boiling water and began to stir the tea. Jane hung her coat on the back of the door and slipped her feet out of her boots, which were giving off a rather malodorous smell, before she crossed to the fire and held her hands out to the welcome blaze.

When the tea was mashed Lil poured it through the strainer and tipped the tea leaves onto a saucer. Minutes later she joined Jane and passed her a steaming mug. Sighing contentedly she took a seat in the chair opposite and slurped at her drink.

'Ah, that's just what the doctor ordered. I needed that, I did.'

Jane raised her eyebrow and grinned. 'I've yet to think of a time when you couldn't make room for a brew, Lil. I've never known anyone like you for tea.'

'My Wilf allus reckoned as I were a tea belly. But it's like I always told him – there are plenty of other things far worse than tea as I could have been addicted to.'

'I won't argue with that,' Jane agreed. 'But it's always nice to see you. You should know that by now. So,

what've you been up to, an' how long are you plannin'
on stayin' this time?'

'In answer to yer first question, not a lot. It were a
bit quiet down at Tamworth. In answer to yer second
question, how long is a piece o' string? Happen I'll just
play it by ear, an' take off when the fancy comes on me.
It don't usually take long before the old wanderlust rears
its ugly head.'

'I'm surprised to see you back so soon,' Jane admitted.

Lil became serious. 'To be honest with yer, pet, I've
been frettin' about that little 'un as yer found on the boat.
I can't seem to get her out of me mind. So I thought I'd
come back this way an' see if you'd heard anythin' about
what's become of her.'

Jane stared down into her mug.

'As a matter of fact, I have, Lil. The coppers came
back the mornin' after I'd found her to return me clobber
– not that I was particularly worried about havin' it back.
But anyway, they told me that the little girl's name was
Alice. She came from up Chapel End way, apparently.
Her dad had reported her missin', an' as far as the coppers
knew, he were goin' to pick her up that mornin'. So that,
I thought to meself, was the end of *that* little bit of excitement. But I were wrong, 'cos on the Saturday after I'd
done on the market I pulled into Henry Street Children's
Home – you know, the one as I supplies the fruit an' veg
to – an' there she is, as bold as brass. I can tell you, it
gave me a rare turn, it did. Nobody's told me why she's
there. All I know is her dad has gone away, an' from
what everyone can gather, he don't want her back.'

Horrified, Lil stared at her. 'What do yer mean, he's gone away? How long for?'

'I ain't got the foggiest,' Jane informed her, and a silence settled between them as Lil digested the information. Eventually she frowned, adding yet more wrinkles to her already creased brow.

'What will happen to the poor little mite if he *don't* come back?' she asked.

Jane swirled the tea around in her mug. 'I've really no idea. I just know her dad ain't gone to get her back yet, which is a bit of a mystery from where I'm standin', an' really sad.'

'Ah well, that's the way o' the world,' Lil said wisely. 'I bet if he don't come back they'll put her up for adoption. Mind, the poor sods as can't have any little ones of their own usually want to adopt babbies.'

'You're right, Lil,' Jane agreed sadly. 'No one's gonna want Alice, are they? For a start-off she *ain't* a babby, and she already has a dad. It ain't like she's an orphan, is it?'

Lil peeped at her out of the corner of her eye. 'Yer know, I'm surprised as you ain't never thought about doin' somethin' like that – adoptin', I mean. Let's face it, this place is far too big fer you on yer own. Yer must rattle around in it like a pea in a pod when I ain't here. An' I reckon as you'd have made a lovely mam.'

The instant she had said it, she saw the colour drain from Jane's face and could have bitten her tongue off. Standing up abruptly, Jane went over to refill their mugs.

'So how's the market goin' nowadays?' Lil was keen to change the subject and Jane was happy to oblige her.

'Not bad at all. Through the summer it's easier when I can grow most o' the produce meself, but through the winter it's a long day 'cos I have to go to the wholesale market in Coventry first to collect some o' the fruit an' veg before I even get to the market to set up me stall. Trade ain't bad though. I'm getting a fair share o' regular customers now. Can't think why. I ain't exactly the easiest to get along with, am I?'

Both women chuckled. They were natural with each other again and for the rest of the night the subject of the little runaway was studiously avoided.

'Are you quite sure that you've got everything?' Glen asked Alice, who was clutching her satchel as if her very life depended on it.

She nodded as he gently placed his large hand in the small of her back and ushered her towards the waiting van. She had just clambered into her seat when Julia appeared.

'All set, are you, love?' she said gaily.

Again Alice nodded but Julia got the impression that she might take flight at any second. The poor child looked absolutely petrified. The housemother resisted the urge to hug her and instead said, 'Don't look so worried, pet. Red Deeps is a lovely school and I'm sure you'll like it there, once you get settled in. I'm just sorry that you had to have a couple of weeks off while we got every-thing arranged. But never mind – you're going now so have a nice day and I'll look forward to you telling me all about it when you get home, OK?'

She slammed the van door and watched as Glen steered it onto the road, then made her way back into the home with a thoughtful look on her face. Sometimes life just seemed so unfair.

'Alice Lawrence?'

Alice tentatively raised her hand, painfully aware of the other children's eyes on her.

'Welcome, my dear. I do hope you'll be happy with us,' the kindly teacher told her. She was a large lady with glasses and an easy smile, but Alice stared back at her straight-faced and sensing her discomfort, the woman went on.

'My name is Mrs Kingdom. I'm sure you'll soon get to know some of your classmates and make some friends once you settle in.'

Alice squirmed behind her desk, wishing that the ground could just open and swallow her up but thankfully, the teacher then addressed the rest of the class and Alice was able to look around her new classroom. It was nice, she had to admit. There were brightly coloured paintings pinned up on the walls and at the front of the class was a large desk where the teacher sat with a big blackboard behind her. The children's much smaller desks and chairs were placed in rows and Alice was grateful at least to have been placed to one side out of the way.

'Right – I think we'll begin writing out this little poem

from the board, shall we?' Mrs Kingdom said, and so Alice's first day at her new school began.

'Well, come on then – tell me all about it. How did it go at yer new school?' Susan clambered onto the bed next to Alice and stared at her expectantly.

'It w . . . w . . . was n . . . nice.'

'Good! Yer see, I told yer, didn't I? I said you'd like it at yer new school. An' there yer were yesterday, frettin' away. Now you've got yer first day over, it'll be plain sailin' all the way, you see if I ain't right. I bet yer made some new friends an' all, didn't yer?'

When Alice solemnly shook her head Susan shrugged.

'Ah well, it's early days yet. What's yer new teacher's name?'

'M . . . M . . . M . . . Mrs K . . . Kingdom.'

Susan chuckled. 'Blimey, that's a bit of a gobful, especially for you to spit out. Is she nice?'

'Y . . . yes.' Alice managed a weak smile as Susan hugged her.

'I don't know. All this excitement in one week, eh? First it's yer birthday an' then startin' a new school – not to mention the two-week gap that you got away with without having to go at all. Yer dead jammy, you are.' She rubbed her stomach as she thought back to the small party that Julia, the housemother, had put on for Alice's birthday. 'Cor, your birthday – that were a good spread, that were. All that trifle an' all o' them cakes. It's a pity I overate an' threw half of 'em back up, ain't it?'

Now Alice did smile as she thought back to Susan's eating binge.

The other girl chuckled. 'That's better. Yer know, when yer *do* smile, I mean *really* smile, you ain't half bad-lookin'.'

Alice was growing accustomed to Susan's backhanded compliments by now. The older girl was the bright spot in her life. But as yet she was still finding everything else about her new life very strange.

She missed her father terribly. He'd shouted at her and not always been kind to her, but even so he was the only father she'd had. Most of all she missed her home and her own little bed. Every day she expected her father to arrive and take her home. If only he would, she promised herself, she would never run away again and she would try to be good. And every night when he failed to come she cried herself to sleep, usually in Susan's arms. Most of the other children in the home left her well alone, apart from Lisa Addison and Steven Mann, who both went out of their way to taunt her whenever the opportunity arose. Alice avoided them both as much as possible, for although she wouldn't admit it to herself she was terrified of them, a fact that they were both aware of and found highly amusing. As she thought about them now she grew depressed again.

Susan hopped off the bed. 'Come on. Nasty Nora's on dinner duty tonight an' yer know what she's like. If we ain't got the tables laid to her ladyship's likin' there'll be hell to pay.'

She tugged Alice unceremoniously off the bed and

together they clattered down the stairs to the dining room.

Julia looked at the young children's officer standing opposite her. They were in the office and could vaguely hear the sounds of tables being dragged into position ready for dinner in the dining room.

Julia thumbed towards the door and grinned. 'Nora's on dinner duty tonight. She can always keep the kids on their toes. I don't know how she does it. It's always chaos when I try to organise it.'

'Perhaps you're too soft on them,' the young woman remarked.

Julia nodded. 'I think you could be right, but still – let's sit down and get on with the business at hand. It's getting late and I'm sure you have a home you want to go to.'

'Yes, of course.' The young woman straightened in her chair and took a file out of her briefcase. 'My name is Carol Woods, and I've just been allocated Alice Lawrence's case. I shall be taking over from Angela Wilson, who was the Duty Children's Officer on the day that Alice came into care.'

'I see.' Julia stared at her. The young woman was very obviously newly qualified and keen to make a good impression. She held out her hand and they exchanged a brief handshake.

'I'm Julia Tuffin, the housemother here at Henry Street. Have you met Alice yet?'

'No, I haven't. The case was only allocated to me

yesterday, but I have read up on the reports. It appears that Alice's coming into care was very sudden and unplanned. How is she coping?'

Julia sighed. 'Not too well, to be honest. Alice is a very withdrawn, timid child. On top of which, as I'm sure you are aware, she appears to have learning difficulties. In fact, she started at the Red Deeps School in Hill Top today. I'm afraid that she's had an awful lot to contend with in the last four weeks, poor little soul. She's a lovely child though.'

Carol nodded thoughtfully. 'Do you think she'll be able to cope here? I mean, in a children's home with so-called "normal children", or do you think she might be better placed in Rugby? Tintersfield, the children's home there, caters especially for those with special needs.'

'I'm not sure yet. It's a little too soon to form an opinion. She does tend to keep herself to herself, but then, considering the trauma she's been through – being motherless then losing her father *and* her home – then I suppose that's only to be expected. Fortunately, Susan Cotton, one of the other young residents here, has taken Alice under her wing – they're almost inseparable. I dare say that by the time you've managed to set up a meeting with your colleagues, I'll be able to tell you more about what I think will be in Alice's interest. All I can say right now is that another move so soon would be totally disastrous for her. She needs time to adjust to the fact that she's in care, before we even think of moving her again. And besides, didn't her father request that she be put up for adoption?'

Carol nodded. 'Yes, according to my records he did. I have written to a forwarding address he left in Leeds, asking if that's still what he wants. As yet he hasn't responded to my letter, but I hope he'll do so soon, otherwise I shall have to drive over and see him.'

'Good. Well, in that case, I think we should leave Alice here for the time being and wait to see what sort of reaction you get from her father.'

'I think you're right,' Carol agreed, closing the file. 'Is there any chance of my meeting Alice? Or will the children have started eating their dinner?'

'No, I shouldn't think so – not yet anyway. Wait there and I'll go and see if I can find her.'

As Julia disappeared into the corridor, Carol began to feel nervous about what this confused child would think of her. She watched the door anxiously and minutes later Julia reappeared holding the hand of a child with startling red hair.

'This is Alice. Alice, this is Carol Woods.' Julia introduced them. 'Carol is going to be your new children's officer, which means that she'll be coming to see you quite often.'

Alice stared at her solemnly as Carol knelt to her level. 'Hello, Alice. I'm very pleased to meet you. I hope that you and I are going to be friends. Are you settling in all right here at Henry Street?'

Alice nodded, her eyes huge in her small face, but she said nothing.

Carol rose. 'Right. I don't want to make you too late for your dinner. It was lovely to meet you, Alice. May I come and see you again soon? And perhaps next time we'll have a little longer to talk, hey?'

Again the solemn nod as Alice inched towards the door. She hovered uncertainly for a second as Carol smiled at her and then suddenly she turned and fled as if the hounds from hell were at her heels.

Carol frowned. 'I see what you mean now about her being quiet and withdrawn. She never said so much as a word.'

'Well, I think Alice says as little as possible because, on top of everything else, she has a terrible stammer. Susan has taken to finishing Alice's sentences for her – when she does speak, that is. But like I said, at the moment Alice needs time to adjust to all that's happening to her.'

'I absolutely agree.' Carol lifted her briefcase and smiled. 'Right, I'll be off. As soon as I have a reply from Mr Lawrence, I'll let you know. With luck, he may have had a change of heart by now. But if he hasn't, well, at least we'll know more about what we can plan for Alice's future.'

The two women shook hands and Carol left. Julia then hurried along to the dining room to supervise dinnertime. She felt vaguely uncomfortable about Alice's new children's officer. Carol Woods was undoubtedly nice, but Julia wished that Alice had been allocated someone with a little more experience.

When she arrived at the dining room she found Alice huddled over her untouched meal as Nora glared down at her.

'Is there a problem here?' Julia demanded.

Susan instantly answered. 'Yeah, there is. *She* had a right go at Alice just 'cos she was a bit late comin' in to dinner.' Susan glared at Nora who glared back at her, and eager to defuse the situation, Julia quickly butted in.

'I apologise for Alice being late, Nora. I have to take full responsibility for it. Her new children's officer had turned up to meet her and I asked Alice to come to my office.'

Nora sniffed and strode from the room as Julia watched in amazement. What the hell was wrong with the woman? It was hardly a hanging offence, to arrive a few minutes late for dinner – yet by the look on Nora's face anyone might have thought that the child had committed a mortal offence.

She dragged her attention back to Alice. 'Come on, love,' she whispered encouragingly. 'Let's see you eat that dinner up now, eh?'

'No, no – *n . . . no!*'

Susan started awake and blinked in the darkness. Then as she realised what was happening she cursed softly and slid her legs out of the warm bed. Sure-footed, she padded across the lino. 'All right, it's all right, Alice, I'm here. Wake up. You're havin' a bad dream again.'

As she gently shook Alice's shoulder the small girl's eyes snapped open. For a moment she stared at Susan, her eyes vacant and confused, then she began to sob as Susan gathered her into her arms.

'Come on, I'm here. Hotch over an' I'll get in. I'll catch me bloody death standin' here, I will.'

Obediently Alice snaked across the bed, and Susan slithered in beside her. She yawned. 'Stop blartin', it's all over. Let's try an' get back to sleep else we'll be fit for nothin' in the mornin'.'

She sounded tired and feeling guilty, Alice tried to relax. She felt Susan go limp, and soon her gentle snores filled the room. But Alice stayed awake; reliving the terrible nightmare she had just been woken from. The loneliness was so tangible that she felt she could have touched it. She was alone with no one in the world except for Susan. But Susan had an aunty, an aunty who loved her. As yet Alice had not met her, although she had waited with Susan for her to come every Saturday since she had arrived. But one day she *would* come, and one day she might want to take Susan home with her. Alice bit back the fear that rose in her throat. Then she would have no one at all. Suddenly very wide-awake, she stayed that way until the first cold light crept into the room. And then at last she slept.

Carol Woods looked at Julia and Margaret across the cluttered desk.

'Well, I've heard from Mr Lawrence, and it's not good news,' she sighed. 'Unfortunately he's still saying that he wants Alice to be adopted. When I received his reply I rang him and, following the conversation we had, I think I can honestly say that there's absolutely no chance of him changing his mind. Off the record, I don't think I've ever spoken to such a cold-hearted man. He obviously has no feelings for the girl whatsoever. He is putting his decision in writing although I have arranged to go and see him.'

'I see.' Julia absently strummed the desk with her fingertips. 'Oh well, I admit I was hoping that he'd have a change of heart. But at least now we can concentrate on doing what's best for Alice long-term. Have you got a date for a meeting yet?'

'Yes, I have. It's next Wednesday at two o'clock. I've already appointed another children's officer to talk to Alice and I'm going to see Mr Lawrence on Monday. Will that be all right?'

Julia thumbed through her diary before nodding. 'Yes, that will be fine. The child has been here for six weeks now, and I need to get a proper care plan drawn up for her future. She's the youngest child here, and in my opinion, if she's not going home then she should be placed with a family.'

'I'm in complete agreement,' Margaret remarked. 'Alice is a lovely little girl. Adoption might be the best thing for her.'

'Let's hope it all works out.' Carol stood up and smiled at them both. 'I'll see you both next week at the meeting.'

Nora, who had had her ear pressed to the office door, stepped back and quickly walked away. She had been angry at not being allowed into the meeting, but as things had turned out it really didn't matter. It had been surprisingly easy to eavesdrop.

Hurrying into the day room she leaned heavily against

the table as she tried to put her thoughts into some sort of order. So Robert had decided that he didn't want his child back, had he? White-hot rage pulsed through her veins, causing her to break out in a sweat. It was time he was taught a lesson he would never forget.

'Julia, I was wondering – would it be all right if I had Friday and Saturday off this week? Something's come up that I need to attend to.'

Her back ramrod straight, Nora Fitton's hands fidgeted nervously as she stared at the housemother across the desk.

Julia looked vaguely surprised. In all the years Nora had worked at the home, Julia had never known her to miss a shift, so she could only assume that whatever it was that Nora needed to do was important.

'Of course you can,' she nodded obligingly, hoping to put the woman at ease. 'I'm sure we can get someone to cover for you, Nora. But is everything all right? You look a little tense.'

'Everything's fine,' Nora snapped.

Julia glanced away. It seemed that no one could get close to this woman and sometimes she wondered why she even still bothered trying. Nora was not the easiest of people to get on with at the best of times and today for some reason she seemed in an even worse mood than usual.

'I'd better get on.' Nora inched towards the door and with a final cursory nod at Julia, disappeared though it.

Julia sighed. Nora had always been a bit of a mystery.

As far as anyone knew, she was somewhere in her late thirties or early forties and lived at home with her elderly parents. Julia assumed that Nora had never been married, for in all the time she had known her she had never once mentioned anyone special. In fact, she rarely spoke of her personal life at all, now that Julia came to think of it. She had never been a popular member of staff, particularly with the resident children, as she could be stern and unyielding, to the point that Julia sometimes worried about the very rare occasions when both she and Maggie were unable to be there and Julia had had to leave Nora in charge. To be completely fair, Julia had glimpsed another, gentler side to her, and that had been when they had a baby staying at the home. Then Nora would become another person, soft and kind and loving.

Julia shrugged her shoulders and turning back to the desk, began to reorganise the staff rota.

Alice took her usual place at Susan's side in the day room. It was becoming almost like a ritual now. Every Saturday afternoon they would sit here waiting for Susan's aunty to arrive, and then as the afternoon wore on and she didn't come, they would give up and go outside to wait for Banana Jane instead. Alice smiled at the thought. She liked Banana Jane. Oh, she knew the staff at the home made jokes about her, but Alice liked her anyway. She was kind, like Glen. He was kind too. Sometimes he would ruffle her hair. No one had ever done that before – not even her father – and it made her feel nice. Sort of special. Today, she settled more comfortably into her seat expecting the usual lengthy wait. It was then that Dawn, the newest member of staff, who Susan had told her was a student children's officer, came in waving an envelope at Susan.

'Look what I've got here for you, young lady. It came by second post at lunchtime. I'm sorry it's so late getting to you, but I've been so busy that I've only just had time to sort the mail. Anyway, better late than never, hey?' She pressed the envelope into Susan's hand, and with a cheeky grin disappeared back the way she had come.

Susan gazed in awe at the letter. *Miss Susan Cotton, c/o Henry Street Children's Home, Henry Street, Nuneaton,* she read. Almost tumbling off her seat in her excitement she leaned towards Alice. 'Come on, we'll go up to our room and read it in private, shall we?'

Intrigued, Alice nodded and trotted after her. Once they were in the privacy of their own room, they clambered onto Susan's bed. The older girl fingered the envelope reverently. Then, unable to wait a moment longer, she tore it open and withdrew a solitary sheet of paper. Falteringly she began to read:

Dear Susan,

I'm sorry I ain't managed to get to see you for a while. Three of the little 'uns is been down with measles. On top of that your Uncle Bert had a forklift truck drive over his foot at work so he's been on the box. Not that he needs much of an excuse anyway. I ain't had any spare cash for bus fares. But still I hope to be able to get to see you very soon.

Love,
Aunty Betty xxxxxxxxxx

P.S. I hope you are bein' good. And not givin' the staff any of your lip.

Susan's chest swelled with importance as she waved the letter at Alice as if it were a trophy. 'Yer see, I *told* yer me aunty loved me, didn't I?'

Alice nodded vigorously, delighted to see her friend so happy. Susan read through the letter again before folding it carefully and returning it to the envelope. 'I think I'll have to put this wi' me special things. Go an' stand by the door an' tell me straight away if yer hear anybody comin'.'

Obediently Alice took her place in front of the door. Intrigued, she kept one eye on the corridor and one on Susan as she hurried to a far corner of the room. Carefully she peeled back the lino before deftly lifting out a short piece of floorboard.

She looked back at Alice. 'Can yer hear anybody about?'

When Alice shook her head, Susan beckoned for her to join her. Closing the door softly, Alice hurried across and stared down at a dusty tin under the floor.

Susan lifted it out. 'This is me secret place,' she confided. 'Nobody knows about it 'cept you. So you have to promise not to tell anyone about it. Do yer promise?'

'I p . . . p . . . p . . . promise.'

Susan nodded with satisfaction. 'Good. In that case

then I'll show you what's inside.' She carefully prised the lid off and lifted a thin gold band out of the tin. 'This were me mam's weddin' ring,' she whispered reverently. 'Aunty Betty gave it me when me mam died. It's too big for me just yet, but one day when it fits I'll wear it. An' this, look, is a picture of me mam. She were lovely, weren't she?'

Alice stared at a faded dog-eared photograph that her friend held out to her. There were features about the woman in it that reminded her of Susan. The same snub nose – the same straight hair – the same smile. She nodded, as Susan lovingly put the treasures back into the tin along with the letter. In no time at all the floorboard and the lino were back in place.

Susan wiped her dusty hands down the front of her skirt. 'I have to keep them under there,' she stated. 'This sticky-fingered lot here – huh! They'd have 'em away in a jiffy if I didn't, but I trust *you*.'

Alice flushed with pleasure at the compliment and was just about to comment when Susan crossed to the window and stared down into the car park.

'Come on. There's no point sittin' in the day room now we know she ain't comin'. We may as well go out back an' wait for Banana Jane to come. Mind you, we'd better put us coats on. It's enough to freeze the hairs off a brass monkey out there.'

Once outside Susan began to stamp her feet and blow into her hands. 'Cor blimey, sod this for a game o' soldiers. Come on, let's go an' see if we can find Glen, shall we?'

They skirted the car park and after hastily glancing around to make sure that no one had seen them, they slipped into Glen's outbuilding. As the warmth met them their faces began to glow. Glen was sitting in an old dilapidated armchair that had been banished long ago from the day room. He was engrossed in a newspaper article about the first ever Hovercraft that had sailed in July from Rhyl to Wallasey across the estuary of the River Dee, reaching a speed of fifty-six miles per hour, and he was wondering what the world was coming to. But the icy blast of air the girls' entrance admitted made him glance up guiltily.

'Oh, it's you two, is it? You gave me a right start then. I thought it was one of the staff coming to check up on me. But seeing as it's only you pair, well, I suppose you'd better share my flask with me. And I don't suppose you'd say no to a bit of chocolate either, would you?'

Two smiling faces answered him as he took a bar of chocolate out of his pocket and divided it into three equal parts.

'There we are then, girls. Share and share alike, that's what I say.'

When Susan's portion was downed in record time, he chuckled. 'I don't know where you put it, love. I really don't. I reckon you must have hollow legs. I've never known anyone so skinny and small eat half as much as you do.'

Susan giggled, holding her hands out to the little electric fan-heater.

'You'll never guess what I've had today,' she challenged him.

Trying hard not to smile, he screwed his face up and frowned as if deep in thought. 'No, I can't guess,' he said eventually. 'You'll have to tell me.'

'I've had a letter off me aunty,' she told him proudly, and by the end of the next hour, Glen could have repeated it word for word. It was only the sound of Jane's van rattling into the car park that halted her flow. She stopped mid-sentence as her eyes flew to the grimy window.

'Come on, little 'un, it's Banana Jane.'

She hauled Alice to her feet and Glen chuckled as he watched Susan almost drag her across the car park.

'Hello, Banana Jane! Guess what? I had a letter off me aunty today – a proper letter through the post with a real stamp on it,' Susan gushed, the second that Jane stepped from the van.

'Did you now? Well, that must have been nice,' Jane remarked.

'Ooh, it were. I've put it away safe. An' she's comin' to see me real soon.'

Jane's amused eyes travelled from Susan and came to rest on Alice, who was standing silently as usual, at Susan's side.

'An' how's life treatin' you, little one?'

Before Alice could answer Susan spoke for her. 'She's doin' all right. Still keepin' me awake half the night but she's settlin' in OK.'

'I'm pleased to hear it.'

As Jane looked down into the solemn little face her heart twisted. It seemed a terrible shame that her own father could have abandoned a child so young. But then, she reminded herself firmly, it's no business of mine!

The two little girls stood aside as she unloaded the van with Glen's help. They then rubbed their hands together as they tried to keep warm whilst they stood waiting for her to return from the office.

Susan began to hop from foot to foot. 'That bloody tea Glen gave us is goin' straight through me. It's no good, I'll have to run in an' use the lav. But you wait here, Alice. An' if Banana Jane comes out before I get back, be sure an' get me a banana – if she's in a good mood, that is.'

Alice nodded as Susan skipped away. Within minutes Jane reappeared and looked around for Susan.

'So where's madam gone?'

'T . . . t . . . to th . . . the t . . . t . . . toilet.'

'Ah, I see.' She knelt down, bringing her face on a level with Alice's, and stared into the green eyes. They were closed and guarded, and Jane found herself wondering what Alice would look like, happy and smiling. There was something about the child that touched her deep inside. She seemed so lost and lonely. Jane recognised the look. She was no stranger to loneliness herself. She sought for some words of reassurance and comfort to offer. But she had never been good at communicating with people and none sprang to mind.

They were still staring at each other when Susan reappeared some minutes later.

'What's this then? What am I missin'? Havin' a heart-to-heart, are yer?'

Flustered, Jane rose quickly and wiped her mittened hands down the sides of her coat. 'Right, let's have a look at what we've got in here. An' then I'd best be off. I've got animals waitin' to be fed back at home.'

Abruptly now she grabbed two large bananas out of the back of the van and thrust them into Susan's hand, studiously avoiding Alice's eyes, afraid of the strange emotions the child could evoke in her. She walked brusquely past them and climbed into the driver's seat. 'I'll see you next week,' she said shortly, and Susan watched in amazement as she drove away without so much as another word.

'Flippin' heck, who rattled her cage then? Have you said somethin' to upset her?'

When Alice shook her head, Susan shrugged. 'Aw well, perhaps she's just havin' a bad day. Here, cop hold of this banana an' then we'll get in out o' the cold and read me aunty's letter again, shall we?'

Alice sighed. She already knew the letter off by heart, but she didn't want to hurt her friend's feelings by saying so, so obediently she followed Susan back inside.

At last, Jane turned into Apple Pie Lane and as she rounded the bend, Canalside Farm came into view. As always she experienced a sense of coming home. The farmhouse was set deep in a hollow at the bottom of the lane. Behind it, she could see the overgrown lawns that sloped towards the banks of the Coventry canal, winding lazily away into the distance towards the Birmingham canal basin. Beyond that, she could see the rooftops of the houses in the nearby village of Fenny Drayton, and further on still she could vaguely see Sibson, which boasted reputedly the oldest inn in England, once haunted by Dick Turpin, the notorious highwayman of bygone times.

To one side of the farmhouse was a small copse that adjoined the field where she kept the goats, and to the other side was the orchard where she grew the fruit that she sold on her stall, and her vegetable plots.

She pulled onto the rough track that led to the barn and sighed with relief. It had been a long hard day and she was glad to be home. Switching off the engine she sat for some seconds enjoying the peace. There was nothing to be heard except the odd animal noise, and the traffic and the town seemed a million miles away. She was trying very hard not to think about Alice, but for no reason that she could explain, the little girl's face kept swimming before her eyes.

Pull yourself together, woman, she scolded herself. *You're goin' soft in your old age.*

Climbing clumsily out of the van she took a deep breath of the cold country air, then glancing at the cottage roof she smiled with satisfaction. Thin straggly wisps of smoke were struggling out of the chimney pot, to be snatched away by the wind.

'At least the fire's still in, that's a blessin',' she mumbled.

She began to walk towards the cottage, her eyes going this way and that as she went, checking that all was as it should be. Really, what happened to the little one wasn't any of her business, she told herself sternly. She pushed open the cottage door and Holly rushed to meet her. Holly – and an overwhelming sense of loneliness.

She crouched in the bottom of the wardrobe. Downstairs she could hear him flinging doors open and screaming her name. He had been drinking. He didn't get drunk very often, but when he did this always happened. She knew that it would be only a matter of time before he found her, so she crouched even lower, as tears slid down her cheeks. She was holding her breath and the tears threatened to choke her. Her nose began to run but she ignored it, too terrified to move. She heard another door slam and then another. Closer now, he was coming closer. Her heart was thumping painfully fast, so loud that she was sure he must hear it. Then another door slammed, so near that it made her jump.

'Where are yer, yer little bitch?' His muffled voice echoed through the solid wooden door and she heard a crash and a muttered oath. He had stumbled and knocked something over. She heard him drag himself to his feet and his footsteps enter the room. Then suddenly there was a silence. The silence was terrible, far more terrible than his drunken stumbling. She could sense him on the other side of the door. Listening – listening and waiting. It was hot in the wardrobe, hot and musty amongst her dead mother's clothes. She felt the urge to sneeze and fought it. She was light-headed and sweating from holding her breath, when suddenly the sneeze erupted, a deafening echo in the silence. 'A . . . a . . . tishoo!'

'Hah!' The wardrobe door was flung open and dim light

penetrated the hidden space, making her blink. 'Got yer. Thought yer could hide, did yer?'

Triumphantly he grasped her thin arm and dragged her out onto the bedroom floor. She looked up at him. Strangely the tears had stopped now and her eyes dulled with acceptance as she watched him unbuckle his belt. There was nowhere else to run or hide.

Chapter Ten

In the faint light from the street-lamp that shone through the car window, Nora peered at the address on the scrap of paper in her hand.

Yes, this was it. Number 34 Claremont Street. Satisfied, she switched off the engine and let the quiet wash over her. She had been driving for three hours and was tired, stiff and irritable. Even so she peeped at the frontage of the house with interest. It was a terraced, three-storey house that looked in need of a new coat of paint. Only one of the downstairs windows was lit but she couldn't see into the room beyond because the curtains were closely drawn. The hall light shone through a half-glazed door, spilling a dim circle of light onto the dirty pavement.

She went over the story she had concocted for the last time. She would tell him that, by a strange coincidence, she was Alice's children's officer – and that there were a few final points she needed to discuss with him before the adoption could go ahead. Then she would lure him to somewhere quiet and teach him a lesson that he would never forget. Drawing a deep breath she climbed from the car, pulling her coat closer around her as an icy blast of wind whipped down the street. This was it then – the moment she had dreamed of. There was nothing to be gained from waiting any longer. She walked to the door in her sensible flat-heeled shoes and rapped on the knocker, starting slightly as the sound echoed through the house.

When Robert himself opened the door her heart leaped into her throat. All the way here she had half hoped that it wouldn't be him. After all, there must be more than one man with the name of Robert Lawrence. But here he was – if anything even more handsome than she had remembered him. Just for a second she wavered, but then as his mouth dropped open and he frowned, the hurt and bitterness returned.

She stared at him coldly. 'Hello, Robert. Long time no see, eh? You could at least *pretend* to look pleased to see me. Aren't you going to ask me in? I have come rather a long way to see you.' She searched his face for some sign that he was remotely pleased to see her, but there was nothing but shock and confusion.

'Nora, I . . . Whatever are you doing here – and how did you know where to find me?' he spluttered.

He had paled significantly but ignoring that, she elbowed past him into the dimly lit hallway. Her nose wrinkled in distaste as she looked around at the peeling wallpaper and the worn carpets.

Noting her expression he began to gabble, 'I er . . . I rent a bedsit here for the time being. I've just moved to Leeds and I thought this would do till I sell my house in Chapel End. I'd just come down to the kitchen to make myself a cup of tea.' His eyes strayed nervously to a door on his right through which she could faintly hear the sound of a television set.

'Look, the landlady isn't too keen on the lodgers having visitors,' he muttered. 'Why don't you come up to my room and then you can tell me what I can help you with.'

'You can't help me with anything,' she told him. Her voice was as cold as ice, but all the same she began to follow him up the steep narrow staircase, smiling with satisfaction as his tea slopped over the edge of the cup onto the threadbare carpet runner. He kept glancing over his shoulder as if he could scarcely believe that she was really there and she flashed him a stiff smile. *'He'll believe it soon,'* she whispered to herself as she fingered the cold steel blade of the knife tucked deep down into her pocket. Once, an eternity ago, she would gladly have laid down her life for this man – but not any more. Now he would pay – and, she hoped – would learn a lesson that would stop him from hurting any other woman as he had once hurt her.

His room was much as she would have expected – spotlessly clean and tidy but bare of ornaments of any kind. There were no photographs, no knick-knacks – nothing but piles of books everywhere she looked.

As she studied the room, Robert in turn studied her as he tried to get over the shock of her presence. It had been seven or eight years since he had last seen Nora and the years had not been kind to her. She had never been the prettiest of women, not even when they

were both younger and he had been seeing her, or
'courting her' as she had always termed it. Not that
that had been of *his* choosing. It was Nora who had
done all the running back then and he hadn't liked to
hurt her feelings. She had never been more than a
casual fling to him, but once their affair had started
he had found it difficult to end it. It had taken a lot
to shake her off back then. *But what was she doing here
now?*

He decided the only way to find out was to ask her
outright, so plucking up his courage he began.

'Look, Nora. It's er . . . nice to see you, but what is
it you've come all this way for?'

Her eyes when she looked back at him were brim-
ming with hatred. 'Oh, don't look so worried, Robert. I
haven't come here on a personal visit, I assure you. This
is purely business. In case you'd forgotten, I'm a children's officer and I now work at the home where your
daughter has been placed.'

When his mouth dropped open she smirked. That had
taken the wind out of his sails all right, and now she felt
that she had the upper hand as guilt and confusion flitted
across his handsome face.

'I see,' he said as he tried to absorb what she had told
him. 'But I still don't see why that should bring you here
on a Saturday evening.'

'Ah well, it's like this . . .' She began to relate the
story she had concocted, savouring the feeling of power
that flooded through her as he chewed on his lip. 'So
you see,' she finished smoothly, 'I need to go through

just a few more points with you before we begin the search for adopters for Alice and get you to sign a few more forms. I realise that you may not feel comfortable doing it here, so why don't we go somewhere a little quieter? I don't wish to get you into any trouble with your landlady. After all, it wouldn't do, would it, for her to think you were entertaining a lady in your room? I passed a nice little pub not far away. We could perhaps go there? I promise it won't take up too much of your valuable time, then I, and Alice too for that matter, will be out of your hair once and for all.'

Ignoring the sarcasm in her voice, he scratched his head in the familiar gesture that had once been able to turn her legs to jelly.

'It seems a bit strange that you couldn't have just phoned me about these things,' he commented. 'Or surely you could have put them in the post and I would have signed and returned them? The children's officer I spoke to said that we would have to go to court before I had to sign anything else anyway.'

'You must have misunderstood her,' Nora lied glibly. 'It doesn't work like that, I'm afraid. These papers have to be signed *before* we can get a court date. The papers you're thinking of are the final ones you sign *after* the court hearing.'

'But on a Saturday night . . . ?'

Nora shrugged. 'Not usual, I'll admit, but seeing as I knew you and had nothing better to do, I offered to come.'

After a moment he sighed. 'In that case I'd better

come and get it over with then. Where was it you were thinking of going? There's a pub just up the road.'

Nora quickly shook her head. 'No, if you don't mind – I'd much sooner go to the one that I passed on the outskirts of the city as I came in. It looked nice and quiet there. The one you're suggesting may be a little crowded on a Saturday night and we need to be able to talk,' she told him. 'I know it must sound very unprofessional, but now that I've driven all this way I'd like to get everything tied up. I assure you I have no intention of taking up a second more of your time than is necessary. We can be there and back within half an hour.'

Robert sighed resignedly as he lifted his jacket and within minutes they were making their way back down the narrow staircase. Nora opened the passenger door of her car for him and as she walked round to the driver's seat she noted with relief that the curtains downstairs were still closely drawn. Everything was going according to plan. Very soon now she would have her revenge. She intended to put the fear of God into him.

The journey was made in silence but when they pulled out of the city and the roads gave way to country lanes, Robert began to grow nervous.

'Where did you say this pub was?' he asked uneasily.

'Oh, it's not much further now,' Nora assured him and the little car sped on through the darkness.

As they passed through a particularly narrow track that was bordered on both sides by thick trees, Nora pulled into the side of the road and parked. The silence when she turned off the engine was all-encompassing, made all the more startling when she switched off the car headlights too and they were plunged into total darkness.

'Nora, just *what* the hell is going on?' There was something wrong about this whole set-up; Robert could feel it in his bones and was wishing that he had never agreed to come.

She withdrew the sharp knife from her pocket and fingered the blade.

'The thing is, Robert, I haven't been altogether truthful with you. You see, I thought it was time that you knew you had ruined my life.'

She felt him squirm uneasily in the seat at her side. 'That's ridiculous,' he snapped. 'Whatever was between us was over a long time ago.'

'It might have been for you,' Nora whispered into the darkness. 'But it certainly wasn't for me.'

Robert turned slightly towards her and now his voice was firm. 'Nora, I have to be perfectly blunt with you. From my point of view there never was *anything* between us other than a fleeting affair. It was *you* who wanted it to continue, not me. I know I should have told you I was married when I first met you, but I wasn't thinking straight then. You know the pressure I was under from Mary because she couldn't have a child, and then you came along and were like a breath of fresh air. With you I didn't have to feel inadequate because I couldn't father a child, but I swear I never meant to hurt you and that's the God's honest truth.'

'So *why* did you leave me then?' she whispered, and

her voice was laden with all the pain he had caused her.

'You know why,' he went on in a gentler tone. 'It was because Mary informed me that she was going to have a child, and at that time I had every reason to believe that the child was mine . . . I couldn't leave her then, could I? It was only much later into the pregnancy that I discovered that the baby was some other man's.'

'And you're *quite* sure that Alice isn't yours, are you?' she spat.

'I think the facts speak for themselves, don't you? We'd been trying for a baby for years and all of a sudden she has an affair and bingo, there's a baby on the way.'

'But you were wrong.' Nora's voice was chilling.

He frowned. 'What's that supposed to mean?'

'What it means is, when you left me *I* was carrying your child, Robert – and believe me, there is absolutely no doubt that it was *your* child. But the thing is, the shock of you leaving me caused me to have a miscarriage. Our little girl was stillborn, and it almost destroyed me. I tried to get in touch with you. I wrote to you time after time, but the letters just kept coming back unopened. Can you imagine how that made me feel? And then when I lost our baby that was the final straw. You simply walked away from me as if I'd meant nothing at all to you, yet *you* had been everything to me. There was nothing in the world I wouldn't have done for you.' Tears were streaming unchecked down her pale cheeks now as she relived the heartache all over again. 'If only you could have seen her,' she sobbed. 'She was so beautiful. If it hadn't been for Alice you wouldn't have left me, and you and I would have our *own* child. But *she* lived and our child died. So what do you say to that?'

His eyes stretched wide with shock as he tried to take in what she had just told him.

'Bu . . . but you must be mistaken. It must have been some other poor devil's brat – some man you chased as you chased and hounded me.'

She recoiled from his insult. 'I really don't think I'd get something like that wrong, *do you*?' she screamed, as white rage pumped through her veins. How *dare* he speak to her like that, question the sacred truth of what she was telling him?

Robert shook his head incredulously as a cold finger of fear traced its way up his spine.

'So – that's why I'm here tonight, Robert. It's got nothing to do with your precious Alice. I'm here to make sure that you never ruin anyone else's life like you ruined mine and our unborn baby's.'

As the moon sailed free from behind the clouds, Robert saw the blade of the knife glint in the silver light and made a grab for it. 'You're stark staring mad, woman!' he gasped.

Hissing with rage, Nora raised the knife and brought it slashing down. She had only intended to scare him. To warn him that from now on she would be watching him, but he had insulted her, doubted the fact that she had once carried his child and that was unforgivable.

The first blow took him completely by surprise, and his body jerked as the blade slid into his stomach like butter. His hand flew to the wound and he stared at her in astonishment as he felt the wet sticky blood on his fingers.

'What the . . . ?'

Before he could say another word she struck again, and then again and again.

'I'm sorry, Robert,' she panted, and tears streamed down her face. 'But I have to make sure you don't ruin any more lives.' She had only ever meant to frighten him, but suddenly all the pain and bitter injustice had caused her to lose control.

Robert could feel his lifeblood ebbing away and he stopped fighting as a strange kind of peace began to wash over him.

A picture of Alice suddenly flashed before him and tears of regret sprang to his eyes. If what Nora said was true then there was every chance that Alice *had* been his child – and all these years he had never allowed himself to love her. Now he would never be able to make up for the way he had treated her . . . The way he had treated both of his daughters . . .

When he became still, Nora sat in stunned silence as she looked at what she had done to him.

After a time she stepped from the car and leaned heavily against the bonnet. Dear God, how could she have allowed herself to lose control like that? Through the windscreen she could see Robert's body slumped in the passenger seat, his dead eyes staring up at the moon. She began to whimper but then slowly pulled herself together. He had deserved to die.

Glancing nervously up and down the lane she satisfied herself that no one was about then hurried around to Robert's side and opened the door. The car stank of blood and death. With a strength that she hadn't been aware she possessed, she somehow managed to drag his body from the seat and into the dense trees that bordered the lane. By the time she was done she was sweating profusely and tears were once more streaming down her face. She gently kissed his cold lips for the very last time as her tears rained down onto his face, and then she covered his body with dead branches and leaves. Turning away, she walked with leaden steps back to her reeking car and left him resting there.

Susan's eyes shone as brightly as the morning sun streaming through their bedroom window as she looked at Alice. 'You'll never guess what! The fair is comin' to the Pingle Fields. I just heard some of the kids going on about it when I was in the showers. I'm goin' to ask Julia if we can go. I don't see why she shouldn't let us. After all, it's only just across the road an' under the Coton Arches, ain't it?'

She had expected Alice to be as excited about the news as she was, but instead, Alice just stared at her from beneath the blankets on her bed.

'Well come on, rouse yerself. I've been an' had a wash an' got changed, an' you ain't even set a foot out o' bed yet. Yer don't want to miss breakfast, do yer?'

A solitary tear slipped down Alice's cheek and realisation suddenly dawned in Susan's eyes.

'Ah, so that's it, is it? You've wet the bed again, ain't yer?'

Alice lowered her head in shame and nodded miserably. This often happened, particularly on school days, and Susan was getting used to it. From the little bits that Alice told her, Susan knew that she was struggling with her lessons and still as yet had made no new friends at all. The older girl felt very protective towards her little friend.

Susan took control of the situation in seconds. 'Come on.' Whipping the blankets back from Alice's slight frame, she ordered, 'Get your arse out o' there an' go an' get washed. I'll strip the bed while you're gone, an' we'll pinch some fresh sheets out o' the airing cupboard an' make the bed back up.'

As Alice slid out of the bed Susan patted her arm reassuringly. 'Don't look so worried, mate. It ain't the end o' the world, yer know? Lots o' people has accidents an' there's only me an' you as knows about it. Get yer nightie off an' put yer dressing gown on. No one will notice as how yer all bare underneath.' As she spoke she was stripping the wet sheets from the mattress, which luckily was covered in a thin rubber sheet that was extremely uncomfortable to sleep on. Bundling them into an untidy pile she thrust them into Alice's arms. 'Drop 'em into the linen basket on yer way to the lav an' I'll make the bed back up. Get a move on! While we're havin' breakfast I'll tell yer all about the fair. Have yer ever been to a fair before?'

When Alice shook her head, Susan grinned. 'You're

in for a treat then, I promise yer that. They do candyfloss there as melts in yer mouth – an' toffee apples. An' there are so many rides to go on yer can't decide which one to choose. I allus go on the Carousel meself. It's lovely, the Carousel is. It's like all these big horses that go round an' round, an' up an' down. Not real horses, o' course.'

Despite herself Alice began to feel a little better, and after she was washed and dressed and the bed was made up with clean sheets, the two girls went down to breakfast. Susan could talk of nothing else other than the fair, and by the end of breakfast Alice was almost as excited about it as she was. Breakfast was a hasty affair as Glen was almost ready to take the children who needed a lift to school in the home's old van. Alice was amongst them, so after snatching up her satchel and coat she smiled at Susan and they went their separate ways.

She was just passing the office when Julia popped her head around the door and beckoned her inside.

'I won't make you late, Alice. I know Glen is waiting for you, but I just wanted to let you know that we're going to have a meeting today about your future.'

When Alice stared back at her from frightened eyes, Julia was quick to reassure her. 'It's nothing for you to worry about, really.'

'Is my f . . . father coming back?' Alice asked timidly.

Julia sadly shook her head as she struggled to keep her smile in place. 'Well – no, my dear. I don't think that will happen, but I'll speak to you soon, and by then I'll know more what your children's officer has in mind for you.'

'I . . . I'm n . . . not going to leave S . . . Susan,' Alice told her, and as she said it her chin jutted stubbornly.

Sensing another side to the usually timid child, Julia gently patted her shoulder. 'Well, we won't worry about it for now. You just get off to school and have a good day. Whatever is decided you can be sure it will all work out in the end.'

She watched Alice walk away before slowly going back inside the office. She had watched the bond between Susan and Alice grow and knew that it would be hard for both of them if they were to be separated. Even so, the chances of Alice staying in the children's home were remote. The younger children rarely did. It was the older children like Susan who were harder to place. It was a sobering thought, and by the time she had seated herself at her desk, the brightness for her had already gone from the day.

'So, are we all agreed then? We're looking for a family who will foster Alice with a view to adoption.' The heads gathered around the table in Julia's office all bobbed in agreement.

'Very well.' Satisfied, Carol Woods told them: 'I shall set up a meeting with the adoption team and see if they have anyone suitable on the waiting list.'

Now that the decision had been made, there was little more to be said, and one by one the people who had attended the meeting gathered together their papers and left. Julia saw the last person to the door before wearily making her way back into the office. Margaret, who was collecting the dirty cups onto a tray, glanced up in concern.

'Are you all right?' she asked.

Julia sank into a chair. 'Yes, I'm fine. It's just . . .' Her voice trailed away as she rubbed her forehead where the beginnings of a headache were just beginning to throb. 'It's these planning meetings. I should be used to them by now, but I must admit I always find them very tiring. I mean, a child's whole future is at stake. And if we make the wrong decision . . . well! It just doesn't bear thinking about.'

'I know what you mean. But what alternative is there for Alice, apart from adoption? She's so young. It would be awful to think of her spending the rest of her childhood in a children's home. If we can only find the right adoptive parents for her, then I think she could settle and be happy. Let's face it – her father obviously doesn't give a jot about her. He couldn't even be bothered to be there when Carol went all the way to Leeds to see him. He knew they had an appointment. It's no wonder she was so annoyed.'

'I suppose you're right,' Julia conceded reluctantly. 'But something must have cropped up for him to just do a disappearing act like that. Didn't Carol say that his landlady hadn't seen hide nor hair of him since the Saturday night?'

When Margaret nodded she said, 'Well, at least he had the good grace to forward on written permission to go ahead with the adoption before he did his vanishing trick. We'll need that to get a freeing order in court.

Looking beyond that, the adopters are going to have to be very special people. Alice doesn't mix easily, especially with adults. She's already had so much to contend with in her short life.'

'That could be said for every child that's living here,' Margaret pointed out gently.

'Yes, I know that, but Alice is so . . . she's . . . Oh, I don't know. She just seems so vulnerable somehow.'

Margaret raised her brows as Julia flushed.

'It sounds to me like someone not a million miles away is at risk of becoming a little over-involved.'

Ashamed, Julia grinned sheepishly. 'I suppose you're right, but don't worry. I'm aware that the adoption team know what they're doing, and I have no intention of interfering.'

'Good. I'm very pleased to hear it. Now get yourself comfortable and I'll go and make us both a nice fresh pot of tea.' Margaret picked up the tray and headed for the kitchen, and for a while Julia was left alone with her thoughts.

'Look, she's comin' – look! She's just turned the corner. I told yer she'd come, didn't I?' Susan hopped from foot to foot excitedly, and curious, Alice followed her pointing finger. A weary-looking woman was walking up the street past the rows of terraced houses towards them. Unable to contain her excitement a moment longer, Susan suddenly ran towards her and flung herself into her arms. Alice could only watch enviously. She was sad for herself and yet pleased for Susan all at the same time. Susan's aunty was nothing at all what Alice had expected. She was wearing a faded headscarf tied firmly beneath her chin and a coat that looked very old. Her shoes were down-at-heel and she looked tired. But even so she returned Susan's hug enthusiastically and her eyes sparkled with pleasure at the sight of her.

'How are yer doin' then, darlin'?'

Susan gazed at her adoringly. 'I'm doin' fine. An' I got yer letter. I've put it away somewhere safe. Are all the kids better now?'

Her aunt chuckled. 'As near as damn it. Mind you, they still argue like cat an' dog. I'll tell yer what. One o' these days I'll end up bangin' their bloody heads together, sure as eggs is eggs.' Arm-in-arm they wandered up to Alice.

'Aunty, this is Alice. She ain't been here fer very long an' we share a bedroom.'

'Well, do yer now?' The woman politely held her hand out to Alice. 'How do yer do, love?'

Alice flushed to the roots of her hair. 'I . . . I'm very w . . . w . . .'

'What she means to say is, she's very well, thank you,' Susan interrupted and her aunt grinned. Together they entered the home and found a quiet corner in the day room. Once she had Alice and her aunt comfortably seated, Susan hurried away to bully Cook into making them all a pot of tea. Her whole face was alight and Alice thought how pretty she looked, which was surprising because she had never thought of Susan as being pretty before.

While Susan was gone, her Aunt Betty took off her scarf and folded it neatly, revealing brown curls that were streaked with grey. She glanced at Alice's clothes and found herself thinking how out of place the child looked in the home. Alice's whole demeanour spoke of good breeding, and if she wasn't much mistaken the clothes she was wearing had cost a pretty penny. She could only wonder at the circumstances that had led to Alice being there. But she didn't have long to ponder, because in record time Susan reappeared, balancing a tray with three mugs on it in one hand and a small plateful of mixed biscuits in the other.

'Look what Cook's sent for us.' She proudly pointed to the biscuits and offered them to her aunt who promptly took a custard cream and dunked it in her tea.

During the next hour Susan and her aunt chatted non-stop. Alice found her eyes straying around the room at the other visitors, and a wave of loneliness washed over her. From time to time she glanced at the wall clock. They were trying to teach her how to tell the time at school, but as yet the numbers meant nothing. Even so, the fast-fading light outside the window told her that soon it would be teatime. And that meant that Banana Jane would be here. She began to fidget and eventually she slid off her seat. Susan paused mid-sentence to stare at her questioningly.

Alice pointed at the door self-consciously. 'I . . . I'm j . . . just g . . . going to s . . . see . . .'

'Ah! You're just going to see Banana Jane.'

When Alice nodded, Susan grinned. 'You go ahead

then, an' tell her I'll see her on Wednesday.' She immediately turned her attention back to her aunt as Alice slipped away.

The little girl barely had time to take up her usual position in the car park when Jane's old van pulled up alongside her. She raised her eyebrows when she saw Alice standing alone.

'So! Where's your mate then?'

Solemnly, Alice pointed towards the building. 'H . . . her aunty's c . . . come t . . . to see h . . . her.'

'Ah!' Jane smiled. 'So how are you settlin' in?' she asked softly.

Alice took a breath and said, 'I . . . I'm all right, thank you.'

'An' your dad – is there any chance of him comin' to fetch you home yet?' To her horror, Alice's emerald-green eyes flooded with tears.

'N . . . no. My father won't e . . . ever f . . . fetch me now.'

'But why?' Jane knew she shouldn't ask, but she couldn't help herself.

Alice hung her head. 'He doesn't . . . love me, be . . . because I'm b . . . bad.'

'*Rubbish!*' The word exploded from Jane's lips before she could stop it. 'You ain't bad. You're . . . well – you're lovely.' She felt colour flood her face but when Alice glanced up at her in surprise she nodded to add emphasis to her words. 'Will you be stoppin' here now then?'

Alice shrugged her slight shoulders. 'I d . . . don't know y . . . yet. J . . . Julia is having l . . . lots of meetings and when they decide what's going t . . . to happen, she s . . . says she'll t . . . tell me.'

'Ah well, I dare say whatever they decide it'll be for the best, eh? But in the meantime, I'd better find you something to do, hadn't I? How would you like to help me take some of this stuff through to the kitchen?' She placed two large cabbages into her arms, and eager to please, Alice skipped away with them. Thoughtfully Jane watched her.

'She's a grand little girl, isn't she?'

She started, unaware that Glen had come to stand beside her. Immediately her manner became brusque and the softness left her. 'Yes, I suppose she is a nice kid, but why don't she never get no visitors?' It was the first time she had ever shown such interest in a child and Glen was surprised.

'I don't rightly know, to be honest. As far as I'm aware there's no one, apart from her children's officer, who has ever come to see her – not since the day she arrived. It's a damn shame if you ask me.'

Jane dropped a heavy box into his outstretched arms, more concerned than she cared to admit. 'Ah well, I suppose it's none o' my business.' Deeply embarrassed, she strode past him and he found himself grinning, but without making a comment he followed her quietly. He had just glimpsed a side of her that he had never seen before, a gentle caring side. And he liked what he saw.

Some time later, unknown to Jane, Glen watched from the grimy window of his outbuilding as she loaded the empty crates into the back of the van. Alice had long since disappeared, clutching three large bananas, no doubt on her way back to the day room to Susan and her aunty. He smiled as he watched Jane. For some reason that he couldn't fathom, she could always lighten his heart, although until the last few weeks she had barely said more than a dozen words to him. He knew that the staff at the home considered her to be somewhat eccentric, and he also knew that she could be more than a little stand-offish, but all the same, he found her refreshingly different. Of all the women he had ever known, Jane was by far the least vain. She never seemed to care how she looked, or what she wore. And today was no exception, as her Wellington boots, shabby coat and woolly hat testified. As usual her face was completely devoid of make-up, and due to her oversized outfit, her face and her fingers, which were poking out from cut-off woollen mittens, were the only bits of flesh to be seen. He watched her reverse the van erratically out of the playground and found himself thinking about his late wife. She had been dead for two years, and as he thought of her he found himself comparing her to Jane.

Lorna had been a slave to every new cosmetic and perfume that came into the shops. She had been a very beautiful woman, and Glen was aware that everyone who knew them had considered them to be the ideal couple. They had never had children, which was one of the biggest regrets of his life. He loved children, which was why he had chosen to work at the home. But Lorna had bitterly resented him working there, for she considered the position to be below him. He screwed his eyes up tight as he remembered the bitter arguments they'd had about it, and then forced himself to concentrate on his next task – raking up the leaves in the car park. Spotting Steven Mann having a crafty smoke by the main gate, Glen wheeled his barrow over and stuck a rake in the teenager's unwilling hand.

'So – what did you think of me aunty then?' Susan was sitting cross-legged on the bed, her face animated.

Alice had never seen her so happy. 'She's n . . . nice.'

'Nice? Huh! She's more than nice. She's lovely, me aunty is. An' guess what? She's told me if I'm good, I can go an' stay at her house fer Christmas. Ooh! I can hardly wait – it's goin' to be lovely. I'll have the best time I've ever had. Me uncle's the best at organisin' a knees-up, I can tell you.'

The words had barely left her lips when she flushed guiltily. 'Oh, I'm sorry, Alice. I weren't thinkin'. If I go to me aunty's you'll be all alone, won't yer?'

'No, she won't. She'll have all of us. So stop worrying, madam. If your aunty invites you for Christmas, then you'll go. Alice will be quite happy here with me, won't you, pet?' Julia had just poked her head around the door and overheard Susan's remark. She looked at Alice expectantly and the girl nodded, sensing that it was expected of her. But inside she was crying. How would she get through Christmas without Susan?

Satisfied, Julia smiled. 'That's a good girl. Now come

on, the pair of you. Cook's dishing the tea up, and if we're much longer she'll tell us off.'

Obediently the two girls trooped after her. But Alice couldn't eat a thing and pushed the beans on toast around her plate. Lisa and Steven were seated directly opposite to her and this only served to make things worse. They smirked at her obvious discomfort.

'What's up then, Carrot-top? Do you need it cuttin' up for you?' Steven grinned spitefully.

Susan bristled and leaned towards him threateningly. 'Push off, you. Why don't yer go an' pick on somebody yer own size, yer big bully.' Her eyes were flashing with rage, which amused him all the more.

'Hark at the little guardian angel then.' Altering his voice he mimicked, '*Push off, you.*'

Instantly Susan was across the table, and before he had time to stop her she had a handful of his hair in her fist.

'Ow, ow, get off, get her off!' His cries echoed around the room and almost instantly Nora, who was on night duty, appeared out of the kitchen.

'Cotton!' Her enraged voice reverberated around the room. 'You let go of Steven's hair right now . . . this minute!'

Susan gave his hair a final vicious tug and slammed back into her seat, her face flushed and furious. A silence descended on the room, and Susan was aware that every pair of eyes was on her. Steven was making a great show of rubbing his head, but his eyes mocked her.

Nora strode to his side. 'Are you all right, Steven?'

He fixed a sad look on his face as he stared up at her innocently. 'Yes, miss, I think so. I was just sittin' here an' she attacked me for nothin' at all.'

'You stinkin' little liar, you. *I never did!* You were pokin' fun at Alice,' Susan stormed.

Nora glared at her with contempt. 'Shut up, Cotton. I've heard quite enough. Lies are only going to make things worse.'

Indignantly Susan sprang to her feet. 'I ain't lyin'. He's always pickin' on Alice but you never do nothin' to stop him, do yer?'

'*Enough*, I said.' Nora's voice erupted in a furious bellow. 'I will *not* tolerate this behaviour. Get to the office immediately!'

'No, I shan't.' Susan stuck her chin out defiantly.

Nora's hand snaked across the table and grasped her arm in a vicelike grip.

'Oh yes, you will! You'll do as you're told, young lady.'

Susan shook off her hand and stamped her foot, her eyes flooding with tears at the injustice of it all.

'It ain't fair. I were only stickin' up fer Alice. But you always take his side. Yer never believe anythin' I say.'

'That is not true, Cotton. But why should I believe you? You're nothing but a troublemaker. And what's more, if you don't get to the office right now, you'll live to regret it. I can promise you that.'

Susan stood her ground as Alice began to cry softly.

'Right then. You have not only been aggressive but now you're being downright disobedient. You leave me no choice. As of this minute, all of your privileges are cancelled for a week. And that includes your right to any visitors at the weekend.'

Susan's face fell. What if her aunty came and she wasn't allowed to see her? Nora knew only too well that this punishment would hurt Susan far more than any other she could inflict.

In that instant Julia, who had heard the commotion in the office, appeared in the doorway. Her eyes swept the sea of faces until they came to rest on Susan. She took in the situation at a glance.

'Come along, Susan. You come with me, and you too, Nora. I think this should be sorted out somewhere a little more private. And then perhaps everyone else can finish their meal in peace.'

Her eyes fixed on Nora's as the enraged woman sniffed loudly and strode indignantly from the room. Hesitantly Susan edged her way around the table, and then after smiling sheepishly at Alice she followed Julia from the room.

As soon as they were out of sight, the innocent look slid from Steven's face. He smirked at Alice. 'Tut tut. It looks like your little friend's gone an' got herself into a spot of bother, don't it?'

She glared up at him as tears streamed down her cheeks unchecked, and he lowered his voice menacingly. 'Hear this, cry-baby. This is only the beginnin'. You don't belong here. You can't even talk proper. You should be locked away with your own kind in Tintersfield. We don't want you – that's a fact.'

Alice flew around the table and clattered up the wooden staircase, and once she had reached the safety of her own room she flung herself onto the bed and sobbed as if her heart would break.

'Very well, Susan, perhaps you would like to explain what's been going on. Did you or did you not attack Steven?'

'Yes, I did.' The girl shuffled from foot to foot as Julia looked at her calmly.

'Do you mind telling me why?'

Arms crossed, Susan glared at Nora. 'Why don't yer just ask *her*?' she said resentfully. 'She won't listen to a word I say, so what's the point o' me sayin' anythin'?'

Julia frowned. 'Well, I assure you, Susan, that I *will* listen. So please go ahead and tell me what happened.'

Falteringly Susan began to explain the sequence of events that had led to her attack on Steven. Julia listened quietly, and when the girl had finished speaking she tapped her chin thoughtfully. 'Mm, it sounds to me as if this has been blown up out of all proportion. I have to say, Susan, that I don't condone violence for any reason. But then I also consider that if Steven has been picking on Alice it should be stopped immediately. I detest bullying and I only wish that you had brought it to my attention before. In this instance I am prepared to accept that you acted under provocation, but I want you to promise me that should it happen again, you will come to me immediately rather than take the law into your own hands. Do you understand?'

Susan gritted her teeth and nodded.

'Very well then, that's good enough. There will be no more said, and I think that we should forget your loss of privileges under these circumstances.'

Nora bristled and opened her mouth to protest, but Julia silenced her with a glare.

'Off you go now, Susan. And leave me to deal with Steven, please. Believe me, he hasn't heard the last of this yet.'

With a final indignant glance at Nora, Susan flounced from the office.

It was then that Nora's rage erupted. 'How *dare* you undermine my authority like that?' she spat. 'I give her a punishment and then *you* tell her to disregard what I've said.'

'That's exactly what I did – I admit it.' Julia's eyes were cold. 'And I was quite right to do so in this case. Perhaps if you had stopped to find out what had caused the trouble in the first place it wouldn't have come to this. Instead, you just assumed that it was all Susan's fault. If Steven *is* bullying Alice, then I intend to address it. While I am housemother here I will not tolerate bullying from anyone. Do you understand? Nor will I tolerate favouritism from members of my staff. I shall be recording this incident in the book, and believe me, from now on I shall be keeping a very close eye on things. Now, if you will excuse me, I have work to do. As I'm sure you have.'

Trembling with rage, Nora stormed out of the office, banging the door behind her. As soon as she had gone

Julia's shoulders sagged and she sank heavily into a chair. Wearily she drew her hand across her brow. She and Nora had never seen eye-to-eye, and she guessed that from now on, things would be even worse between them. If she were any judge then Nora could prove to be a formidable enemy. Julia sighed. Only time would tell.

Chapter Eleven

On a cold November afternoon Susan and Alice sat in the day room with Susan's aunt.

'Yes, he's a good lad is Dave – our Michelle could do a lot worse. He's takin' her to buy the ring next week. So o' course we'll be havin' a little knees-up come Saturday. To celebrate like.' Aunty Betty winked at Alice. 'Which leads me up to what I come here to ask yer.'

Intrigued, Susan leaned closer. 'Go on, then. Spit it out,' she urged.

'I were just wonderin' if yer might like to come? To the party, I mean. An' then yer could perhaps stay the night? It would mean you sharin' a bed wi' our Sharon, an' we ain't the Ritz, as yer know. But you are family an' it seems a shame fer yer to miss it. I'm only sorry as there ain't room for yer mate here.'

'Oh, yes please! I'd *love* to come – an' I won't mind sharin' a bed at all. I usually end up in Alice's bed most nights anyway. Thanks, Aunty.' Susan threw her arms around the woman's neck, beside herself with excitement.

'Right. That's settled then. Now you wait there an' I'll just go an' square it wi' the staff.'

Susan watched her leave the room and hugged herself, barely able to contain her delight. 'Fancy that then, eh, Alice? Me goin' to our Michelle's engagement party!'

Alice smiled, pleased to see her friend so happy, but already she was dreading the night that she would be forced to spend alone.

Susan's aunt returned within minutes. 'That's all sorted then. No objections there. I expect they're glad to get rid of yer fer a while if truth be told,' she teased. 'Anyway – I'd best be off.' She lifted her bag and scarf. 'I've got a lot to do if I'm to be ready for this here party, an' in the meantime I want yer to be on yer best behaviour.'

'Oh, I will be,' Susan promised, and when her aunt was fully dressed she and Alice accompanied her outside. In the car park, her aunt kissed them both warmly.

'I'll be here to pick yer up on Friday, our Susan, straight after school,' she promised, and her niece nodded, her eyes sparkling.

Once Aunt Betty had disappeared around the corner, Susan lifted Alice and swung her into the air as if she weighed no more than a feather. 'Let's go an' tell Glen me good news,' she shouted, dumping her down, and sprinting towards the outbuilding. Alice followed, her steps dragging.

Some time later, Alice noticed the sky darkening through the window. It must nearly be time for Banana Jane to come.

Susan, who could barely sit still, jumped up. 'I'm just

goin' to check me wardrobe an' see what I've got to wear fer the party.'

Alice blinked, amazed. 'B . . . but what about B . . . B . . . Banana J . . . Jane?'

'Oh, I ain't got time to hang about today. You wait here wi' Glen. Get me an orange or a banana if yer can. Anythin' will do. An' I'll see yer later.'

The door banged resoundingly behind her as Alice looked at Glen.

He saw the bewilderment in her eyes and smiled at her kindly. 'Don't worry, Alice. She'll only be gone for the one weekend. I'll still be here, and I'll tell you what: while she's gone you can help me. How's that?'

She nodded, keeping her eyes downcast, and he sighed. Alice was such a quiet child and the fact that she had come to rely on Susan was more than obvious. It was also a little worrying from where he was standing, but there wasn't much he could do about it. When they heard Jane's van pull into the car park they went to meet her hand-in-hand.

'What's this then? What's happened to the rest of me welcomin' committee?' Jane looked from one to the other enquiringly.

'Susan's looking through her wardrobe. She's going to stay at her aunt's for the weekend. Her cousin's getting engaged so they're having a party,' Glen explained.

'Oh, I see.' Jane looked at Alice's dejected face. 'So what are you plannin' to do with yourself then, little 'un, without your buddy?'

Alice's lip quivered, and immediately Jane wished that

she could have bitten her tongue off. 'Aw, come on, lass. It's not as bad as all that. You'll hardly have time to miss her before she's back again.'

Glen nodded in agreement. 'That's what I've told her. Now come on, Alice. Cheer up. You can help us carry all this through to the kitchen. Here you are. You take these apples.'

Without protest she took the bag from him and went into the home, her shoulders stooped.

Jane shook her head. 'The poor little mite,' she muttered, and without another word she heaved a sack of potatoes into her arms and followed her. Twenty minutes later when the van was unloaded and Jane had been paid she hurried back to the van, expecting Alice to be waiting for her. But there was no sign of her, although half a dozen other children were hovering around expectantly. Distracted, she handed them their treats and waited until they had all wandered away. But still there was no sign of Alice. She scratched her head then quickly reaching a decision, she strode across the tarmac and tapped at the outhouse door. Almost immediately Glen answered it. His eyebrows rose with surprise. Usually he got the impression that it took Jane all her time to even bother speaking to him, and yet here she was seeking him out.

'Is there a problem?' he asked quizzically.

Deeply embarrassed, she shuffled from foot to foot. 'I'm not sure. Alice weren't waitin' for me when I come out of the home like she usually is, an' I wondered if perhaps she were in here with you?'

'No, she isn't. I expect she's gone to find Susan. She's like her shadow, she is. I think perhaps she's fretting about her going off to her aunt's next weekend. You know – worried that she won't come back.'

Self-consciously, Jane plucked at a button on her coat before looking him directly in the face. For the first time he noticed that her eyes were a lovely shade of green.

'Glen, do you know why Alice is here? What I mean is . . . why has she been put into care?'

He bit his lip. Although he was only a handyman at the home, he heard a lot that went on. He had always prided himself on keeping any information that he picked up strictly confidential, but something told him that Jane was enquiring out of genuine concern, and he felt instinctively that he could trust her. He opened the door wide enough to admit her.

'Come on in a minute,' he urged, and when she had stepped past him he closed the door firmly behind her. He took a deep breath. 'I don't know too much about Alice's circumstances,' he admitted, 'but I have heard that her mother died giving birth to her. Apparently her father never took to her. Why, I can't imagine, because from where I'm standing, Alice is a lovely child. Anyway, it seems that it got to the point where he couldn't cope any longer. That's when he put her into the home and cleared off, by all accounts.'

He paused, and when Jane made no comment he hurried on. 'There was a big meeting here a couple of weeks back. One of many, I can tell you. And it seems that her father wants to let her go for adoption.'

'No, surely not!' Jane was shocked to the core.

Glen nodded. 'It's true, I promise you. Of course, I couldn't say if they've begun looking for anyone yet. There was some talk of them transferring her to Tintersfield, the home for mentally and physically handicapped children in Rugby. But again I couldn't say what's been decided.'

Jane was genuinely appalled. 'How could a man turn his back on his own child like that?' Immediately the words had left her lips she realised that she was becoming overly involved, and she cursed herself. Unwittingly, Glen had answered a question that had been plaguing her. If Alice's mother had died bringing her into the world, that was probably what the girl had meant on the night Jane had found her, when she told her that she had killed her mother. The poor little mite obviously blamed herself for her mother's death.

She swung around. 'I'm sorry, Glen. I shouldn't have asked. It's really none of my business what happens to her.'

'Hey!' When he gently took her arm, she flinched away from him as if she had been stung. 'It's all right, Jane. Really. There's no shame in caring about somebody.'

'Ah, but that's just the point, ain't it? I *don't* care. I suppose I was just bein' nosey. It makes no difference to me one way or the other what happens to her. I've never been very maternal. So – I'll bid you good day.'

She stamped away, her face a mask of false unconcern, and bemused, Glen watched her go. Then he found himself smiling. Jane might be trying to fool herself but she wasn't fooling him, not for a second. She might not know it yet, or it could be that she didn't want to admit it, but from where he was standing, Jane cared about Alice very much. And, if truth be told, so did he.

All through the following days a little germ of an idea kept wriggling its way into Jane's mind. She tried to ignore it but it was there all the time. By Wednesday when she was due to deliver to the home again it would not be ignored.

As she and Glen unloaded the van he noticed that she was even quieter than usual. But he was a tactful man and he said nothing. Susan and Alice, who were waiting for her in their normal position, stood back patiently while Jane went to the office to be paid. Jane hovered nervously outside the door. She could hear Julia and Nora going over the week's menus on the other side and she sighed gratefully. She was glad that Julia was on duty. She liked Julia. Margaret was nice, too, but Nora . . . Well, she was a different kettle of fish altogether. Still, she found comfort in the fact that Julia was the housemother and was therefore superior to Nora. This was just as well, because she guessed that what she was about to ask her would be highly irregular. She drew herself up to her full height and tapped on the door before her courage failed her.

'Come in.'

Obediently she stepped into the room.

Julia smiled. 'Hello, Miss Reynolds – all done, have you?'

Jane nodded as she placed the invoice on the desk. Julia immediately crossed to the safe and returned with the petty cash box. Counting out the money she placed it in a neat pile on the desk. 'There you are then, thank you very much.'

Jane pocketed the money, but instead of leaving immediately as she normally did, she paused. 'I was wonderin', could I have a word? In private, like.'

Julia nodded. 'Why yes, of course you could.' She glanced at Nora. 'Would you mind just giving us a minute, Nora?'

Nora sniffed and pushed past Jane indignantly, glaring at her as she went. Once the door had closed none too quietly behind her, Julia said encouragingly, 'What can I do for you? Take a seat, make yourself comfy.'

Jane shook her head. 'No, it's all right, thanks. I'd rather stand. I er . . . I've got somethin' to ask you. Of course I do realise that what I'm askin' might not be possible.' She paused, her cheeks flaming, and Julia laughed.

'Yes, well, ask away then. The worst I can do is say no, and I assure you I've never been known to bite.'

'It's about little Alice Lawrence. I've noticed that her and Susan have grown close, like. An' Susan tells me that she's goin' away to her aunty's for the weekend.'

'You're right on both counts. Susan and Alice are close. And yes, Susan is going on a visit.'

'Ah well, that's it, see. I've got a feelin' that Alice will be lost to death without her, an' so I were wonderin' – would it be possible for Alice to come and spend the day with me? I usually run a market stall on a Saturday as you know, but it wouldn't hurt to miss it just for once. An' I thought Alice might enjoy a day out.'

'Mm.' Julia tapped her lip with her forefinger thoughtfully. Then she looked back at Jane. 'I have to be honest with you. Most of the children here usually visit their extended families or foster parents when they have a break from the home, but . . .' She smiled as Jane's face fell. 'I think we could make an exception in Alice's case. She has no extended family – or at least, none that we know of or who take any interest in her. And I do feel that a day out would do her the world of good. She's had an awful lot to come to terms with in the last few months. And it's not as if you're a stranger to us, is it?'

Jane visibly relaxed as the two women looked at each other.

'The only stipulation I will make at this stage is that you bring Alice home for bedtime. Could you do that?'

Smiling now, Jane nodded.

'Good, that's settled then. We'll bring Alice in now and see how she feels about it. If she wants to come, then I'll raise no objections at all.'

Shortly afterwards, Jane pulled out of the car park with an enormous grin on her face. In her mind's eye she could still see the way Alice's face had lit up when Julia asked her if she would like to visit Canalside. Now it was all arranged. Jane would fetch her at eight o'clock on Saturday morning. She found herself looking forward to it – she had never had a child visit the farm before. In fact, she had very few visitors at all apart from old

Lil and a few more of the boat people who called in briefly from time to time. That was how her father had always preferred it. But Alice would be her visitor. Her very first, and she could hardly wait. The cottage had seen so much sadness . . .

The red-haired child lay perfectly still. Downstairs she could hear her father moving from room to room, switching off lights and locking the doors. Her heart began to thump painfully in her small chest, and then she heard his footsteps on the stairs, and for an instant her heart seemed to stop beating. She screwed her eyes tight shut, and strained her ears into the darkness. Thump, thump, thump. The footsteps were drawing nearer – then, just as she had feared, they stopped outside her door. She tried to concentrate on the light that was spilling through a crack in the curtains, casting a pool of silver onto the bedroom floor. Slowly the door creaked open and her father entered the room. He stood directly in front of the window and the comforting light was gone. She watched as his hand went to the leather belt around his waist. Slowly he began to undo it as he stared down at her. 'You've been a bad girl. A very bad girl.'

She began to tremble. But she did not deny it, nor did she argue. She had learned a long time ago that it was pointless.

He approached the bed and she felt a warm trickle of urine warm the top of her thin legs.

'Daddy is going to have to teach yer a lesson. Teach yer to be a good girl, ain't he?'

She nodded numbly.

He stepped closer, allowing the light to once again spill through the curtains and reflect from the belt buckle as it rose and fell.

Chapter Twelve

As Alice and Susan skipped past her in the corridor hand-in-hand, Nora glared at them. The girls ignored her and hurried on their way. They were used to Nora being in a bad mood, and recently she had seemed to be even more miserable than usual.

'Walk!' she snapped, and raising her eyebrows at Alice, Susan slightly slowed her steps. When they came to the office door, Susan tapped on it and dragged Alice inside without waiting to be invited in.

When the door had closed behind them, Nora glanced up and down the deserted corridor and once she was sure that there was no one else about, she hurried to the door and pressed her ear against it. It looked to her as if Susan was up to something if the bright smile on her face was anything to go by. Nora glanced at her watch. It was already after six o'clock on a Thursday evening, which meant the girls had both got to go to school in the morning. It also meant that she had a good excuse to collar them as soon as they left the office and send them to bed early.

Her lip curled with contempt as she heard Susan's pleading voice through the door. Asking a favour, was she? Well, she'd soon put a stop to that if she had her way.

Sometimes the power of her hatred for Alice frightened her. Each time she saw her, the need to punish the child as she had punished her father became stronger, to the point that her hand itched to lash out at her. Added to this were her feelings about Robert. Sometimes she was glad that he was dead, but at other times she would slip into a deep depression as she realised that because of her actions she would never see him again. At least before, she had always harboured the hope that one day he *might* come back to her. Even on her journey to Leeds she had imagined the look of surprise and delight that would surely cross his face when he saw her, after all the time they had been apart. But instead he had looked at her as if she were a ghost from the past, a ghost that he would rather not remember, and that had cut her to the quick. She pressed her ear closer to the door. No, the root cause of it all was Alice – and now it was her turn to pay.

'But *why* can't we go? The Pingles is only a stone's throw away, an' I promise as I'll hold her hand all the time.' Susan's cheeks were suffused with colour as she stared at Julia.

'I know that, Susan, but look.' Julia nodded towards the window. 'It might only be six o'clock but it's dark already and I don't think it's safe for you and Alice to be wandering off to the fair all on your own.'

'Well, couldn't you come with us then? Just for an hour?'

Julia felt a stab of guilt sharper than a knife as she looked into Susan's expectant face. 'There is nothing I'd like better, love. But you know I can't just go off and leave the rest of the children to their own devices. It wouldn't be fair on Nora to leave her here all alone to cope.'

As she realised that she was fighting a losing battle, Susan's shoulders sagged. 'Ah well, that's it then. We might as well forget it.'

Alice's eyes as she looked up at her friend were equally disappointed. Susan took her hand and they trudged miserably out of the room. Nora was pinning something up on the noticeboard on the wall outside the office and as Susan caught her eye she grinned smugly.

They had just turned to make their way to their room when Glen came in at the front door. Immediately noticing their glum expressions, he asked jovially, 'What's this then, girls? Have you lost a bob and found a shilling?'

Susan couldn't laugh; she choked back her tears. 'Julia won't let us go to the fair 'cos it's dark,' she told him forlornly. 'An' I saved all me pocket-money specially this week – look. An' Alice did too an' she ain't never been to a fair before.'

As she held her palm open, displaying the shiny sixpences she had saved, Glen frowned.

'Well, that's too bad. I can understand Julia not wanting you to go on your own though. It's not the end of the world, mind, because there is a way round it from where I'm standing.'

'How is there?' Susan asked as her eyebrows rose enquiringly into her mousy fringe.

He smiled. 'Well, I *was* just on my way home, but I certainly wouldn't say no to an hour around the fair. I haven't been to one for years, so if you two young ladies will allow it, I'll take you.' He watched with amusement, as their faces lit up.

'You ain't havin' us on, are yer?' Susan hardly dared to believe that he meant it and when he shook his head she squealed with delight and dragged Alice towards the stairs to go and get ready. It was then that Nora reappeared as if out of nowhere to glare at him.

'If Julia has said no to the girls, then she meant it, Glen.'

He stared coolly back at her. 'There's only one way to find out, isn't there?' Looking back at the girls, whose faces had fallen a foot, he nodded towards the stairs. 'Go and get ready both of you. I'm sure there won't be a problem.'

Skirting around Nora, whose face had turned a livid red, Susan dragged Alice on.

'Come on, quick. Let's go an' get us coats on before he changes his mind.'

Glen chuckled, wondering what he had let himself in for. Then studiously avoiding Nora, who looked as if she were about to erupt, he went into the office to clear it with Julia.

In no time at all they were on their way. Susan skipped along, in her excitement holding fast to Alice's hand.

Alice was still a little subdued following the brief encounter with Nora, for although she had only been at the home for a comparatively short time compared to most of the children there, she had already picked up on the fact that Nora seemed to have it in for her, more so following an incident that had happened that very morning. She had left her hat in her room, and had run up to get it before leaving for school. Nora had seen her go, and was waiting at the bottom of the stairs when Alice came back down. Nora had shouted at her and accused her of wasting everyone's time, which had resulted in Alice going to school in tears. Now she had begun to really fear her.

However, Susan's excitement was so infectious that by the time they had turned out of Henry Street into Edward Street she was happy again. When they came to the corner, Glen paused outside Mallabones General Store. Susan stared at the boxes all lined up in neat rows along the front of the shop. They contained all manner of fruit and vegetables, plus there was a big bucket full of mops and brushes of all shapes and sizes, illuminated by the light that spilled from the shop window, casting shadows onto the pavement.

As Susan longingly eyed the enormous glass jars of sweets stood on the shelves behind the counter, Glen said, 'Come on, girls. Let's go in and get us something nice to eat on the way, hey?'

'I want to save all me money fer the rides,' Susan told him regretfully.

'That's fine. This is my treat.' Glen winked and pushed

the door open as the two girls, hardly daring to believe their luck, filed into the shop behind him. Mr Mallabone, the shopkeeper, a large red-faced man in a clean white coat, was serving a lady at the counter.

'Will that be all for today then, Mrs Bradshaw?' he asked.

She sniffed. 'Ah, that should be enough to keep the greedy little sods quiet for a day or two, Mr Mallabone. Put it down on tick will you, till Friday.'

He nodded, and as she loaded the last of her shopping into a large brown paper carrier bag with string handles, he took a small book from beneath the counter and, after licking the lead of a stubby pencil, wrote an amount next to her name.

'Thanks, Mr Mallabone. I'll be seein' you come Friday then,' she smiled.

'You will that, Mrs Bradshaw,' he replied, and as she left the shop, setting the shop bell tinkling, he turned his attention to Glen and the girls.

'Right then, sir, and what can I do for you?'

Glen grinned at the girls. 'Go on, both of you – choose something nice,' he encouraged, and Susan's eyes grew as round as saucers as she stared at the vast display. After much thought she chose a long liquorice stick and a huge bright green gobstopper that Glen declared would never fit in her mouth. Alice was a little more conservative and settled for a Wagon Wheel and a Walnut Whip.

They left the shop and crossed Coton Road and soon they entered the tunnel that ran under the railway lines alongside Coton Arches that would lead them into the Pingle Fields. It was very dark in the tunnel and Alice was a little afraid, but when they emerged on the other side she gasped with amazement at the sight that met her eyes. In the centre of the field was the fair, so brightly illuminated that the sky above it was ablaze with light. Everywhere she looked were gaily painted stalls and rides, and as they approached, she hardly knew what to look at first, so mesmerised was she by all the different sounds and smells. Susan made a beeline for the carousel and Alice watched in wonder as the metal horses with their tails flying in the breeze, floated round and round and up and down. Susan joined the queue and Glen took Alice's hand and joined her.

'We'll go on one together,' he whispered, and she smiled in anticipation. In no time at all they were climbing the steps that led to the gaily painted horses and when Glen swung Alice into the air and put her astride one, she flushed with pleasure, savouring the safe feel of his strong arms around her. After the carousel they went on the bumper cars, then Susan dragged them into the Hall of Mirrors, where she had them in fits of laughter as she posed comically in front of each one. 'Look at me,' she cried. 'I'm as tall as a house.' Swiftly moving on to another mirror she pulled a face. 'Now look, I've shrunk to be a dwarf.'

Alice was totally bemused by it all and stared at Glen questioningly.

He smiled at her kindly, enjoying himself far more than he cared to admit. 'You can be anything you like

171

in here,' he explained patiently. 'You can be long or short, fat or thin.'

'C . . . can you b . . . be good?' Alice asked him solemnly, and suddenly some of the joy was gone from the evening as he sensed her pain.

'What do you mean?' He stared at her enquiringly.

'My f . . . father told me th . . . that I was b . . . bad, and I just w . . . wondered if there was a mirror th . . . that would make m . . . me be good.'

Glen had to swallow very hard to get rid of the lump in his throat. 'I think you're *very* good already, Alice,' he said quietly, and slightly reassured, the little girl cheered up again.

After the Hall of Mirrors Susan dragged them towards the coconut shy, where lots of young men all dressed the same were throwing balls at coconuts on sticks.

'Why are they all dressed like that?' she asked, poking a finger towards them.

Glen's eyes followed her pointing finger. 'Oh, they're all sailors who are stationed at HMS *Gamecock* at Bramcote. They're all dressed the same because they have to wear a uniform.'

'Do they sail on that river there?' Susan nodded to the perimeter of the field where the River Anker ran sluggishly by.

Glen laughed aloud. 'No, love. They sail on great big ships on the sea.'

'Well, *I've* seen boats on the river, through that tunnel there in Riversley Park,' she declared, with a toss of her head.

'They're rowing boats, love,' Glen patiently explained. 'I'll tell you what. We'll walk back home through the park when we've finished here and then Alice can have a look at them.'

Susan's attention returned to the coconut shy. 'Do yer reckon as you could win a coconut, Glen?'

'I could have a try,' he said, and reaching into his coat pocket he withdrew a sixpence, which he gave to the stallholder who then handed him some rather misshapen balls. Susan held her breath as he took aim and flung the first one. It was way off target and missed the coconut by a mile. Concentrating now, he flung another, again with no luck. Eventually he was left with the final ball and he drew himself up to his full height and concentrated on his target. With an almighty swing he flung the ball into the air and to Susan's amazement, a coconut toppled from its perch.

Susan whooped with delight and when the stallholder handed Glen his prize, he placed it in her hand. She flushed with pleasure.

'Right then, madam. We'd better see if we can't win you something now, hadn't we?' Glen smiled at Alice and she smiled shyly back.

'I know – why don't yer let her have a go on the Hook a Duck?'

'That's a very good idea, Susan. Come on, we'll go and try our luck now while we're on a winning streak.'

The girls followed him through the throngs of noisy people until at last they came to a stall where bright yellow little plastic ducks bobbed on the water.

173

'Now, do you see that little ring on the ducks' heads, Alice? What you have to do is get the stick with the hook on through the ring, and if you do you'll win a prize. Look – they're all hanging up there.'

Alice could see that, at the back of the stall, lots of little dolls and teddy bears were hanging. Glen gave the man some money and in return he handed Alice a long pole.

Glen positioned himself behind her and steadied her two hands as she clutched it. 'Easy now,' he urged as she directed it towards the water. Alice held her breath and watched as a little duck floated towards her.

'Now!' Glen almost shouted, and Alice obediently swooped the pole towards the duck.

It connected with the ring and Glen helped her pluck the little dripping duck out of the water. Alice was trembling with excitement as she stared up at him, her eyes full of wonder.

'Have I w . . . won?' she gasped.

He laughed. 'You most certainly have. Now all you have to do is choose your prize.'

She gazed in disbelief at the array, completely spoiled for choice, but then eventually she chose a little brown teddy bear with a pretty red ribbon tied around his neck. When the man on the stall handed it to her she grasped it tightly and smiling broadly, she trotted off after Susan and Glen again. Eventually, Glen paused at a stall that smelled wonderful.

'Right then, girls. We can't have a trip to the fair without a candyfloss or a toffee-apple, can we? So what's it to be?'

'I'll have a candyfloss, ta,' Susan told him without hesitation, and after a great deal of consideration Alice decided on a toffee-apple.

As they were standing eating them, Glen glanced at his watch. 'I'm sorry, you two, but I'm afraid all good things must come to an end. It's getting late now and you've both got to get up for school in the morning, so we'd better be making our way home. Let's go back through the park so that Alice can see the boats.'

He led them into another tunnel and after stumbling along blindly in the dark for some seconds they eventually emerged on the other side in Riversley Park. Glen steered them towards the centre of it where the River Anker flowed, and pointed to the rowing boats that were tied to the side of the boathouse.

'In the summer you can hire them out and sail up and down the river,' he told them as Alice stared in awe at the huge weeping willows whose branches dipped to trail in the water. She was sure that she had never seen anything quite so pretty, and pleasantly tired now she leaned into Glen's side and took his hand. He stared down into her contented little face, revelling in the feel of her small warm hand in his. All at once he was engulfed in regrets and if onlys. If only he could have had a child of his own. If only Lorna had felt differently. But he knew that the time for if onlys was past now. He sighed into the darkness and led them on, pointing out the places of interest as they passed.

'That there is the bandstand,' he told them, gesturing at a rather splendid building that took pride of place in the centre of the park. 'In the summer the bands play in there and you can come along and listen to them.'

They moved on and he pointed again. 'That building over there is a museum.'

'What's a museum?' Susan asked, through a mouthful of candyfloss.

'Well, it's a place where things of interest from the past are kept so that people can go and see them. You've learned about George Eliot at school, haven't you?'

She nodded.

'Well, some of her dresses and some of the furniture from her house is kept in there.'

'Who is G . . . George Eliot?' Alice asked.

'She were a writer as lived in Nuneaton, an' she were very famous,' Susan said bossily. 'I thought everybody knew that. But what I don't understand is, why did her mam call her George if she were a girl?'

Glen chuckled. 'George Eliot wasn't her *real* name. Her real name was Mary Ann Evans.'

'So why did she call *herself* George then?'

Feeling a little out of his depth, Glen coughed and decided to opt for the easy way out. It had been a long day and he was feeling tired. 'I'll explain some other time,' he promised and satisfied, Susan turned her attentions back to the fast-disappearing candyfloss.

Much later, when they were tucked up in bed, Susan sighed contentedly.

'Do yer know, Alice – I've had the best time o' me life.'

Alice nodded in agreement. 'S . . . so have I.'

'What were yer best thing?' Susan asked curiously.

Alice screwed her eyes up as she tried to think. 'A . . . all of it,' she said eventually.

Susan giggled but then as she remembered something she stopped smiling and frowned. 'What did yer mean when we were in the Hall o' Mirrors an' you asked if there were one as could make yer be good?'

Alice gazed into the darkness as sad memories flooded back.

'My f . . . father always said that I w . . . was bad, and st . . . stupid.'

'Phew, he sounds like a bad kettle o' fish. If that's the case I reckon as you're better off where you are. *I* don't think as yer bad, nor does Glen.'

A silence descended as Alice thought on Susan's words. Then she thought of the wonderful evening she had just spent, and for the first time since coming to the home she fell asleep without tears on her cheeks.

Chapter Thirteen

It was a bright Saturday morning as Jane manoeuvred the van into the car park of the Henry Street Children's Home. She parked, then sat for a moment trying to put her thoughts into some sort of order. They were in turmoil and she was questioning whether or not she had done the right thing in inviting Alice to the farm in the first place. After all, Alice was really nothing to do with her. Oh well, it was too late now to renege on her offer, so she clambered down from the seat and made her way into the home, nodding at the children who were playing hopscotch on the playground as she passed.

The first thing she saw when she entered the long hallway was Alice standing all alone next to the office door. The child immediately turned to her and she looked so small and vulnerable that Jane's heart immediately melted. Unused to such feelings and unsure how to handle them, Jane became brusque.

'Come on then if you're comin', there's animals waitin' to be fed.' Never one to waste words, she stared down at Alice who was struggling with the buttons on her coat. 'Come here.' She knelt and fastened them quickly. As Alice looked solemnly back at her, Jane winked.

'Don't mind me, Alice. Me bark's far worse than me bite, I promise.' Standing back up she awkwardly took the girl's hand. 'Right then, we'd best be off. And yes, I'll have her back for bedtime.'

Julia, who had just emerged from the office, looked on and smiled, secretly amused. 'Yes, you do that, Miss Reynolds. And Alice, you have a lovely day. You can tell me all about it when you get back.'

Without another word Jane led Alice away, and it was all Julia could do to stop herself from laughing aloud. She hurried across the corridor and watched them walking to the van from the boot-room window. They made an unlikely couple, Jane in her unflattering coat and Alice in her little patent-leather shoes and yet, even so, Julia sensed a bond between them, and hoped that the day together would do them both good. She watched until the van had disappeared, then as she remembered the report on her desk the smile slid from her face. There were lots of plans being made at present for Alice's future, and as yet she had not approved of any of them. Still, she comforted herself, Alice was very young and would probably adapt to whatever was decided. Sighing, she turned and slowly trailed back to the office.

The first part of the journey was made in absolute silence. Alice, who had never travelled further than her school, which was in the opposite direction, stared out of the window, her eyes blank. Every now and then Jane peeped at her, wishing that she could think of something witty to say. But then as they drove through Stockingford and up Bucks Hill, past Camp Hill, which was one of the largest council-house estates in Nuneaton, Alice sat straighter in her seat and Jane saw a flicker of interest appear in her eyes.

'M . . . my h . . . house is d . . . down there.'

As they reached the crossroads at the top of the hill, Alice pointed excitedly towards Chapel End. Although it meant a slight detour, Jane immediately steered the van in that direction. They went down the steep hill past the post office and the florists, with its buckets of brightly coloured flowers outside that Alice remembered so well.

'Th . . . there it is! . . . look!' Halfway down the hill, Alice pointed at a house set well back from the road and Jane drew the van to a shuddering halt. Alice leaned across her and stared up the familiar drive. But then she frowned in bewilderment. It was still her house, and yet it looked different. The blue front door she remembered was now a bright pillar-box red, and flowered curtains had replaced the plain velvet ones that used to hang at the windows. As she stared, a young woman opened the front door and began to manoeuvre a pram out through it.

Jane saw the confusion flit across her face and squeezed her arm gently. 'Your house has been sold now, darlin'. I should imagine that's the lady who's bought it.'

Alice's shoulders sagged and the closed look came back into her lovely green eyes. Without another word she sank back into her seat, and feeling the girl's distress, Jane restarted the van and drove on, regretting taking her there in the first place. When they were turning into Apple Pie Lane, Jane pointed.

'Canalside is down there in the dip. Look – you can see it from here. There's the canal runnin' alongside it.'

Immediately Alice brightened again and she stared at Jane with a look of wonder on her face. 'Y . . . you h . . . have g . . . goats.'

'How do you know that? It were dark as I remember it, the last time as you set foot on the farm.'

'I saw th . . . them on my w . . . way to the boat.'

Jane laughed, amazed that Alice remembered. 'Good grief! Yes, there's Tilly and Moses and another one as you ain't seen yet. They had a baby, though I ain't come up with a name for her as yet. Perhaps you could think of one? And then, of course, there's the pigs an' the chickens. An' there's Holly, me dog, and a fat old cat called Tabitha who is so idle she can't even be bothered to catch the mice half the time. I just hope you like animals, that's all.'

Alice's head bobbed furiously and her eyes began to sparkle. Jane suddenly noticed how pretty she was when she smiled. She found it strange that she had never noticed it before, but now that she had it was hard to concentrate on the road. She was relieved when they turned into the farm drive, and she could park the van in its usual place in front of the old barn.

Jane watched in silent amusement as Alice's head swivelled from left to right as she stared at all the new sights. Everything looked so much nicer in the daylight. Jane hurried to lift her out of the van. Immediately a fat chicken waddled up to them and Alice clapped her hands with delight, causing it to scuttle indignantly away.

Grinning broadly, Jane took her hand. 'Come on, little 'un. Let's go an' meet Holly. Then we'll have us a bit of breakfast an' I'll take you to see Tilly an' Moses an' the pigs.'

Obediently, Alice trotted alongside her. It was a cold clear morning and the frost on the grass sparkled in the weak sun that was struggling to break through the clouds. To one side of the farm a bonfire that Jane had lit the night before sent lazy little wisps of smoke up into the misty morning. Alice sniffed appreciatively at the air. There was nothing here to remind her of the smells that she associated with living in a town; everything here smelled clean and fresh.

As soon as they entered the cottage, Holly launched herself at them, skidding on the red-tiled floor. Without hesitation, Alice dropped to her knees and hugged her as Holly licked her furiously and her tail wagged to and fro. Alice giggled, enjoying the attention.

Jane was amazed, but wisely made no comment. She had expected Alice to be nervous, and yet looking at the two of them rolling about on the floor, anyone would have thought they had known each other for years. She hung up her coat, and went to put the kettle on. When she came back, Holly and Alice were still frolicking and the little girl's laughter rang around the room.

'It looks like you've made a friend there,' Jane commented, and when Alice looked up at her she was pleased to see that her small face was alight.

Breakfast was a merry affair with very little said but lots of laughter. Jane turned a blind eye to the numerous titbits that Alice passed under the table to Holly. And slowly all the misgivings she had suffered over the last few days about inviting Alice here slipped away.

The morning passed quickly and pleasantly. Together they built the bonfire back up and then they cleaned out the pigsties. More than once Jane glanced worriedly at Alice's clothes. They were already very grubby, and she wondered what Julia would say when she saw the state of her. But Alice was totally oblivious to anything except the fact that she was enjoying herself. At lunchtime, Jane made them both huge doorstep cheese sandwiches, and instead of picking at her food as she normally did, Alice wolfed them down hungrily. While she was eating, Jane cleaned her patent shoes as best she could. But it was a waste of time, for within minutes of Alice being outside again they were as dirty as ever. The cold air made her cheeks glow and her green eyes sparkled as she helped Jane to fork hay into big hessian sacks in the barn.

'These are for the goats' hut,' Jane informed her. 'We'll be cleanin' them out next – that's if you're not too tired?'

Alice shook her head.

'Good, but just be warned. Tilly and Moses are as soft as butter, but the little one . . . Well, she can give you a right nasty nip, so don't go getting too close. I don't want to end your day out with a trip to the hospital Casualty Department.'

Alice giggled, and soon they were dragging the sacks across the field. Tilly and Moses hurried to meet their mistress, keeping their baby protectively between them.

They sniffed at Alice curiously then to her immense delight they nuzzled up to her. Jane was amazed. Alice showed no fear whatsoever, not even when the little kid approached her and sniffed at her. She was a pretty little creature with a black body, white legs and a smattering of white on her face. Jane stood back and watched as the child and the young goat surveyed each other, ready to rush to the rescue if need be. Then her mouth fell open as Alice suddenly flung her arms about the animal's neck and hugged her. The small goat nestled into her arms as Alice kissed her soundly.

'Look, Banana Jane, she likes me.' Her words hung on the frosty air as Jane's mouth gaped even further. There was no stammer. Nothing. She gulped, sure that she must have imagined it, before asking tentatively, 'What did you say, Alice?'

'I said – look. She likes me. And I think you should call her Susan. Susan is my very best friend's name.'

Jane was so shocked that she was rendered temporarily speechless. Eventually she nodded. 'Right. Susan it is then, if that's what you want. I suppose it's as good a name as any. You can stay and play with her for a while if you like, while I go an' put this fresh beddin' in their hut.'

She walked on, dragging the sacks behind her and didn't stop until she reached the goats' hut. There she paused to look back over her shoulder. Alice was still chattering away to the goats. She shook her head in disbelief. It was almost as if another child had emerged from the withdrawn little shell that was Alice. Entering the hut, she deftly began to throw down the fresh hay, talking to herself the whole time.

'I just wish Julia were here. She'll never believe me, not in a million years she won't.'

When the job was done she emerged and looked back across the field. Alice was skipping along the hedgerow with all the goats in hot pursuit, and it was hard to tell from where she was standing who was enjoying themselves the most. She dragged the soiled bedding to the bonfire and tossed it on and within minutes, Alice, the goats, and Holly had all joined her. The flames licked at the hay and sent a shower of sparks into the air, causing Alice to shriek with glee. Holly was barking and scrabbling in the cold ashes in the perimeter of the bonfire. She emerged more black than white and, highly amused, Alice scooped her up into her arms, covering the front of her coat in sooty black stains. Jane inwardly cringed; Alice was so grubby that she barely resembled the clean child she had picked up from the home only hours before. But even so, Alice was obviously enjoying herself and Jane hadn't the heart to stop her playing. She just prayed that Nora wouldn't be on duty when it was time for Alice to go back to the home.

I'll get her something more suitable to wear for knocking around the farm in the next time she comes, Jane thought – and then she frowned. What was she thinking of? Today was supposed to be just a one-off visit. At least, that was what she'd told herself. But now she had to admit that she was not quite so sure. After all, Alice was enjoying herself, wasn't she? So where would the harm be if she were to come again? She looked thoughtfully at Alice. The child was standing contentedly with her hands outstretched to the bonfire, her new friends clustered around her feet, and a cold finger touched Jane's heart. 'Pull yourself together, woman, you're getting in way too deep,' she scolded herself silently. But that was something that was proving to be much easier said than done.

By teatime the farm was cloaked in darkness. Alice helped Jane bed down the animals before reluctantly following her back into the kitchen. A great fire was roaring up the chimney and the room was filled with the mouthwatering smell of sausages gently sizzling in the pan.

'There we are then, little 'un. Get your teeth round them.' Jane scooped four fat bangers and a large fried egg onto Alice's plate. 'An' don't get leavin' any. You need your energy after all the work you've done today.'

She winked at Alice, as the child grabbed up her knife and fork and attacked the food as if she hadn't eaten for a month. Within minutes she had cleared her plate. Jane hurried happily away to reappear seconds later, carrying a homemade sponge cake, oozing jam and cream. Alice licked her lips in anticipation. She could never remember having enjoyed a day so much and wished that it could go on for ever.

Once the meal was finished Jane cleared the dirty pots into the sink, then disappeared into another room and returned wielding a large wooden hairbrush.

'Right, little 'un, come here and let's see if we can

make you look more respectable. Julia will have a fit if she sees you like this. You look like a walkin' haystack.'

The happy look disappeared from Alice's face at the prospect of going back to the children's home, but obediently she stood still while Jane plucked bits of straw out of her hair and attempted to brush the tangles out of it.

'So. Have you enjoyed yourself?'

'Oh y . . . yes.' The stutter was back and Jane bit down on her lip.

'Well, that's good. I'm glad.' She deliberately kept her voice light as she continued to gently brush the child's hair.

Suddenly Alice swung around to face her. 'B . . . Banana J . . . Jane. C . . . can I come again a . . . another d . . . day?'

With an effort Jane kept the fixed smile on her lips. She had an overwhelming desire to snatch Alice into her arms and hug her. But she resisted it. 'I don't see why not. That is, if Julia has no objections, of course.'

Alice visibly relaxed and turned around again, allowing Jane to finish brushing her hair. The woman made a final attempt at cleaning her shoes. Next she washed her hands and face with a wet flannel, and finally she stood back to survey her. Alice's socks were filthy, and her coat was covered in soot, made worse by Jane's attempts to remove it. But there was nothing more she could do about it.

'Aw well. I'm afraid that's about the best we can do for now. Come on, little 'un. Let's get you back – else they'll think you've got lost.'

Alice stared at her and then suddenly, with no warning, she flung her arms around Jane's waist. 'I . . . I . . . love you, B . . . Banana Jane.'

A great lump swelled in Jane's throat and a rush of emotions, the like of which she had never experienced before, surged through her as she returned Alice's hug.

'Aw, get away with you. You hardly know me, child.' Gently disentangling herself from Alice's arms, she tried to blink away the tears that were rushing to her eyes. She sniffed noisily. 'Now come on. Say goodnight to Holly an' then we'll be off.'

Julia was just leaving as they arrived back at Henry Street. She was due for two days off and was looking forward to it. But she stopped abruptly when she caught sight of Alice. Taking in the child's bedraggled appearance at a glance, she burst out laughing, much to Jane's relief.

'My goodness, Alice. Whatever happened to you? You look as if you've been pulled through a hedge backwards.' She smiled at Jane. 'Has she been a good girl then?'

Jane nodded, as deeply embarrassed, she released Alice's hand. Her own suddenly felt very empty. 'She's been as good as gold. I ain't known I've had her.'

'Well, I didn't really expect anything else. Alice is always good, aren't you?'

'Huh! That's a matter of opinion,' sniffed Nora, who had come to stand behind them. Instantly the closed look came down on Alice's face as Nora swept past Julia, and grasped Alice's arm none too gently.

'Come on, you look like you need a good bath.

Whatever have you been doing? Just *look* at the state of your coat. That will have to go off to the cleaners. And your shoes are all but ruined.'

Abruptly Jane turned about. 'I'd better be off then.'

Julia glared at Nora, before saying, 'Yes, of course, Miss Reynolds. And thank you very much for taking Alice out. I'm sure she's enjoyed it.'

She held out her hand but Jane ignored it and strode towards the door. Her temper was in danger of getting the better of her and she thought it wise to make a hasty exit, before she told Nora exactly what she thought of her or worse. Just once she glanced back over her shoulder to see Nora hauling Alice up the stairs. The little girl looked back at her imploringly, and in that moment Jane hated Nora more than she had ever hated anyone in her whole life. 'Bloody ferret-faced old bitch,' she muttered beneath her breath, and as Julia looked on helplessly she stormed out into the cold night air, slamming the door behind her.

As Nora turned on both of the taps the cold bathroom instantly began to fill with steam. She unbuttoned Alice's coat and flung it into a corner in disgust.

'Ugh! We might as well put that in the bin – it will never come clean,' she grumbled. None too gently she tugged Alice's jumper over her head. When the child was at last standing naked in front of her she glared at her with distaste. 'Just look at you. You're a disgrace. Now get in there.'

Fearfully, Alice glanced at the steaming water.

'Get in, I said – or are you deaf as well as daft?'
Viciously, Nora grabbed her arm and began to
manhandle her into the water.

Alice screamed as the scalding water burned her
tender skin. 'It's t . . . too h . . . hot,' she gasped, but
Nora ignored her and snatched up a bar of soap and a
coarse flannel.

'Oh, stop being such a baby. Of course it isn't too hot
– though looking at the state of you it ought to be. My
God, you look like you've been down the pit. Now shut
up while I try to get you clean.' She soaped the flannel
and spitefully proceeded to scrub Alice's face. The soap
went in her eyes, making them sting. But too terrified to
move she sat perfectly still. At last her ordeal was over
and Nora pulled the plug and yanked her out onto the
cold lino. Alice began to shiver uncontrollably as Nora
flung a rough towel at her.

'There then.' She wiped her damp hands on her tweed
skirt. 'Now get yourself dried and into bed. And I warn
you: if I hear so much as a peep out of you tonight,
you'll be sorry. Do you understand?'

Alice nodded, her teeth chattering, and when Nora
swept out of the bathroom she let out a sigh of relief
and leaned back against the bath. Her eyes were red and
raw, and she felt sick from all the soap she had swallowed. But even so, Nora could not take away the
pleasure from the day she had just spent. Nothing and
no one could – ever.

The little girl dried herself and slipped into her nightdress. Then she hurried along the bleak landing and

hopped into her cold bed. She snuggled down, listening to the sounds of doors opening and shutting on the landing. Slowly she relived in her mind every moment of the wonderful day she had just spent. She thought of Holly and the goats, the pigs, the chickens and the cat. But most of all she thought of Banana Jane, and a warm feeling grew inside her. She was lovely, was Banana Jane. Alice didn't care that certain people in the home laughed at the woman and the way she dressed, because she could see beyond the shabby clothes to the person that Jane was inside. 'Oh yes!' she told herself. 'Banana Jane is really lovely.' On that happy thought she sank into a restful sleep.

Jane tossed the van keys onto the table and wearily looked around.

Everything was just as she had left it. Holly was fast asleep in front of the fire. The dirty pots were piled in the sink, and the fire was still burning brightly. She was home. Jane had lived with loneliness all her life, but never had the cottage felt quite as empty as it did now. She lifted the flannel that she had used to wash Alice's face with and sniffed it as if the act would somehow make her feel close again. Then slowly the tears welled in her eyes. Bitter scalding tears of regret.

She stared at the chair by the side of the fireplace, her father's chair, and choking with emotion now, she cursed. 'Look, Dad. *Look at me.* Nearly forty years old an' what have I got? Nothin', that's what – and it's all your fault. I could have had a child, couldn't I? But no! You always had to come first, didn't you? An' now it's too late. I'm too old; I've missed me chance. It's funny, ain't it? Until today I never missed what I'd never had. But now I do. Oh by God, I do. An' now all I've got to look forward to is a lonely old age.' And as she lowered her head into her hands she wept for what she knew could never be as bitter memories came flooding back . . .

The weak watery sun turned her hair to a burnished gold as she shrank back against the playground wall. The taunts of the other children still rang in her ears. But now thankfully they were gone, and she was left alone with her thoughts – terrible thoughts that seemed to fill her every waking moment. She shuddered involuntarily as she recalled the events of the night before. She vividly remembered waking to find her father standing at the side of her bed. A feeling of dread had engulfed her as she imagined the beating that would surely come. But she had not been beaten. Instead her father had stared at her with a strange light in his eyes.

'You're goin' to be a good girl now. A big girl, ain't yer?'

Fearfully she had stared back at him, too terrified even to answer. Then slowly he had peeled away the blankets until her shivering body was revealed in the moonlight that spilled through the window. He sat down on the edge of the bed and almost tenderly stroked the skin of her inner thigh. She was bewildered. Confused. What was he doing? Her father never touched her usually. He began to tremble and his eyes became glazed. Her terror intensified. Then to her horror he stood and slowly began to undo his belt and she watched in horrified fascination as his trousers slithered down his hairy legs.

'Now remember what I told yer. You've got to be a good girl, ain't yer?'

He dropped heavily onto the bed and snaked towards her. And as she recalled what had happened next, a great fat tear slid from the corner of her eye. She still did not quite understand exactly what had happened. But her every instinct told her that it was wrong – bad. Far worse than any beating he had ever inflicted on her. She felt sore and bruised inside. And somehow she knew that she would never be the same again.

Chapter Fourteen

Carol Woods placed her cup back on the saucer on Julia's desk. She had called into the home to give the house-mother an update on what was happening regarding Alice's father, and the news she had just imparted was not good.

'So that's about it,' Carol told a worried-looking Julia. 'It seems that Robert Lawrence has just disappeared off the face of the earth. No one has seen so much as a sight of him since the Saturday evening before I went to visit him in Leeds. When I phoned his landlady at the house in Claremont Street where he was renting a grotty bedsit, she said she thought she'd heard him speaking to someone in his room on that Saturday evening. Apparently it sounded like a woman. She reckoned he left the house at about nine o'clock and he hasn't been seen since. After a week or so she got worried and went into his room, but all his stuff was still there – suitcases, clothes – the lot. That rather rules out the possibility of him doing a moonlight flit, doesn't it? I suggested that she ought to call in the police, which she did, and they have been able to tell me that he hasn't attended the new school he had started teaching at either. Going on that, they have now registered him on the Missing Persons List.' She sighed. 'Bit of a rum do, isn't it? Luckily, I do have his written permission to go ahead with adoption proceedings for Alice so I suppose we should just do that, don't you?'

Julia nodded. 'It doesn't look like we have much option. Oh dear. How do you tell a child that her father has just disappeared into thin air?'

A day or two later, Julia had another meeting with Carol in her office at the Henry Street home. Alice's doctor, Nora and Carol's manager were also present. They all listened avidly to what Carol was telling them as they sat closely around Julia's desk. Nora, who had only been allowed into the meeting in Margaret's absence, was constantly butting in and Julia stifled her annoyance as best she could whilst making a mental note to prevent the woman from becoming involved in any more business that concerned Alice.

'Nora, *please* – could you allow Carol to finish?'

Carol glanced at Julia gratefully and continued, 'I have two couples who I think may be ideal for Alice. One couple is childless, but not necessarily looking for a baby. The other couple are in their late thirties with two teenage sons. Personally, I feel that the second couple may be the most suitable. As you've already admitted, Alice is a very withdrawn child, and I feel they already have the parenting skills to help her. That, plus the fact that they have specifically asked for a girl puts them high on my list. They could also offer her the sort of home that Alice was accustomed to when she lived with her father. What do you think?'

The children's officer looked at Julia for a response, but before she could answer her, Nora butted in yet again.

'Well, *I* don't think that adoption is the right road for Alice. I *still* think she would be far better placed in Tintersfield in Rugby.'

Julia flushed with annoyance. 'I totally disagree with you. Alice is far too young to be institutionalised, and as for her being placed in Rugby . . . Well! I have very grave doubts as to whether Alice is even Special Needs at all. Jane Reynolds told me that when Alice was at her farm for the day, she was like a totally different child. Her stammer disappeared! I believe that her so-called psychological problems stem from neglect, emotional deprivation, plain and simple. Her father, or should I say, Mr Lawrence, openly admitted before he abandoned her that he had never bonded with her. Therefore we can only assume that Alice lacked any stimulation and affection in her early years. If she can respond as she did to Miss Reynolds after just one day – then imagine how she could develop if we can only find the right family for her on a long-term basis.'

Nora crossed her arms across her flat chest, and her lips set in a grim line of disapproval. 'Huh! Who's to say that Miss Reynolds was telling the truth?' she sniffed pettishly.

Losing her patience, Julia glowered at her 'There is absolutely *no* reason for Miss Reynolds to lie, from where I'm sitting.'

'Of course there is. She would hardly want us to think that the day out was a failure, would she? So it's more than obvious that she's going to make out that it went better than it really did. I mean, look at the facts – Alice losing her stammer indeed. Have you ever known her to say so much as a single word without taking about five minutes over it? Because I certainly haven't.'

Julia felt her temper rising, but thankfully she was saved from having to reply by a tap on the door. All eyes turned towards it as a small freckled face appeared.

'Sorry to interrupt, Aunt Julia, but it's Becky. She's fallen over outside an' she's cryin' fit to burst. An' her knee's all bleedin' too.'

'All right, Jeremy, thank you.' Julia smiled at the little boy before looking pointedly at Nora, glad of an excuse to get her out of the meeting.

'Nora, would you mind attending to it, please?'

Nora almost bounced out of her chair and followed the child to the door, slamming it behind her. Julia let out a sigh of relief. Nora was not a particularly popular member of staff with any of the resident children, but her blatant hostility towards Alice was becoming a problem – to the point where Julia could no longer trust her to give an unbiased opinion on what would be best for Alice in the future. The meeting continued, those remaining agreed that it would be best for both couples to be approached, and so it was decided.

When everyone had left, Julia sank back into her chair. She considered Nora's approach to Alice to be very unprofessional. But then again she was forced to admit to herself that her own was, too. For, as much as Nora disliked the child, Julia was drawn to her, far more than she should have been. She thought back to the short visit that she'd had from Jane Reynolds following Alice's day out at the farm.

'I'm tellin' you, that child is no more backward than my elbow,' Jane had insisted. 'When she were on the farm with the animals she were like a different child. Laughin' – happy – an' hardly a trace of a stammer. I couldn't believe it. All that child needs is a bit of love an' attention an' she'd be as right as ninepence.'

Julia still found it hard to believe, and yet Jane had spoken with such sincerity that she had no cause to doubt her. She shook her head sadly. It would be best for all concerned when Alice *was* placed.

To Alice's delight, another trip to Canalside Farm was arranged. This time though, it would be on a Sunday so that Jane wouldn't have to miss her Saturday market day. When Julia told her about it Susan was green with envy.

'Why, yer jammy bugger, you,' she complained. But her eyes were twinkling. 'So what's the farm like then?'

They were heading towards Glen's outbuilding hand-in-hand and Alice's eyes were dreamy.

'Ooh! It's l . . . l . . . lovely. Th . . . th . . . there's H . . . H . . . Holly. Sh . . . sh . . . she's a l . . . l . . . little d . . . dog. And th . . . there's T . . . Tilly and M . . . Moses. They're g . . . g . . . g . . . goats.'

Susan sighed enviously at the wonderful picture Alice had conjured up.

'Cor, it sounds smashing. I reckon Banana Jane has took a right shine to you.'

Glen looked up from his newspaper as they entered and noticed the smile on Alice's face.

'What's this then? It isn't Christmas for another four weeks. Has Santa Claus come early and I've missed him?'

Susan playfully slapped at his arm. 'It's her,' she cocked her thumb at Alice. 'She's just been told that she's off fer another day out at Banana Jane's farm on Sunday. I tell yer – she's got more bleedin' jam than Hartley's, she has. If she fell in the cut she'd come out wi' a pocket-ful o' fish. An' she's more than likely to, an' all, 'cos from what she's told me, the cut runs right through Banana Jane's garden.'

'Well, I'll be . . . That's grand, Alice. Something to look forward to, eh?'

Alice nodded vigorously, and when the two girls finally left, Glen watched them thoughtfully from his window. Who would have thought it? Jane Reynolds going soft. Perhaps he had been right all along. It seemed that there *was* a heart under that brash exterior after all.

He wondered vaguely what Jane would be doing at her cottage that evening, then sighing he lifted the newspaper and turned to the television page. *The Black and White Minstrel Show* was on tonight; it was one of his favourites. He didn't need to wonder what he would be doing – his evening would be spent alone in front of the television set as usual.

* * *

Alice woke on Sunday morning to an eerie grey light. Across the room she could hear Susan, softly snoring. Swinging her legs out of the bed she padded across the cold floor to the window, drew the curtain aside and gasped with amazement. The glass was covered in a thin layer of ice that had formed a pattern. Leaning forward she breathed on it then furiously began to scrub at it with the sleeve of her nightdress. At last she had cleared a little circle just big enough to peep through. The sight that met her eyes made her squeal with delight and brought Susan springing awake. The tarmac outside was covered in a crisp white blanket of snow, and the whole world was white and glistening. In a second Susan was beside her, elbowing her impatiently out of the way.

'Hotch over then, let's 'ave a look.' She pressed her eye to the glass and a smile spread across her plain features as Alice watched her adoringly, thinking how pretty she looked.

'Bloody 'ell. Just take a gander at that. We'll be able to build a snowman if we get a shufty on. What time is Banana Jane pickin' yer up?'

'N . . . n . . . nine o'clock.'

'Right then, get yer togs on. I reckon it must still be early. I can't hear anyone up an' about yet. So if we're quick, we'll have time to have a play before yer go.'

Alice nodded eagerly and soon, hand-in-hand, they crept down the stairs. Apart from Cook, who they could hear clattering about in the kitchen, they felt as if they were the only two people in the world. Susan struggled with the key in the massive front door, and then they were outside. In no time at all the virgin snow was covered in their footprints, and snowballs were flying to and fro. Curtains began to twitch and small sleepy faces began to appear at the bedroom windows. Within minutes, almost every child in the home had joined them, and the white car park rang with the sounds of their laughter.

Eventually Cook, a large rosy-cheeked woman, poked her head precariously out of the kitchen window. 'All right then, you lot,' she bellowed. 'Breakfast is on the table. Get yourselves in *now.*' She slammed the kitchen window to, just in time to avoid a hail of snowballs.

Hungry from their exertions, the children began to troop into the boot room and kick off their shoes, dumping their soaking wet scarves and gloves and coats before filing into the dining room. As usual Susan tucked into her breakfast with a vengeance, but Alice was far too excited to eat and kept glancing at the clock above the door. The teachers at school were still trying to teach her how to tell the time, but it was an art she had not yet mastered.

'Wh . . . wh . . . what t . . . time is it?' she whispered to Susan.

Her friend sighed as she noisily swallowed a large mouthful of sausage. 'Christ, Alice. It's two minutes past since yer asked me the last time. It's ten to nine. She'll be 'ere to fetch yer in a minute. So stop frettin', will yer?'

Satisfied, Alice nodded and settled back into her chair to wait. Soon the other children began to drift away from the tables, until eventually only Susan and herself were left. Nine o'clock came and went. Then it was a quarter past nine. Susan crossed to the high window and peered up and down the street.

'Look, little 'un, she'll be here in a minute – you'll see. It'll be the weather that's held her up. Don't forget she's got a good way to come. An' I bet the roads are bad.'

Alice stared at her from huge concerned eyes, and Susan hurried across to her. Grasping her hand she yanked her none too gently off the chair. 'Now don't yer dare start blartin'. Do yer hear me? Come on. We'll go an' get yer coat on, an we'll wait fer her in the boot room.'

She dragged Alice unceremoniously out into the corridor where they almost collided with Steven and Lisa.

Instantly Steven grinned spitefully, as he bent to look into Alice's eyes. 'Well, well. Look who's still here then. Has your precious Banana Jane let you down, hey?'

Without thinking, Susan kicked out. Her foot connected firmly with his shin, and caught offguard he toppled over and landed with a resounding thud on his backside.

'Ouch! *You bitch.* What did you bloody do that for?'

'I did it 'cos you're a big-mouthed bully. That's what for.' Susan's eyes flashed dangerously, but just then Margaret, who was on weekend duty, appeared further along the corridor at the office door.

Ignoring the trouble that had obviously just broken out and the fact that Steven was on his backside, she called, 'Ah! Alice. Just the one I wanted. Could I have a word, love?'

Alice tore her eyes away from Steven's outraged face. Then with Susan close behind her, she slowly approached Margaret.

The tall fair-haired woman smiled at her kindly. 'Come into the office, please.' She walked back inside and Alice and Susan trooped in after her. Kneeling down, Margaret took Alice's small hand and looked into her face. 'I've just had a phone call. It was from Miss Reynolds – or should I say Banana Jane? I'm afraid she's having problems with her van. Apparently she just can't get it to start. It's probably the cold weather, so unfortunately it looks like your visit will have to be postponed until another time.'

Alice's face mirrored her disappointment and her lip trembled, but before she could say anything, they all became aware of someone standing in the doorway.

'Morning, Margaret. Morning, kids.' It was Glen. 'I just popped by to pick up my shed keys. I left them here last night. I'll tell you what, I'm getting worse in my old age. I'd forget my head if it was loose . . .' Then, noticing Alice's tear-filled eyes, he asked, 'What's the matter, pet? And what are you still doing here? I thought you were supposed to be going to Banana Jane's today. Surely I haven't got it wrong? It's all I've heard off you for days.'

'No, Glen. You didn't get the wrong day. Unfortunately Miss Reynolds can't get her van to start. So it looks like the visit's going to have to be postponed,' Margaret explained.

Glen frowned. He knew how much Alice had been looking forward to this outing. He stroked his chin thoughtfully, his smile slowly returning.

'The way I see it, there's only one solution to this problem,' he announced. 'If Banana Jane can't come to you, then I shall have to take *you* to her, won't I? That is, if it's all right with you, of course, Margaret.'

The woman's face broke into a grateful smile. 'Oh Glen, that would be really kind. Are you sure you don't mind?'

'I wouldn't have offered if I minded, would I? Besides, I haven't got anything better planned. But I think that Susan ought to come along for the ride as well. She can keep me company on the way back.'

When he winked at her, Susan's face lit up.

'Right, that's settled then. Go on, you two. Be sure to get your warm togs on and hurry up, or else it'll be time to come back before we even get there.'

Shoulder-to-shoulder the two girls rushed through the doorway as he chuckled.

'Oh Glen, this is really very kind of you.'

Embarrassed, he flushed at Margaret's praise. 'Ah, get away with you. As I said, I've nothing better planned. In fact, to tell the truth I'll be glad of the distraction. Sunday is never my favourite day of the week. It can get a bit lonely when you're on your own, so I'll probably enjoy the outing. Anyway, I've been curious about this farm of Jane's for some time. It will give me a chance to have a nosy at it.'

At that moment the two girls burst back in, giggling

as they shrugged their arms into their damp coats. Glen herded them towards the front door.

'Right, kids. Let's get this show on the road, shall we?'

They skipped ahead of him, and soon they were all seated in his car, Susan in the front, and Alice in the back.

From the window of the boot room, Steven watched the girls climb into Glen's car. His hands clenched into fists of rage. 'Look at that,' he spat at Lisa. 'Talk about blue-eyes. Margaret never even told Susan off for pushin' me over. I reckon them pair can twist the staff round their little fingers.'

'Yeah, I suppose yer right,' Lisa agreed. 'But who cares, eh? I'm sure we can find us somethin' to do, startin' with this.' She took a rather bedraggled Park Drive from the pocket of her skirt and after straightening it out as best she could, she struck a match on the wall, lit it and handed it to Steven.

He grinned as he inhaled a lungful of smoke. 'Our day will come,' he said ominously.

Susan kept up a continuous stream of excited chatter all the way. Glen drove slowly as the roads were treacherous, and it was almost ten o'clock before he finally turned into Apple Pie Lane.

'L . . . l . . . look! Th . . . th . . . there it is!' Alice pointed at the farm below them as she jiggled excitedly in her seat.

Glen whistled. 'Goodness me, it looks like something off a picture postcard.'

And it did. The cottage roof was covered in snow. Smoke drifted lazily from the chimney, and behind it lay the canal, with its thin coating of ice stretching away into the distance like a shiny silver ribbon.

He negotiated the downhill lane very slowly, as the car slithered dangerously this way and that, making the girls squeal in nervous excitement. At last he pulled onto the driveway that led to Canalside Farm. He saw Jane's van with the bonnet still up parked next to a barn, and pulled up alongside it.

Alice threw open the rear door, and almost spilled out of the car into the snow in her haste. At the same moment the cottage door burst open and Jane stepped out, still in her old slippers. When she saw Alice a mixture of emotions flitted across her features. Then she opened her arms and the little girl flew into them.

'What? I mean . . . how?' Jane raised her eyebrows as Glen and Susan walked towards her. 'Well, I'll be . . . I never expected this,' she said, amazed. 'I couldn't get the bloody van goin' an' I were feelin' really bad at havin' to let the little one down. This is really good of you, Glen.'

He shrugged. 'Think nothing of it. It was just lucky that I popped into the home to pick up some keys. I wouldn't normally be there on a Sunday. What's wrong with the van anyway?'

Jane frowned. 'Beats me. I can turn me hand to most things. I have to, livin' on me own. But I'm afraid when it comes to engines I'm lost.'

'Well, seeing as I'm here, I may as well take a look at it for you.'

When she stared at him uncertainly, he laughed. 'It's the best offer you're likely to get,' he pointed out. 'You'll not get a garage to come out. Not on a Sunday you won't.'

'Oh, go on, Banana Jane. *Please* let Glen have a look at it. Then we won't have to go straight back, an' Alice can show me around the farm.'

As Jane looked into Susan's sparkling eyes she grinned. 'Well, all right then, but on one condition. I've got a leg of pork roastin' in there that would feed an army. If you'll all agree to stay for dinner it's a deal. I'll phone Henry Street an' tell them that you're stoppin'. What do you say?'

Glen glanced at Susan and Alice to find that they were both watching him intently. When he beamed back they both relaxed.

'Seeing as you put it like that, how can I refuse? But now, point me in the direction of your toolbox and get yourself inside, else you'll be catching your death of cold.'

He nodded down at Jane's slippered feet and following his glance she flushed, clearly embarrassed.

'Right. You'll find the toolbox to the right-hand side of the barn door.'

He nodded and strode away, as Jane ushered the two girls towards the cottage.

She could hardly believe what she had just done. What had possessed her to ask them all to stay? She, who had always prided herself on needing no one? And now here she was with three guests for dinner. Strangely, it felt nice, if somewhat confusing. Anyway, she reasoned, it was too late to do anything about it now so she might as well make the best of it.

She mashed a pot of tea, and while Alice introduced Susan to Holly and Tabitha, the cat, she carried a cup out to Glen. By the time she returned, the two girls were longing to get outside. But first Jane had a surprise for Alice. In fact, she had a few. Self-consciously she lifted a variety of carrier bags out of the cupboard.

'I got you these. I thought they might be a bit more suitable than *them*.' She nodded down at Alice's little patent shoes. 'I had to guess your size, but I think they'll fit. Don't worry if they don't. I can always take them back an' change them.' As she spoke, she withdrew a pair of shiny black Wellington boots.

Alice gasped with delight. 'Ooh! The . . . the . . . they're l . . . l . . . lovely.' Excitedly, she kicked off a shoe and tugged one boot on. They were slightly too big but comfortable nonetheless. The next bag contained a small pair of denim dungarees and a warm red woolly jumper. In the last bag was a thick woollen duffel coat, and a red hat and gloves to match the jumper. Alice was overwhelmed, and suddenly with no warning she flung her arms around Jane's neck. When the woman felt the small soft cheek against her own, something deep inside her, stirred again.

'Oh, B . . . Banana J . . . Jane. Th . . . th . . . thank you.'

Brusquely, Jane disentangled her arms and stood back up. 'Now don't you dare get goin' all sloppy on me, they're only a few bits o' clothes. So come on, get them on an' then clear off from under me feet. You can take Susan to see the animals an' collect the eggs for me, while I get on with the dinner.'

She crossed to the sink and began to peel potatoes into a large pan. But out of the corner of her eye she watched as Alice struggled into her new outfit.

Susan looked on approvingly until at last Alice was ready. 'Cor, yer look a million dollars. Don't she, Banana Jane?' She herself was wearing sensible clothes – a pair of old trousers and two thick jumpers under her school mac.

'She'll do,' Jane grunted. 'Now get off with you an' make yourselves useful.'

The girls needed no second bidding, and scampered off outside into the snow. Jane watched from the window as they skipped towards the canal. Within seconds they were throwing snowballs onto the ice, and her hands became still as she smiled with amusement at their antics. When they tired of that they disappeared, no doubt off to see the animals, and she turned her attention back to preparing the meal.

Almost an hour later Glen appeared in the kitchen doorway. Avoiding his eyes, she passed him an old rag.

He wiped his hands, feeling as awkward and ill-at-ease as she did. 'Well, I managed to get her going,' he told her eventually.

Jane ushered him towards the sink. 'That's marvellous. I was wonderin' what I was goin' to do, come market day. What were wrong with her?'

'Oh – nothing too serious. It was the distributor got damp in it, that's all. I've pulled her into the barn. And while it's really cold like this, it might be a good idea to keep her in there and throw an old blanket over the engine at night.' He soaped his hands as she nodded at him gratefully.

'I'll do that,' she mumbled.

He looked out of the kitchen window. 'It's a nice place you've got here,' he commented for want of something to say.

She shrugged, noticing for the first time how threadbare the hearthrug was. In fact she was noticing just how outdated everything was, as Lil was always telling her. She had been nagging her for ages to treat herself to a television set and a twin-tub washing machine for a start, but up until now Jane had always managed very well with a dolly tub and a mangle, just as her mother had before her. As for a television set, Jane had always been quite happy with her transistor radio and her daily episode of *The Archers*, but now she began to wonder if she shouldn't perhaps splash out on a few mod cons after all.

'It does me. Though I'll admit there's a lot that needs doin'.'

'Well, if ever it gets too much for you, just give me a shout. I'm always free on a Sunday and there isn't much that I wouldn't do for a good roast dinner.' He sniffed the air appreciatively. 'In fact, I can't remember the last time I had one. It must have been just before . . .'

His voice tailed away, and Jane glanced at him

sympathetically. She guessed that he had been about to say, 'just before my wife died'.

'Well, let's just say I haven't had one for a long time,' he finished briskly. 'There doesn't seem much point going to a lot of trouble just for one, does there?'

'I know what you mean,' Jane agreed. 'I don't very often bother meself. I . . . er . . . don't usually have guests. In fact to tell the truth, until Alice began to visit, I'd never had one. Apart from Lil, that is, but she's me aunty an' family don't count. Just don't go expectin' anythin' too posh, that's all.'

He chuckled and went to sit at the kitchen table, watching as she bustled about putting the finishing touches to the meal. The smell of roasting pork and cabbage was making his stomach rumble with anticipation.

He was amazed at how different Jane looked without her thick layers of clothes. She was dressed in jeans and an old pair of down-at-heel slippers, the whole look completed by a sweater that appeared to have been washed at least a hundred times. It was also more than obvious that she had never visited a hairdresser's in her whole life. Luckily the haircut she sometimes administered to herself was saved from being a complete disaster by the fact that her hair had a tendency to curl. The steam from the saucepans was making it do that now, and he found himself thinking how much softer she looked as it framed her face in soft red waves . . . His thoughts were interrupted by the noisy entrance of the two girls. They were covered in snow from head to foot and giggling uncontrollably, obviously enjoying every minute of their adventure.

'Look, look – Susan's gone all misty.' Delighted, Alice pointed at Susan, whose coat was steaming from the heat of the roaring log fire.

Glen's mouth dropped open with amazement. Alice had not stammered even once. His head whipped around to meet Jane's eyes, but guessing what he was about to say, she cast him a warning glance. Obediently he clamped his mouth shut and watched as Alice ran for a towel and began to dry Holly, who shadowed her every move. Soon they were all seated around the old oak table with their plates piled high in front of them.

'Cor, look at this.' Susan stabbed a crispy roast potato with her fork, as if she hadn't eaten for a month.

'She's always hungry,' Alice informed them, and laughing they all began to eat. A steamed jam roly-poly pudding swimming in thick creamy custard followed the first course. Susan's eyes almost popped out of her head at the sight of it, and in record time she had consumed double helpings.

When she had finally eaten her fill, she leaned back in her chair and patted her swollen little stomach. 'That were one o' the best dinners as I've ever had,' she informed them. 'Not better than one o' me aunty's, o' course. But close, very close. I don't think I'll be able to eat again fer at least a week.'

'What you mean is – you won't be able to eat again at least until teatime,' Alice teased, and everyone chuckled.

Once the girls had gone back outside again Jane began to clear away the dishes. The atmosphere was more relaxed now and Glen rose and started to help her.

'You sit down an' let your dinner settle,' she protested, but he shook his head.

'No, many hands make light work. That's what they say. So you wash and I'll dry.'

He snatched up a tea-towel and took a stand at the side of the sink, and seeing that he meant it Jane did as she was told.

'You know, Alice loves coming here, Jane,' he told her softly. 'She's taken a right shine to you, there's no doubt about it. But I'll tell you what, if I hadn't seen it with my own eyes, I'd never have believed how outgoing she can be. She's like a different child when she's here. Back at the home she wouldn't say boo to a goose. Yet look at her now. And what about that stammer, hey? When she's here it's non-existent. It's bloody incredible.'

'Yes, well, I think that's because she feels at ease with the animals here. We don't know, do we? What I mean is, we don't know what happened to her before she went to Henry Street. I've noticed she's very edgy around people. But with animals . . . well – I suppose they've never hurt her so she can relax with them.'

Glen dragged his eyes away from the window to stare at her in amazement. 'Do you know, Jane, I think you've missed your vocation. For someone who's never had any kids, that's a very astute observation.'

Jane chuckled. 'Well, hark at you turnin' out the big words.'

214

'You shouldn't judge a book by its cover,' he told her. 'Just because I'm an odd-job man doesn't mean that I haven't got any brains, you know. I could tell you things about myself that might shock you.'

Jane had secretly always thought that Glen seemed a little out of place as an odd-job man, so she grinned and said, 'Go on then, I'm all ears.'

He shook his head and she was shocked to see the raw pain in his eyes. 'No. Some things are just too difficult to talk about.'

She frowned. At least she could agree with that – if he did but know it, she felt exactly the same. She became silent and turned her attention back to Alice and Susan who were once more frolicking in the snow.

Once the pots were all put away she produced two bottles of beer out of a refrigerator that Glen felt sure must be an antique. Handing one to him, she motioned towards the fire.

'Come on,' she commanded. 'Shift the cat off that chair and put your feet up for half an' hour. You ain't got to rush back, have you?'

'Not at all,' he admitted. 'I might as well hang on now and run the girls back when they're ready. It's silly for you to have to get the van out in this weather, when I'm going that way anyway.'

She nodded in agreement, and after switching on the radio, they each took a seat at the side of the fire and settled into a companionable silence.

Eventually Jane smiled. 'Old Lil will never believe me when I tell her I've had *three* guests for Sunday dinner.

She's always telling me what an unsociable bugger I am.' She sneaked a look at Glen. He looked totally at home, and the combination of the big dinner and the warmth of the fire were making his eyes droop. Sighing with a strange feeling of contentment she leaned back in her chair.

Mid-afternoon it began to snow again. Jane came back to the kitchen from playing with the girls, just as a log cracked on the fire and Glen woke with a start. He looked around, confused, to see Jane looking at him in amusement as she slung her coat across the back of a chair.

Hastily knuckling the sleep from his eyes he glanced anxiously at the window. 'Goodness me, I must have dropped off, I'm so sorry. I think we ought to be thinking of going soon. The way this is coming down, if we don't, we're liable to get snowed in. You should have woken me.'

Jane smiled. 'Didn't like to. You looked so comfortable, an' anyway, you're goin' nowhere till you've had a good tea inside you.'

He groaned. 'Good Lord, woman. You'll have me fit to burst. My dinner hasn't had time to go down yet.'

Jane laughed. 'Well, all the same you'll have to find room for a bit of tea. Besides, you stand no chance of draggin' them pair away just yet. I got me old sledge out of the shed for them an' they're havin' a rare old time.'

She crossed to the window and watched as Susan tugged Alice along on the wooden sledge. Glen came to stand beside her and laughed at their antics.

'It's nice to see them enjoying themselves so much, isn't it?' he remarked quietly, and Jane nodded in agreement.

It was almost six o'clock before Jane's guests finally left, and by then it was pitch dark and the snow was coming down with a vengeance. Susan had eaten the most enormous pile of ham sandwiches that Alice had ever seen, and between the two of them they had devoured a delicious homemade jam sponge cake.

Alice was yawning and contented as Jane lifted her into the back seat of Glen's car. He had cleared the windows and run the engine with the heater on for ten minutes to warm the car up. 'Now you be good girls and I'll see you both on Wednesday when I deliver to the home,' Jane said. 'All right?'

Without stopping to think, Alice snaked her arms around Jane's neck, and planted a wet sticky kiss on her cheek. 'I love you, Banana Jane.'

Jane felt her heart do a somersault in her chest. Deeply touched, she said gruffly, 'I'll see you on Wednesday. Now go on, off you go, the pair of you, else you'll be asleep before Glen gets you home.' She closed the door firmly and stood up.

Her eyes met Glen's; he was watching her curiously over the car roof. 'Thanks, Jane,' he said softly, 'for a lovely dinner, a lovely tea, and a lovely day. Do you know something? I can't remember when I last enjoyed myself as much.'

Glad of the darkness that would hide her blush, Jane shrugged. 'Think nothin' of it. It should be me thankin' you, for bringing the girls an' fixin' me van.'

An awkward silence settled as they looked at each other. Then abruptly Glen climbed into the driver's seat and put the car into gear. Jane waved to them as they drove away. She stood in the falling snow and watched the small car labour its way up the Lane until at last the headlights disappeared around the bend. Then suddenly cold, she shivered and picked her way across the yard to the cottage door. Holly was fast asleep in front of the fire, totally exhausted from her day's exertions. Jane closed the door on the darkness and gently fingered the cheek that Alice had kissed.

Chapter Fifteen

When Lil suddenly appeared at the cottage just before Christmas, Jane was delighted. The thought of spending yet another Christmas alone had been weighing heavily on her mind and Lil was like the answer to a prayer.

As they sat in front of the cosy fire enjoying a cup of tea, Jane was thinking of a way to invite Lil to stay, but as things turned out she didn't have to, for her aunt suddenly asked tentatively, 'I were wonderin' if yer wouldn't mind very much if I were to moor up till the weather improves?'

'Of course I wouldn't mind, Lil. I've always told you – you can stay as long as you want. It's nearly Christmas anyway, so why don't you stay until after that? You might as well come in an' spend it in the cottage with me as both of us be on our own.'

'Mm.' Lil beamed at Jane over the rim of her mug. 'I might just do that. I ain't as young as I used to be, and the thought of another Christmas alone on *Firefly* is a bit dauntin' to say the least.'

'There you are then. That's settled.'

'So, what yer been up to, gel?' Lil enquired conversationally.

Jane shrugged, keeping her eyes directed at the fire. 'Nothin' much,' she muttered, and Lil settled further back in her chair. As her eyes swept the familiar room they came to rest on a small pair of Wellington boots at the side of the door.

'So whose are those?' she queried, as she pointed at them.

Jane flushed. 'Oh, those? Er, they belong to Alice. You know – the little girl who lives at Henry Street Children's Home. She's been to visit a few times and I got her those to wear when she's here.'

'YOU WHAT?' Lil could hardly believe what she was hearing. 'You mean the little girl yer found on me boat that night?'

When Jane nodded, a grin spread across her face. 'But I thought yer said that what happened to her from now on were none o' your business. Why the sudden change o' heart? If yer buyin' her boots to wear about the place it sounds to me like you an' this little Alice are gettin' close.'

'Course we're not,' Jane retaliated quickly. 'It's nothing like that. It's just . . . Alice is . . . Well, she's a bit lonely, that's all. So I bring her here occasionally because she likes to be with the animals.'

Lil noticed Jane's colour rising and she said gently, 'There's no need to go on the defensive, gel. I think it's brilliant. I've been tellin' yer fer long enough that yer spend far too much time on yer own. An' if you an' the little 'un enjoy each other's company, then that's all to the good. So what's she like? That night yer found her on the boat she hardly said a word.'

Jane chewed on her lip thoughtfully, thinking of how best to describe Alice.

'She's seven years old,' she said eventually, 'and I suppose she's small for her age. But then you already know that much – that she's dainty, like. Her hair reminds me of mine when I were a nipper. But I'd have to say that her eyes are her best feature. They're green as you saw, an' when she smiles, well – they just seem to sort of light up her whole face.' The colour in her cheeks deepened as she saw Lil grinning and she snapped, 'Anyway, that's enough said about Alice. If you're going to be stayin' here for a while, I dare say you'll meet her again an' you can judge for yourself. But now come on, it's your turn to tell me what you've been up to since I saw you last.'

Lil stifled a chuckle, aware that Jane was trying to change the subject, and for the next hour until Lil returned to her barge the subject of Alice was studiously avoided.

Following one of Susan's aunt's much-anticipated visits, Susan swept Alice off the bed and danced her around the sparsely furnished bedroom. 'It's all arranged. Me aunty's just been in to see Julia an' she's agreed I can spend the whole o' Christmas with her! I'm goin' the day before Christmas Eve an' I won't be comin' back till the day after New Year's Day. Oh Alice, it's goin' to be brilliant! I'll have the best time I've ever had.'

She suddenly stopped dead in her tracks and the smile slid from her face as she stared down into her friend's pale face. 'Oh, Alice, I'm sorry. I am a selfish cow, ain't I? I weren't thinkin' about you. What are you gonna do?'

'I . . . I . . . I'll b . . . b . . . be all right,' Alice assured her bravely, not wishing to spoil her friend's mood. 'S . . . S . . . Steven and Li . . . Lisa are g . . . g . . . going away too, s . . . so you n . . . needn't worry about me.'

'Huh! Them an' half the rest o' the kids here an' all. There's only gonna be a handful of yer left. Are yer sure as you'll be all right?'

'C . . . Course I w . . . will b . . . be.' As Alice smiled bravely up at her, Susan squeezed her hand.

'Just so long as you're sure. Now come on. We'd best get downstairs else we'll miss Banana Jane.'

Side by side they clattered along the landing and down the wooden stairs, and they were only just in time, for as they passed the window of the boot room they saw Jane's van pull into the car park.

As Jane drew the rusty old Bedford to a halt and switched off the engine, a loud bang and a belch of thick black smoke exploded from the exhaust. 'I really must get that fixed,' she muttered to herself, as she clambered out and picked her way through the snow to the back doors.

Almost immediately Glen appeared. 'Afternoon, Jane,' he greeted her, and she mumbled a greeting back.

He chuckled good-naturedly as he patted the bonnet. 'I reckon you're going to have to think about replacing this old girl soon, Jane. Seems to me like she's only keeping going on a wing and a prayer.'

'You could be right there, Glen. But you know what

it's like. It's one of those things that I'm always goin' to get around to doin' tomorrow, but somehow tomorrow never comes.' She tightened the string that served as a belt around her over-sized coat as together they leaned into the back of the van and began to lift out the boxes.

'So, how's the farm doing?' he asked.

She shrugged. 'I can't complain really, I suppose. Things are always a bit slower in the winter. It just means that I have to pay a few more visits to Coventry whole-sale market before I set the stall up, that's all. I never have enough room to store enough to see me all through the winter.'

'Even so, I take my hat off to you, Jane. The produce is always top quality, and it can't be easy managing all by yourself.'

She flushed at the praise and turned her attention to the job at hand.

Inside, Susan tugged Alice to a halt as a thought suddenly occurred to her. 'Alice, do me a favour, would yer? Run upstairs an' fetch me a scarf. It's bloody freezin' out there.'

Puzzled, Alice stared up at her. Susan rarely even wore a coat, let alone a scarf. But still, there was nothing that she wouldn't do for her friend, so obediently she retraced her steps. Susan watched until Alice had disappeared around the bend in the dog-legged staircase. Then she tore outside and battled through the ever-deepening snow to Jane's van. Jane was talking to Glen and they both turned to look at her as she came rushing up.

Jane frowned. 'Hello, Susan. Where's Alice?'

Breathlessly Susan explained, her face a comical mask of sorrow. 'She's upstairs. She's a bit upset, like.'

'Upset? What for?' Jane's face mirrored her concern.

'Oh! She's just found out I'm off to me aunty's house fer Christmas. Most o' the kids here are off somewhere. But still – Alice will be all right all on her own, won't she?' Susan watched Jane's face, a crafty little smile playing on her lips. *That's it, gel,* she praised herself. *I've planted the seed, now all I've got to do is sit back an' watch it grow.*

Silent again, Jane began to unload the van, and after a few minutes Alice joined them.

'I c . . . can't find your sc . . . scarf,' she told Susan apologetically.

The other girl shrugged innocently. 'It don't matter. I don't need it after all. It ain't as cold as I thought.' Bending, she lifted a string sack of onions. 'You stay here an' help Banana Jane unload an' I'll take these through to the kitchen.'

Jane and Glen exchanged a puzzled glance, and continued unloading.

'You look perished,' he commented, as he noticed Jane's blue fingertips peeping from her fingerless gloves.

'I am,' she confessed. 'It were freezin' stood in that marketplace today. I don't mind tellin' you, I shall be glad to get home tonight.'

'I'll tell you what. Why don't you come over to the hut when you've finished, and I'll make you a nice hot cup of tea to see you on your way?'

'I might just do that,' she told him shyly, and twenty minutes later she tapped on the outhouse door.

'Come in.'

She stamped the snow off her boots and stepped inside.

Glen was just pouring tea into two chipped mugs from an equally chipped teapot. 'Here,' he said, pushing one of the mugs towards her. 'Get that inside you and sit down and take the weight off your feet for a few minutes. You look fit to drop, woman.' He motioned to a dilapidated old chair and Jane sank into it gratefully. For a while neither of them spoke.

Glen watched her troubled face, before asking, 'You're fretting about Alice being on her own at Christmas, aren't you?'

'I am a bit,' she admitted. 'I'd gladly have her to spend it with me at the farm, but I don't think they'd allow it, do you?' Once again she could hardly believe that she was voicing her thoughts aloud but somehow Glen was easy to talk to.

'Well, I know most of the staff here like the kids to have a break away from the home at Christmas whenever it's possible. And it isn't as if they don't know you, is it? I'd say this is a case of nothing ventured, nothing gained. Why don't you just go ahead and ask? But not tonight, mind. Nora's on duty. If I were you I'd wait and ask either Julia or Margaret.'

'When will they be on?' she enquired.

'I don't know,' Glen said, 'but I can soon find out. Leave it with me. As soon as it's quiet I'll go into the office and take a peek at the duty rota. Then I'll phone you. Would that suit you?'

She smiled at him gratefully. 'It certainly would. Thanks, Glen. But don't go stickin' your neck out. I wouldn't want you gettin' into any trouble on my account.'

He flapped his hand, waving aside her concerns. 'Consider it done. I'll phone you as soon as I can.'

Jane drained her mug and rose stiffly, handing it to Glen. 'I'll wait to hear from you then.'

He nodded, and she walked towards the door. There she paused to look back at him briefly. He was kind, was Glen. Oh yes. As far as she was concerned, he was a kind man, and wasted here. Everything about him told her that he could have done far better than to land up as an odd-job man in a children's home. But then, as she told herself, there must be a reason for it, and, like so much else, it was none of her business.

'Right then, Miss Reynolds. Thank you. Thank you very much indeed. I'll have a word with Alice straight away. I'm sure that she'll be absolutely delighted. Goodbye.'

Julia replaced the phone receiver and smiled. Deciding that there was no time like the present she hurried into the corridor just in time to see Steven about to disappear into the boot room. 'Ah, Steven,' she called. 'Would you mind going and fetching Alice for me, please? Tell her I'd like a word with her in the office.'

Tutting, he swung about and stamped off towards the day room. He saw Alice and Susan immediately, engrossed in a game of Ludo. Crossing to them unseen, he nastily upended the board, scattering counters all over the floor.

'What did yer bloody have to do that for?' Susan spat indignantly.

He ignored her and looked at Alice. 'Julia wants you in her office . . . right now,' he said coldly.

Susan rose to go with her, but he pushed her viciously back into her seat.

'She wants *her*, not you. Little Miss Goody Two Shoes must be in trouble.'

Alice visibly paled as he sniggered, 'Go on then. I told you, didn't I? She's waitin' for you.'

With a last frightened glance at Susan, Alice scurried from the room. By the time she reached the office her legs were trembling, but thankfully when Julia answered her timid tap on the door she looked calm and friendly, and Alice relaxed a little.

'Come on in, love. I've got something to tell you.'

Alice clambered onto a hard-backed chair and looked at the housemother apprehensively.

'Don't look so worried, dear. You're not in any trouble. In fact, I think what I have to say will please you. At least, I hope it will.'

Alice left the office ten minutes later with a smile on her face that stretched from ear to ear. She felt as if she were floating, and almost ran to the day room to tell Susan her good news.

'Well, I'll be damned. That's great. So you're goin' to Banana Jane's fer Christmas, are yer?' Susan tried to sound surprised, delighted at the outcome of her scheming as her arm slid around Alice's slight shoulders. 'Looks like we're both set to have a good time now then, don't it?'

As soon as Jane had put the phone down, Lil looked at her expectantly. 'Come on then. Don't keep me in suspense. What did she say?'

'She said it would be fine.' Jane was trying hard to hide her delight.

'Well, you'd better let Glen know the good news, hadn't yer? Seein' as he had a hand in it.' She watched Jane's colour rise, with amusement.

'Yes, I suppose I had.' Jane began to fumble on the cluttered mantelshelf, looking for the piece of paper with Glen's number written on it.

'He sounds like a really nice chap, this Glen does,' Lil commented innocently. 'Didn't I hear yer say he was a widower?'

'Yes, he is. He lost his wife about the same time as me dad died.'

'Ah, that's a shame. I dare say that poor bugger will be spendin' Christmas on his own an' all. It's a shame he couldn't have come here to us, ain't it? After all, yer know what they say. The more the merrier.'

Jane chewed on her lip thoughtfully as she tossed the idea around in her mind. 'I suppose I could ask him,' she said eventually. 'Though I dare say he will have already made other arrangements.'

'I dare say he may have. But it wouldn't hurt to ask, would it?' Lil hauled herself painfully out of the chair.

'Anyway, my old bones are achin'. I'm away to me bed to leave yer to make yer phone call in peace.' She hobbled towards the door. 'Goodnight, luv.'

'Goodnight, Lil. I've put a couple of hot-water bottles in your bed and one bar of the electric fire's been left on.' Jane stared at the phone for a time before slowly pulling it towards her. With shaking fingers she dialled Glen's number, half hoping that he would be out. He answered on the second ring.

'Hello?'

'Hello, Glen. It's me . . . Jane. I'm just ringin' to let you know that Julia has agreed to let Alice spend Christmas here at the farm.'

'Why, that's marvellous news.' He sounded genuinely pleased.

'Yes, it is. But there was something else I was wantin' to ask you as well.' She gulped, suddenly losing her nerve – then she began to gabble. 'Of course, I realise, you'll probably say no. An' of course it's quite all right for you to say no. I'm sure that you'll already have somethin' else arranged. But I were wonderin' – if you hadn't . . . Well, I were wonderin' if you'd like to come an' spend Christmas Day here too . . . with us?' She felt the heat burn into her cheeks and was thankful that he couldn't see her.

There was silence for what seemed like an eternity before Glen's voice floated down the line. 'Thank you, Jane, that's really kind of you. As it happens I haven't got anything planned. So if you're quite sure you don't mind – I'd love to accept your invitation.'

Still feeling very flustered, Jane laughed nervously. 'Right then, we'll expect you on Christmas Day, bright an' early.'

'You certainly can. I'll be there, and I shall look forward to it.'

But he was there before Christmas Day. It was 23 December and Jane was taking advantage of the fact that the snow had temporarily stopped falling. She was raking the dirty straw out of the goats' hut when Lil's head popped up over the hedge.

'Here, duck, leave that a minute. You've got a visitor. Come on.'

Her excited face disappeared as quickly as it had come, and frowning, Jane propped the rake against the wall. She brushed some of the straw from the front of her coat and made for the gap in the hedge. She was puzzled. She rarely had visitors, and had no idea at all who it could be. When she emerged from the field to see Glen standing at the side of his car she felt her legs go weak.

He smiled at her nervously, suddenly wondering if this had been such a good idea. 'Hello, Jane.'

'Hello, Glen.' She was acutely aware of Lil watching them. 'So, what brings you here, then? It ain't Christmas Day yet, you know,' she joked awkwardly.

He laughed. 'I'm well aware of that. But I just thought, seeing as you've been kind enough to invite me, that I ought to make some sort of a contribution. I'm just hoping now that you haven't already got one.'

'Got one what?'

Self-consciously he opened the rear door of the car and dragged out a freshly cut Christmas tree. He stood it on its end and Lil was amused to see that it reached well past his shoulders. 'I wasn't sure what size you'd prefer.'

Jane burst out laughing. 'I ain't had a Christmas tree since I was a little girl, Glen. You should know as I ain't one for frills and furbelows. Why! I ain't even got a single bauble to dress it.'

'That ain't a problem,' Lil butted in. 'I've got some down on the boat. They ain't seen daylight fer years, but I know they're still there under one o' the seats somewhere. I never throw nothin' away, I don't. Yer never know when it might come in handy. You bring it in, luv, an' I'll go an' fish 'em out.'

Glen began to drag the tree towards the cottage as Jane hurried away to find something to stand it in. By the time Lil returned, laden down with two dilapidated carrier bags, the tree was standing in pride of place at the side of the fireplace in a sturdy bucket filled with earth.

'Here we are. I knew I still had 'em somewhere. A bit o' spit an' polish an' they'll be as good as new.' Lil dropped the bags onto the hearthrug.

'Oh! I nearly forgot. There's something else in the car as well.' Glen hurried back out into the freezing evening, and as he opened the door an icy gust of air made the fire flicker and spit. He was back in seconds with a box that he handed to Jane. She looked at him questioningly.

'It's fairy-lights,' he explained. 'I picked them up on

231

the way. Good old Woolworth's. You can't have a tree without fairy-lights, can you?'

Totally at a loss for words, Jane thrust the box at Lil. 'Here, you'll have to deal with 'em. I've got animals as still needs seein' to.' She brushed past Glen and headed for the door, her cheeks burning.

'Thanks very much, Glen,' she muttered. And then the door slammed behind her.

Glen looked at Lil. 'Oh dear. I think I've offended her.'

'Ah! Stuff an' nonsense. That's just Jane's way. She's chuffed to bits, I can tell. But she ain't much of a one for words, is our Jane. I would have thought you'd have known that by now.'

'I don't know her that well actually,' Glen admitted, and Lil chuckled. He coughed to clear his throat and edged towards the door. 'I'd best be off anyway. I've held you up enough.'

'Rubbish. Have you 'ell as like. Now plonk your arse down on that there seat an' I'll make us a nice cup o' tea. Oh! An' by the way, I'm Lil, Jane's aunty. I'd best introduce meself 'cos she didn't think to. Ain't never been much of a one for niceties, has our Jane.'

He took her outstretched hand and shook it firmly. 'I'm Glen.'

'Well, I did gather that. Jane's talked about you, an' the little girl from the home. What's her name . . . Alice?'

'Yes, it is.' He began to relax a little. 'I think you'll like her, Lil. She's a grand lass.'

'I'm sure she is. Jane obviously thinks so anyway.'

She pottered away and filled the kettle at the sink, setting the old pipes rattling, then while she was waiting for it to boil she fetched the tea caddy and carefully ladled two spoonsful of leaves into the teapot before pouring milk into two mugs. Staring at him curiously she eventually asked, 'Are yer from around here, Glen?'

He shook his head. 'Not originally, no. My late wife and I came to live in Nuneaton quite some time ago now. Not very far from the children's home, actually.'

'Well, yer made a wise choice then. Ain't nowhere in the world as beautiful as Shakespeare's country. An' it must be handy livin' so close to work. Do yer like working there?'

'Very much,' he admitted. 'I've been there for years. I like being around the children.'

'Did yer never have any of yer own then?'

Glen's face clouded. 'No, I'm afraid we didn't.'

Lil poured boiling water into the teapot and stirred it, watching him all the while. Wisely she changed the subject, sensing that somehow she had touched a raw nerve. Twenty minutes later he drained his mug and stood up. 'Well, I really have to be off now, Lil. Thanks for the tea and the chat – I've enjoyed it. I'll look forward to seeing you again on Christmas Day.' She walked with him to the door, but when she made to follow him outside, he gently pushed her back into the room.

'Don't come out, Lil. It's freezing out here.' He smiled at her kindly, and she smiled back. She liked Glen. In fact, she liked him very much. She watched him pick his way through the snow to his car, his broad shoulders hunched against the bitter cold. He's a good-lookin' chap, Lil thought to herself. Perhaps not in the classical sense, but good-looking all the same. His nose was just fractionally too big and his mouth slightly too wide. His hair was still thick, greying slightly at the temples, and he was tall and well-made. But it was his eyes that struck her most of all, big grey eyes that twinkled when he smiled. Mentally she tried to assess his age but found it difficult. Probably somewhere in his early forties, she supposed.

He started the car and seconds later the car headlights sliced through the darkness. She waved as he drove away, and he tooted his horn. As soon as he pulled into the lane Jane appeared from around the side of the cottage.

'That were bad timin'. You've just missed Glen.' Lil had the feeling that Jane had missed him on purpose, and her feeling was borne out by the shrug of Jane's shoulders and the way she avoided her eyes.

'So!' She made to elbow past Lil, and the old lady remarked casually, 'You never told me when you was on about him that he were so good-lookin'. He's a bit of all right he is, an' well-spoken into the bargain.'

Jane blushed furiously. 'I can't say as I've ever noticed,' she muttered, and as Lil followed her into the cottage, she smiled to herself.

'Here we are then, young lady.' Julia handed Susan a brightly coloured envelope. 'The postman's just been – very late on his round admittedly, but then it is the day before Christmas Eve. It looks like someone loves you enough to send you a Christmas card.'

Susan's head snapped up from the jigsaw that she was bent over in the day room, and as she fingered the envelope reverently, Julia winked at Alice.

'Cor, I bet it's from me aunty.' Susan gazed at the familiar handwriting, and unable to contain her curiosity a second longer she tore it open to reveal a card with a glittery robin displayed on the front of it. She opened it and as she read the greeting she trembled with pleasure.

'It *is* from me aunty,' she beamed, and her smile was so infectious that Alice found herself smiling too.

Julia headed back towards the door. 'Right, well just make sure that you put it away safely in your room. If you leave it lying about in here it might get thrown away and that would be a shame.' She disappeared the way she had come and glancing up, Susan saw Lisa and Steven sneering down at her.

'*Put it away safely now!*' Steven mocked.

Susan glared at him before turning back to Alice. 'Here.' She passed it under the table into her friend's hand. 'Wait until them pair ain't lookin' an' then nip up to our room an' put this in me tin – but make sure as no one sees yer, all right?'

Alice nodded solemnly and some minutes later, when Steven and Lisa had turned their attention back to the television, she slipped quietly from the room. She paused on the stairs for a moment to make sure that she wasn't being followed. Once inside their bedroom she switched on the light and crossing to the corner, she carefully peeled back the lino as she had seen Susan do. She had removed the loose floorboard and was just about to put it to one side when suddenly the door swung open. Steven and Lisa stood there, watching her every movement.

'Well, well. What have we here then, hey? A little hidey-hole if I ain't very much mistaken.' As Steven glared at her, Alice felt the colour drain from her face, and she held tight to Susan's precious card. She froze as he sauntered towards her and leaned over the hiding-place to try to prevent him from seeing the tin. Lisa joined him and when they were so close that she could have reached out and touched them, they suddenly stopped.

'So . . . what you hidin' then, Carrot-top?'

Alice clutched the card as if her very life depended on it. 'N . . . nothing.'

'Huh – you don't hide nothin'. Come on, shift out of the way an' let's have a look.' Reaching across, Steven viciously gripped her arm and with ease he swung her out of the way. 'Haha, what have we here then?'

Alice began to struggle but Lisa held her tightly as his hand dipped into the hiding-place and came out holding the box. The fact that Alice was crying by now seemed to heighten their pleasure.

'L . . . leave th . . . that. *P . . . please!* It's S . . . Susan's.'

'Is it now?' Steven rattled the tin. 'We'll just have a little look an' see what's inside, shall we?'

'N . . . no!' Alice was no match for Lisa and she could only watch helplessly as Steven opened the tin and tipped the contents onto the bare lino. Susan's mother's wedding ring hit the floor with a *ping!* and would have rolled away beneath the bed, had Lisa not put her foot on it.

'Blimey!' Her eyes lit up as she bent to pick it up, still holding Alice in an armlock. It was then that the door burst open and Susan stormed in. She took in the situation at a glance and flung herself at Steven, who was fingering the photo of her mother.

'You just put that down, yer lousy bastard. That's *mine*.'

'Huh, I can see that,' he laughed, holding her at arm's length. 'Only someone as ugly as this could be anythin' to do with you.'

Tears of rage stung at her eyes as she swiped at him, and loosening her hold on Alice, Lisa tottered over to her on ridiculously high-heeled shoes and pulled her arms behind her back as Steven stood up and waved the photo in her face.

'That's me mam. *Give it back*,' Susan sobbed furiously, but he only sneered as he studied the photo.

'Now I see where you get your looks from. My God, she *were* ugly, weren't she? I reckon I'd be doin' you a favour if I got rid of this once an' for all.'

Alice watched in horror as Steven slowly started to tear the photograph to shreds. By now Susan was almost hysterical with grief as the only photograph of her mother that she possessed was slowly destroyed in front of her very eyes. Lisa pushed Alice away from her, and as she slipped the ring onto her finger, Alice began to inch towards the door, intent on going and getting help. But Susan just stood there with tears streaming down her face as she watched the shreds of paper slip from Steven's fingers to the floor. It was as if there was no fight left in her, for the ring and the photo were all that she had left of her mother and Alice knew that she treasured them above anything else in the world.

Thankfully, just then there was a tap at the door and before Lisa could stop her Alice made a dash for it and flung it open. Julia stared past her open-mouthed into the room, then as she realised what was happening she stormed in.

'Just what the hell is going on in here?' she demanded. Breathlessly, Alice tried to tell her between sobs. Julia's face hardened and her eyes glittered dangerously as she stared at Susan's hunched shoulders and tear-stained face.

'*You two* . . .' As she stabbed a finger towards Lisa and Steven, their bravado disappeared and they paled. 'Get downstairs *now* and be waiting for me in my office. You're going to regret this, I promise you. And you, Lisa, give that ring back to Susan RIGHT NOW.'

Fearful now, Lisa pulled the ring from her finger and put it onto the bed then meekly she and Steven filed from the room. The instant they were gone, Susan dropped to her knees and began to gather up the shreds of the desecrated photograph.

'I . . . I'm s . . . sorry, Susan. I d . . . didn't know they were following m . . . me,' Alice sobbed, but Susan was so distraught that she didn't even seem to hear her.

Julia lifted the ring from the crumpled bedspread and gently pressed it into Susan's hand. 'Here you are, love. Let me go and deal with those two and later on we'll have a go at Sellotaping that all back together, eh?'

Susan nodded numbly, and angrier than she had ever been in her life, Julia Tuffin turned on her heel and went to deal with Steven and Lisa.

When they were alone again, Alice approached her tentatively. 'I'm so s . . . sorry, Susan.'

Gone was the brash manner and the brave front that Alice had always so admired. Now instead, Susan was just an orphaned ten-year-old child who had lost the most precious possession she owned. For a long time Susan said nothing; she just stared in shock at the ruined picture in her hand. Then suddenly she sank down onto the floor and as Alice held her tight, she began to weep again, with such bitter tears it seemed as if her heart would break.

Much later that evening, Julia stole quietly up the staircase and paused on the landing outside the girls' bedroom door. All was silent, so she crept into the room. Alice and Susan were huddled together in Susan's bed, their arms tight about one another, and Julia's heart twisted as she looked down on them. They looked so small and vulnerable that it was all she could do to stop herself from gathering them both into her arms there and then. But that would not have been professional behaviour, so instead she placed the photograph she had spent the whole of the evening Sellotaping back together as best she could, on the chest of drawers and with heavy steps left the room.

On the landing she passed Lisa who was just coming back from the bathroom. The girl glared and elbowed past her in a sulk and Julia sighed. Both Lisa and Steven would be leaving tomorrow to spend Christmas with their extended families, and for that Julia was grateful. When they returned after Christmas they would begin their punishment. Julia had stopped all their privileges and their pocket-money for a whole week. She hoped that there would be no further repercussions on Alice and Susan, but just in case there were, she would be keeping a very close eye on them.

She yawned and wearily descended the stairs. There were still the daily reports to write up before she could go to bed. It had been a very long day.

Chapter Sixteen

At the top of the stairs Susan put her suitcase down and hugged Alice warmly. Downstairs in the hallway she could see her aunt waiting for her. 'Right, Alice. Have a lovely Christmas, I know I will. Let's just forget about what happened to the photo yesterday – it weren't your fault. Julia made a crackin' job o' fixin' it all back together again. An' next week when we both get back we'll be able to tell each other all about what we've both been up to.'

Alice clung to her, missing her already, as tears slid down her cheeks. 'I . . . I . . . I'll m . . . miss you,' she whispered.

Susan laughed softly. 'Well, I ain't goin' fer good, yer know. An' neither are you. Banana Jane will be here to pick yer up any minute now. So come on, dry yer eyes. Yer don't want her to see yer cryin', do yer?'

Alice sniffed loudly and managed a watery smile, glad that Susan had forgiven her.

'That's better. Now I must go. Me aunty will think I've got lost.' She bent and planted an awkward kiss on Alice's damp cheek, then snatching up her suitcase she clattered away down the stairs. Alice watched until Susan had disappeared through the front door with her aunt.

Then her slight shoulders sagged and she leaned back against the bare plaster wall.

Seconds later, Nora swept along the landing like a ship in full sail. She stopped abruptly at sight of Alice, and her thin lips pursed in disapproval. 'What are you standing there for, girl? You should be getting your bags packed. Miss Reynolds will be here to fetch you soon, though what she sees in you, or why she would want *you* to stay, I'll never know.'

The closed blank look that never failed to infuriate her settled across Alice's face. Roughly, Nora gripped her arm and almost dragged her up on to the top landing and towards her room. The majority of the other children had already left to spend Christmas with their extended families, and it was unnaturally quiet. Their footsteps echoed hollowly on the cold linoleum floor and when they reached Alice's door, Nora flung it open and viciously pushed her inside. 'Now you stay there until you're called,' she spat.

But Alice only stared back at her indifferently, enraging Nora all the more. She bounced out of the room, slamming the door behind her so hard that it danced on its hinges. Alice stuck her tongue out. 'I hate Nora and Lisa and Steven,' she muttered to herself. Then, silent again, she sat on her bed to wait. After what seemed like a very long time, she heard footsteps on the landing. They stopped outside, and someone tapped on her door. After a moment it creaked open and Julia's smiling face appeared. Alice visibly relaxed.

'Are you all ready, love? Miss Reynolds is waiting

downstairs for you.' She crossed to Alice's case and snapped down the catches. Lifting it, she held her other hand out to the girl. 'Come on, miss. Let's get you on your way. We don't want to keep her waiting, do we?'

Smiling broadly now, Alice slid off the bed as a little bubble of excitement began to form in her stomach. She was here! Banana Jane was really here! Alice had hardly dared to believe that she would come. But she had, and suddenly Nora and the latest unfortunate incident was forgotten.

Jane was waiting for her outside the office door and when she saw Alice, she smiled. Not knowing what to say, she awkwardly took the suitcase from Julia. 'Right, we'd better be off. The roads are like a skatin' rink, an' the snow's comin' down thick an' fast. If we don't get off soon we may have to spend Christmas here.'

Julia bent and kissed Alice gently. 'Have a wonderful time, my dear. I shall look forward to you telling me all about what you've been doing when you get back.' She glanced up at Jane. 'This is really very kind of you, Miss Reynolds.'

Jane was saved from having to reply, for just then Nora appeared and bore down on them like an avenging angel. She elbowed past Julia, her face a mask of disapproval. 'This is all *highly* irregular, if you ask me. Miss Reynolds is not even related to Alice.'

Julia's face hardened. 'We *didn't* ask you, Nora. And fortunately decisions like this are left to the discretion of the housemother – who happens, in case you'd forgotten, to be me.'

Nora sniffed and slammed into the office as Julia turned back to Alice and Jane.

'Don't mind her,' she advised. 'I think she's suffering from a severe case of pre-Christmas blues.' She ushered them towards the door, and watched as Jane reversed the van out of the car park.

At last they were on their way, and Jane frowned as she thought of Nora's snide comments. She had realised a long time ago that Nora had no fondness for her. That was acceptable. After all, the feeling was mutual. What did worry her was the fact that Nora's dislike of Alice seemed to be getting stronger.

Jane gripped Alice's hand as they slithered across the icy yard. Lil appeared at the door to welcome them. She beamed at Alice and the little girl shyly smiled back.

'Alice, this is Lil, me aunty. I never got to introduce you properly the last time you met, but we won't harp on that now, eh? She's got her boat moored at the bottom of the garden. It's called *Firefly* and I bet she'll take you on it for a proper look around if you ask her nice. Lil's going to be spending Christmas here with us, so hopefully we'll all have a fine old time.'

Jane pushed the suitcase through the door and stamped the snow off her boots before drawing Alice into the warm kitchen. Alice's eyes immediately fell on the Christmas tree and she clapped her hands with delight. 'Ooh! The tree's lovely!'

Jane flushed with pleasure at her response. But then as suddenly as it had come, Alice's smile vanished. She was thinking back to another Christmas, at Chapel End. Mrs Skeggs had cooked the dinner, and the three of them had pulled a couple of crackers each. Her father had been kinder to her than normal, after he and the nanny had drunk a glass of something he called 'egg nog'. Alice remembered the funny name. But this Christmas her father – he hadn't even sent her a Christmas card. Nothing. And she had been so sure that he would. The little girl was suddenly confused. She missed her father – but not because she loved him; she missed him because he had been the only stable person in her life. And now he was gone. Julia had told her that no one even knew where he was and she wondered if he was thinking of her.

Jane and Lil exchanged a worried glance as they saw the conflicting emotions flitting across Alice's small face. Lil took control of the situation immediately.

'Right then, little 'un. It might be nearly Christmas, but I'm afraid there are still animals as need seein' to. Fer a start off, Tilly an' Moses an' little Susan need feeding. An' then there's the pigs to see to – not forgettin' the chickens, o' course. There's the eggs to collect – an' then . . . well, I shall need somebody to help me make the mince pies.'

Alice's expression lightened as Lil's eyes twinkled. 'That's better.' She chucked Alice gently beneath the chin and pointed to her Wellington boots. 'Get them on. As I said, there are jobs to be done an' there's no time like the present. Time an' tide wait fer no man.'

Eagerly, Alice scrambled into her boots and Lil

watched through the window as she and Jane trudged towards the gap in the hedge that led to the goats' field. She shook her head sadly. They looked so right together. 'It's a cryin' shame as Jane never had no kids of her own,' she muttered to the empty kitchen. And then she returned to the unenviable task of plucking the turkey.

By teatime, Jane and Alice had completed all the outside jobs. Lil, meantime, had cleaned the cottage from top to bottom. The normally untidy main room looked cosy and inviting, and there was a huge log fire roaring up the chimney. Freshly cut holly adorned the mantelshelf, and Lil had hung a bunch of mistletoe from the low beam that ran across the centre of the ceiling. In the corner, the fairy-lights on the tree reflected all the colours of the rainbow. And on the table was a rack where delicious, if somewhat misshapen, mince pies were spread out to cool, a testimony to Lil and Alice's hard work.

Alice sat at the side of the fire with Tabitha contentedly purring on her lap and Holly curled up at her feet. And suddenly, Steven, Lisa and the Henry Street Home seemed a million miles away.

Whilst Jane made them all a delicious tea, Lil took the little visitor on her lap and told her a story just as Mrs Skeggs used to do. Alice felt as if she would burst with happiness, particularly when Lil asked, 'Are you ready to put the mince pie and the sherry out for Santa now?'

Bemused, Alice stared back at her and Lil laughed as she cuddled the child closer.

'The thing is,' she said as she looked deep into the girl's enraptured eyes, 'every Christmas Eve Santa comes calling on all the children who've been good and leaves them some presents.'

When Alice looked dismayed and opened her mouth to speak, Lil gently pressed a finger to her lips. 'He'll *definitely* be coming to you 'cos I happen to know that you've been *very* good.'

Alice sighed with relief as Lil went on, 'Now the thing is, Rudolph the reindeer brings Santa every year. He has a red nose that glows in the dark so that Santa can see where he's goin', and it's him that has some milk and an apple. Santa has the sherry and his mince pie then he moves on to the next house and the other girls and boys.'

'But how will they get in if Banana Jane locks the door?' Alice's small face creased in concern.

Jane looked at her fondly. 'Don't you get worrying about that. Santa and Rudolph climb down the chimney with the biggest sackful of toys you ever did see.'

'But how can they do that without getting burned?'

Jane lowered her voice. 'He's magic, Alice. Magic . . .'

Alice's eyes were almost starting out of her head and she wondered how she would ever be able to wait until morning.

She was speechless with delight, and when Lil allowed her to place a mince pie on a plate and pour the sherry for Santa she shook with excitement. She poured out a saucer of milk, then went to great trouble to choose the rosiest apple in the fruit dish for Rudolph. All through their tea, Alice could barely take her eyes from the treats awaiting the Christmas visitors and the meal was a merry affair.

'What time will Santa and Rudolph be coming?' she asked through a mouthful of Christmas cake.

'Ah well, this is it, you see.' It was all Lil could do to keep a straight face. 'He'll only come when all the girls and boys are tucked up fast asleep in bed.'

Alice almost choked in her haste to swallow her food and get changed into her nightie whilst Lil and Jane cleared the table.

When she came back from the chilly bathroom, wearing her dressing gown and slippers, she found Jane reading a newspaper at the table, her glasses perched precariously on the end of her nose. Lil was sitting opposite, her knitting needles clicking furiously, so Alice curled up in the chair at the side of the roaring fire. Slowly the combination of the warm flames and a comfortably full stomach made her eyelids droop. In no time at all she was fast asleep.

'Here, look at this.' Jane looked up, and following Lil's pointing finger she gazed down at Alice. Her long eyelashes were curled on her pale cheeks and her hair shone red-gold in the firelight.

'She looks like a little angel, don't she?' Lil whispered, noticing the way Jane's face softened as she gazed at the sleeping child.

'Yes, she does, and a tired little angel if you ask me. I think I'd better get her up to bed.' Jane lifted Alice gently into her arms and headed for the stairs door. She had spent the whole of the day before airing and cleaning the room next to hers. And it was there that she carried Alice now. In no time at all she had tucked her into bed, warmed by two hot-water bottles wrapped in old towels, then she stood back to stare down on her. She smiled as Alice snuggled further down into the blankets and jammed her thumb into her mouth.

'Sleep tight, me lovely,' she whispered and self-consciously she bent and kissed the small cheek before creeping from the room.

It was Lil who woke them bright and early the next morning. She had spent far too many lonely Christmas Days in recent years, so she had every intention of enjoying each minute of this one.

'Come on, me darlin'.' She nudged Alice, as excited as a child herself, and Jane, who was close behind her, smiled.

'We've got to go an' see if Father Christmas has had the sherry an' the mince pie we put out for him. An' what about Rudolph? Do you think he'll have had his apple, an' his milk?'

Alice was instantly awake, feeling far more excited than she had ever felt in her short life. Putting out the mince pie and the sherry for Santa was a ritual that she had never performed before, and she had loved every second of it. Now she was quivering with anticipation.

'Right – now we have to do this proper.' Lil, who was at the head of the procession, winked at them over her shoulder. 'We have to creep down as quiet as mice, an' then we'll open the door. If the sherry an' the mince pie has gone off the table . . . well, we'll know he's been. An' if he has, there'll be presents under the Christmas tree.'

Alice's excitement was so great that she had the urge to push her, but she managed to stop herself. And slowly, step-by-step, they all crept down the stairs. The journey to Alice's mind seemed to take for ever – but at last they were at the stairs door. The tension in the air by now was so tangible that it could almost be felt.

'Ssh!' Lil put her finger to her lips as painfully slowly she inched the door open.

Alice held her breath. What if Santa hadn't been? The thought was unbearable.

At last Lil glanced back at her. 'Look – over there.' She held the door open just enough to reveal the table. An empty plate containing a few crumbs, an empty sherry glass, and an apple core met Alice's eager eyes.

A look of wonder spread across her face. '*Has he been?*'

Jane and Lil nodded in unison, and the door was pushed wide. Alice stared in absolute amazement at the pile of brightly wrapped presents beneath the Christmas tree.

Jane took her hand and led her, open-mouthed, towards them. 'Looks to me like you'd better get started. Half of them at least look to have your name on 'em, an' they ain't goin' to unwrap themselves.'

Eagerly, Alice bent and lifted the first present. Carefully she unwrapped it to reveal a book of fairy-stories. It was the most wonderful book she had ever seen, and although she couldn't read very well as yet, she could hardly wait to look at all the beautiful pictures.

'That's from me,' Lil informed her, and Alice gulped, lost for words to express just how much she liked it. Jane handed her another present. And so it went on until Alice looked in danger of disappearing under a pile of toys and games.

'You'll need another suitcase to take this lot home,' Lil chuckled, enjoying herself as much as Alice.

'Now, this is the last one.' Jane handed her the final gift. 'I chose it meself,' she smiled. Excitedly, Alice peeled away the wrapping paper from a large box and gasped with delight. Inside was a doll, a beautiful doll with long blonde hair and shining blue eyes. 'I shall call her Susan,' she declared, staring down adoringly at her new treasure.

'Hang on, all these Susans is goin' to get a bit confusin',' Jane teased her. 'We've got Susan Cotton, Susan the goat, an' now Susan the doll.'

'Don't care.' Alice was adamant. 'Susan is my best friend in the whole world, next to you, Banana Jane. And I'm going to call her Susan.'

Deeply touched, Jane smiled. 'So be it then. Susan it is.' And she bustled away to start the breakfast.

Glen arrived punctually at ten o'clock laden down with yet more presents. There was a lovely teddy bear for Alice, who declared she would be naming him Billy, a bottle of perfume for Lil, who immediately sprayed copious amounts all over herself, almost choking them all and finally, a tiny parcel tied with gold ribbon that he handed to Jane. She took it self-consciously, aware that all eyes were on her. With fumbling fingers she peeled away the paper to reveal a small leather box. Carefully she opened it and gasped. Inside was a gold locket on a fine gold chain.

'Glen, I can't accept this . . . it's too m . . . much,' she stammered.

He laughed. 'Don't talk so daft, woman. It's nothing. But if you don't like it, I could always change it.'

'Of course she likes it,' Lil answered for her, and crossing to Jane she lifted the necklace from the box. 'Turn around,' she ordered bossily, and as Jane obeyed her, she fastened it around her neck. 'There.' Lil stood back to admire it. 'It looks a fair treat, that does. Especially on that nice blue jumper I bought you.'

Jane fingered the locket. It was the only piece of jewellery that she had ever owned, apart from her late mother's wedding ring.

'Thank you, Glen,' she said simply. The words sounded totally inadequate for such a wonderful gift. But it was all she could think of to say. An awkward silence hung between them until Lil broke it. 'Let's get a move on, then. There's animals waitin' to be fed, Christmas Day or not.'

Jane crossed to the door and unhooked her coat from the back of it. 'Are you' comin', Alice?' This was one of the jobs that Alice loved best. But today she was so enthralled with all her new treasures that even the offer of feeding Tilly and Moses fell on deaf ears.

Amused, Glen followed Jane to the door. 'Let her be. She's too taken up with all her new toys to be dragged away. I'll help you feed the animals.'

'Yes, you do that, Glen.' Lil nodded approvingly. 'And while you two are busy I'll get the dinner on the go.'

She watched them walking across the yard, an arm's length apart, and smiled smugly to herself. This Christmas was turning out to be even better than she had hoped it would be.

By the time the couple returned, any awkwardness that had been between them had disappeared, and the atmosphere was easy and lighthearted. Lil had laid the table with Jane's mother's finest china, which had not seen daylight for years, and the appetising smell of roasting turkey made Glen's mouth water with anticipation. At last, Lil staggered to the table with the bird on a huge platter and they all took their seats. Crackers were pulled amidst much laughter and soon they were all sporting party hats and reading jokes and mottoes to each other. Glen carved the meat while Lil piled the plates high with sprouts, carrots, parsnips and crispy roast potatoes. When that was gone the plates were cleared, and Jane carried the largest Christmas pudding that Alice had ever seen to the table. A sprig of holly poked out of the top.

'I wonder who'll be lucky enough to get the sixpence,' she mused as she winked at Glen.

Alice looked confused. 'Why would there be a sixpence in a pudding?'

Lil was horrified. 'Surely you know that whoever finds the sixpence gets to make a wish?'

Solemnly Alice shook her head. 'I d . . . didn't know. We never had them in our Christmas pudding before.'

Jane ladled a generous portion into her dish. 'Well, let's hope that today's your lucky day then.' She covered the pudding in thick yellow custard and Alice's eyes sparkled greedily as she snatched up her spoon.

Minutes later she whooped with delight. 'I've got it! I've got it! Look!' She held up the sticky brown sixpence triumphantly.

'Right, quick. Make a wish. Close your eyes an' wish very hard for somethin' you really want.'

Alice stared at the faces around the table before screwing her eyes tight shut as a silence settled on the room. 'I wish . . .' She concentrated very hard. 'I wish that we were a real family. That Glen was my dad. That Banana Jane was my mum. And that Lil was my grandma and that we could all be together for ever and ever.'

She opened her eyes to find them all staring at her in amazement. Suddenly Lil sniffed loudly, and blew her nose noisily into a paper napkin. Jane herself placed her spoon down, unable to eat any more for the large lump that had formed in her throat and was threatening to choke her, and Glen smiled at Alice to break the tension.

'That was a lovely wish. I'll take it as a compliment. And I don't see why, just for today, we can't pretend that we *are* a real family. But now come on. Finish your pudding up, else it'll get cold.'

Smiling, Alice obediently tucked in again. This was Christmas as she had always imagined it to be. It had taken on a magical quality and she knew that she would never forget this day for as long as she lived.

Although Glen had declared when dinner was over that he might never be able to eat again, he managed to put away a sizeable tea.

Beyond the cottage window the snow was falling softly and the whole world looked clean and bright. Inside, Alice was sitting cross-legged beneath the Christmas tree, totally absorbed in her doll Susan as she rocked her to and fro and nursed her. Lil was sitting in the fireside chair watching her fondly, and Jane and Glen were sitting at the table.

Nora pulled her scarf more tightly about her throat as she peeped through the window at the cosy scene. Rage turned her blood to ice, as like a slap in the face it hit her that they looked like a family. A happy family, as she and Robert would have been, had it not been for Alice. The realisation was almost more than she could bear and as her hand flew to her mouth, she stepped back and her leg connected with a bucket that Jane used for feeding the animals. Had it not been so close to the door the snow would have muffled its fall, but instead it clattered resoundingly against the wood. Nora quickly scuttled away to her car, which she had left parked further down the lane.

Instantly the commotion outside made them all look towards the window.

'What the hell was that?' As Jane made to rise, Glen pressed her gently back into her chair.

'You stay there in the warm. I'll go and look.'

'Be careful!' Lil watched anxiously as Glen strode to the door and threw it open. All he found was an over-turned bucket. Bending, he moved it to the side of the door and peered into the darkness. There was nothing to be seen but the soft falling snow. Closing the door quickly he hurried over to the fire and held his hands out to the welcoming blaze.

'Probably just a fox on the lookout for his supper,' he remarked, unaware that, had he looked more closely, he would have seen footprints in the snow.

Lil chewed on her lip. 'I ain't so sure about that. To be honest I've had the feelin' that there's been somebody prowlin' about the place on a couple of occasions. I've thought I've glimpsed somebody out in the lane, but when I've gone out there's been nobody there.'

Jane chuckled. 'I reckon you've had a drop too much sherry, Lil. Your mind's playin' tricks on you.'

Not wanting to spoil what had been such a lovely day, Lil forced a smile to her face. 'Happen you're right,' she grinned, but even so her eyes stole back to the window.

That night, Alice lay in bed and stared up at the ceiling. Downstairs she could faintly hear Banana Jane banking down the fire and moving from room to room as she checked that the windows and doors were locked. Lil had retired to bed and Glen had gone home. She snuggled her new doll closer to her, and a feeling of wistful-ness washed over her. Today had been perfect, like a fairy-tale, but Alice knew that soon it must end. There were no children's homes in fairy-tales, but there was one in her life, and soon she would have to return to it. She sighed. 'You know, Susan,' she cuddled her new confidante tightly to her, 'I'd do *anything* to make the wish I made earlier come true. But I don't know how to.' Her plastic friend stared back at her from blank blue eyes. Alice looked around the room. The wallpaper was dated and faded, as was the furniture. The curtains were threadbare, and the carpet was worn. But for all that, it was homely. She smiled as she thought back to Glen leaving.

Lil had positioned herself under the mistletoe. 'Come on, give us a kiss fer Christmas. I shan't let yer leave until yer do.'

Laughing, Glen had planted a big wet kiss on her wrinkled cheek.

'Right, little 'un. It's your turn next.'

Delighted, Alice had flung herself at him, all her in-hibitions forgotten. He had swung her so high into the air that she had thought she would hit the beams, and she had kissed him full on the lips. And then it had been Jane's turn. Alice was highly amused to see Banana Jane flush a dull brick-red as she approached him cautiously. And even more amused to see that Glen was equally as embarrassed as she was.

'Well? Gerron with it, woman! Kiss the man, fer God's sake. He don't bite, yer know,' Lil had laughed.

Hastily, Glen had pecked Jane's lips, and then they had sprung apart as if they had been burned.

'Bloody hell! Do yer call *that* a kiss? Why, if I were

a few years younger I'd show yer both how it should be done.' Lil's eyes had twinkled as she winked at Alice. What a wonderful day it had been! The happy feeling was back again. As Alice wriggled further down into the warm bed her eyelids drooped. And soon she had slipped into a contented sleep.

On the first night back at the home Susan and Alice lay in their beds talking about their holiday.

'So, you had a good time, did yer?' Susan said finally, when they were all talked out.

Alice's dreamy sigh was her only answer.

'I did an' all.' Susan leaned up on her elbow. 'In fact, it was the best time I've ever had!'

Alice grinned into the darkness, and content to be together again, the two girls were soon fast asleep.

Chapter Seventeen

Alice perched uncomfortably on the edge of a hard-backed chair in Julia's office. Her heart was pounding, and her eyes looked enormous in her small face. 'S . . . s . . . so w . . . won't I b . . . be able to go to Banana Jane's o . . . on S . . . Sunday then?' she ventured timidly.

'No, love, I'm afraid you won't. Not this week anyway. As I just explained, Mr and Mrs Webb are coming all the way from Leicester especially to meet you, and I'm sure you'll like them,'

Julia sighed. Alice looked so frightened. Adoption was a very difficult subject to discuss with a seven-year-old, and the housemother was not at all sure that Alice understood what it meant, even though she had tried to explain it to her. At the moment, all Alice seemed to care about was missing her day out at Jane's. It was now nearing the end of January 1962 and Alice had gone to Jane's every Sunday since Christmas. But still, Julia consoled herself, if the meeting with the Webbs went well, Alice might soon be placed with a family. And that, as far as she was concerned, was much more important than missing one day out.

'You can go now, dear, unless there's anything you'd like to ask me, of course.'

Alice shook her head miserably and slithered off the chair. Once outside the office she scuttled away to find Susan. She was upstairs in their bedroom waiting for her.

'So – what did she want yer for then?' she asked the second that Alice walked into the room.

'She said th . . . th . . . that I c . . . can't go t . . . to Banana Jane's o . . . on S . . . Sunday.' Alice's voice was choked with unshed tears, and instantly Susan slid an arm around her shoulders. She knew how much her friend looked forward to those days at the farm.

'Aw, that's a bloody shame. But why can't yer go?'

'B . . . because some p . . . people are co . . . coming to m . . . meet me.'

Susan raised her eyebrow. 'What people are them then?'

'They're c . . . called Mr and Mrs Webb, a . . . and th . . . they're adopters.'

'Phew!' The older girl whistled through her teeth. 'It sounds like they've found a new family fer yer.'

Alice nodded miserably, and suddenly the tears she had tried to hold back spurted from her eyes. 'The trouble is, I d . . . don't want a new family. I . . . I've got y . . . you and B . . . Banana Jane.'

'Yer mustn't see it like that,' Susan replied wisely. 'I think the world of yer, yer know I do, but the trouble is, I might not be here for ever. Yer see, I found out last week that our Michelle's in the club. Yer know, the puddin' club.' She pushed her stomach out comically. 'I weren't supposed to know, but I were passin' the kitchen door an' I heard me aunty an' me uncle talkin' about it. Seems like the weddin's goin' to be a lot sooner than they planned. An' well, who knows? Me aunty always said that if she had room fer me I could go an' live there. Our Michelle is on the waitin' list fer a council house up Hill Top, an' once she's gone, her mam an' dad might take me.'

Alice stared at her from stricken eyes as Susan squeezed her hand. 'Don't look like that, you'll make me feel bad. If it weren't for me aunty I could end up here for ever. Nobody's goin' to want to adopt *me*, are they? I'm plain as a pikestaff. I've got a gob like a parish oven. An' on top of all that, I'm too old. But you . . . Well, you've got everythin' goin' fer yer. You're only a babby, an' a pretty one at that. It would be awful if you had to stay here. These people, the Webbs, they could wind up bein' yer new mum an' dad. Yer could end up livin' with 'em happy ever after. So just give 'em a chance, eh?'

Alice hung her head as a solitary tear slid down her cheek. The way she saw it, she didn't have much choice in the matter.

When Jane entered the cottage Lil saw at once that she was not in a good mood. She struggled out of the fire-side chair and headed for the sink to fill the kettle. 'Had a bad day, love?'

Jane flung her coat over the back of a kitchen chair. 'I've had better,' she replied shortly.

'Aw, well. If we never had a bad day then we'd not appreciate the good ones,' Lil commented philosophically. She glanced out of the window. The snow had melted and now everywhere looked wet and miserable. 'I've been down on the boat – gave it a bit of an airin'. I thought I might hang on till Sunday to see Alice an' say goodbye, an' then be on me way. Happen I've imposed on yer long enough.'

Jane stared at her. 'You ain't imposed on me at all, Lil. I've enjoyed your company, but as for waitin' for Sunday, well . . . You'll be waitin' a long time if it's Alice you're hopin' to see, because she won't be comin'.'

Lil turned to stare at her. 'What do yer mean, she won't be comin'? She allus comes on a Sunday.'

'Not this week she ain't; she's got people comin' to visit her. Glen just told me when I dropped the order off at the home. It appears as they've found someone who is interested in adoptin' her and they're comin' to meet her.'

Lil sank heavily into the nearest chair, her eyes never leaving her niece's face. It was more than obvious that the news had affected her badly, but being the sort of person that she was, Jane was trying to hide it.

Suddenly Lil knew that she must say what she had been longing to say for weeks. 'So, what are yer goin' to do about it?'

Jane frowned. 'What the bloody hell *can* I do?'

'Yer could adopt her yerself, me gel – *that's* what yer could do. Why, it's as clear as the nose on yer face that yer love the child. An' what's more, I think she loves you. So I say again, what are yer goin' to do? Are yer goin' to just let them take her away without even puttin' up a fight?'

Jane's mouth dropped open in astonishment. '*Me!* Adopt Alice?' Her voice was incredulous. 'Don't talk so bloody daft. They'd never consider *me* adoptin'.'

'Why not? You've got a steady income. You've got yer own place. Admittedly, it could do wi' tartin' up a bit, but that's nothin'. Glen's a dab hand at decoratin', he told me so himself. An' I'd lay odds that he'd help like a shot if we were to ask him. Wi' a lick o' paint, some new carpets an' curtains, this place could be like a little palace in no time. Fit for anybody to live in.'

Jane looked around at her home and tried to see it as other people would. She knew that Lil was right. The cottage was long overdue for a face-lift. She felt a little stirring of excitement. 'Do you really think that they'd consider me?'

'I don't see why not. An' you'll never know unless yer try, will yer?'

Jane chewed on her lip thoughtfully. 'How would I go about it?'

'Ah! Now there I'm afraid I can't help yer. I reckon the best thing to do would be to make a few enquiries. Why don't yer have a talk to that nice woman down at the home? Yer know, the housemother – what's her name? Julia or somethin'. I reckon as she'd put yer on the right road.'

When Jane's shoulders sagged, Lil's voice became

hard. 'You just listen to me, me gel. You've been on yer own fer far too long. Chances like this don't come every day. You're still a young woman. Well, young compared to me, any road. An' I can tell yer, it's a bloody lonely life when yer get old an' you've got nobody. I know first hand, so you just think on what I'm sayin'.'

She pulled herself stiffly out of the chair and went to attend to the evening meal. But Jane didn't even notice, she was too deep in thought.

Jane tapped tentatively on Julia's office door. She was exactly on time for their appointment, and after two days of soul-searching, felt that she was doing the right thing. As Julia admitted her, the housemother raised her eyebrows appreciatively at the new coat and shoes that Lil had bullied Jane into buying the day before. She smiled and motioned her to a chair.

'You're looking very nice, Jane,' she remarked, and Jane flushed furiously at the compliment. 'Now, how can I help you?'

Jane coughed nervously to clear her throat. 'Well, I were wonderin' . . . How do you go about adoptin'?'

Julia blinked, and tried unsuccessfully to hide her surprise. 'Are you asking for yourself?'

'Yes, I am.' Jane nodded vigorously as Julia sat down heavily in the chair opposite her.

'Well, I think it only fair to warn you that if you were hoping for a baby it could take a very long time. There is already a long list of people who are waiting for an infant.'

Jane shook her head impatiently. 'I don't want a baby.'

'That's good, then. The waiting list is not nearly as long for people who are prepared to take older children, once they are approved. Although I think I should warn you, the Department's attitude to single adopters is still quite strict in most cases, particularly if you are already a single parent, which thankfully you aren't. There is still quite a stigma attached to them, which I totally disagree with. After all, we're not living in the Dark Ages now, are we? This is the sixties, for God's sake, and personally I think it's high time more single carers were appointed, but the Department is still very family orientated. Still, if you're quite serious about this I would certainly approach them and see what they have to say.'

She began to rummage through her desk drawer. 'Ah, here we are. This is the number of the person who you will need to speak to at the Central Recruitment Office in Rugby. She will be able to explain exactly what the approval process involves in detail to you.' She handed Jane a leaflet.

'Thank you, Julia.' Jane rose abruptly and held out her hand.

Julia shook her hand warmly. 'You're very welcome. I must say, you've completely taken me by surprise though. I had no idea at all that you were considering adoption.'

Jane grinned wryly as Julia followed her to the door. 'I wasn't until recently,' she admitted.

The two women faced each other.

'I hope all goes well for you, Jane, if you're sure this is what you really want. Good luck, and be sure to let me know how you go on.'

'I will,' Jane promised, and once again Julia was amazed at the transformation in the woman when she smiled. In fact, she appeared to have undergone a transformation in all ways in the last few months. She was softer somehow, easier to approach. Julia wondered why Jane Reynolds had never considered adoption before. Single adopters were a rarity – but still, if that was what Jane wanted, then she wished her well. There was no denying that both Susan and Alice had taken a shine to her, which only went to reinforce what she herself had always believed, that it took all sorts.

Now that she came to think of it, she supposed that it was the contact with Susan and Alice that had made Jane think of adoption. It was a shame really that neither of them was available, Susan because she already had extended family and Alice because prospective adopters had already been found. Thankfully, Jane must be aware of the fact, for neither child had been so much as mentioned, but then, there were so many children who needed a home . . .

On the way back to the van Jane met Glen. He, too, looked her up and down appreciatively. 'What brings you here today?' he asked.

Feeling self-conscious, she lowered her eyes, then glancing back over her shoulder to make sure that they were not being overheard, she whispered, 'Glen, I have a favour I need to ask you, but not here. Do you think you might be able to come to the farm tonight?'

He nodded, intrigued.

'Good. I'll see you later then. An' I'll explain everythin' there.'

'Right you are.' He watched her climb into the van, and in seconds she was gone, leaving him to scratch his chin in bewilderment. Bye heck, she scrubs up all right, he thought to himself, and wondered how he would ever contain his curiosity until the evening.

It was dark, drizzly and cold when he pulled into the farmyard at almost eight o'clock that evening. The first thing he saw when he entered the kitchen was a pile of wallpaper and paint samples spread out across the kitchen table with Lil busily thumbing through them.

'What's this?' he said, taking off his coat. 'Thinking of doing a bit of decorating, are we?'

'No, *we* ain't . . . *you* are,' Lil informed him cheerily, and as he glanced quizzically at Jane she lowered her eyes and blushed.

'Go on, madam. Get that kettle on,' Lil ordered bossily. 'You're about as much use as an umbrella in a snowstorm. You make the tea while I tell Glen what we have in mind. No use leavin' it to you to tell him, you'll end up getting all tongue-tied.'

She manhandled Glen towards the table and as he stared at her open-mouthed she began to explain. 'The thing is, Jane has decided that she'd like to adopt Alice. *But* – we ain't goin' to tell them straight off that it's

Alice she wants. The way I see it, it might go against her if she starts to get picky an' tell 'em she's only interested in one specific child. Far better from where I'm standin' to get herself approved an' *then* tell 'em who she wants.'

Ignoring the frown that had creased his brow, Lil rambled on.

Half an hour later Glen sat staring at both women with a look of amazement on his face.

'So that's about the long an' the short of it,' Lil finished breathlessly. 'Jane's got a children's officer comin' out to see her at the end o' next week. So I reckon we should make this room our priority. First impressions count, I always think. Do yer reckon between us we could get it finished? I'm more than happy to stay on a while longer an' help. I don't profess to be any good at paper-hangin', but I'm a dab hand on a sewin' machine. We've already chosen the material fer the new curtains. An' I can wield a paint-brush as good as the next man.'

Glen began to pace the room, roughly calculating how many rolls of wallpaper they would need. 'I don't see a problem at all. I'd have to come straight here from the home though, and work through Sunday.'

'Good. Then that's sorted. You do that, me lad, an' there'll be a hot dinner waitin' fer yer every night when yer get here. Me an' Jane will go an' choose the wallpaper tomorrow.'

When he arrived the next evening he found Jane busily stripping the walls. On the table were some rolls of wallpaper in a pretty flowered design, and Lil was busily sewing new curtains in a warm pink shade on Jane's ancient treadle Singer sewing-machine.

'Hello, Glen.' Jane greeted him cheerfully. Her cheeks were flushed with exertion and her eyes were shining. Glen could scarcely drag his eyes away from her and found himself thinking, She doesn't need make-up. She's beautiful – her kind nature shines through. Perhaps she wasn't beautiful in the conventional way, he had to admit. But he suddenly realised that she *was* beautiful all the same.

By the time he and Jane had finished that night, they had painted all the skirting boards and doors in a brilliant white that made everything appear brand new. The furniture had been pushed into the middle of the room and as they sank down exhausted, Jane chuckled. 'It's a bloody good job that children's officer ain't comin' tomorrow. The place looks like a bombsite.'

'We'll have it done,' Glen informed her confidently. 'You won't even recognise the place this time next week.'

He was true to his word. Five days later, he and Jane manhandled the old oak dresser back into place. Lil had polished it until it shone, and now she carefully placed all Joan Reynolds's treasured china back onto its shelves. Finally they all stood back to admire it. The walls were all freshly papered. The new curtains had been hung at the windows, topped off with pretty frilled pelmets. A large soft-pile rug, in the same shade as the curtains, took pride of place in front of the fire, and the brass fender had been polished until they could see their faces in it.

Glen wiped his hands on a towel and smiled with satisfaction. 'Not a bad job, even if I do say so myself.'

'Not bad! Why it's bloody lovely,' Lil quipped. 'Yer could invite the Queen herself for a cup o' tea now.'

'I'm more worried about the children's officer comin' than the Queen,' Jane admitted.

Glen laughed. 'You'll be fine,' he reassured her. 'Just be yourself and she'll soon see that she's on to a winner. I'll tell you what. You can adopt me if you like.' He patted his stomach. 'I've never had so many good dinners inside me.'

'Why's that then? Didn't your wife like cookin'?'

'No, she was more into salads and such . . .' His face clouded, and once again Jane wished her words unsaid. It was obvious that Glen still found it difficult to talk about his late wife. Jane envied him in a way. His wife must have been very special for him to still miss her as he did, but at least he had loved and lost, whereas she had never loved at all. The mood became sombre until Lil hurried away and returned with a bottle of wine and some glasses.

'I think this calls fer a toast.' Never needing much of an excuse, she quickly filled three glasses and handed them round. 'To our New Look room.' She raised her glass and they all dutifully took a drink.

'An' one more toast.' She topped up the glasses. 'To Jane. Wishin' her luck. Because I'll tell yer now, her and Alice were meant to be together.'

'I'll second that.' Glen smiled, and Jane experienced her first real concern. What if the children's officer didn't share their opinion? What if they wouldn't consider her for an adoption?

Alice's footsteps slowed as she approached the day-room door.

Nora dug her painfully in the back. 'Go on, you ungrateful girl,' she hissed. 'These people have come all the way from Leicester to meet you, and here you are dragging your feet.'

She pushed Alice through the doorway and as they entered, a man and a woman stood up. The man was tall with dark hair that was fashionably greased down; he reminded Alice a little of her father. The woman was of average height with fair hair that was teased into a bouffant. She was immaculately dressed in a smart linen suit with a straight fitted skirt and matching box jacket. She looked as if she had stepped straight off one of the pages of the fashion magazines that Alice and Susan were so fond of looking at. A huge diamond ring sparkled on her left hand but as she smiled, Alice noticed that the smile didn't quite reach her eyes.

Nora frogmarched her towards them. 'This is Alice.' She introduced them with a fixed smile on her face. 'Alice, this is Mr and Mrs Webb.'

Nervously Alice sat down in front of the couple, painfully aware of the way they were staring at her.

'I'll just go and make you some tea,' Nora said with a grimace of a smile, and Alice was left alone with them.

'So, how old are you, Alice?' Mr Webb asked. Alice

was sure that he must already know, but she answered him politely all the same.

'I . . . I . . . I'm s . . . s . . . seven.' As always when she was nervous her stutter was at its worst. She saw Mrs Webb glance at her husband, but he ignored her and concentrated his attention on Alice, and for the next ten minutes kept up a constant flow of light-hearted chatter. Even so, the atmosphere was strained to the point that Alice was almost relieved when Nora reappeared.

'Here we are.' She placed a tray of tea onto a small table. 'I'll leave you all to it, and let you get to know one another. If you should need me I'll be in the office.'

As she strode away she grinned to herself. The meeting was obviously tense and didn't appear to be going well at all. But that was what she wanted. As far as she was concerned, Alice was trouble, just as her father had been. *Been* – the word made a nervous smile hover about her thin lips. He would never be trouble to anyone again. *She had made quite sure of that.* Not that she had intended to. She had only meant to frighten him on the night she'd visited, but somehow things had got out of control. Still, the way she saw it she had gotten away with murder and as time passed she was feeling better about it. Now all she had to do was to get rid of Alice. Why should *she* find happiness when her own child had died? If it hadn't been for Robert finding out that Alice was on the way he might never have left her; they might be together still, and *her* child might still be alive.

No, she couldn't allow Alice to be happy. She'd hoped

that she would be placed in a home for children with severe handicaps – children far worse than herself – where she would never settle or know a moment's happiness. But seeing as the Department obviously thought otherwise, then this was the second-best option. Alice obviously didn't like the Webbs, and she had the strangest feeling that Mrs Webb wasn't all that taken with Alice either. What better punishment for the child than to be placed with someone who would never love her? She could feel Alice's eyes burning into her back as she walked away and turned just once to give her an insincere and sickly smile.

Alone with the Webbs again, Alice stared at them warily. They were not what she'd expected at all, especially Mrs Webb, who despite her fashionable clothes was almost plain and very quiet. In fairness she had to admit that Mr Webb seemed nice, and he was obviously trying very hard to make her feel at ease. But even so she was determined not to like him.

'I'll be Mother, shall I?' he smiled, lifting the teapot. Alice sat back and let his cheerful chatter go in one ear and out of the other, only answering when it was absolutely necessary, and wishing fervently that the visit was over. The afternoon wore on painstakingly slowly, until at last it was time for them to go.

Nora escorted them to the door, with Alice trotting obediently along behind them, her little shoes making click-clacking noises on the dull tiled floor.

Mr Webb smiled down at her. 'It's been lovely to meet

you, Alice. I do hope that you'll let us come and see you again.'

Alice nodded numbly, sensing that it was expected of her, and he beamed.

'Excellent. In that case, we'll come again next Sunday, won't we, dear?' He peered at his wife and she nodded and smiled, that curious little smile that still didn't quite reach her eyes. Alice's stomach lurched. Next Sunday. That would mean missing another day at Banana Jane's. She bit her lip, but her distress went unnoticed.

Mr Webb bent unexpectedly, making her jump, and whispered in her ear, 'Until next Sunday then, Alice. Be a good girl and we'll bring you a little present. Would you like that?'

Alice longed to tell him that she didn't want a present. That she didn't even want them to come. But instead she just smiled politely. Then they were gone, and free to go at last she wearily climbed the stairs back to her room and Susan, who she knew would be waiting for her.

Susan was watching the Webbs' departure from behind the thin curtains. 'So how did it go?' she asked, noticing Alice's glum expression.

'I . . . i . . . it w . . . w . . . was all right.'

Susan turned her attention back to the Webbs, who were just climbing into a shiny new Wolsey. 'Cor, it don't look like they're short of a bob or two. Just look at that car. An' her outfit must have cost a small fortune, an' all. That's the latest fashion, that is – they reckon straight skirts are goin' to take over from the flared ones. Can't see it meself. I mean, how would you do the twist in one o' them? Mind you, she don't exactly look the laugh-a-minute type, does she? She looks like she's bin suckin' a lemon. In fact, she's a sour-faced old sod altogether if yer ask me.'

'H . . . he w . . . was a . . . all right,' Alice volunteered.

Ever the optimist, Susan laughed. 'There yer go then. Yer in. As long as you've got him on yer side you'll be laughin'.'

'I . . . I . . . I don't like them.'

'Oh, now come on, little 'un. You ain't hardly given 'em a chance. She might be all right when yer get to know her. She's probably just nervous.'

Alice shook her head adamantly. 'I . . . I d . . . don't want t . . . to give them a chance.' As a big fat tear rolled from the corner of her eye, Susan frowned, for once at a loss for words.

Lil paced the tiny living room impatiently. Every few minutes she opened the barge door and listened for a sign that the children's officer, who was in the cottage with Jane, was leaving. She seemed to have been there for hours! But then at last the throbbing of a car engine pierced the quiet country air and she snatched up her coat. She waited for a few minutes to give the car time to pull off the dirt track and move into the lane. Then she stepped off the barge and marched purposefully up the sloping lawn.

'Well?' Breathlessly she stared at Jane. 'So how did it go?'

'I think it went all right. She's explained all about what the approval process involves. An' she asked lots of questions. But then I expected that.'

'So, what happens next?'

'She's given me a week to think about it. And then if I still want to go ahead, which I will, she'll start the ball rollin'. You know, police checks, medical checks, et cetera. I'm tellin' you, there's more to this adoption lark than I expected.'

'Did she ask yer about what age an' sex of child you'd prefer?'

'Yes, she did. But don't worry. I didn't mention Alice, as you advised. I just said that I'd prefer a girl of around about six or seven.'

'Good.' Lil nodded, satisfied that Jane had followed her advice. 'I think you've done right not mentioning a specific child just yet. Now you've set the wheels in motion an' it's all in God's hands. If it's meant to be, it will be.'

'I hope you're right,' Jane muttered. 'I want this more than I've ever wanted anythin' in me whole life.'

Lil saw the determination on Jane's face and her heart went out to her. She had loved Jane since the day she was born, more so than Jane could ever know. And now, here she was, trying to adopt a child of her own. As far as Lil was concerned, Jane had missed out on a lot, and Alice had come along just in time to save her from a lonely old age. To Lil's mind, Alice was the best thing that had ever happened to her, and if needs be she would fight tooth and nail to help Jane get her. She didn't really envisage any problems, mind, and content with the way the meeting had gone, she bustled cheerfully away to put the kettle on.

The smell of new leather filled Alice's nostrils as she climbed into the back of the plush new car. The Webbs had been visiting her for four weeks now, but this was the first time that she'd actually been allowed to go out with them, although she wasn't at all sure that she wanted to. Because of the Webbs' visits, her Sundays at Banana Jane's had been changed to Saturdays. Jane had temporarily cancelled her Saturday market and was now doing a Friday market instead, in the nearby town of Bedworth. Alice thought of Banana Jane as Mr Webb leaned into the car to tuck the plaid rug around her, and suddenly wished that she were going to the farm now instead of to the Webbs' home. Somehow she had just not taken to them. Mr Webb was nice, admittedly. He always arrived with sweets for her, which were more than appreciated by Susan after he'd gone. But to Alice they meant nothing, and no matter how hard she tried, and underneath she had to admit that she hadn't tried very hard, she just couldn't take to Mrs Webb. The woman was always immaculately dressed, and always pleasant enough in her manner. But as far as Alice was concerned, she wasn't half as nice as Banana Jane, and never would be.

The car pulled smoothly away as Alice raised her hand half-heartedly at Susan, who was hanging precariously out of the bedroom window frantically waving to her.

She found herself comparing the smooth gliding car to Banana Jane's bone-shaking old van, and smiled to herself.

'Are you quite comfortable, Alice?'

She looked up to see Mr Webb studying her in his rearview mirror. 'Y . . . yes, th . . . thank you, Mr Webb.'

He laughed. 'I've told you – my name is Andrew. Why don't you call me that? "Mr Webb" sounds awfully formal.'

She was saved from having to reply by Mrs Webb, who turned to look at her over the back of the seat. 'You'll meet Adam today, Alice. I'm sure that you'll like him. Adam is seventeen and attends a college in Leicester. His brother Alexander is nineteen, but he's away at university at present, so unfortunately you won't get to meet him just yet. But I'm sure that when you do, you'll get along famously.'

There was pride in her voice as she spoke of her sons, but Alice stared out of the car window tight-lipped, unsure of how to reply. The roads were quiet and soon they'd left the town behind and were driving through the countryside. Despite herself Alice peered with interest from the window.

'Have you ever heard of Kirby Muxloe?' Mr Webb enquired.

Alice shook her head.

'Oh, I think you'll like it. It's on the outskirts of Leicester. We've lived there since we were married.'

'Yes,' chipped in his wife. 'But of course we have done a lot of improvements to the house over the years, including adding a rather large extension. We have four bedrooms now *and* two bathrooms.'

Alice really didn't care if they had a dozen bathrooms, but she listened politely and said nothing.

'I think I can promise you a really nice dinner when we get home,' her husband continued. 'We left Mrs Martin, our daily, busily preparing vegetables. She does an excellent roast beef with all the trimmings, including the best Yorkshire puddings that you've ever tasted.'

Alice was bored by now and simply stared out of the window, wishing with all her heart that she was already on her way back to the home.

After what seemed a long time, the countryside gave way to houses again, and they entered a long tree-lined avenue. She noticed that the houses were all large and imposing, as if each one was trying to outdo its neighbour for grandeur. Mr Webb turned the car into a shrub-lined drive. At the end of it stood the biggest house that Alice had ever seen. She gaped, wishing that Susan were with her to see it. The car slowed to a stop in front of an impressive front door and Mr Webb climbed out and opened Alice's door.

'Here we are,' he said proudly. 'This is home.'

Alice stared at the shining windows before slowly following him to the front door. Mrs Webb fumbled in her handbag for the key, and once she had found it, unlocked the door and led Alice into an airy hallway. 'Take your shoes off,' she ordered, and within seconds Alice was standing in her socks staring up at an ornate galleried landing.

'Adam – we're home, darling!' Mrs Webb called, and taking Alice's hand she led her along the hallway. They entered a room that seemed to be covered in books from floor to ceiling.

In the centre of the room was a large desk, and sitting at it in a leather chair was a bespectacled, spotty-faced youth.

'Alice, this is Adam.' Mrs Webb introduced her and the boy glanced up. He nodded but then his head was bent again over the book that he was studying. His mother beamed. 'Adam's a bit of a bookworm, as you can see,' she told Alice proudly. 'Come on, we'll leave him in peace. He hates to be disturbed when he's studying.'

Alice followed her from the room, feeling more uncomfortable by the minute. Mrs Webb led her into a drawing room that was as impressive as the rest of the house, and Alice perched on the edge of a leather settee, afraid to lean back in case she disturbed the cushions, gazing in awe at the walls, which were covered in elaborate flock wallpaper. She sat through a lunch that was as delicious as Mr Webb had promised it would be, but she was so nervous that she barely tasted it. The silver cutlery was heavy, the bowl of fresh-cut roses in the centre of the table kept making her sneeze, and when she spilled a drop of gravy onto the snow-white damask tablecloth, she glanced at Mrs Webb fearfully.

'Don't worry, dear,' Mr Webb smiled. 'It's nothing that won't come out in the wash.'

She noticed that Mrs Webb didn't say anything; she

just looked at her disapprovingly, and that only served to make Alice even more nervous. Adam didn't speak to her at all, not even once, although she looked at him from time to time, hoping that he would. After lunch Mrs Webb went into the kitchen to supervise the washing-up. Alice realised then that they must be very rich indeed to have someone who did almost all the cooking and cleaning for them. In his wife's absence, Mr Webb took Alice for a stroll around the gardens, pointing out and naming the different flowers and shrubs that grew in abundance there. Alice was quite taken with them, they were so pretty that it would have been hard not to be, but still she longed to get back to Susan and the sanctity of the home. When at last, late in the afternoon, Mr Webb led her back to the car for the return journey, she breathed a sigh of relief.

Once they arrived back at the home the Webbs said goodbye to Alice and followed Julia into her office. And then at last Alice was free to go and find Susan.

'So what were their house like then?' she enquired eagerly. 'Were it posh?'

'Y . . . yes,' Alice nodded. 'I . . . it was, b . . . but I didn't like it. I d . . . didn't like A . . . Adam either. He hardly sp . . . spoke to me. N . . . not even at d . . . dinnertime.'

'Aw, come on, gel. Give him a chance. It must have been as awkward fer him as it was fer you.'

Alice shook her head. She'd already formed her opinion of Adam and nothing that Susan said would change it. 'I didn't l . . . like him. And I don't think he

I . . . liked me. And what's more, I . . . I d . . . don't like the Webbs either, and I n . . . never shall.' She was so adamant that Susan was temporarily lost for words, and when Alice burst into tears she simply held her in her arms and let her cry.

Downstairs, Julia was talking to the Webbs. 'So – how did the visit go?' she asked pleasantly.

'Oh, very well, I think,' Mr Webb said immediately. 'Alice and Adam seemed to get on famously. She was very quiet, admittedly, but then I should imagine that's to be expected. After all, it was her first visit and everything must have seemed very strange to her. Even so, all in all I feel that it went well, and as far as I'm concerned the placement can go ahead as soon as you like. What do you say, darling?'

Mr Webb looked at his wife, and she nodded. 'I'm in full agreement.'

'I'm pleased it went well,' Julia said pleasantly. 'But you do understand, don't you, that these things can't happen overnight? We have to feel absolutely certain that Alice, and yourselves for that matter, feel quite comfortable with each other before we can think of placing her with you permanently. Even then, when Alice *is* placed with you, the adoption won't be legalised overnight. We still have to get the Freeing Order in court. That isn't even scheduled until next month. Not that I foresee any problems. Alice's father still hasn't shown up and even if he does, I can't envisage him putting up any objections. But then you will have to go back to court again for the adoption and that could take months, even a year or more before everything is finalised.'

'I understand perfectly. We just wanted you to know that we will be more than happy to take Alice as soon as possible.'

'Very well then, leave it with me. And in the meantime can I assume that we will see you at the same time next week?'

The man nodded, and standing, he held out his hand. Julia smiled and saw the couple to the door. But once they had left, the smile slid from her face. There was something wrong. It was nothing that she could quite put her finger on, just a gut feeling. Mrs Webb seemed nowhere near as keen about the adoption as her husband did, and it was more than obvious that Alice hadn't taken to her either. Still, she consoled herself, it was early days yet. Things would work out right in the end. They had to, for Alice's sake.

'I'm telling you, Alice is not happy. Her stammer is worse than ever and the home is getting bad reports back from school. Her face falls a foot every time the Webbs are so much as mentioned.' Glen shook his head worriedly as he paced the floor. They'd just finished papering the bedroom that Alice slept in when she stayed at the farm, and they were all tired. 'How are the assessment visits going anyway? Are there many more?' He paused in his pacing to peer at Jane over the rim of his mug and she shrugged.

'I've had four visits now. An' everything, as far as I

can tell, seems to be in order. All the checks are under way. No problems there, I don't think. I reckon they know all me habits now as well as I do meself. The questions are endless. About the only thing they ain't asked me as yet is what time I go to the toilet! There is just one thing that concerns me. The children's officer keeps on sayin' that she thinks I might be more suited with an older child. You know – because of me age. But I'm standin' me ground. I've told her, I don't want a child no older than six or seven. But I still ain't mentioned Alice. Not yet. I just hope to God that the Webbs don't take her before I'm approved, that's all.'

Glen finally found the courage to say what had been on his mind. 'Jane, I hope you won't think that I'm interfering, but the thing is, I have to wonder if you're doing right in not mentioning Alice?'

Jane shrugged. 'Bit late to worry now, ain't it? I reckon I've just got to let things take their course.' She rose to go and make another pot of tea.

Lil looked from one to the other of their gloomy faces. 'Lord love us. Look at the pair o' you, fearing the worst before it's even happened. If I've told yer once I've told yer a dozen times, what's meant to be will be. God moves in mysterious ways. An' if the Webbs do take her an' Alice ain't happy, well . . . then we'll fight 'em to get her back. Anythin' worth having is worth fighting for, ain't it?'

Glen chuckled. 'As usual, you're right, Lil. Now come on, Jane. Get a move on with that refill. I'm as dry as a bone.'

Long after Glen had gone and Lil had retired for the night, Jane tossed and turned in her bed. Her eyes were heavy with exhaustion but sleep eluded her until the early hours when at last she sank into a fitful doze.

Her eyes snapped open and she wiped the damp red curls from her sweating brow. For a second she was disorientated in the darkness, and her heart thumped painfully in her chest. Her father had been standing over her, his belt in his hand. He was so close that she could feel him, smell him even. But now slowly, as she recognised the familiar surroundings, she knew that it had just been a nightmare. Alfred Reynolds was gone. He could never hurt her again, only in her nightmares. This was the legacy he had left her.

Chapter Eighteen

'I'm bored,' Susan moaned. She was lying on her bed with her hands behind her head, staring up at the faint criss-cross of cracks on the ceiling.

Alice glanced up from the book she was looking at. 'Wh . . . what do you w . . . want to do then?'

'I'm not sure,' Susan confessed, then suddenly she grinned and flipped over onto her stomach. 'Let's go into town an' have a look at the cattle market.'

'W . . . will Julia let us?' Alice enquired.

Susan shrugged. 'I can't see why not. I want to call in at the library anyway, an' I won't tell her as we're goin' anywhere else if you don't.'

Alice frowned. It all sounded a bit naughty to her, but if Susan said it was all right she supposed it was.

'Have yer ever been to the cattle market before?' Susan asked, and when Alice nodded she was surprised.

'Once,' Alice told her solemnly. 'I w . . . went once with Mrs Skeggs.'

'Who the hell is Mrs Skeggs?' Susan asked.

Alice smiled sadly. 'She w . . . was a lady who looked a . . . after me once for a f . . . few months when m . . . my father w . . . as at work.'

This was the first time that Susan had heard Alice mention anyone other than her father and she was intrigued. 'Was she nice?' she asked.

Alice nodded. 'Ooh, yes. Mrs Sk . . . Skeggs was l . . . lovely.'

'So why did she stop lookin' after yer then?'

Alice looked sad. 'She died and w . . . went to heaven t . . . to be with George.'

'An' who the hell was *George*?' Susan demanded.

Alice stared off into space as she remembered. 'George was m . . . my goldfish. Mrs Skeggs bought him for me w . . . when I was fi . . . five.'

'Cor blimey, yer never told me that before. You're a bit of a dark horse, you are.' Susan was greatly impressed. 'It must have been nice to have a pet of yer own.'

'It wasn't n . . . nice when he died,' Alice told her solemnly. 'Mrs Skeggs helped me plant him in the garden but he n . . . n . . . never grew back.'

'Well, of course he wouldn't, not if he were dead, would he?' Susan sighed again. There were times when she really didn't think that Alice knew much at all. 'Anyway, are yer game fer a trip into town, or what?'

Alice nodded and stood up from her position on the bedroom floor. The cold lino had given her pins and needles in her legs and she rubbed them as Susan got their coats out of the wardrobes.

After helping Alice to put her coat on, Susan collected her library books together, and soon they were strolling along Coton Road. As they passed the Rose Inn, a popular local pub, a man appeared out of the door wobbling dangerously. Susan waited until he had passed them, then giggled and nudged Alice in the ribs.

'Did yer see that? He had a right old sway on. I wouldn't like to be in his shoes when he gets home. No doubt his missus will be takin' the rollin' pin to him.'

Alice had no idea at all why anyone should want to take a rolling pin to their husband. But Susan was walking so fast that she was breathless just trying to keep up with her, and so she didn't bother to ask.

When they came to the impressive wrought-iron gates that marked the entrance to Riversley Park, the older girl's footsteps slowed.

'What do yer reckon? Should we go in here or carry on to the cattle market?'

'G . . . go in here,' Alice replied without hesitation. She hadn't been very keen on going to the cattle market in the first place. When she went there a long time ago with Mrs Skeggs it had upset her. There had been cows, and chickens and pigs and sheep, all cramped into cages and pens that looked far too small for them, and it had made her cry. Just like the day when she had gone into a butcher's and seen a poor dead pig hanging from a hook. Ever since then she didn't even look in a butcher's shop if she was forced to pass one.

They turned into the entrance, passing Mr Dicks the Dentist's Surgery, and started to walk through the Memorial Gardens that would lead them into the park. It was almost the end of February and bitterly cold. Alice had forgotten her gloves and when she looked down at her fingers she saw that they were turning blue.

Susan put one of her mittens on Alice's right hand, and then tucked their bare hands together in her pocket. 'Perhaps this weren't such a good idea after all,' she admitted, as the biting wind whipped at her hair, turning it into a mass of tangles. As her eyes lit on the museum an idea suddenly occurred to her. 'How's about we go an' take a peep in the museum? Remember, Glen told us some of George Eliot's clothes an' things were in there?'

Alice nodded enthusiastically. The entrance was very impressive and both girls had a sense of stepping back in time as they passed through the enormous double doors. They gazed in awe at a sweeping staircase that led to the upper floor and looked with wonder at the huge paintings that were displayed on the walls. 'Cor, I bet they're worth a bob or two,' Susan remarked, and Alice nodded in agreement. They moved on, and after passing through another huge doorway, found themselves in a room that was full of artefacts from the days when the town had relied partly on its mining industry. Old black and white photographs of men, covered in soot and naked to the waist, filled glass display cases.

Susan whistled through her teeth. 'I wouldn't have liked to wash their clouts,' she remarked, and Alice had to stifle the urge to giggle. In the next room were cases full of ribbons, made many years ago in the ribbon factories that had dominated the town centre.

'I know about this,' Susan told Alice smugly. 'We did about this at school in history. Did yer know that in the last century, Nuneaton were the place where nearly all the ribbons were made? The women used to spend sixteen hours a day at their looms an' then most o' the ribbons were taken by horse an' cart to Coventry, where they were used to dress ladies' bonnets. Some of 'em went to Atherstone an' all to the hat factory there.'

Alice was clearly impressed with her knowledge and Susan's small chest swelled with pride. They spent some time admiring the old-fashioned looms and the numerous ribbons before they passed through yet another doorway and found themselves in an old-fashioned room setting. This was the place where George Eliot's clothes and some of her personal possessions were kept.

Alice's breath caught in her throat as she stared at the dresses that told of a bygone age.

'Phew, I wouldn't have fancied ironin' them neither,' Susan whispered, as she stared in awe at the yards and yards of silk and the dainty lace collars. 'An' look how tiny they are. You could put yer hands round the waists. She must have bin really small. Not that much bigger than me, in fact.'

Again Alice nodded as they turned their attention to a small glass case that housed an assortment of fountain pens and nibs, and solid silver inkpots. 'Just think, Alice. She might have written some of her books wi' them very pens. It's weird when yer come to think about it, ain't it? I mean – that she's long gone an' yet we can still read her books. Spooky like, ain't it?'

The girls stood in silence for some seconds as they reflected on Susan's comment, and when they'd seen their fill they moved on and made their way back to the entrance. The second they stepped outside, the cold hit them like a douse of freezing water.

Susan shuddered as her eyes swept the almost deserted park. 'Come on,' she said. 'Let's take the short cut. We can go across the bridge that runs over the river to the library an' cut out the marketplace. It's too flippin' cold to be messin' about out here.'

They hurried past the bandstand with its ornately carved roof that Glen had pointed out to them on the night he'd taken them to the fair, and soon came to the banks of the River Anker. The wind was whistling through the weeping willow trees, which seemed to be thrashing their barren branches into the water in protest. Now that the snow had thawed the water level was dangerously high and the boats that were tied to the boathouse bobbed furiously in the water as if they were trying to escape. Alice shivered as Susan took her hand and yanked her along. They crossed the bridge and at last the library was in sight. By now, Alice's teeth were chattering with cold.

Susan breathed a sigh of relief. 'Not much further now,' she encouraged, and soon they were climbing the steps to the library. As they entered, the warm air met them and brought a glow to their cheeks.

'Phew, that's better,' Susan declared, going with Alice towards some seats that were placed along one wall. 'At least we can take the weight off us feet fer a minute.' She reached into her pocket and withdrew a small chocolate bar. She broke it neatly in half and handed one piece to Alice.

'So – are the Webbs comin' to see yer again this week?'

Alice nodded as she eyed a pigeon that had landed on the windowsill and was watching them curiously.

'Yes, they're coming tomorrow.'

Susan noticed that, as usual, now that they were alone and away from the home Alice's stammer was almost non-existent.

'I reckon as yer should at least give 'em a chance,' she said matter-of-factly. 'After all, it ain't every day as yer get a brand new mum an' dad offered to yer on a plate. What is it as yer don't like about 'em anyway?'

'It's not so much them – I'd like a mum and dad. 'It's just . . . I . . . I'd miss Banana Jane.'

'Is that all that's botherin' yer, yer daft ha'porth? There's ways round that. I mean, I'm sure they'd still let yer visit her from time to time.'

Slightly heartened, Alice stared at her. 'Do you really think th . . . they would?'

'No doubt about it.' Susan swallowed the last square of chocolate and licked her fingers as she glanced through the window of the crowded library. Outside, the skies were leaden. It seemed to be getting darker by the minute and she was sure that they were in for a downpour.

'Come on.' Grabbing Alice's hand she hauled her to her feet. 'I need to choose some more books then I reckon as we'll just about have time to get back to the home before the heavens open, if we get a shufty on.' She and Alice rushed back down the aisles, with Susan snatching some books randomly from the shelves as they went.

Once the books had been stamped at the counter, the

293

girls reluctantly went back outside and hurried towards the town, skirting the cattle market. Alice kept her eyes averted from the large cages of chickens that were clucking indignantly at their imprisonment.

As they passed the Newdigate Hotel, Alice glanced curiously in at the window. She could vaguely remember her father mentioning somewhere called the Newdigate, but as she didn't want to stir up unhappy memories she pushed the thought from her mind and let Susan rattle on without comment. It was very smoky inside and she could see lots of big red-faced men talking and gesticulating loudly.

'That's where most o' the farmers do their deals over a pint,' Susan informed her, as they shouldered their way between the crowds of people and moved on.

They managed to get back to the home just as it was starting to rain. Breathless and giggling, they almost collided with Nora as they burst in through the door.

At the sight of Alice, a surge of rage rushed through Nora and it was all she could do to keep herself from slapping her. The force of her feelings took her by surprise and she began to shake. What was happening to her? she wondered. She managed to control herself enough to address them. 'You *do* know that it's almost dinnertime, don't you?' she said tersely.

Susan wiped her nose on the sleeve of her coat, ignoring the tone of Nora's voice. 'O' course we do. Ain't never known me to be late fer me snap, have yer?'

She took Alice's hand and strolled past the woman as bold as brass. Side-by-side they picked their way upstairs to their room. Alice's face was miserable but Susan grinned at her and said, 'Don't let old Ferret-face get to yer. If yer show her you ain't scared of her she'll start to lay off yer a bit. That's what bullies are like.'

Alice nodded. She knew that what Susan said was probably true but the problem was, one glance from Nora could reduce her to a quivering wreck.

'Anyway,' Susan was keen to change the subject, 'this here Mrs Skeggs that used to look after yer – you liked her, did yer?' Although she had shared a room with Alice for some time now she still knew very little about her background and was curious.

'It was Mrs Skeggs who t . . . told me about the fairies that live a . . . at the bottom of the g . . . garden,' Alice told her solemnly.

Susan rolled her eyes, but said nothing. She had stopped believing in fairies years ago.

'Sometimes at night when my f . . . father was asleep I would get out of bed and peep out of the window to see if I could spot them at the bottom of the garden. B . . . but I never did,' Alice said sadly.

'Ah well, happen yer never dropped on the right night,' Susan said kindly. 'Yer can bet they were there all the same.'

The conversation was interrupted when the bell sounded for dinner and hand-in-hand they trooped off to the dining room.

In Canalside Cottage, Glen stepped off the ladder and wiped his hands. 'Two more rooms to go,' he smiled.

Jane looked around the room and nodded. 'Yes, just

two more and the whole place will have been decorated from top to bottom. I could never have done it on me own though, Glen. I don't know how to thank you. And Alice will feel the same, next time she comes to stay. You've done marvels with this room. She'll love it, I know she will.'

Glen looked around at his handiwork, hoping that she was right. The room was pretty, he had to admit, although in fairness that was more due to Jane's choice of paper and the colour scheme. It was the sort of room that any little girl would love, all in soft shades of lilac.

As they were admiring it Lil bustled in balancing a tray of hot chocolate and biscuits.

'Ah! So you've finished it.' Her eyes roved appreciatively around the room. 'It looks bloody lovely. I must say, you two make a fine team. Alice is goin' to love it. I know she will.'

Jane laughed, delighted. 'That's what I was just sayin' to Glen.'

She had gone to more trouble with this room than with any other room in the house. Because this, she hoped, would be Alice's permanent room if all went well. She and Glen lifted a mug each from the tray. It was getting late and they were both tired, but more than satisfied with their efforts.

'I'll get the new curtains up tomorrer,' Lil said as she bit into a custard cream, and Jane nodded.

'So – which room were you thinking of starting on next?' Glen asked.

Jane shrugged. 'Well, there's no panic about the other two rooms. There's only mine an' . . . an' me dad's left to do. I reckon as both of them could wait a while longer. I think you've earned a rest.'

He noticed the way she seemed to find it painful to mention her father, and his heart went out to her, but tactfully he chose to ignore it, and instead said cheerfully, 'Rubbish! I've started the job and I'll finish it. So I ask again: which room would you like doing next?' Glen was so insistent that she laughed.

'Well, if you're sure that you've not had enough I suppose that we ought to start on mine. To be honest, it's a disgrace. I can't remember it ever bein' decorated. It's been like that since I were knee high to a grasshopper. So, be warned.'

Glen's eyes twinkled. 'I like a bit of a challenge.' He placed his empty mug back onto the tray. 'But now, if you don't mind, I'm going to get myself away to my bed.'

As he yawned, Jane felt a surge of guilt. He looked desperately tired, and so he should. Over the last weeks he'd spent almost every spare minute at the cottage, and in that time he had totally transformed it.

'Go on, lad. You look all done in,' Lil urged him, as one behind the other they made their way down the stairs. In the warmth of the kitchen Glen shrugged his long arms into the sleeves of his coat.

'We'll make a start on your room tomorrow,' he promised Jane, and with a friendly nod to Lil he walked to the door.

Jane followed him out to his car. 'I've got the children's officer comin' again tomorrow. That will be seven visits in all up to now.'

Hearing the concern in her voice, he said to her gently, 'That's good. It can't be much longer now, can it?'

'I hope not.' Jane frowned. 'I'm seein' less an' less of Alice lately an' the Webbs are seein' more an' more of her. Though I have to say, she don't seem to be very happy about it. Surely it ain't right that she has to go on seein' them if she don't want to?'

'I know what you mean,' Glen sympathised. 'But don't forget, she's only seven years old, and the home has to do what they think will be in her interests, long-term. Try not to worry. It can't be long now until you're approved and then if Alice is given a choice, well . . . I'm sure that she'll choose to be with you. It goes without saying. She obviously thinks the world of you.'

'Yes, but *will* she be given the choice? Or will the authorities make the decision for her? That's what troubles me.'

Unable to answer her, Glen climbed into his car, wishing there was something he could say to comfort her. The lonely hoot of an owl pierced the silence as he wearily wiped his hand across his eyes. 'I'd better be off, else I'll be falling asleep at the wheel.'

'Yes, of course, Glen. I'm sorry. You look all done in an' here's me chewin' your ear off. Go on. Get yourself off to bed an' I'll see you tomorrow.'

Just before he turned out of the drive, Glen glanced in his rearview mirror. Jane was standing where he had left her, staring up at the clear, star-dotted sky. He sighed. He'd watched the closeness between Alice and Jane blossom and had no doubt at all that Jane loved Alice. Furthermore, he felt sure that her love was returned. But would the authorities think the same, and even if they did, would love be enough? The way he saw it, on the one hand they had the Webbs, wrapped in a cloak of middle-class respectability. They could offer Alice every material thing that she might ever need: a private education, two ready-made brothers, a beautiful home and a mother and father with parenting skills already to their credit. On the other hand they had Jane, a spinster with a very moderate income, no parenting skills at all, but enough love to light Alice's life for ever.

To Glen's way of thinking, Jane should have made her intentions towards Alice known. Although he could understand her reasons for not coming forward just yet, still he wondered if she was doing the right thing in remaining silent. Sometimes he longed to voice his opinions on the subject again, more strongly, but he didn't want to be seen as interfering, so he stayed tight-lipped. All he could do was pray that Jane would be approved very soon, and then at least the Department would be able to make a choice. A little worm of unease gnawed away in the pit of his stomach. Again he asked himself the same question, the one that was haunting Jane's every waking moment. Would love be enough? He could only pray that it would be, for both Jane and Alice's sake. For if ever two people were meant to be together, it was those two.

* * *

The children's officer closed her notebook and smiled at Jane. 'Well, Miss Reynolds, that's about it. I think I have all the information that I need now, so I won't need to trouble you again.'

Jane let out a sigh of relief and leaned anxiously forward in her chair. 'So what will happen now?'

'Well, your police and medical checks have been completed and there were absolutely no problems there. So I shall be going away now to write up a report. Once that's done it will be submitted to my manager and the final decision will rest with her and her colleagues.'

Jane swallowed hard, before asking tentatively, 'Do you think I stand any chance at all of becoming approved?'

'Oh, absolutely! In fact, I see no reason at all why you shouldn't be. Of course, that's just my personal opinion. I can't promise that the rest of the panel will feel the same. As I've told you on numerous occasions, they do prefer families when it comes to adoption. Single adopters are still to my mind far too much of a rarity. But as I said, I shall be writing up my report and hopefully I shall have it finished in time to go before the approval panel next month. And then it's up to them. But I do assure you, I won't prolong your agony. As soon as I'm made aware of their decision I shall inform you of it either by post or phone.'

The tall slender woman rose and held out her hand. 'Goodbye, Miss Reynolds, and thank you for being so patient with me. I know the questions I've had to ask you must have seemed endless, and possibly rather intrusive at times. But I'm sure you'll understand why we have to do it. Adoption is a very serious step and we have to be sure that the people we are approving are genuine and suitable.'

'It's all right, I do understand,' Jane said. 'You can't go placin' children with just any Tom, Dick or Harry. I never expected it to happen overnight. But I must admit I'm anxious now, to put it mildly.'

'Well, try not to be. The worst part is over, and I promise to be in touch immediately I get any news. All that remains to be said is "good luck".'

Jane smiled at her gratefully. 'Thank you.' She followed the woman outside to her car and watched her drive away. Then she went back into the cottage to confront Lil who had been hovering between the boat and the cottage, waiting for the children's officer to leave.

As she stared into her aunt's kindly face, Jane's eyes suddenly filled with tears. 'That's it then,' she said shakily. 'It's all done an' in the lap of the gods. All we can do now is just sit back an' wait.'

Lil placed a comforting arm around her shoulders. 'Then wait we will. What's worth havin' is worth waitin' for,' she told Jane philosophically. Her voice became gentle. 'Try not to fret, love. The worst bit is over now. You'll soon know one way or another. But personally I don't think you have a thing to worry about. You've done everythin' by the book.'

She watched as Jane rose and crossed to the sink and with a little shock she noticed for the first time how Jane's trousers were flapping loosely around her legs. She had lost a lot of weight lately, although until now Lil hadn't realised just how much. She imagined it was due to a combination of overwork and worrying about Alice, but even so the weight loss suited her. She was still not what Lil would have termed as thin, but curvy, and her hair had grown too, making her look younger, softer somehow. Lil smiled to herself. For years she had worried about Jane's lonely existence, but soon now it might be over. If all went well, Jane might shortly be adopting a daughter. Her thoughts turned to Glen. Who knew what else the future might hold for the lass? She settled back contentedly in her chair.

Alice shyly held out her present to Jane. 'Th . . . these are for you.'

Jane's face lit up as she took the small posy of spring flowers from the child's grubby hand.

'There are only two daffodils,' Alice informed her solemnly. 'Cos Tilly and Moses ate the rest.'

Jane stifled a laugh. 'I'll just think meself lucky to have these, in that case. Them goats are terrible. Be careful – they might try eatin' *you* if you stand still for too long.' She poured out a glass of milk and placed it in front of Alice, and as the child clambered onto a chair, Jane took a seat beside her. It was the first whole day that they'd been able to spend together for weeks, and they were both determined to make the most of every single minute. Alice had been spending whole weekends at the Webbs'. But this weekend, they had been called away to visit Mr Webb's father who had been taken ill.

'So, how are things?' Jane asked softly, and she was disturbed to see Alice's green eyes fill with tears.

'They're all right, but I wish I didn't have to keep going to their house. I don't like staying with the Webbs, Banana Jane. I'd rather be here with you and Grandma Lil.'

Jane had an overpowering urge to tell Alice that soon she might never have to see them again. That soon *this* might be her home. But she dare not. As yet she still hadn't heard if she was to become an approved adopter, and until she did she would not raise Alice's hopes. That would be cruel, so instead she simply smiled at her. 'Why don't you like goin' to the Webbs', Alice? They seem to be nice enough people.'

Alice pouted. 'Mr Webb is all right,' she admitted grudgingly, 'but Mrs Webb makes me sit still all the time. She says children should be seen and not heard. And Adam keeps telling me to be quiet, too. He is their son and he's very clever. He's always reading and he gets very cross with me if I make a noise.'

She bent to stroke Holly who was sitting at her feet, and Jane and Lil frowned at each other, but said nothing. Lil eventually struggled out of her chair. Her Christmas stay with Jane had already extended into the spring, and in that time the cottage had been totally transformed. Nearly all the rooms were newly decorated, and fresh curtains had been hung at all the windows. Only one room remained untouched, and that was Alfred Reynolds's room. Jane seemed reluctant to even enter it. Lil had not pressed her; nor had Glen. They both felt that Jane would tell them why she felt like that when the time was right.

Lil crossed to the table and lifted an ancient wicker basket. 'Come on, little 'un. Get that milk down yer, an' then yer can come an' help me collect the eggs.'

Alice drained her glass, and Jane watched with amusement as she took Lil's hand and almost dragged her towards the door. Once they'd gone she stepped outside and peered up and down the lane, hoping to catch a glimpse of the postman. She looked for him every day now. It had been almost three weeks since the children's officer's final assessment visit. Three whole weeks that had felt like three long years, and the waiting was becoming unbearable. 'It can't be much longer now,' she sighed, trying to console herself, but another little unwelcome voice whispered, 'It mustn't be. Or it may be too late.'

Angry with herself, she fled back into the house to check on the steak and kidney pie that was baking in the oven. It was Glen's favourite. He was out there now, repairing a fence. She found herself wondering what she would have done without him and Lil over the last few months. It was now late March and they'd both worked tirelessly to help her bring the cottage up to the standards that the Children's Department would expect of a prospective adopter. But more than that, they had both encouraged and supported her. She would never forget that. And she knew that they were true friends indeed.

* * *

Later that day, Alice clung to Jane as tears coursed down her cheeks. 'I don't want to go back.'

'I know you don't, love, but don't cry. You can come again next week. You know you can.'

Alice shook her head. 'Next week Mr Webb's father might be better, and then I'll have to go to their house again!'

Jane's heart twisted painfully as she stroked Alice's hair, and feeling totally out of her depth she glanced at Glen imploringly.

Taking control of the situation he opened the car door. 'Come on, Alice. There's a good girl. You're upsetting Banana Jane, and Julia will be getting worried about you if we're much later. Like she said, you can come again next week, all being well. Think of Susan. She'll be missing you and wondering where you've got to.'

'No, she won't. She's been at her aunty's all weekend and she won't be back yet.'

'Oh, I see.' Glen frowned and now it was Lil's turn to try and coax Alice into the car.

'Come on, babby. Let's be havin' no more o' this now. We've all had a lovely day, an' we don't want to spoil it, do we?' Gently prising Alice away from Jane's side she led her towards the Morris Minor. 'That's a good girl now. In yer get.' She planted a kiss on Alice's cheek as she winked at Glen. 'Didn't I hear yer say that yer might be stoppin' off at the chippy on yer way back?'

Glen grinned and nodded. 'You most certainly did. We'll call in at Toppers, hey, Alice? They do scallops there that make your mouth water.'

Slightly appeased, Alice's sobs subsided to hiccuping gulps and she managed a watery smile.

Sighing with relief, Jane leaned into the car to kiss her soundly. 'You be a good girl now and I'll see you soon, eh?'

Alice nodded as Jane and Lil stood side-by-side and watched as Glen drove away.

'Shall I go in an' put the kettle on?' Lil asked.

Jane nodded absently. 'What? Oh, yes. Yes, Lil, you do that.'

Lil started towards the door but then stopped abruptly to look back at Jane. 'Well, are yer comin' or what?' she asked.

Jane looked past her. 'You go ahead, I'll be in shortly.'

'Just as yer like.'

Lil pottered away and Jane stood in the yard, alone except for the chickens that clucked about her feet. Her thoughts were in turmoil. Until the last few months she had always prided herself on being fiercely independent, and yet lately she'd found herself relying on Glen, more and more. That was worrying enough in itself, but worse still was the fact that she'd been forced to admit to herself that she looked forward to his visits. Sometimes when they were working together, she would find herself watching him from the corner of her eye. She'd noticed the way his hair had a tendency to flop across his forehead, and more than once had resisted the urge to reach out to him and wipe it away. And then there was that funny little feeling she got sometimes when he first arrived, like butterflies fluttering in her stomach. It was all very confusing. Added to this were her feelings for Alice. Each time the child visited now it was harder for both of them to separate. But it had never been as hard as it was this evening, and Jane's heart was aching. If she'd ever had any doubts at all about whether she was doing the right thing, tonight had dispelled them.

As the rear lights of Glen's car disappeared up Apple Pie Lane, Nora shrank further into the shadows of the hedge. Sensing her presence, Holly, who was standing at Jane's feet, suddenly looked towards her and began to yap.

'What's up with you then?' she heard Jane ask as she too looked towards her hiding-place. Turning quickly for fear of being seen, Nora bent low and scuttled away. It wouldn't do for Jane to find her there. She didn't stop running until she reached the shelter of some trees and there she stopped to catch her breath.

Strangely, the hatred she felt for Alice extended to Jane too now, for it was obvious that the woman and the child cared for one another. Their tearful parting had confirmed that.

Gloatingly, she thought of Alice's prospective adopters, the Webbs. With luck, the little bitch would soon be placed with them and then Jane would be alone again – just as she was.

Chapter Nineteen

Alice tripped into Henry Street with a large smile on her face, her school bag slung across her shoulder. She was feeling happy today, and as the week progressed she was feeling happier still. Today at school Mrs Kingdom had read them the story of *Cinderella* and it had reminded her of the day when she had watched the Royal Family on television going to church in a coach just like the one in the story.

Grandma Lil had been nagging Banana Jane to get a television, but as yet she hadn't. She'd said that she couldn't be doing with all these new-fangled devices and Alice and Lil had laughed at her. Mr Webb's father's illness had meant that she'd been able to spend two whole weekends with Banana Jane, and with any luck she would be spending another one there at the end of this week, in her lovely new bedroom. She hummed to herself as she discarded her shoes in the boot room, and she was still humming when Nora's voice halted her.

'Alice Lawrence, *wait*. I want a word with you.'

The smile immediately slid from the girl's face as she sidled into the office, her eyes tight on Nora. She noticed with surprise that her children's officer was there, too.

But even more surprising was the fact that Nora seemed to be in a good mood. In fact, she could hardly stop smiling.

Nora waited until Alice was in the room then she closed the door behind her and motioned her to a seat. 'As you can see, your children's officer has come to see you. And I think you'll find that she has some very good news for you.'

She stared at the child in front of her, knowing that what the woman was about to impart would be far from good news to Alice. Over the last few months she'd been forced to watch the bond between Alice and Jane Reynolds grow and blossom. Unseen, she had spied on them together on the farm, although she was having to be more careful now, because on more than one occasion that nosy old woman that Jane had staying with her had almost spotted her. Theirs had been a relationship that she herself was strongly opposed to, and yet Julia in her wisdom had chosen to ignore her advice and had openly encouraged it. She smirked. Well, now it was her turn, and she sat back and listened with satisfaction as the young children's officer explained the reason for her visit.

'Hello, Alice. As Nora said, I'm here to give you some good news,' she began. Alice tried to concentrate on what she was saying, but there was something about Nora's smug expression that made her feel uneasy.

'As you know, the Webbs have offered you a permanent home with them. That's why you've been spending so much time with them, so that you could all get to know one another. Normally the introductions before you actually moved in with them would span a few more months. But as you also know, Mr Webb's father has been taken quite seriously ill, which is why he has been forced to spend the last two weekends with him. Now Mr and Mrs Webb are more than aware that they can't be with you *and* visiting Mr Webb senior at the same time, and they are very concerned that you may feel that they are neglecting you, as obviously they can't be in two places at once.' She paused, waiting for Alice to see the joke but when the child remained straight-faced she went on, 'Due to this fact, Mr Webb has approached us and asked if you could move in with them a little sooner than planned. That way, you could accompany them on their visits to his father at the weekends. Normally, of course, the final decision as to when you should move would be left to the housemother who, as you know, is Julia Tuffin or Margaret, her deputy. But unfortunately Julia is off sick, and Margaret is taking some leave she's owed, so in their absence the decision rests with Nora, who has been able to tell me that your visits with the Webbs have gone very well indeed.'

Alice glared at Nora who watched with satisfaction as the colour drained from the child's face.

'Anyway,' the children's officer continued, completely oblivious to Alice's distress, 'on Nora's advice I have decided that there is no reason why you shouldn't move in with the Webbs sooner rather than later.'

Alice dragged her eyes away from Nora's hated face, and plucking up every ounce of courage she possessed, she looked back at her children's officer and asked falteringly, 'H . . . how much s . . . sooner?'

She saw the cruel gleam in Nora's eyes, but the children's officer merely smiled.

'Tomorrow, my dear. You will be leaving to live with the Webb family tomorrow. And may I just say that I hope you'll be very, very happy.'

Lil lifted the mail from the doormat, and as her eyes rested on a long brown envelope her stomach seemed to turn a cartwheel. This was it, she was sure of it. This was the letter that Jane had been waiting for. She tightened the belt on her dressing gown and tore along the corridor at a speed that would have done credit to a woman half her age. Jane was sitting at the kitchen table balancing toast in one hand and juggling a newspaper in the other when Lil dropped the envelope in front of her.

'There yer are then, gel. I think this might be what you've bin losin' sleep over. Look – it's from the Department. This must be the decision from the approval panel.'

Jane gulped and licked her lips, which had suddenly gone dry as she stared at the envelope.

'Go on then, open it,' Lil urged. 'It can't bite yer. Whatever it says, at least you'll know one way or the other. To my mind there can't be nothin' worse than this not knowin'. You've been walkin' around like a bear wi' a sore head fer weeks. So go on. Fer God's sake open it an' put us both out of us misery.'

Slowly, Jane inserted a shaking thumb into the end of the envelope and slit it open. She withdrew a sheet of headed notepaper and began to read. Lil held her breath and looked on silently as a wealth of emotions flitted across Jane's face. At last she put the paper down. Her face was parchment white and Lil's heart sank.

'Well?' she breathed, hardly daring to ask.

'I've been approved. It's all over. I can adopt. Now God willing I can give Alice a home.'

Tears of joy spurted from Lil's eyes as she grabbed Jane and hugged her fiercely.

'There you are, yer see? I told yer things would work out, didn't I?'

Jane hugged her back, laughing and crying all at the same time.

'I must tell Glen,' she said chokily.

Lil's head nodded vigorously in agreement. 'Yes, yer must. An' this weekend we can tell Alice an' all. We can tell her that you're goin' to try to bring her home fer good. Oh! An' you'll need to speak to Julia and—'

'Whoa!' Jane held up her hand and stopped Lil in full flow. 'Slow down a bit – one step at a time. I'll go an' get dressed, an' then I'll phone Glen and tell him the good news first. Then we'll take it from there.'

Lil chuckled. 'You're right,' she admitted. 'It's just I'm so chuffed I were gettin' carried away. Go on – get off an' get yerself dressed. Then we can phone Glen, as yer say.'

With a spring in her step, Jane headed towards the stairs. She was halfway up them when the phone rang.

'Damn.' Cursing softly, she hurried back down and snatched up the phone.

'Hello, Jane – it's Glen.'

She smiled, delighted to hear his voice. 'Now that's what I call good timin'. I was just about to call you. I've got some good news for you.' When he didn't immediately answer her she babbled on, 'It's come – the letter. And it's official now. I've been approved as an adopter. So we can go ahead now and try to get Alice.'

She waited for a reaction and when after a few moments none was forthcoming she asked, 'Are you still there, Glen?'

'Yes. Yes, I am,' he replied hesitantly.

Suddenly, for no reason that she could explain, a cold hand closed around her heart. 'Well, ain't you goin' to congratulate me then?'

Again that terrible silence until after what seemed an eternity he spoke. 'Jane, I don't quite know how to tell you this, but . . .'

'But what?' She was really concerned now. Something was wrong – she could feel it, hear it in the tone of his voice. 'Come on, Glen. If somethin's amiss, spit it out. You're frightenin' me.'

He took a deep breath. 'I'm afraid your approval has come too late. You see – Alice has just left with the Webbs.'

'What do you mean, she's just left with the Webbs? Where have they taken her?'

'They've taken her home, to their home. Jane – they're going to adopt her. It was awful, her and Susan were both in a right state. There's nothing we can do now. It's too late – I'm so sorry.'

Jane felt the room spin around her, and she gripped the phone as she leaned heavily against the wall. After a moment she said quietly, 'I'll speak to you later, Glen. I've got to go.'

She dropped the heavy black phone back into its cradle. Lil found her still standing there ten minutes later. She stared at her bewildered. Jane seemed to have aged ten years in as many minutes, and was deathly pale.

'Lord love us. Whatever's the matter now? You're as white as a sheet.'

Jane slowly raised her eyes, and Lil was shocked when she saw the raw pain in them.

'Come on, lass – tell me. What's the matter? Is somethin' wrong with Alice?'

Jane shook her head as if in a daze. 'No, there's nothin' wrong with her.'

Lil let out a sigh of relief. 'Thank God for that. Did yer tell Glen the good news?'

'Yes, I did, Lil. But he was in a bit of a state. I don't think he really took it in. You see, the good news has come too late. They've just taken Alice.'

Lil was really bemused now. 'What do yer mean, they've taken Alice? Who's taken her – where?'

'The Webbs have taken her. They beat me to it.' Jane laughed – a hollow sound that was chilling to hear. 'Alice has gone to be adopted by somebody else, on the very day that I could have told her how much I loved her an' wanted her. An' now she'll never know.'

She walked unseeing past Lil and back into the kitchen. There she sank heavily onto the nearest chair as all her hopes and dreams crumbled around her.

Chapter Twenty

Alice paused outside the kitchen. On the other side of the door she could hear the Webbs talking. Unashamedly, she eavesdropped.

'I'm telling you, Andrew, if things don't improve soon I'll . . . I'll . . . Well! I don't know what I'll do. But what I *do* know is that I'm about at the end of my tether.' Stella Webb's whining voice reached Alice through the slight gap in the door. She inched forward soundlessly, and peeping through the gap she saw Mr Webb seated at the kitchen table with a pained expression on his face. But before he had time to say anything, Stella went on.

'I've managed to get her in at the convent, the best school in the area. No mean feat, let me tell you. She has a wardrobe full of the finest dresses that money can buy. I've got a speech therapist seeing her twice a week. I've booked her music and ballet lessons. And yet she still barely speaks to me. She just comes home from school and shuts herself away in her room, and yesterday when Mrs Forsythe-Smythe from the Women's Guild visited me, Alice was downright rude to her. I was utterly mortified. The child is turning into an embarrassment, instead of an asset.'

She paused for breath, and now her husband answered her, and his tone was cold. 'I didn't realise that Alice was *supposed* to be an asset, Stella. I thought she was supposed to be the daughter that we never had. Let's face it, you haven't exactly given her much of a chance, have you? It's still very early days yet as far as I'm concerned. The poor child is still trying to settle in, and as for her being rude to Mrs Forsythe-Smythe, all I can say is, "Well done, Alice". Let's hope that the ghastly woman was offended enough to keep away permanently, the stuck-up snob. I don't know why you ever bother with her anyway. And I find it very hard to believe that Alice could be rude. What's she supposed to have done?'

His wife shrugged. 'Well, I suppose she wasn't exactly *rude* as such, but every time the poor woman tried to talk to her she just hung her head as if the cat had got her tongue.' Realising that she'd upset him, Stella quickly changed her tack. 'I'm sorry, Andrew. You're right, of course. I suppose I'm just expecting too much too soon, and trying too hard.'

Sensing that he was still annoyed, she edged towards the door, her tone sweet now. 'I'll go and see if she's managed to get her uniform on, then she can come and have a cup of tea with you before you leave for the office.'

Not wishing to be caught listening, Alice pushed the door open and walked into the kitchen.

'Ah! There you are, Alice. I was just coming to fetch you. Daddy would like a few minutes with you before he leaves for work. Wouldn't you, darling?' As she smiled across at him, Andrew Webb sighed. It was more than obvious that Alice was nowhere near ready to call him Daddy as yet; she had only been with them for a couple of months. But still Stella pushed it. Stifling his irritation, he looked past her at Alice.

'Good morning, sweetheart. Come and sit down. I must say you're looking very smart in your new uniform.'

Silently, Alice slid past Stella and took a seat at the table. He poured out a glass of orange juice and pushed it across the tablecloth towards her. 'Did you sleep well?' he asked.

Alice shrugged and kept her eyes downcast. She lifted the glass and sipped at her drink to avoid having to speak to him.

'I've got you a nice cooked breakfast keeping warm in the oven,' Stella told her, smiling falsely, and lifting a pair of oven gloves she slipped them on and crossed to the oven. It was then that Adam came into the kitchen and without a word sat down next to her. Within seconds his head was bent over a book. His mother carried two plates to the table, one for Alice and the other for him, and Alice watched fascinated as he lifted his fork and stabbed at his food, without his eyes ever once leaving the page.

The voice that Alice was coming to hate dragged her attention back to her own meal. 'Come along now, dear, eat your breakfast up. It would be such a shame for it to go to waste after I've gone to all the trouble of cooking it for you, wouldn't it?' Stella shook out a starched white table napkin and went to a great show of placing it across Alice's lap.

Andrew Webb rolled his eyes, far more concerned than he cared to admit. Alice hadn't spoken so much as a single word since she had entered the room. He'd noticed that she seemed to be saying less and less of late, and suddenly wished that he could have run her to school himself; could have given her a little time, just the two of them. A glance at his watch told him that this would be impossible. His first appointment was booked for nine o'clock and if he didn't leave now he would be late for his client. He rose slowly and smiled at her as he lifted his briefcase. 'How about we go to the pictures tonight, Alice?'

'That's impossible, I'm afraid. Alice has a ballet lesson booked for four-thirty, and by the time that's finished it will be time for her to have her tea and a bath.'

Exasperated, Andrew glared at his wife then turning on his heel he strode away without so much as another word. Stella bit on her lip as she watched him leave and once the car had disappeared down the drive she turned to glower at Alice. It was all her fault. The child seemed to be nothing but trouble. Not for the first time in the last month she wondered if she'd done the right thing in bringing Alice home. She was turning out to be nothing at all like the daughter she had imagined having. The daughter she'd always yearned for. Her mind slipped back over the years to the day of Adam's birth. Complications had arisen during the delivery that had led to her having to undergo a complete hysterectomy. And with the loss of her womb had gone all her hopes of ever having a daughter of her own. The pain this had caused her was far worse than any after-effects of surgery. But she'd settled somehow over the years into a dull acceptance of the situation, convincing herself that it had not been meant to be. Until, that was, Andrew had suggested adoption. At first she'd been totally opposed to the idea. But then gradually she had begun to consider it, and now here was Alice. She looked at her and sighed. Already wisps of unruly red curls were threatening to escape from the tightly braided plaits, and the recent sunny weather had caused a spattering of freckles to erupt across her nose. Moodily she snatched Alice's untouched meal away from her.

'Go and get your shoes on,' she ordered shortly. 'The school minibus will be here to pick you up soon.'

Alice scuttled gratefully away into the spacious hall where her newly polished shoes were neatly placed at the side of the impressive stained-glass door. Her stomach was already twisting into a knot at the thought of the day ahead. She hated it at the convent. She hated the religious ceremonies that she was forced to partake in daily. She hated the silly uniform that she was forced to wear. She hated the other girls, who formed into tight little groups and made fun of her and the way she spoke. But most of all she feared the nuns. She'd convinced herself that none of them had legs, for they all seemed to glide along soundlessly, their legs concealed by their long black habits, and now her fear had grown to such a pitch that just the mere sight of one approaching her could strike terror into her heart. Being at home was only slightly less formidable, for Stella could have the same effect on her. So now, rather than risk yet another telling-off she slipped her feet into her shoes and obediently walked down the long drive to wait for the minibus.

Alice stared miserably from her bedroom window. Stella had sent her to bed over an hour ago, but sleep eluded her. She didn't want to go to sleep anyway, because if she did she might wet the bed again, and then Mrs Webb would be cross with her. She never shouted at her or anything, she just sighed and made Alice feel very silly and dirty. Which was why she was standing now, gazing out across the lush green fields at the back of the house. The sight bought her no joy. In fact, it only heightened her longing for a glimpse of the fields that surrounded Banana Jane's farm. Banana Jane had never minded when she wet the bed. She would just strip the sheets off and tell her not to worry, and then together they would fill the copper and wash them before feeding them through the mangle and hanging them out to flap on the line in the wind. Her eyes filled with tears of loneliness and despair. She missed Susan, and Glen, and Grandma Lil. She missed Holly, and Tabitha, and Tilly and Moses, and her very own baby goat. But most of all she missed Banana Jane. She wondered what she would be doing now, and salty tears coursed down her cheeks. She licked them away. When she'd first come to live with the Webbs they'd promised her that she could see her friends whenever she wanted, but up until now she hadn't been allowed to visit anyone, not even once. Whenever she asked Mrs Webb if she could, she always told her that it wasn't convenient, and now she was beginning to wonder if she would ever see any of them again.

Life was unfair, she thought to herself. It felt as if for all of her short life she had lived with people who didn't want her, didn't love her. Stella was included amongst those people. Only one person had ever truly loved her, the way Alice saw it – and that was Banana Jane. So why had they sent her away from her? Perhaps it was because she was truly bad, as her father had always told her; after all, he had left her, hadn't he? Perhaps bad people weren't allowed to be happy. She cuddled her beloved doll more tightly against her. She was all that she had left of Banana Jane now. But even loving her as much as she did, the doll was no substitute for the person who had given it to her. The realisation made her tears turn into soft hiccuping sobs.

The next morning was Saturday. As yet Mrs Webb hadn't gone into her room, but Alice knew that when she did she would be annoyed because she'd wet the bed again. The thought made her push her breakfast around the plate, a fact that Mr Webb was quick to pick up on.

'What's wrong, Alice, not feeling too hungry?' He smiled at her kindly, and after glancing fearfully across at Mrs Webb, who was at the kitchen sink, she shook her head.

'She barely eats enough to keep a sparrow alive,' his wife complained. 'I sometimes wonder why I bother going to all the trouble of cooking for her at all.'

He frowned at her, and stifled the urge to tell her that

breakfast was the only meal she ever cooked anyway. Mrs Martin came in to clean and cook the rest of the meals, whilst Stella was gallivanting off to the hairdresser's or some social event or another. Turning back to Alice he winked. 'You know, I think we ought to go out somewhere nice today. What do you think, Alice?'

Before she could say anything Mrs Webb chipped in: 'I thought you were going for a game of golf today, Andrew? And anyway, Alice has a dancing class immediately after lunch.'

'Yes, I was going to have a game of golf, but I can change my mind, can't I? It's about time we did something as a family. I thought a trip to the zoo might be nice. As for Alice's dancing class, it won't be the end of the world if you miss it just once, will it, dear?' He watched a flicker of interest grow in the little girl's eyes, but before she could answer him his wife spoke again and her carefully painted lips pursed in disapproval. 'Do you have *any* idea at all just how much these classes cost? And I couldn't come anyway, because I've got to do the flowers in church.'

He saw the disappointment settle on Alice's face and in that moment his mind was made up.

'It's a shame that you can't come, Stella. But I think Alice and I should go anyway.'

The child looked from one to the other of them. To her surprise, Mrs Webb didn't argue although she certainly didn't look very happy.

'Have it your own way, dear. I'm pleased that you have time to waste. Unfortunately I haven't.'

Ignoring the sarcasm in her voice he rose from the table and beckoned Alice towards the door. She slithered off her seat and followed him into the hallway. Once he'd closed the door behind them he smiled at her and took her hand.

'Come on. Let's go and see what we can find for you to wear. You've got some dungarees that you brought with you, haven't you?'

'I haven't g . . . got them any more,' she said sadly, 'She – M . . . Mrs Webb – thought they were b . . . boyish and threw them a . . . away.' She struggled with the expression Mrs Webb had used and frowned.

Quickly swallowing his irritation, Andrew Webb said, 'Well, never mind. I'm sure that we'll find something suitable. It's still a bit nippy out so we'll need to wrap up. I thought we might go to Dudley Zoo. Have you ever been there before?'

When she shook her head he grinned. 'You're in for a treat then. Dudley Zoo is on a big hill on the outskirts of Birmingham. They've got everything there: lions, tigers, bears, elephants, camels – even a castle. You name it, they've got it.'

He was pleased to see the little girl's eyes widen with anticipation. By now they were entering her bedroom and he saw her glance nervously at the bed.

'Had a little accident, have we?' he probed gently.

Chewing on her lip, Alice nodded as she stared up at him fearfully.

'Not to worry. It's not the end of the world. We'll soon sort that between us, although I have to admit I'm not that brilliant when it comes to bedmaking. You start to strip it and I'll go and get some fresh sheets out of the airing cupboard, hey?'

Minutes later they stood back to admire their handiwork. Alice was feeling much more cheerful now.

'Right – let's see what we can find for you to wear.' Andrew hunted through her wardrobe. All it contained apart from her school uniform were rows of pretty flowery dresses. Aware that Alice was watching him closely he forced a smile to his face and reached one down for her. 'We'll just have to make do with one of these then, won't we? You can always put a warm cardigan on over the top. That should do the trick. Now you get ready and I'll meet you downstairs in ten minutes.'

Alice nodded solemnly and after hastily changing and combing her hair she made her way down to the hall. Mr and Mrs Webb were in the kitchen and it sounded like they were arguing.

'*Surely* to God you could break your routine just this once,' she heard him say. 'We have to make an effort, you know? It can't be easy for the child.'

'It isn't easy for me either, Andrew. I'd forgotten what hard work younger children can be. It wouldn't be so bad if she'd show a bit of gratitude now and again but she doesn't even do that.'

'Why *should* she?' he stormed.

His wife sighed so loudly that Alice could hear her from the hallway. 'I would have thought it was more than obvious why! For a start-off, we've spent a fortune on her in one way and another. She should be grateful and happy to be here, but all she does is ask when she can go and see her friends. I mean, she should be forgetting about them by now and making new ones, but I don't think she's even trying.'

'Oh, for God's sake, Stella, grow up and act your age! You were never like this with Alexander and Adam.'

'No? Well, that's because *they* were mine.' The second the words had left her lips she saw his expression darken, and knew that she'd said the wrong thing. But he didn't retaliate; he simply turned and strode away without giving her so much as a backwards glance.

In the hallway, all the pleasure that Alice had felt at the proposed trip to the zoo evaporated. Mrs Webb didn't want her, just as her father hadn't wanted her. And it was all because she was bad – like her father had always told her.

The outing was not a success, despite all Mr Webb's attempts to make it so. All Alice could think about was the things that she'd heard Mrs Webb say about her and the fact that soon she would have to return to her. She followed Mr Webb from one enclosure to another, gazing at animals that she'd only ever seen in books before, but the only ones that brought forth any sort of response from her were those inside the Pets Corner. There, for the first time, Andrew saw a flicker of interest flare in her eyes as she released his hand and ran to a little pen that housed four small goats.

'There are goats on Banana Jane's farm,' she told him animatedly, and his mouth gaped in amazement. For the first time he saw another side to the usually quiet, with-drawn child as she leaned over the low railings and cooed at them. From there she skipped across to an old donkey and began to fearlessly stroke his mane. Standing back, Andrew allowed her to roam at will until the afternoon began to darken. Glancing at his wristwatch he called her reluctantly to his side.

'I'm afraid we're going to have to leave now, Alice,' he told her. 'Stella will be waiting to serve the tea and we don't want to upset her, do we?'

The closed look that he'd come to know so well immediately settled across her face, but she went obediently to his side, and with a last regretful glance at the animals followed him back down the winding path that would lead them to the exit of the zoo.

When they got home, Stella's mood had not improved. If anything it seemed worse and it was all she could do to be civil to either her husband or Alice. She slammed their evening meal down in front of them then stormed out of the kitchen.

Mr Webb winked at Alice. 'Take no notice,' he whispered when his wife was out of earshot, but Alice couldn't eat a thing, which enraged the woman even further when she returned to the kitchen. Mr Webb had retired to his study by then to tackle a pile of paperwork so Alice took the full length of her tongue.

'You wasteful, ungrateful child,' Stella ranted as she tipped the meal into the bin. 'Get yourself upstairs and into your nightwear.'

Alice was so keen to escape that in her haste she knocked her drink flying all over the tablecloth as she clambered down from her chair.

'*You idiot child*, can't you do anything right?'

Suddenly, Alice was back in the kitchen with her father when she had done exactly the same thing. Her whole body started shaking.

'I think what you're lacking is a damn good hiding, my girl, and I've a good mind to give you one!'

'You so much as raise your hand to that child and you'll have me to answer to.' Andrew, who had heard the noise from his study, stood in the doorway. His voice was ominously quiet. He looked directly at Alice and in a gentler tone told her, 'Go and get yourself ready for bed, there's a good girl.'

Needing no second bidding, she flew past him and as the door closed behind her she heard the couple begin to shout at each other.

Once in the privacy of her room she threw off her clothes and after slipping into her nightdress, she scrambled into bed. Pulling the pillow over her head she tried to shut out the raised voices that could be heard even from there. But it was no good. They just went on and on and on. Sobs shook her slight body and she began to rock back and forth. She knew now without a shadow of a doubt that she would never be happy. In that moment, as small as she was, she wished that she were dead.

'What do you mean, Alice wouldn't go to school?' Back home from work the next day, Andrew loosened his tie, and greatly agitated, began to pace up and down the length of the kitchen.

Stella shrugged defensively. 'Just what I said. She ignored me when I called her to get up this morning. She refused to get dressed. She refused to eat. So what was I supposed to do? Physically drag her out of bed?'

He paused in his pacing to stare at her. 'You didn't try to make her wear one of those damned silly frilly dresses again, did you?' he snapped accusingly.

'No, I did not. Though may I tell you, those "damned silly frilly dresses" as you call them cost the earth!'

'Oh, for God's sake, woman. The child isn't a doll to dress up. She *does* have feelings and preferences. Why don't you just lay off her a bit? You're on at the poor kid all the time. "Alice, do this. Alice, do that. Alice, sit up straight". It's no wonder she barely speaks. When she does, either you or Adam tell her to be quiet. In all the weeks that she's been here you've only ever asked her *once* if there was anything that she wanted – and then when she said yes, you didn't like it. She wanted a little dog of her own. What was it she wanted to call it? Holly or something? Personally I didn't think it was an un-reasonable request. It might have helped to make her feel more settled. But what did you do? You went mad and said definitely *not*, and all because you were afraid of a few dog hairs on the carpets.'

'It wasn't that at all,' Stella defended herself, as she studied her perfectly manicured nails. 'You know I don't like dogs, or cats for that matter. They're dirty un-hygienic creatures.'

'Oh Christ, Stella.' He strode towards the door, greatly agitated. 'Where is she now?'

She sniffed indignantly. 'She's in her bedroom, where do you think she is? I just told you, didn't I? She's been there all day.'

Without saying another word, he left her sitting there and took the stairs two at a time. Once outside Alice's door he stopped abruptly and tried to compose himself. Then tentatively, he tapped, calling out, 'Hello, Alice. It's me, Andrew. May I come in?' He strained to hear the response but none came. He tapped again, a little louder this time. 'Look, I only want to talk to you. I'm going to come in, all right?'

He inched the door open and saw Alice, still in her pyjamas, sitting at the bedroom window. She was clutching her doll and her thumb was jammed tight in her mouth. Softly closing the door behind him, he crossed to her and bent to look into her pale face. Her eyes were blank and unseeing, and a stab of pity sliced through him. She looked so small and alone, as if she had locked herself away from the world.

'Look, darling, I know it must be hard for you right now. You have a lot to get used to, a new home, a new school, a new family. But we can work through this together. You'll see – things will get easier. We all need just a little time to adjust to each other, that's all.'

His pity turned to fear as she remained unmoving, unseeing. He rose slowly and left the room with a sick feeling of dread in the pit of his stomach.

When he walked back into the kitchen, Stella stared at him enquiringly. 'Well, is she in a better frame of mind?'

He looked back at her and she noticed his pallor.

'I think you'd better ring the doctor and tell him to get here as soon as he can. And you should feel very proud of yourself, because by threatening to hit her last night, I believe you tipped her over the edge.'

The woman opened her mouth to object, but something about the set of his jaw silenced her. Realising that something was terribly wrong, she lifted the phone and dialled the doctor's number with shaking fingers.

Glen dropped the bunch of flowers onto the table and flushed self-consciously. 'These are for you,' he muttered, glancing at Jane. 'I thought they might cheer you up a bit.'

She looked absently at them and smiled, then heaving herself out of the chair, she headed towards the door. 'Thanks, Glen, they're lovely. Lil, put the kettle on, would you? I've just got to go an' see to the pigs. I'll be back in a minute.'

Glen waited until the door had closed behind her before saying to Lil, who was filling the kettle at the sink, 'So, how is she?' He sounded anxious.

Lil sighed. 'As you just saw, she ain't good, Glen. I'd be lying if I told yer different. She's off wi' the fairies half the time. I thought after a couple o' weeks she'd settle down a bit, an' up to a point I think she has. What I mean is, I think she's had to accept that there's nothin' more to be done. Alice is gone. She's grievin' though, I know it. I hadn't realised just how much she'd come to think o' the child. I blame meself now, for tellin' her *not* to mention that it were Alice as she wanted. It's a bloody shame it is, if yer ask me. But then life ain't never been a bed o' roses fer Jane, has it?'

'What do you mean? I thought Jane had lived a rather sheltered, privileged life. You know, just her and her dad. No worries and only each other to care about?'

'Huh! Things ain't always what they seem, lad. You believe me.'

Glen frowned and would have questioned her further, but something about the set of Lil's mouth told him that she would say no more. In fact, he got the impression that she felt she had said too much already. Silent now, he sat back and watched as she mashed the tea, musing on the strange comments she had passed.

Much later that evening he drove back to his own home. The sight of the dark windows made him shudder. What had Lil meant when she said that Jane's life had not been a bed of roses? And what was the other comment? *Things are not always what they seem.* He let himself into the empty house. The last comment he could understand, for that could be applied to himself as well. The world saw him as a grieving widower, bereft at the loss of a perfect wife, a perfect marriage. But no one knew. They only believed what they saw from the outside. He smiled bitterly as he thought how he could have enlightened them.

'May I come in?' As Julia peeped around the bedroom door, Susan nodded. Tiptoeing into the room, Julia went to sit on the end of the bed. Susan's knees were drawn up tight to her chin with her thin arms wrapped around

333

them. Julia saw straight away that she'd been crying. 'Are you all right, love?' she asked softly, and Susan nodded slowly. The rest of the home was cloaked in silence. Everyone else was fast asleep. But Julia had guessed that she would find Susan still awake, just as she had been every night since Alice had left. The housemother wished desperately that there was something she could say that would ease Susan's loss. But there was nothing, so instead she waited for the question that she knew the girl would ask – and she didn't have to wait for very long.

'Have yer heard how Alice is doin'? Have the Webbs phoned to say as they'll be bringin' her to see us yet?' She asked the same thing every single day. And every day Julia gave her the same answer.

'I haven't heard personally, Susan. But Alice's children's officer will be visiting her regularly to make sure that the placement is going well.'

A wave of resentment swept through her, just as it did every time she thought of how Nora had slyly allowed Alice's move to the Webbs to be brought forward. Had she not been off ill, she herself would never have sanctioned it so soon. She was not at all sure that Alice had been ready to go, and she would have hoped for a much lengthier introductory period. Unfortunately, due to unforeseen circumstances the decision had been taken out of her hands, and now she could only hope that Alice was settling with her new family. Poor Susan was missing Alice dreadfully. The child had changed almost beyond recognition in the weeks since her younger friend had left. The brash front and loud voice had vanished as if into thin air. She no longer even bothered to argue with Lisa or Steven. Instead, to Julia's concern, she kept herself to herself, and spent a lot of the time alone in her room.

Julia squeezed her thin arm reassuringly. 'Try not to worry about her, love. Alice will be fine, I'm sure she will. Oh, and by the way – your aunty rang earlier this evening. She says you can go and stay for the weekend. So that's something for you to look forward to, isn't it?'

Slightly cheered, Susan slithered down under the blankets as Julia tucked her in.

'Goodnight then, love,' she whispered.

'Goodnight, Julia.' Susan listened as Julia quietly slipped from the room and after a time she felt her eyelids grow heavy. Her last waking thought was, *I hope Alice is all right*. And then at last sleep claimed her.

'Now are you quite sure that you'll manage on your own?' Lil's voice was heavy with concern.

Jane said affectionately, 'Of course I'll manage. I'm used to bein' on me own, ain't I? You can't stay here and hold me hand for ever. But sayin' that, I really appreciate all you've done for me over the last few months, Lil. I don't know what I would have done without you – or Glen, for that matter. Just remember, me door's always open to you, day or night. I've really enjoyed havin' you stay.'

'I've enjoyed it an' all.' Lil grinned. 'But now I've got the yen to be back on the water fer a while. I reckon as I must have a bit o' gypsy blood in me veins. Me old man allus used to tell me that.' As she glanced around the room her eyes misted with tears. 'Do yer know, luv, our Joan would have been proud if she could see what you've done to the cottage. She loved this place, she did. An' she loved you an' all, don't yer never doubt it fer a second. She were a good woman an' it's a crime as she were took so young, though if I were to be honest wi' meself, it wasn't totally unexpected.' She sighed. 'Even when we were kids she was a sickly little gel. Never grew out of her TB that she had as a nipper. There ain't a day as goes by as I don't still miss her, an' that's the truth. Still, the past is the past, ain't it?'

'You're right there, Lil. But you know, even though I was only a kid when she died, sometimes I have the weirdest feelin' as she's still here with me.' Deeply embarrassed, Jane rubbed her face and then suddenly the two women moved a step forwards and hugged each other fiercely.

'Now you be sure an' take care o' yerself, do you hear me?' Lil said. 'An' make sure as yer get some decent snap inside yer. If yer lose any more weight we'll be able to stand you in the field an' use yer as a scarecrow. An' don't think that I won't know if yer go neglectin' yourself. Glen has promised to keep his eye on yer fer me. If yer need any help with anythin', before I get back, you see him. He's a good man, is Glen, an' don't yer forget it. If you had any sense you'd be eyein' him as husband material. You could do a lot worse, I'm tellin' yer.'

Jane went as red as a beetroot. 'Oh Lil, don't be daft. Me an' Glen are friends, nothing more. Glen would never look my way – I'm too long in the tooth. Now be off with you.' She gently pushed Lil towards the barge that was all ready to go. Lil had polished *Firefly* from top to bottom and its brightly painted roof shone in the warm July sunshine.

'Now, are you quite sure that you've got everything?' Jane asked for the tenth time.

Lil stepped from the canal bank onto the freshly mopped deck. 'I've got enough supplies on here to take me on a round-the-world cruise,' she joked. 'If I try to load any more on I reckon as the bloody boat will sink, an' then I won't be goin' nowhere.' Her face became serious. 'Keep yer chin up, luv, an' just remember – things always happen fer a reason. The darkest hour is allus afore dawn.'

Seconds later, Jane heard the low throb of the barge's engine. She waved as *Firefly* pulled away from the canal bank, and then slowly turned to look back at the cottage.

During the summer months Glen had given the whole of the outside a rubdown and a much-needed coat of paint. Now with the roses and clematis climbing around the door, Canalside Cottage resembled a picture off a chocolate box. But the sight of it brought Jane no joy. It was empty. Just as her life was empty yet again, and now she knew that it always would be so. She had missed her chance at happiness.

As Lil steered the barge around a bend in the canal the cottage and Jane disappeared from sight. The bright smile slipped from her face and her eyes filled with tears. She felt guilty at leaving Jane to face her heartbreak alone, and yet she knew that she had to get away, for she could not live a minute longer with being so near to her and denying her the truth that she had long deserved to hear. The truth had eaten away at Lil every day of her life, since Jane had drawn her first breath, and over the last weeks the old woman had come dangerously close to revealing the secret that she had sworn to her sister she would never tell. Now Lil felt that she had done Jane yet another huge injustice – for hadn't it been she herself who had urged Jane not to tell the authorities that it was Alice she wanted to adopt? Looking back, Lil felt that had she done so, things might have turned out very differently. Jane and Alice might have been together by now.

She sighed as she looked up to the azure blue sky. *You should have taken me instead of our Joan*, she told God, as she had a thousand times before. *That poor woman loved Jane with all her heart.*

Julia chewed on her lip as she read the report informing her of Alice's progress. She'd just received it from Alice's children's officer, and as far as she was concerned, it didn't make very good reading at all. 'Withdrawn, aggressive, rude' were just a few of the comments that had been made, and yet she found it extremely difficult to associate any of them with Alice. While she'd lived at the home Alice had been a shy, timid child, happy to hide behind Susan's formerly extrovert personality. Crossing to a large metal filing cabinet, she withdrew Alice's file and slipped the report inside it. She felt now, more than ever, that she had been right in her assumption that Alice had been placed with the Webbs too soon. She had felt all along, without Alice saying a word, that the child was not comfortable with them. An older child might have said so outright, but Alice, being the quiet child that she was, had been too afraid to object.

Her thoughts moved on to Nora. Why had the other woman been so keen to get Alice away from the home? And why had she taken such an obvious dislike to her? It was a mystery. Nora had never before, in all the years that Julia had worked with her, been so blatantly unpleasant to a child. It wasn't even as if the dislike had grown as she got to know her, for it had been there from the moment she had seen Alice's name on the register.

Julia grimaced as she thought of the pleasure that Nora would get when she read today's report. She would delight in the fact that Alice's placement was not going well. Still, there was nothing that Julia could do now, only hope that the little girl would settle eventually. She wondered fleetingly what she should tell Susan the next time she asked how Alice was doing. But she knew, without having to think too hard, that she would lie and tell her that everything was fine. Far better a little white lie than cause even more heartache to what was fast becoming a heartbreaking situation.

Chapter Twenty-One

As Jane inched the door open, light from the landing spilled into the long-disused bedroom. Everything was just as it had been on the day her father had died, even down to the unmade bed. The dirty blankets and sheets were pushed to the end of the mattress as if he had just climbed out of it. The thought made her shudder, but she steeled herself to stand there and look around the room. Even now she could smell him: the reek of stale sweat and tobacco seemed to hang in the air. The lampshade was covered in cobwebs, and the dust on the furniture was so thick that she could have written her name in it. At the side of the bed were his hastily discarded boots, exactly where he had kicked them off for the very last time, despite the many occasions when Jane had asked him to take them off in the scullery. The mud had long since dried on them and now it had disintegrated into little piles of grey dust on the bedside rug. Beside them were his socks, crumpled and coated in a covering of evil-smelling green mould.

An old jacket was flung carelessly across the tarnished brass footboard of the bed, and one wardrobe door hung drunkenly open, displaying the rest of his motley assortment of clothes. Alfred Reynolds had never been one to waste money on clothes. In fact, he had never been one to waste money on anything. Jane imagined his rage if he could see the cottage now, all clean, fresh and newly decorated. He would have considered the whole exercise to be a wild extravagance.

Jane gripped the old sack in her hand and slowly her resolve slipped away. She had thought that she was ready to clear the room of his vile belongings, to rid the cottage of his presence once and for all. But now she knew that she did not have the strength. Not yet. He was still here. His presence was so tangible that she almost expected him to appear. A terrible shudder ran through her, and hastily she backed out of the room onto the landing, slamming the door to behind her. Another day, she promised herself as she had a thousand times before. And then dejectedly she walked away, leaving the room untouched yet again.

Jane had just handed out the children's treats at the Henry Street Home when Glen hurried across the car park to her. He waited impatiently until the last child had drifted away, and then drew Jane into the shelter of the open van doors.

'I need to talk to you,' he whispered urgently. 'But not here – it's more than my job's worth.'

She neither questioned him nor argued. She knew Glen well enough by now to know that it must be important, and she trusted him implicitly.

'Come to the farm tonight,' she told him. 'In fact, if

you're not doin' anythin' else, come straight from work and I'll do us both a bit of dinner.'

He nodded, and without so much as another word hurried away.

Driving back to the farm, Jane's mind was working overtime. What could be so important that Glen couldn't have told her about it there and then? Unless . . . her heart began to pound . . . unless it was something to do with Alice. She hardly dared allow herself to hope that he'd had word of her. But even so, by the time she arrived back at the farm she had worked herself into a high state of agitation, and could concentrate on nothing until his car at last swung into the yard that evening.

'It's Alice, isn't it?' she demanded, the second he put his foot through the door. 'You've heard something about her, haven't you?'

He stared at the woman he had come to care about and nodded, his face a mask of concern. Looking back now he had no idea when the liking he had always felt for her had turned to love. It had been a gradual thing. A slow awakening, but now he couldn't deny it. He loved Jane as he had never loved anyone else in his whole life, but the realisation brought him no joy, for he knew that his love would never be returned. It seemed that Jane had no room in her heart for anyone but Alice, and he respected that, as he respected her.

Her patience was about to snap. 'Come on, Glen, *please*. If you've heard somethin', for God's sake tell me what it is, and put me out of me misery.'

He went with her to the table and sat down, facing her, knowing all too well that what he was about to say would cause her pain. He had wrestled with his conscience all day, wondering whether he should tell her anything at all. But then he'd decided that he really had no choice. Jane was longing to hear how the child was, and he could only assume that any news was better than no news at all.

'Well, it's like this,' he began slowly. 'There was a big meeting down at Henry Street today. Just before it started I heard Alice's name mentioned so I guessed that it must be about her.'

Jane leaned forward in her seat, hanging on his every word.

He coughed and went on. 'Going on that I decided that it was time I got around to painting the boot-room door. It's needed doing for some time now. The boot-room door is nearly opposite to the office, see, and happen I might get to hear a bit of what's going on. Anyway, off I go to get the paint and brushes and what have you, and by the time I get back there was already a ruck of people arriving.'

He began to count them off on his fingers. 'There was that woman from the adoption agency, Alice's children's officer, another chap that I hadn't seen before – I think he was Alice's doctor – plus another woman who I heard introduce herself as Alice's children's officer's manager, and then the Webbs rolled up, looking none too happy, may I add. Anyway, off they all went into Julia's office and the review began. Two hours it lasted. I tell you, it's never taken me so long to paint a door, and all the time I'm straining to try and hear what they're saying.'

'And?' Jane breathed.

He could see the tension in her face. 'And I'm afraid what I did manage to hear didn't sound too good. Alice's placement with the Webbs is over, Jane. It's broken down and I heard Mrs Webb say that they didn't want her back. Apparently, the lass left them some weeks ago.'

Panic replaced the worry in Jane's face as without meaning to she snapped at him, 'What do you mean, she left them some weeks ago? So where is she now?'

Glen screwed his eyes tight shut, but then he slowly opened them again and said, 'From what I could gather, the poor little mite's in a hospital somewhere. She's had some sort of a breakdown, apparently.'

'*No!*' Jane sprang to her feet as Glen grabbed at her arm to try and restrain her.

'Calm down, love. That won't get us anywhere. I'm going to try and find out where she is, and then we'll take it from there. We'll find her, I promise you.'

Jane sank heavily into a chair. Her face was a picture of misery and suddenly she began to cry, hot scalding tears that spurted from her eyes. In a second Glen was around the table, cradling her in his arms. It was the first time he had ever held her and it felt right. But now was not the time for thinking of his own feelings, instead he tried to consider Jane's.

'There now, love, don't cry. We'll find her. Come hell or high water. I promise you we will.' He pushed her back gently into her seat, and crossing to the old oak dresser he withdrew a bottle of brandy from the lower cupboard. Swiftly he tipped a generous measure into a glass and thrust it into her trembling hand. 'Here, take a good swig of that,' he ordered. 'It will calm you down a bit. Then we'll decide what's to be done.'

She gulped at the spirit, coughing and spluttering as it burned its way down her throat.

'That's better,' he encouraged. 'Now try and get a grip on yourself. You're no good to neither man nor beast like this, are you? Let alone Alice.'

She saw the sense in his words and with a superhuman effort, took a deep breath and tried to calm herself.

When he saw that she was once more in control he squeezed her hand reassuringly. 'That's better. Now we'll talk and see if we can't salvage something out of this mess. I tell you, if that bloody Nora were here now, I'd wring her scrawny neck with my bare hands. It's all her bloody fault. Julia would never have let Alice go so soon, not until she was sure that she was ready to leave. But still, it's no good crying over spilled milk. Now we have to decide what we can do to put things right.'

Jane fetched another glass and tipped more brandy into each, pushing one across to Glen. She rarely drank alcohol, only on high days and holidays, but tonight she felt the need for it. Slowly the matter-of-fact, down-to-earth woman that he had come to love emerged from the panicked creature of minutes before.

'So what do you think we should do?' she asked him pointedly.

He took a swallow of his drink. 'The way I see it, the

first thing we need to do is to try and find out exactly where Alice is.'

She nodded in agreement. 'I think you're right. But how do we go about it?'

'I could have a word with Julia first. Tell her the truth and then . . . well, if I have no joy there, I'll have to go to more desperate measures, won't I?'

She raised an eyebrow. 'Exactly what do you mean?'

'I'll have to get access to Alice's file.'

'Won't that be difficult? I mean, ain't they kept under lock and key?'

'Yes, they are,' he admitted. 'But don't forget I've worked at Henry Street for a long time. I know where all the keys are kept. In fact, I have access to most of them.'

She was suddenly concerned for him. 'Glen, I don't expect you to do anythin' that could get you into trouble.'

His eyes twinkled. 'Don't you go worrying about me – I'm not stupid, you know. Anyway, if it comes to that I'd be doing it as much for myself as you. I care about Alice as well. If I'd ever been fortunate enough to have a child, I would have been proud to have one just like her. To my mind the poor little soul's had a raw deal all the way round. What with her dad abandoning her, then this on top, it's no wonder she's switched off, is it?'

Suddenly remembering the dinners that were being kept warm in the oven, Jane went and carried them to the table. But for once, Glen seemed to have lost his appetite and they both merely pushed the food around their plates.

He stayed for a further two hours, and during that time the conversation centred on Alice and the plight she was in. By the time he left, the gleam of determination that had been absent for so long was back in Jane's eyes.

'I'm going to rescue her, Glen,' she told him. 'No matter what I have to do, I'm goin' to bring Alice home.'

'That's my girl. That's what we need, a bit of fighting talk,' he said approvingly. 'But before you put the gloves on, let me see what I can find out first. Unfortunately, it's Julia's day off tomorrow and Nora's on duty. So I'll get no joy there. But I promise that I'll speak to Julia the second she walks in on Thursday, and then I'll be straight on the phone to you. Somehow I feel that Julia will help us if she can. I reckon she had a soft spot for Alice.'

'Thanks, Glen. I don't know what I'd do without you and that's the truth.'

He had the urge to tell her that he would *always* be there for her, but instead he remained silent. When she looked at him he saw the loneliness in her eyes.

'I'll tell you somethin', Glen. I wish Lil were still here. Right now Thursday seems a bloody long way away.'

That wish at least was granted to her, for the very next morning Jane came downstairs to see *Firefly* moored at the canal bank as if it had never been gone and her aunt sitting at the kitchen table.

Lil held her arms out to her and Jane tumbled into them. The older woman tenderly stroked her hair.

'I had to come back,' Lil whispered softly. 'I got this funny gut feelin' that yer might need me.'

'Oh I do, Lil, I do.' Burying her face in her aunt's neck, Jane began to cry.

'Have you seen the newspaper today?' Julia threw a copy of the *Nuneaton Tribune* onto the desk as she shrugged out of her coat, and Margaret, who was busily writing a report, glanced up at her. Seeing Julia's white face, she immediately reached for the paper. The headlines seemed to jump off the page at her.

MURDER INVESTIGATION UNDER WAY

A man walking his dog yesterday in woodland on the outskirts of Leeds found the partially hidden body of a man. The victim had been repeatedly stabbed, and the police are combing the area for the murder weapon.

The body has been identified as that of Mr Robert Lawrence, a former Nuneaton teacher, who left the town last year to work in Leeds. Mr Lawrence had been reported missing from his lodgings some months ago, after his landlady heard him speaking to a woman in his room. Police are appealing for this woman, or anyone who might know her, to come forward as she was possibly the last person to see Mr Lawrence alive . . .

Margaret gasped. The paper slipped from her fingers and she stared up at Julia, appalled.

'My God. That's Alice's father, isn't it? As if the poor little mite hasn't gone through enough. She has no one in the world now.'

'I know.' Julia was on the verge of tears and a heavy silence settled on the office as both women tried to take in the latest tragic event. Eavesdropping outside the door, Nora gave a strange little grimace, then she darted noiselessly away.

'So, how are we feeling today, Alice?' The young doctor in the white coat knelt down to the child's level and smiled at her but she simply stared blankly past him, rocking her dolly to and fro. He straightened and sighed then moved to the end of the bed where he unhooked her charts and glanced briefly through them. Motioning to a waiting nurse, he walked away with her down the children's ward.

'Have there been any signs of improvement at all?'

'None at all, Doctor,' the woman told him. 'She hasn't uttered so much as a single word since the day she was admitted. A children's officer came to see her and broke the news that her father was dead, but even that had no effect on her whatsoever. She just sits at the window all day sucking her thumb and rocking her dolly. She seems to be completely oblivious to everything going on around her. You know, Doctor, in all my years of nursing I've never seen anything quite like it. Physically, Alice is a healthy little girl. But she seems to have locked herself away in her own little world where no one can reach her.'

He nodded. 'After what she's gone through it's hardly surprising, but there must be something or someone that she'll respond to.'

The nurse sighed. 'I just hope that you're right – and

I also hope that whatever or whoever it is turns up very soon, because every day Alice Lawrence seems to be slipping a little further away.'

The doctor looked troubled as, side-by-side, he and the nurse went to attend to their next young patient.

Glen waited until all the children had left for school before tapping at Julia's office door. She opened it and gave him a friendly smile.

'Hello, Glen, and what can I do for you today?'

He felt the colour flame in his cheeks.

Seeing his discomfort, she asked, 'Is something wrong?'

'Not wrong with me, but there is something that I need to ask you . . . I was wondering if you could tell me how little Alice Lawrence is going on.'

A closed look came over her face. 'You should know by now, Glen, that I'm not at liberty to divulge that kind of information.'

'Yes, of course I do know that, but you see, I'm not just asking out of idle curiosity. Someone who cares for Alice very much indeed wishes to know where she is, and you of all people should realise that Alice needs someone special right now.'

Julia was visibly surprised. 'Who on earth is that?'

Once again Glen had to grapple with his conscience. Would Jane mind him revealing her interest in Alice?

He was forced to make a decision, and decided that, if it led to discovering Alice's whereabouts, he should reveal everything.

'It's Banana Jane,' he confessed, using the nickname that the children had given her. 'She's been worried sick ever since Alice left. It would mean a great deal to her if she could at least know where Alice is, and visit her, particularly since the adoption broke down and the girl has lost her father.'

'I see.' Julia tapped her chin thoughtfully with her forefinger. 'I know that she used to have Alice to stay at the farm, but when she came to see me, and asked me how to go about being approved as an adopter, she never mentioned Alice, so why should she be so worried about her now?'

Once again, Glen was in a dilemma. And once again, he opted to tell the truth. 'Jane didn't want to adopt just *any* child,' he said in a low voice. 'She applied to become approved because she wanted to adopt Alice.'

Julia was amazed by this revelation. 'Then why on earth didn't she tell me that?' she asked.

He shrugged. 'She thought that if the authorities found out that she wanted to become approved for one specific child, it might have gone against her. But I'll tell you now – she loves Alice.' His voice grew stronger. 'I mean, *really* loves her. It almost destroyed her when Alice went away with the Webbs. Oh, I know Jane might not come across as the maternal type, but she is – at least where that youngster is concerned. Over the last few months I've got to know her quite well, and I'll tell you now: Jane could really help that little girl.'

Julia sat silent for a few minutes as she digested Glen's

news. Eventually she looked up at him. 'Could you get in touch with Miss Reynolds, Glen?'

He nodded eagerly. 'Yes, I could.'

'Right. What I'm about to do is rather unorthodox, so I would prefer it if it could be kept between the three of us.'

'Of course.'

'I'd like you to ask Miss Reynolds to come and see me here, at, shall we say, two-thirty this afternoon? Do you think she could manage that at such short notice?'

'I'm sure she could.' Smiling broadly, he stood and strode purposefully towards the door.

'You won't regret this, Julia,' he promised.

She frowned nervously. 'I just hope that you're right, Glen, because this could cost me my job.' What she was about to do was totally unprofessional, against every single rule in the book. But then she consoled herself with the undeniable truth that some rules are made to be broken.

Jane arrived punctually at two-thirty, and Julia ushered her quickly into the privacy of the office. As Jane perched on the edge of a hard-backed chair the two women eyed each other uncertainly.

At last Julia spoke. 'Miss Reynolds, whyever didn't you tell me that it was Alice you were hoping to adopt?'

'I was worried that you might not approve of the idea.'

Julia sighed, pulling the cardigan of the pretty blue twin set she was wearing more tightly about her. 'May I call you Jane?' she asked suddenly. 'Miss Reynolds is awfully formal, isn't it? And we have known each other for a while now.'

'Of course you can,' Jane agreed, relaxing slightly.

'The final decision as to who is or is not approved is not solely down to me as you now know,' Julia went on, 'but if only I'd been aware that you had a special interest in adopting Alice, I could at least have put in a good word for you – and, believe me, I would have done so. I have seen her thrive through her contact with you and her trips to Canalside Farm. The question is: what do we do now? I find myself in a dilemma. You see, as you are not related to Alice, it would be totally unprofessional of me to divulge her whereabouts to you.'

She watched Jane's face fall with disappointment, and rose from her chair slowly.

'However, should you find out where Alice is by some *other* means, then it would hardly be down to me . . . would it?'

Jane's brow creased with confusion as Julia walked towards the door.

'I'm going to make us both a cup of tea now. After all, that is the least I can do for a guest. And whilst I'm gone – well, obviously I'm sure that you wouldn't dream of reading anything that was confidential.' She nodded towards a large file, strategically placed in the middle of her desk. As Jane followed her eyes she saw *Alice Lawrence* typed across it, and her mouth gaped.

Julia grinned. 'I shall be about ten minutes, Jane,' she said meaningfully, and then she quietly left the room.

Keeping one eye on the door, Jane quickly opened

the file and with trembling fingers, turned to the back page. There, neatly typed, was the latest report on Alice's progress. She skimmed the page swiftly and as she read what had been recorded there, a large lump formed in her throat. Glen had overheard correctly. Alice *was* in hospital and had been there for some time. But worse still was the fact that she was in the George Eliot Hospital, which was literally just a stone's throw away from the children's home. Jane must have passed it a dozen times without knowing that Alice was so close. She read on, and suddenly her heart skipped a beat. It appeared that once Alice was deemed well enough to leave the hospital, there were plans to transfer her to the Tintersfield home in Rugby. Jane was enraged. 'They'll move her there over my dead body,' she muttered, and slammed the file shut.

Julia returned to find her seated sedately in her chair.

'What can I do?' Jane asked her bluntly the moment the housemother had shut the door behind her.

'Well, completely off the record, of course, the first thing I would do if I were in your shoes would be to visit her. See how she responds to you. I can only think that if you were to get any sort of reaction at all, that it would have to go in your favour. If you do, come back to me and we'll take it from there.'

Leaving her tea untouched, Jane rose and stared for a long moment at the woman in front of her. 'I don't think you can have any idea how much this means to me,' she told her gently. To her surprise she saw Julia's eyes grow moist.

'I think I'm beginning to, Jane. I must have been blind not to see it before. Good luck.'

Jane found Glen hovering anxiously at the entrance, waiting for her.

'Well?' he demanded.

She grabbed his arm and dragged him towards the van. 'You and me are off to pay a hospital visit,' she informed him, and unprotesting he clambered into the passenger's seat beside her.

'Can you believe it? Alice has been in the George Eliot Hospital all this time. So near without us even realisin' it.' She drove out of the car park at breakneck speed as Glen hung on to the side of the seat and shook his head in disbelief. Within minutes they turned into the hospital entrance.

Jane was suddenly nervous. 'What will I do if she don't remember me?' she whispered.

Glen threw back his head and laughed. 'Don't talk so daft, woman. Alice would never forget you. Why! She worshipped the very ground you walked on.'

'I hope you're right. She's been through so much, what with the adoption breakin' down an' losin' her dad,' Jane muttered, and after haphazardly parking the van, she got out with Glen and they followed the signs to the children's wards. A smart nurse in a crisp blue uniform looked at them enquiringly as they reached the main entrance area.

'We've come to see Alice Lawrence,' Jane informed her with a confidence that she was far from feeling.

'Are you related?'

'Yes.' The lie slipped easily from Jane's lips. 'We're her aunty and uncle.'

'Oh, wonderful.' The young nurse smiled. 'It will be nice for Alice to have some visitors. I wasn't aware that she had any relatives left after her father . . . well, you know? But I think I should warn you. Don't expect too much. Alice is in a very disturbed state. She hasn't uttered so much as a single word since the day she was admitted.'

'I understand.' Jane nodded calmly, but she felt as if her heart were breaking, and when Glen took her hand, sensing what she was feeling, she gripped it gratefully.

They followed the nurse down a long ward full of beds and cots of various shapes and sizes. In the centre of the ward a cleaner was idly swinging a mop this way and that, seemingly oblivious to the cries of the children that hung on the air. Jane shuddered and hurried on, until at last the nurse paused in front of a side ward.

'She's in here,' the nurse informed them, and standing aside she allowed them to enter then followed them in, softly closing the door behind her. She nodded to them, indicating that they should stay where they were. Then, crossing to Alice, she took the limp little hand in her own and gently shook it. 'Look, darling. Aren't you a lucky girl? Your aunty and uncle have come to see you.'

Alice was in her usual position at the window, gently rocking back and forth, with the doll Susan that Jane had bought her clutched tightly in her arms. She gave no sign at all that she had even heard the nurse, and when Jane glanced at Glen for reassurance she was shocked to see that his cheeks were as wet as her own.

Rosie Goodwin

The nurse sighed and stood up, shrugging her slim shoulders despairingly.

'This is how she is all the time,' she told them sadly. 'I doubt that she'll even know that you're here. But of course you're very welcome to stay for as long as you like.'

Reluctantly releasing Glen's hand, Jane approached Alice. She knelt down and looked into the lovely face that haunted her day and night, as she tenderly wiped a stray red curl from Alice's forehead.

'Alice, can you hear me, darlin'? It's me, Banana Jane. Everything's goin' to be all right now. I promise.'

Alice continued to rock to and fro, her empty eyes staring at the window.

Jane stroked her fingers, desperately afraid that she had lost her for ever. 'Alice, *please* come back to me, darlin'. I need you an' I miss you so much.'

Again for some moments there was no response, but then to the nurse's amazement Alice suddenly stopped rocking and became still. A glimmer of recognition appeared in her eyes. Excitedly the nurse urged Jane on. 'Go on, please. Keep talking to her, I think she heard you.'

Jane caressed Alice's hair. '*Do* you hear me, darlin'? Look, I'm here. I've been to see Julia, and I've told her that I want to bring you home to the farm. Think about Holly an' Tabitha, and Tilly an' Moses an' your little Susan. We all miss you so much, sweetheart, and look – Glen's here as well. He's goin' to fix that swing up for you in the apple tree that you wanted. Please come back

358

to us, Alice, and I promise that I'll never let anyone hurt you again.'

The nurse and Glen both held their breath as Alice slowly turned her head to stare at Jane. She seemed to be struggling to come back from a faraway place. A thin film of sweat broke out on her forehead as conflicting emotions flitted across her face. But then at last, after what seemed an eternity, her mouth began to work.

'B . . . Banana J . . . Jane.' Suddenly she flung herself into Jane's arms and wrapped her thin arms tight around her neck, and they were both laughing and crying all at the same time.

'Oh, my darlin',' Jane sobbed. 'I've missed you so much. Don't cry, you're safe now, I promise.'

Delighted, the nurse sped towards the door. 'I must go and get Dr Philips. He's never going to believe this,' she laughed, and so saying she disappeared down the corridor.

Meanwhile, Alice clung to Jane as if she would never let her go again. Jane offered up a silent prayer of thanks as she held the child close to her. They had both suffered so much, but hopefully soon now they would be able to put their pain behind them.

The child watched in horror as the glass dish slipped from her hands and smashed on the tiles. A terrible silence descended on the room as she and her father watched the fragments of glass spin across the floor. Appalled at what she had done, she raised her frightened eyes, and when she saw the look in his she began to tremble.

'I . . . I'm sorry.' Her apology fell on deaf ears as he rose from his seat, slowly unbuckling his belt. She backed away from him, her hands outstretched as if to fend him off. But then she felt the kitchen sink behind her and knew that she could go no further. She watched him advance as if in slow motion and noted the way his lips twisted with contempt.

'You clumsy little sod, you. Can't you ever do anythin' right?' he ground out.

Her heart began to thump in her thin chest and her breath came now in short, painful little gasps. His hand shot out and grabbed a handful of her vibrant red curls. Then he shook her so hard that her teeth chattered and sank into the tender skin of her tongue. She tasted blood. It was warm and sticky and she began to cry, although she knew that this would only make things worse. He began to drag her across the kitchen, and as she suddenly realised where he was taking her, she struggled wildly. He paused to bring the belt down hard across her bare legs. She felt the soft skin split and swell and she screamed in agony. He ignored her and proceeded to hoist her along the hallway. When they came to the cupboard under the stairs he flung the door open, and her terrified eyes almost started from her head.

'N . . . n . . . n . . . no, please. I d . . . didn't mean to b . . . b . . . b . . . break it. It w . . . were an accident.'

'Yes, well. Perhaps an hour in here will teach you to be more bloody careful in future.'

Viciously he swung her into the cupboard and she landed with a sickening thud against an old metal box. Pain scorched up her arm, but she ignored it and threw herself at the door as he closed it. Her strength was no match for his and she found herself in darkness. Sliding down the wall she wrapped her arms around her knees and sobbed. She heard the sound of the bolt being shot home and then his voice reached her from the other side of the door.

'Sleep tight!'

She shuddered as she realised that he intended to leave her there the whole night. The air was musty and stale and she felt something crawl across her sock. With a scream of revulsion she swiped it away, and immediately her mind began to conjure up pictures of great fat-bodied spiders with hairy legs.

'Oh Mam, Mam, where are you?' she whispered. Eventually her sobs calmed to dull hiccuping whimpers as the darkness wrapped itself around her, and suddenly the stifling cupboard was filled with the scent of lavender, and then at last, despite her terror, she fell into a deep and peaceful sleep.

Chapter Twenty-Two

'Aunty Julia!' Alice's eyes lit up, as bright as the summer sky outside, at the sight of her friend. The housemother beamed back, as pleased to see Alice as the child was to see her.

Crossing to a bedside chair she sat down and folded her hands sedately in her lap. 'So, how are you feeling, love?' she asked kindly.

Alice clambered across the crumpled sheets to dangle her legs over the side of the bed.

'Much b . . . better, th . . . thank you, and B . . . Banana Jane is c . . . coming to see m . . . me later.'

Julia grinned. 'Is she now? Do you like Banana Jane, Alice?'

The smile that stretched from ear to ear answered her question, as did the words, 'Ooh, yes! I love B . . . Banana Jane.'

It was uttered with such sincerity that Julia's heart skipped a beat. Already plans were under way to have Alice transferred to Tintersfield in Rugby, but the woman knew now, without a shadow of a doubt, that this must not be allowed to happen. If it did, then Alice might again lapse into that terrible state of limbo from which Jane Reynolds had somehow managed to release her.

The old familiar gut feeling was back in the pit of Julia's stomach; the one that told her that Jane and Alice should be together. It was increasingly obvious that they adored each other. The only problem was that Julia seemed to be the only one as yet who recognised it. How could she convince her colleagues? Admittedly, on paper it seemed that Jane Reynolds was a totally unsuitable candidate for adopting Alice, because although she was now approved to adopt a child, she had no experience of caring for a child, especially one who was 'backward'. But then, Julia was not at all convinced that Alice was any different from any other 'normal' child. Jane had always insisted that her timidity, stammer and poor schoolwork were the result of deep-seated and chronic insecurity – stemming from the fact that she had never known a loving home. And now, more than ever, Julia was inclined to agree with her. According to the Department, Alice needed to be placed with a family with previous parenting skills and siblings with whom the little girl could bond. But they had tried that with the Webbs and the results had been disastrous. She pulled her thoughts back to Alice, who was humming softly as she brushed her doll's hair. Julia's kind heart went out to the child. She had endured so much in her short life. Surely now she deserved to be happy?

'How would you like me to bring Susan in to see you?' she suggested brightly. 'I know she's longing to come. She's missed you very much.'

Alice laughed aloud. 'Ooh! Yes, p . . . please.'

Julia grinned. 'I'll do that,' she promised, and then she became serious as she remembered the purpose of her visit. 'Alice, I have something to ask you, and it's very important that you answer me truthfully. Do you think you could do that?'

The hairbrush paused in mid-air as Alice nodded solemnly.

Satisfied, Julia continued, 'That's a good girl. Now, I want you to think very carefully before you answer my question, because as I told you, it's very important. The question is – where would you like to live when you leave hospital, if you could have a choice?'

Without hesitation, Alice replied, 'With Banana Jane.'

Julia nodded slowly; the answer had been exactly as she had expected. 'Very well. Alice, I'm going to be completely honest with you now. When I leave here I shall be going to see your children's officer to tell her what you've said. Unfortunately, I think it's highly unlikely that you would be allowed to go to Banana Jane straight away. So what I'm going to try and do is arrange for you to come back to Henry Street, so that you can be with Susan whilst I try and arrange it. Would that be all right?'

Alice nodded, relieved that she was not going to be sent back to the Webbs'. Julia ruffled her red curls as she took a variety of chocolate bars and two little white sugar mice from her bag and placed them on the bedside table. She winked at the girl. 'Don't eat them all at once, else you'll get me into trouble.'

As she stood up, Alice's eyes followed her. 'I have to go now, love,' the housemother told her, 'but I'm so pleased to see you on the mend. I'll be back this evening with Susan, I promise. And I'll make you another promise too. I'm going to do all that I can to try and have you placed with Banana Jane.'

Alice's eyes shone with hope, and when Julia had gone she hugged herself. Julia was nice, so much nicer than that Nora. Ugh! She shuddered as she thought of her, and wondered again why the woman had always seemed to hate her so. Her expression clouded as she remembered the loathing on Nora's face, every time the woman so much as looked at her, and her lip trembled as she thought again of what they had told her about her father. He would never come for her now because he had died. But then she remembered Banana Jane, and Susan's visit, and the smile returned.

The children's officer frowned at Julia. 'I must be honest,' she said. 'It would be very difficult at this stage to alter all the arrangements for Alice's move. The home in Rugby has already agreed to take her; in fact, they have a bed ready and waiting. Why do you feel so strongly that she would be better off returning to Henry Street?'

'I would have thought that it was more than obvious why. Alice has just suffered a terrible breakdown. She's only just recovering from it, and on top of that, she's also having to come to terms with the fact that her father is dead. Personally I feel that if she's moved to yet another strange place at this point, it could have a very detrimental effect on her. The child needs to be with people she knows. For now at least.'

'Mmm, I can see what you mean.' Carol Woods shifted to a more comfortable position in her chair and chewed on her lip thoughtfully. 'I'll tell you what, Julia. I'll bring it up at the team meeting next week. You *do* understand that the decision is not just mine to make? I shall have to discuss it with my manager. But I have to admit that what you've said does make sense. Leave it with me and I'll get back to you as soon as I can.'

'Of course.' Julia rose, pleased with the way the brief meeting had gone, and after saying her goodbyes returned to Henry Street to write up her own report. She also phoned Jane, and asked her to come in and see her as soon as it was convenient.

Jane arrived less than an hour later, while Julia was still writing up the report. The housemother quickly ushered her into the office and shut the door. Nora was somewhere about, and Julia was very aware that, for some unknown reason, Nora was not to be trusted. At least, not in having a say in Alice's future. As far as Julia was concerned, the less Nora knew about it all the better.

She explained quickly about her visit to Alice and her children's officer, as Jane smiled at her gratefully, feeling that she had found an ally.

'Basically, I've set the wheels in motion,' Julia told her. 'But now it will be very much up to you. There's only so much that I can do.'

'Fine, I appreciate that.' A determined glint appeared in Jane's eyes. 'So what do you suggest?'

'Well, I think you should get in touch with Alice's children's officer yourself now, Jane. It's time to lay your cards on the table. Tell them how you feel about Alice. How she feels about you. And then, ask them to get a report from the hospital. That will *have* to go in your favour, when they know how Alice responded to you. I'm already writing up my own report, as you can see. That will corroborate theirs, and I'll make sure that they get it before any decisions are made.' She leaned across and squeezed Jane's hand; a friendly gesture that brought tears stinging to the woman's eyes.

'Do you think I stand a chance?' she asked huskily.

Julia struggled to answer the question truthfully. 'I don't know,' she admitted eventually. 'On paper I have to admit that you're nothing at all what they're looking for, but in real life, well, it rather speaks for itself, doesn't it? Alice obviously loves you and you love her, which in my book scores points. All I can say is that I'm behind you one hundred per cent. I really feel that you and Alice should be together. I can't imagine why I didn't see it sooner. Looking back now, it was as plain as the nose on my face. I just hope that you can be reunited.'

'So do I.' Jane stood up slowly. 'Otherwise all of my life would have been for nothin'.'

Enraged, Nora turned the pages of the open file. So! Alice was almost well enough to be discharged, was she? But why the change of plan? All the arrangements had been made to have her transferred to Tintersfield, where she belonged. Yet according to the reports that had been added to the file, it seemed that those arrangements were now in doubt. She had no chance to read on and find out why, because at that moment, Julia walked into the office. She scowled when she saw what Nora was reading, noting her guilty body language.

'What are you doing, Nora?'

Nora hastily slammed the file shut. 'I was just bringing myself up to date on Alice Lawrence's progress.'

'I see no reason why you should be concerning yourself with Alice.'

'I w . . . wasn't,' Nora stammered. 'Only I just read that the transfer to Tintersfield has been postponed, and I thought it a little strange. After all, Alice *is* backward. That's more than obvious, and the home at Rugby is geared up to cope with children like her. Far more than we are, I would have thought.'

'That's a matter of opinion, on more than one point as far as I'm concerned. I still maintain doubts as to whether Alice *is* backward, as you are well aware. As for the move being postponed, let's face it – we've already made one dreadful mistake about where she would best be placed, haven't we? Alice should *never* have been placed with the Webbs so soon. It would not have happened, had I been here. It was doomed to failure.'

Nora flushed indignantly at the criticism in Julia's voice. The housemother went on: 'It is absolutely imperative that the *right* decision for Alice Lawrence's future is made before she's moved on again to a permanent placement. Her father abandoned her before he died. Her placement with the Webbs has broken down, and the poor child is not even eight years old yet. I'd say she's had rather a lot to contend with in her short life, wouldn't you?'

Nora shrugged. 'It all depends on how you look at it. Alice is not an easy child to deal with, and I personally feel that the Tintersfield home would be the best place for her.'

'In that case, it's a good job that the final decision is not down to you, isn't it? Because I wholeheartedly disagree with you. If we can find the right home for Alice, she could settle very well indeed. What she needs more than anything right now is a little tender loving care, and someone who has the time and patience to give it to her.'

'I think you'll find that Alice is going to be very hard to place now,' Nora said spitefully. 'How many people are going to want to take on the responsibility of a child like *her*?'

Julia smiled smugly. 'I shouldn't concern yourself too much on that score. You see, I have already been approached by someone who would be only too happy to take Alice tomorrow.'

Nora's eyebrows almost disappeared into her hairline as she stared at Julia in disbelief. '*Really* – and who's that?'

Julia saw no point in lying. Jane had already made her intentions clear to Alice's children's officer, and this would soon be common knowledge. So she looked Nora in the face, feeling a measure of satisfaction as she said, 'Actually, it's Jane Reynolds.'

Nora was rendered temporarily speechless. Then she sneered, 'You can't mean *Banana Jane*!'

'Yes, I can.'

Nora drew herself up to her full height. 'I told you that no good would come of allowing the kid to go gallivanting off to the farm, didn't I?'

'Yes, Nora, as I recall, you did. But it seems that you were wrong, doesn't it? Miss Reynolds has now been approved to adopt a child, and personally I feel that she and Alice would suit each other very well indeed.'

'Rubbish!' The word shot from Nora's lips like a bullet from a gun. 'How can you even *consider* it? Jane Reynolds would be totally unsuitable for Alice.'

She began to pace agitatedly up and down the confines of the small room.

'For a start,' she spat, 'Jane Reynolds has never even *had* a child, so that will go against her. She has no previous parenting skills at all.'

'You are quite right,' Julia agreed, 'but what she *does* have is all the time in the world for Alice, and a lot of patience. To my mind that means an awful lot – particularly to a child who has been pushed from pillar to post.'

'I still don't agree.' Nora's lips pursed in disapproval.

Julia simply smiled, enraging her all the more. 'I'm sorry that you feel that way. But at the end of the day, neither you nor I will make the final decision as to where Alice will be placed. I *will* tell you that I have suggested Alice should return here whilst the decision is being made. Furthermore, I will also tell you that I intend to do everything in my power to ensure that Alice *is* placed

371

with Miss Reynolds, and I have already submitted a report to that effect.'

Nora looked as if she were about to burst with rage. Her mouth gaped, emphasising the sharpness of her features, before she wheeled about and stormed from the room, slamming the door behind her.

Julia let out a sigh of relief. *One to me*, she prided herself.

Alice was in heaven. All the people she loved most in the world were gathered about her bed. There was Banana Jane, Grandma Lil and Glen, and Susan, whom they had picked up on their way to the hospital. Even Susan seemed more like her old self now that she was reunited with her friend, and she chattered away merrily.

'Our Michelle's gettin' married this Saturday. Cor! You should see her. She's as big as the back end of a bus.' A ripple of laughter ran through her captive audience. 'An' you should just see the frock me aunty's bought me to wear. Ugh!' She grimaced comically. 'It's horrid. All pink an' frilly.'

Alice giggled, trying to picture Susan in a frilly dress, and failing dismally. Unbidden, a picture of a wardrobe full of such dresses back at the Webbs' sprang to mind, and the smile slid from her face. But it was hard to be sad for long when Susan was around.

'O' course, the good thing is, once our Michelle is married there will be a spare bed at me aunty's, an' I'm hopin' that she'll have me to live wi' her then. She's as good as said it already. But I think she just wants to get the weddin' out o' the way first. Just think, Alice. Soon I could be livin' wi' me aunty, an' you could be livin' at the farm. It would be great, wouldn't it? I could come an' see yer. We'd have some rare old times.'

Alice nodded excitedly. The disappointment that she'd felt earlier in the day had subsided slightly. Her children's officer had visited her with Julia, and they had told her that in two days' time, she would be returning to the Henry Street home. But, they had explained, there were lots of forms to be filled in and lots of meetings to be held before she could be placed with anyone, even Banana Jane. Julia had promised her faithfully that she was doing all she could, and Alice believed her, which made the delay bearable. And at least it meant that she would be with Susan again.

When her visitors eventually left, the small room that had seemed to be full to overflowing suddenly felt very empty, but Alice could bear it now. She had something to look forward to, so bravely she blinked back her tears and cuddled her beloved doll.

On the way back to the farm Jane called in briefly at the home to drop Susan off. The little girl was in fine high spirits, and after planting a hasty peck on Jane's cheek, she skipped merrily away, content in the knowledge that soon Alice would be rejoining her.

Glen fished his car keys out of his pocket. 'She's a card, that one is,' he commented, and Jane and Lil nodded in unison.

'So, what are yer goin' to do with yerself this evenin' then?' Lil asked him.

He thought for a minute then shrugged. 'I suppose I'll do myself a bit of dinner and then watch the telly.'

Lil sensed his loneliness. 'You'll do no such thing, me lad. I know what you men are like when yer left to yer own devices. I suppose dinner will be a tin o' soup or some such. Come on. Get in yer car an' follow us back. I were a bit heavy-handed when I made the stew earlier. It's brimmin' over the pan. So you'd best come an' help us eat it – else me an' Jane will be livin' off it fer a fortnight.'

'You're on,' he smiled, only too happy to oblige, and Lil watched in the van mirror as he climbed into his car and followed them out of the car park.

Much later that evening, after Glen had helped Jane bed down the animals, they wandered into the orchard and sank down onto an old wooden bench. It was a beautiful summer evening, and they sat in silence for some time, watching the hedgehogs scuttle around in the dusk, hunting for food. The rope swing that Glen had hung especially for Alice swung to and fro in the soft breeze, and above them a galaxy of stars twinkled in the sky.

'It's looking promising then, is it, you bringing Alice home?'

'Up to now it is.' Jane flashed him a smile that made his heart miss a beat.

'The trouble is,' she went on more soberly, 'we've still got a long way to go. I just thank God that Julia's on our side. She's been wonderful. She's already managed to swing it so that Alice can come back to Henry Street, instead of her bein' sent off to Rugby. But the final decision doesn't rest with her, unfortunately. An' there's so much red tape to cut through it's unbelievable. I've already spoken to Alice's children's officer, and now I've got the woman from the adoption team comin' back out to see me. It's a right old rigmarole, I can tell you.'

'I know, love. But everything will come right in the end, you'll see.'

'That's what Lil keeps tellin' me,' Jane smiled sadly. 'But I know one who's against us for a start, and that's Nora. She's cut me dead for the last week every time I've delivered to the home.'

'Huh! I shouldn't worry too much about her,' Glen snorted. 'I'm beginning to wonder if that woman's right in the head. She's as sweet as a nut to me, but I haven't forgotten how hard she was on Alice, the last time she was staying at the home. The poor kid couldn't do a thing right for her. But I'll tell you now, I shall be keeping a very close eye on her when Alice gets back, and the first time she so much as says a wrong word to the child, she'll feel the length of my tongue. Don't you doubt it!'

'Oh Glen, you're a good man, you are.' Impulsively, Jane reached across the seat and squeezed his hand. Then, just as swiftly, she snatched it away as if she had been stung, glad of the darkness that would hide her blushes.

Glen had an overpowering urge to tell her how he felt about her there and then, and before he lost his courage he slid his arm around her shoulders and suddenly blurted out, 'Jane, there's something I have to tell you . . .'

'Yes?'

When Jane turned to look at him expectantly his heart did a somersault and his courage deserted him as quickly as it had come. He slowly withdrew his arm and stared up at the canopy of stars overhead, silently cursing himself for being such a coward. He had come dangerously close to telling her how much he loved her, but what was the point? Jane had room in her heart for no one but Alice. 'Oh, it's nothing really. I just wanted you to know that I'll always be here for you. You've come to mean . . . Well, what I'm trying to say is, you're very . . . important to me.'

'Oh.'

Did he detect a note of disappointment in her voice? His head snapped back to look at her but she was fidgeting with the buttons on her cardigan and studiously avoiding his eyes.

'You're . . . very important to me too, Glen,' she whispered. Inside she was crying even while she scolded herself for being a fool. What had she thought he was going to say? That he loved her? That he couldn't live without her? Huh! As if a man like Glen would ever want *her*. She stood up, suddenly feeling the need to be alone.

'It's getting late.'

'Yes, yes of course. I er . . . I should be going.'

They began to walk towards his car and Lil, who had

been spying on them from the cottage window, smiled. She had noted the intimacy between them with satisfaction. If she had her way, it would not just be Alice who was coming here to stay.

Back at the home again, Alice sat on her old bed and listened contentedly to Susan rattling away as she hastily emptied the contents of Alice's suitcase into the drawers and wardrobe, as she had first done so many months ago.

'Well, at least we've got tonight together,' she said happily. 'An' then first thing in the mornin' I'm off to the weddin' an' you're off to Banana Jane's. I bet you're lookin' forward to it, ain't yer?'

'Y . . . yes I am,' Alice said dreamily.

'I'd be lookin' forward to the weddin' an' all, if it weren't for havin' to wear that soppy frock,' Susan grumbled.

Alice giggled as Susan, who had finished unpacking the case, flung it into a corner. Swiftly crossing to her own wardrobe she drew out the offending article. 'Look at it,' she said in disgust, and began to parade comically up and down the room holding it in front of her. Alice laughed so hard that she got the hiccups, but the laughter stopped abruptly when the door was suddenly flung open.

'What the *hell* is going on in here? You're making enough noise to waken the dead. Mind you, I should have known to expect trouble now that *you* are back.' Nora glowered at Alice, as Susan defensively took a stand in front of her.

'Leave 'er alone, you. We was only havin' a bit o' fun.'

'Yes, and that might be all the fun you do have if you don't mind your mouth, young lady. One more word out of you and you can forget your cousin's wedding.'

Susan's eyes glittered dangerously, but nevertheless she clamped her mouth tight shut, knowing that Nora only needed an excuse to carry out her threat.

'That's better,' Nora mocked her. 'Now be told. Be quiet – *or else*!' And she whirled away, banging the door behind her.

Susan stuck her tongue out. 'Bleedin' old witch,' she muttered. 'All she's missin' is a broomstick.' She saw the amused twinkle return to Alice's eyes, and flinging the dress over the end of the bed, she hopped up beside her, happy that they were together again.

'Take no notice of her, Alice. She's never had a life,' Susan whispered, wise beyond her years, as her arm slid protectively around her friend's shoulders. 'But you an' me, we've got our whole lives in front of us. An' do yer know what? I've got a good feelin'. We're goin' to be happy – both of us. You just wait an' see.'

Jane took a last look around the rarely used lounge, checking that everything was as it should be. Apart from decorating, this was the first time she had been in this room since the day her father's coffin had been carried out of it. But later today, it would be used again when Alice's children's officer came to visit her. Behind her in the hallway Lil watched Jane's anxious eyes travel around the room. She stepped forward to place her arm comfortingly around Jane's diminishing waist-line.

'If yer don't feel comfortable in here, luv, yer could allus speak to her in the kitchen.'

'No, Lil.' A new determination shone in Jane's eyes. 'This is a lovely room. Just look at the view from the window over the garden. It's high time it was used properly again.' She took a deep breath. 'This ain't the only room that needs some air in it neither. I'm going to shift some of me dad's stuff out of his bedroom today, an' all.'

Lil bit down on her lip, guessing what a momentous decision this was. 'Are yer quite sure that yer ready fer that, love?' she asked softly.

Jane nodded. 'Yes, I am, Lil. It's time I laid me dad's ghost to rest once and for all. This house has seen enough sadness and enough tears to last a lifetime. It's about time it saw a little happiness.'

'Well, if yer sure, I'll help yer. We could perhaps bag up some of yer dad's clothes an' take anythin' decent for the church jumble. The rest can go to the rag an' bone man.'

Jane laughed mirthlessly. 'You must be jokin', Lil. There ain't nothing in there as anyone would want. You know what Dad was like. He'd never spend a penny where a ha'penny would do. No. The whole bloody lot is goin' on the bonfire, and while I appreciate your offer of help, this is somethin' that I have to do on me own.'

She marched past Lil and went straight up the stairs. From below, the older woman could hear her pad across the landing and pause outside her father's door.

Slowly her mind drifted back across the years as a vision of Jane's father swam before her eyes. She cursed softly. 'Damn you, Alfred Reynolds. May you rot in hell where you belong!'

The words were uttered with so much venom that Holly, who was sitting at her heels, scooted away to the kitchen with her tail between her legs.

With an effort Lil slowly pulled herself together before she followed her.

Chapter Twenty-Three

As Alice's children's officer crossed the farmyard, she paused. A lazy spiral of smoke was rising into a clear blue sky from the direction of the orchard, and she sniffed at the air appreciatively. It was hard to believe that the farm was on the outskirts of a town, for it was so peaceful here. A large rooster strutted majestically past her, and she smiled, amused. This, she had to admit, was an ideal environment in which to bring up a child and yet she still had doubts. She had come straight from a meeting with Julia, who had made it more than clear that she felt this was the right place for Alice to be. But then they had thought that the Webbs would be the right family for her, and that had gone horribly wrong, which was why Carol Woods was so determined to get it right this time. The thought of the consequences if she did not were unthinkable. She continued across the yard, but before she had time to knock at the door, Jane, who had been waiting for her, opened it.

'Hello, Miss Woods.'

'Hello, Miss Reynolds.'

Jane ushered her inside, but instead of leading her into the kitchen where their previous meetings had taken place, she led her along the hallway and into a pleasant sitting room.

'What a lovely room. And what a marvellous view.' Carol Woods crossed to the window and gazed appreciatively down the lawn that led to the canal.

Unused to compliments, Jane blushed, before ushering her guest to a seat. 'Would you like a drink?' she offered awkwardly.

The young woman shook her head. 'No, thank you. I've only recently had one, down at Henry Street with Julia. I just wanted to pop in and let you know what is happening. Julia has been telling me about the good effect that you seem to be having on Alice.'

When a glimmer of hope sprang into Jane's eyes, Carol sighed. 'I'm going to be brutally honest with you, Miss Reynolds. I'm fully aware of your intentions towards Alice, but I have to admit to having grave reservations as to whether this would be the right long-term placement for her.'

'But why?' The words slipped from Jane's lips before she could stop them and her blush deepened.

'Well.' The woman chose her words carefully. 'First of all, as you know, you are a little bit of a rarity. What I mean is, it's still quite unusual for a single person to be approved as an adopter. Within the next few years the Department is planning to look into the possibility of closing down some of the children's homes in Warwickshire, the reason being that they consider most children, particularly the younger ones, would be better placed within a family unit. This of course means that we will need a considerable number of foster parents and adopters to be approved to make this possible. So luckily, with that in mind, it went in your favour. However, during your assessment I did consider, because of your age, that you might be better suited to a slightly older child, and preferably one that didn't have special needs.'

Jane's face hardened. 'I am three years younger now than Alice's mother was when she gave birth to her. So I'm afraid I can't agree with that statement.'

Carol nodded. 'Point taken. But that would not be my only concern. Alice has suffered a lot of trauma and neglect in her short life. So to be truthful, we were looking for people who already have children, people who could cope with any problems that Alice may present in the future.'

'People like the Webbs, you mean?' There was a note of undisguised sarcasm in Jane's voice and now it was the children's officer's turn to blush.

'I admit that placement was a disaster, but that is all the more reason for me to be sure that it's right next time. Another such disruption could have disastrous consequences for Alice, so I don't want to rush into anything. I need to feel quite sure next time that I've got it right.'

'I can understand that,' Jane admitted grudgingly. 'But surely Alice herself should have a say in her future? She wants to be here with me, and I want her. Children do have *some* rights, don't they?'

'Of course they do. I'm not disputing that. But my main concern with that would be . . .' She paused, choosing her words carefully. 'I think what I'm most concerned about is how you would cope with Alice on a long-term basis. It seems that you've led a rather sheltered, protected life here, and I wonder if you are fully aware of just how difficult Alice could become in the future, because of her past experiences. Believe me, I haven't been doing this job for all that long, but already I have seen more adoption breakdowns than I care to remember. People tend to look at fostering and adoption through rose-tinted glasses. They think that a child will be placed with them and that they'll all live happily ever after, much as the Webbs did. Unfortunately, that is seldom the case. Every single child that comes into care, for whatever reason, is damaged – simply by the fact that they are no longer with their natural family – and in the majority of cases, even if it doesn't happen straight away, this can lead to problems.'

'I do understand that, and I could cope, I know I could.' Jane was so adamant that Carol was even more uncertain of what she should do. Her every instinct told her that Jane would be the perfect person to adopt Alice, but unfortunately, her manager still seemed to be leaning towards finding a family for her.

'Just how many people are involved in making this decision?' Jane asked quietly.

Carol shrugged. 'There's my manager. Then there will be Alice's doctor and the head of the adoption unit. Also, although we won't be present, the reports from myself and the housemother will be taken into account, of course.'

She watched Jane's face fall. 'Thank you for seeing me again, Miss Reynolds,' she said, and got up from her chair. 'I won't take up any more of your time, at least not today. I only called in to tell you that we are seriously considering your offer, believe me, and I'm sorry that it's taking so long. But this time we must get it right, for Alice's sake.'

She walked towards the door and Lil, who was eavesdropping in the hall, scuttled away to the kitchen.

'Would you like to see Alice's room before you go?' Jane asked quietly. 'We've just decorated it in her favourite colours.'

Detecting a note of pleading in her voice, Carol smiled kindly. 'I'd love to,' she agreed, and followed Jane up the stairs and along the landing until she stopped and flung a door open.

'This is Alice's room,' she told her proudly. 'I chose all the colours myself, and the bedspread and the curtains.'

Carol stepped past her and looked around. It was a lovely room. The soft shades of lilac made it feel warm and cosy, and she was surprised to see an assortment of toys and books already lovingly arranged on the shelves.

'Alice loves books,' Jane informed her, following her eyes. 'She can't read properly yet, of course, but she's gettin' better all the time. When she stays over she loves me to read her a story at bedtime.'

Carol glanced curiously at a fat comfy cushion positioned on the floor at the side of the bed.

Jane laughed. 'That's there for Holly, my dog. She

likes to sleep in here with Alice. Though why I bothered to put that cushion there I really don't know, 'cos nine times out of ten she ends up on top of the bed. Alice and her are inseparable. I think animals can be very therapeutic for little ones like Alice, don't you? You know, kids that have had a bad time of it.'

Carol frowned. 'I'd never really given it much thought,' she admitted. 'But thinking about it now, I can see that you could be right. Does Alice like all the animals on the farm?'

'Oh yes, every last one of them. Look, I'll show you something.'

Carol followed her to the window and Jane pointed. 'See the goats grazin' in the field over there? Well, Alice has adopted the little one. She named her Susan. She adores her, she does. I reckon she'd have her up here sleepin' in the bedroom an' all if I'd let her.' She chuckled, but then when she turned to find Carol watching her intently she became embarrassed. 'I'm sorry. Hark at me rattlin' on, an' you with things to do. Come on, I'll show you out now, shall I?'

When Carol nodded, Jane hurriedly led her back down the stairs. At the door Carol shook her hand formally, but her eyes were warm and kindly. 'I shall be in touch very soon,' she promised. 'But just one last question. If Alice doesn't come to you, would you be prepared to take some other child?'

Jane shook her head sadly, aware that she might be saying totally the wrong thing. 'No, I wouldn't,' she said flatly. 'You see, if I hadn't met Alice I would probably have lived the rest of me life here alone. But I *did* meet her an' she's changed everythin'. I suppose what I'm trying to say is, I love her, and I can't imagine livin' me life without her now.'

'Well, one thing is for certain. We both have Alice's best interests at heart. So rest assured I shall make sure that the panel are aware of everything you've said before they make a firm decision.'

Jane nodded, worry clouding her face as she watched Carol pick her way through the chickens and back to her car.

The second the door was closed Lil descended on her, her face red with rage. 'You bloody little fool. *Why* in God's name didn't yer tell her the truth?'

'I d . . . don't know what you mean,' Jane stuttered, quickly looking away from Lil's blazing eyes.

The elderly woman would not be put off. 'Don't give me that shit, me gel. I've known yer too long. That woman has gone away wi' the impression that you've led a sheltered, cosseted life. Huh! Well, I happen to know bloody different. I ain't blind as to what was goin' on here, yer know? But all these years I've kept me mouth shut to save yer feelin's. I could see the shame it was causin' yer an' it fair broke me heart. Do yer really think that I don't hear yer cry out in the night, even now?'

Jane screwed her eyes tight shut, as tears squeezed out of the corners and ran unchecked down her cheeks.

Exasperated, Lil grasped her arm and shook it. 'It don't give me no pleasure to get on at yer like this, yer know. But are yer goin' to let him beat yer? He's dead an' buried, an' good riddance to bad rubbish, that's what I say! Yet rather than admit to what you've been through, you'd lose Alice, would yer? Well, I'm shocked, I don't mind tellin' yer. I thought yer had more guts than that. You've nothin' to be ashamed of, luv. The shame was all his, that bastard of a father o' yours. He sent yer mother to an early grave an' had he not gone when he did, I reckon as you'd have followed her. But now, for the first time in yer life, you've a chance to be happy. If only you'd told that woman how you've suffered, then she'd have known that yer could cope wi' anythin' that Alice could throw at yer. Yer should have been honest with her, Jane. I just hope to God as you ain't missed yer chance. 'Cos as sure as eggs is eggs, then he'll still be runnin' yer life from beyond the grave. You just think on what I've said.' With that she stormed away, leaving Jane to ponder on her words.

Glen scraped the unappetising meal into the bin and dropped the dirty plate into the sink. Sinking heavily into a chair he picked up the newspaper. He was surprised to see that it was 10 October already and he wondered where the days were going. It will be 1964 before we can blink, he thought to himself, and began to read the headlines that were blazened all across it.

HAROLD MACMILLAN ANNOUNCES HIS RESIGNATION AS PRIME MINISTER DUE TO ILL HEALTH.

Normally Glen took a great interest in politics but tonight he couldn't concentrate on what he was reading, and eventually flung the paper away. He switched on the radio and tried to concentrate on that, but then switched that off too. Restlessly, his fingers strummed the arm of the chair. Quickly making a decision, he stood up and took his car keys from the table. It was no good. He would have to pay Jane a visit or he would never sleep tonight. He had expected her to phone, hopefully with good news following the children's officer's visit. But he had heard nothing, and now he was beginning to fear the worst. Surely she would have phoned him if the meeting had gone favourably? There was only one way to find out.

A red sunset hung over the farm as he pulled into the drive, giving it a peaceful look. But the second that he walked into the kitchen he sensed that the atmosphere was far from peaceful. Lil was standing at the sink and she greeted him with less than her usual good humour. Immediately he began to wish that he hadn't come. The atmosphere was so thick between the two women that he could have cut it with a knife. He had barely sat down when Lil headed for the door.

'I'll be off to the boat then, fer an early night.'

'Ain't you sleeping in here tonight?' Jane asked meekly.

Lil shook her head, setting her steel-grey curls bobbing. 'No, I ain't. I've got a yen for me own mattress, so I'll wish yer both goodnight.' With that she inclined her head towards Glen, and flounced away.

He glanced at Jane uneasily. 'So, what's the matter with her?'

A guarded look came over Jane's face. 'Oh, I think she's just got one on her. She'll be all right in the mornin', no doubt.'

He sensed that she was not telling him something, but wisely didn't push it. 'How did the meeting go? I was expecting you to phone me,' he said, changing the subject.

Jane flushed guiltily. 'Sorry, Glen. I should have, though there's really nothin' much to tell. I'm no further forward than I was before she came. They still ain't decided. It seems that they're worried because I've had no kids of me own. They reckon that because of that, I may not be the right person to look after Alice.'

Outraged, Glen thumped the table with his fist. 'What a bloody load of twaddle. Haven't they got eyes in their heads? Can't they *see* how much you and Alice care for each other?'

Jane ran a hand through her hair wearily. 'Carin' alone obviously ain't enough. If it were she'd be here now, Glen.'

To his horror she began to cry, great tearing sobs that racked her body. He could only watch. As much as he longed to take her in his arms and comfort her, he dare not. He was afraid that she wouldn't want him to. Instead he crossed to the dresser and returned with the almost empty brandy bottle. He was rewarded when a glimmer of a smile shone through Jane's tears.

'If they don't hurry an' make their minds up soon, I'll be a bloody hopeless alcoholic,' she sniffed.

Laughing with relief, Glen filled two glasses.

Before he left an hour later, he asked Jane if she would mind if he had a word with Lil. She raised her eyebrows curiously and shrugged but made no objection, so instead of going out of the door that would take him to the farmyard as he normally did, he bade her goodnight and slipped out the back way. He stood on the sloping lawn for some minutes gazing at the star-studded sky before slowly making his way down to the boat, hoping that Lil wouldn't have already gone to bed. As he neared the barge he saw that a light was shining from the small cabin window so he swung himself aboard and tapped tentatively at the door. He heard Lil shuffle towards it and when she threw it open and peered out into the darkness to see him standing there she blinked with surprise.

'I thought you'd have gone off to your bed long since, lad,' she muttered, pulling an old dressing gown about her skinny frame. 'What can I do for yer then?'

He saw from her red-rimmed eyes that she had been crying and he smiled kindly.

'I think it's more a case of what *I* can do for *you*, Lil. Forgive me, but I couldn't help but notice earlier on that things weren't as they should be between you and Jane, and I just wondered if there was anything I could help you with?'

She opened her mouth to send him packing but then seemed to change her mind. 'Actually, Glen, I could do wi' talkin' to somebody.'

'I'm your man then,' he grinned, and standing aside

she let him walk past her into the small room. It was much like Lil herself, he thought – bright and colourful and surprisingly homely. She motioned him to a padded seat that ran along the length of the cabin. After sitting down he looked at her expectantly.

'So, Lil – what is it that you need to talk about?'

She sighed, and for the first time since he had met her he was shocked to see that she suddenly looked very old and very tired. She seemed to be struggling for the right words and so, hoping to make things easier for her, he asked gently, 'Is it all the indecision about Alice that's getting you down?'

She nodded slowly. 'That ain't helpin',' she admitted, 'but it goes deeper than that. You see, Glen, I've done Jane a grave injustice. Since the day she were born I've had to keep a terrible secret from her. Should she ever find out what the secret is, she might never forgive me an' I'll lose her for ever. It's a secret as I vowed to her mother I would never tell her. But you know, I may not be long for this world an' I don't want to go an' meet me Maker with this to answer for. More importantly, if I told Jane the secret it might encourage her to reveal a few of her own. A few that might make the difference between her gettin' Alice or not. What do you think I should do, lad?'

Glen scratched his head and thought for a few moments. 'Well, Lil, from where I'm sitting I don't think that you have a choice. I don't know what the secret is, of course, nor do I wish to. But I do know that Jane wants Alice more than anything else in the world. Also, from the little I've heard about your sister, I'm sure that Joan would forgive you for revealing the secret if it meant that her daughter could be happy. And Jane *would* be happy if she could have Alice, we both know that. Lastly, I doubt that there's anything in the world that could turn Jane from you, Lil. She loves you far too much.'

'Thanks for yer opinion, lad,' she said. 'I'll sleep on it and happen I'll know what to do by mornin'.'

'Good. I'm sure that whatever decision you reach, Lil, it will be the right one.' He rose and walked to the door but just as he was about to leave she placed her hand on his arm and stayed him.

'Yer love her, lad. Don't yer?'

A denial hovered on his lips, then he nodded wordlessly and slipped away into the night, leaving Lil alone with her thoughts.

'Now you ain't havin' me on, are yer? Yer do *really* mean it?' Susan's whole face was alight as she stared at Julia.

'Yes, I do really mean it. And no, Susan, I'm not having you on. Your aunt and uncle now feel that they are in a position to offer you a permanent home with them.'

Although Susan had hoped and prayed for this to happen, still she hardly dared to believe that it had come to pass, and she was so excited that she could barely keep still.

Pleased with her response, Julia chuckled. 'Am I to take it then that you're in favour of this proposal?'

Susan nodded as hard as she could.

'Very well, if everything goes to plan and I can get all the necessary paperwork completed, I can see no reason why you shouldn't be able to move within the next couple of weeks. Luckily you've had ongoing access with your aunt since you were placed here, so really all we need to do now is cut through all the red tape.' Her eyes twinkled. But then to her dismay she saw the smile fade from the girl's face. 'You are quite sure that this is what you really want, aren't you?' she added.

'Oh yes,' Susan quickly reassured her. 'It's just . . . what about, Alice?'

'Don't you worry about her, love. She'll be fine, I promise you.'

'But how much longer will it be before she goes to her new home? Yer know, to Banana Jane's?'

Julia bit her lip. 'Unfortunately I can't answer that question, Susan. You see, her move is not quite as straightforward as yours.'

'But she *will* be goin' to Banana Jane, won't she? It's all she ever talks about. Promise me that it'll be OK.'

Julia looked away from the pleading in her eyes. 'It isn't just up to me, Susan, I'm afraid. Other people have to be involved in a decision like this. All I *can* promise you is that if I can do anything, anything at all to make sure that she *does* go to Banana Jane, then I will.'

Slightly comforted, Susan hopped down from the chair. She had great faith in Julia and believed what she had told her as she had never, in all the time she had lived at the home, had cause to doubt her word.

'That's good enough then.' She grinned. 'Now I'm off

to tell Alice me good news.' She flew out of the office and almost collided with Nora, who was just coming down the corridor.

'Slow down and look where you're going!' she barked.

For once Susan was too happy even to bother retaliating. Instead she simply flashed the woman a brilliant smile and sped on her way, leaving Nora to scratch her head in bewilderment.

Nora stuck her head out of the bedroom that was reserved for overnight staff and cocked her ear to check if anyone was still awake. Luckily, only silence greeted her. Tightening the belt on the old dressing gown that she kept at the home, she trod stealthily along the landing. Pausing halfway down the stairs she listened again; all was as silent as a grave so she hurried on, her slippered feet making no sound on the tiled floor. When she came to the office she slid soundlessly inside and clicked the light on, closing the door softly behind her.

She blinked, and waited for her eyes to adjust to the harsh fluorescent light before crossing quickly to the filing cabinet. After fumbling in her pocket for the keys she unlocked it and withdrew Alice's file. Dropping into a chair she laid it on the desk and stared at it.

Alice Lawrence – even the name could make her tremble with hatred. But there was no time to dwell on that now, so she carefully withdrew the last two reports that had been entered. The first was written by Julia and contained nothing that she had not expected. Julia had already made her feelings abundantly clear as to where Alice should live. But the second, and as far as Nora was concerned, most important report was from the girl's children's officer.

Her eyes flew greedily back and forth across the page, and the more she read, the more outraged she became. In fairness, the officer *had* listed her concerns about the proposed placement. But she had also listed the positive things that she felt Jane Reynolds could offer Alice. It was more than clear that as yet, no decision had been made either way, but it seemed that the woman was leaning towards Jane's offer, which meant that Alice could well end up living at the farm. She could be happy.

Nora ground her teeth. It mustn't be allowed to happen. Why should Alice be happy when . . . She shook her head to stop her train of thoughts running on to things that were just too terrible to remember, even now after all these years. The report fluttered from her shaking fingers and landed noiselessly on the desk, and it was then that she made her vow.

'You will never know a day's happiness, Alice Lawrence. Not so long as I have a breath left in my body. You are evil. As the Bible says, the sins of the fathers shall be visited upon the children.'

She gathered the reports together and placed them, exactly as they had been, back into the file. Then she returned it to the cabinet and after relocking it she switched off the light and crept back to her room. She lay there in her lonely bed, her tortured mind working overtime. Robert was gone to an early grave, which as far as she was concerned was no more than he had deserved – but that was not enough. His daughter must never be allowed to know happiness. Whatever she had to do to stop it happening, Nora would do it, regardless of the consequences.

Chapter Twenty-Four

Pointing to a pile of freshly cut sandwiches on the table, Lil told Glen, 'There you are, lad. Get some o'them inside yer before yer get yourself off home. The tea's mashin' – but where's our Jane?'

Glen thumbed towards the ceiling. 'She'll be down in a minute. She's just washing her hands.'

Satisfied, Lil poured milk into the mugs. 'She'll work herself into the grave, she will,' she grumbled. 'An' you won't be that far behind her, the way yer goin' on.'

He helped himself to a sandwich from the plate. 'I wouldn't go so far as to say that, Lil. Though I won't be sorry to see that room finished, and I don't think Jane will be either. I must admit I was surprised when she suddenly decided to tackle it. There isn't a thing of her dad's left in there now. She hasn't kept a solitary item to remember him by. Not so far as I know, anyway. It seems a bit strange, to my mind. What I mean is – I can understand that it must be painful for her. But if they were so close, why has she burned every single thing he owned?'

'You're best not to question, lad,' Lil told him sadly. 'Happen if ever the time is right she'll tell you herself.'

He frowned in confusion but had no time to comment, for just then Jane appeared. She looked tired but happy. 'I reckon at this rate we'll be done by the weekend,' she said.

'You could be right,' Glen agreed, then teased her, 'and then no doubt you'll find me something else to do.'

'No, I won't, Glen. You've done far too much for us already. I think when we've finished that room you'll have earned a damn good rest.'

'Look, I've done what I've done because I wanted to do it. In fact, I've enjoyed it,' he said robustly. 'It certainly beats sitting at home night after night with only myself and the TV set for company.'

Again Jane sensed his loneliness. But wisely this time she passed no comment. Instead she took a seat at the table and sipped at her tea.

'So – whose bedroom is it to be when it's finished?' Lil piped up. 'It's bigger than yours, luv. Are you thinking of claiming it?'

She shuddered at the thought. 'No, I won't be claimin' it. I'm quite happy where I am, although I do have *someone* in mind for it.'

Both Glen and Lil stared at her curiously, as she swiped a stray red curl from her forehead. 'I got to thinkin', Lil. With your arthritis the way it is, you won't want to be floatin' up an' down the cut for ever, so I'm doin' that room up for you. Oh, I know you shout me down every time I tell you I want you to live here permanent, like, but perhaps if you've got your own room done up the way you like it, then you might change your mind? What I'm sayin' is . . . There's a room an' a home waitin' here for you whenever you want it.'

Lil's mouth gaped open. 'What, you mean *live* here? Proper – like all the time?'

'That's exactly what I mean. An' I don't know why you should be so surprised. I've certainly hinted at it enough times in the past. You know I ain't one for fancy speeches an' such, but you're the nearest thing to a mother I've ever had. I can't remember much about me real mam, though strangely enough, there have been times when I've sort of felt as if she was near. Anyway, I never had her for long, but I have had you. Ever since I was a little one you've kept your eye on me. Always poppin' in and out, an' this is my way of sayin' thank you. Though of course, you only need come if and when you want to.'

'I'll bear that in mind,' Lil said gruffly, her voice thick with emotion. Then she scuttled away, leaving Glen and Jane alone.

Admiration shone in his eyes as he looked at her. 'That was a really nice thing to do,' he said fondly. 'You aren't quite as hard as you like to make out, are you?'

She laughed self-consciously. 'Old Lil's the salt of the earth. She must be knockin' on in age now, an' over the years I've been glad of her. This is the least I can do for her after all she's done for me, an' anyway I enjoy her company. So I'm askin' her as much for meself as her.'

Unconvinced, he grinned and said nothing, but again he found himself thinking, *She really is beautiful, inside and out.*

* * *

Lil strolled stiffly up the garden towards the cottage, her feet leaving shiny footprints in the dew-laden grass. She paused for a second, sure that she had caught a glimpse of someone lurking in the orchard, and strained her eyes in that direction. But she saw nothing, and thinking that she must have imagined it, she hurried on. She had risen early to make Jane a cup of tea before she left for market, but when she walked into the kitchen she found Jane already dressed and sitting at the table. The dark bags under her eyes told Lil their own story.

'You ain't slept again, have yer?' she scowled.

'Not much,' Jane admitted as she pushed the teapot towards her. 'There's a fresh brew in if you want one.'

Lil poured out a mug of tea and joined her at the table. 'There's another meetin' today, ain't there?'

Jane nodded. 'Yes, there is. I'm just hopin' that it will be over before I deliver to the home. I don't mind tellin' you, Lil, this waitin' is drivin' me mad. Why can't they just make a decision?'

'Happen they would if you'd come clean with 'em,' Lil told her philosophically, then leaning across the table she gently squeezed Jane's hand. 'I know it must seem like I'm keepin' on at yer, love. But yer know, I truly think it would go in yer favour if they knew what yer own childhood had *really* been like. It breaks me heart to see yer frettin' so.'

Jane gave no reply as she rose slowly from her seat, though her mind was working overtime. 'I'd better get off. I'll see you around teatime.'

Lil nodded, and tried one final appeal as she followed Jane to the door.

'Promise me that you'll at least think on what I've said. Yer might live to regret it if yer let this chance go. I know that it's goin' to be hard for yer to talk about what happened, but surely Alice is worth swallowin' yer pride for, ain't she?'

Lil's mind went back to the conversation she'd had with Glen, and in that moment she made her decision. It was time to cleanse her soul of the secret that had haunted her for all of Jane's life. If she didn't, then Jane might never find the courage to tell the truth and she might lose Alice for ever.

'Come an' sit back down, gel,' she said quietly, her heart beating fast. 'There's somethin' as I have to tell yer.'

Jane frowned. 'Can't it wait till tonight, Lil? I'm late as it is.'

'What I have to say has waited fer too long already, me luv. If I don't say it now I may never say it.'

Jane saw the colour drain from her aunt's face and watched in alarm as she sank heavily onto a kitchen chair. Sensing that whatever it was that Lil was about to tell her was important, she took a seat opposite her aunt. After a while, Lil raised her eyes and looked Jane straight in the eye.

'What I have to tell yer may change the way yer see me from now on. I just hope to God as you'll find it in yer heart to forgive me for the terrible wrong I've done yer.'

Lil closed her eyes for a moment and then began.

'For you to understand, I have to go back to when me an' yer mam were nippers. As I always told yer, we were as different as chalk from cheese, but close nonetheless. Right from when our Joanie were small, all she dreamed about were getting wed an' havin' a family. Me, huh! I was the total opposite, a bit of a rebel. Our mam allus said as I had a wild streak in me an' I were the black sheep o' the family.

'Anyway, we comes to our teens an' that were when yer mam met yer dad. In no time at all they was wed an' yer mam were as happy as Larry fer a time. She loved this place, she did, an' she loved yer dad an' all. After a couple of years he starts to get on at her about havin' a family. Wanted a lad, he did, to carry on the farm. Yer mam were all for it but as time went on an' nothin' happened she got more an' more concerned. After another couple o' years, it started to be a bit obvious that somewhere along the line somethin' weren't quite right. O' course, yer dad blamed yer mam. *"What use are yer to me if yer can't even give me a son to carry on the family name?"* he'd say to her. It fair near broke her heart, I don't mind telling yer. Anyway, round about that time I had a bit of a fling with a fairground bloke. It were nothin' serious, an' after a couple o' weeks the fair moved on an' I ain't never seen nor heard of him from that day to this. The only trouble was, a couple of months later I finds out I'm pregnant. Me mam an' dad hit the roof. *"There ain't no bastard goin' to darken our door,"* they told me, an' they chucked me out on me ear. Well, there I was with nowhere to go an' not a penny piece to me name, so I come to yer mam an' she took me in. It were yer dad as first suggested that they should keep the baby; he were worried as people would think he couldn't make one, yer see. Yer mam were all for it an' the more I thought about it, the more it made sense. There were me with nothing to offer, an' there they were longin' fer a child, so I stayed here until it were born. An' then . . .' Lil gulped as tears streamed from her eyes. 'An' then I hands the baby over to 'em an' made 'em promise as they'd love it as their own. Yer dad was disappointed that the baby were a girl, but I suppose by then he'd told everybody as yer mam were expectin' an' he couldn't back out. I cleared off then. It was too hard to be near the child an' not claim it as me own.'

Jane stared at her and for a while she was speechless.

'I was that baby, weren't I, Lil?' she whispered eventually.

Lil nodded miserably. 'Yes, yer were, love, an' all I can say is I'm sorry from the bottom o' me heart. I thought at the time as I was doin' right by yer.'

'But why didn't you claim me back when me mam died? Why didn't you tell me before now?'

'Because by then I had my Wilf, an' he had no idea that you were my child. Plus I'd swore to yer mam on her deathbed that I'd take the secret wi' me to the grave. I felt as if I were trapped between the devil an' the deep blue sea. So all I could do was keep poppin' in an' tryin' to keep me eye on yer, although there were times when I did come close to tellin' yer. The day of yer dad's funeral was one of 'em.'

Jane hung her head and after a time Lil rose slowly from the table.

'I'm only telling yer this now, Jane, because if yer don't tell the children's officer yer secret yer might lose Alice like I lost you, an' I couldn't bear that. To lose a child that yer love with all o' your heart is a terrible thing, I should know better than any. So I beg yer, whatever yer may think o' me, think on what I've said. All that matters now is you an' Alice.'

A silence descended on the room for a time and then Lil wearily made her way to the door, but before she could leave, Jane's voice stayed her.

'Don't go, Lil. I think I understand why you did what you did. The fact that you're me mam though is goin' to take some gettin' used to.'

'I were never yer mam, pet, not from the second I placed you in her arms. Our Joan is dead an' buried, God rest her soul. But I'd like to hope as yer could still think o' me kindly.'

Suddenly, Jane began to sob and in an instant Lil was across the room and had her tightly in her arms.

'I'll always think of you kindly, Lil. I love you.'

'An' I love you an' all. Have done since the very first breath yer took. Now though, will yer think of Alice?'

'Of course I will,' Jane answered her huskily. 'I'd better think about gettin' to work an' all, else I'll lose me pitch.'

She sniffed loudly and dried her eyes on the sleeve of her coat then quietly made her way to the door. 'Will you be here when I get home?' she asked.

Lil nodded. 'I'll always be here fer yer, fer just as long as yer need me.'

All the way to market Lil's words rang in Jane's head. 'Surely Alice is worth it?' she had said, and Jane knew without a doubt that she was.

By the time she was ready to pack up the stall and deliver to the home later that afternoon her mind was in turmoil. She loaded the last of the produce into the back of the van and drove away, leaving the council workers to dismantle the stall. The first thing she saw when she pulled into the home was Carol Woods's car in the car park. The second thing was Alice, patiently waiting for her with her trusty mate Susan.

Her heart swelled at the sight, and suddenly her mind was made up. She hopped out of the van and beckoned. 'Alice, would you and Susan start taking some of these things through to the kitchen for me? I just need to go an' have a quick word with Julia.'

Feeling very important, Alice and Susan nodded in unison. Satisfied that they were occupied, Jane drew herself up to her full height and entered the home.

There was a *Do Not Disturb* notice on the office door but Jane chose to ignore it. She rapped sharply. After what seemed an eternity, it was flung open and Julia's face appeared. 'Jane!' Her voice registered her surprise. 'Is there something I can do for you?'

'Yes, I think there is,' Jane nodded. 'For a start-off you could give me a few minutes of your time.'

Julia glanced uncomfortably across her shoulder. 'To

be honest, now isn't a good time. Alice's children's officer and I are in the middle of a meeting.'

'Well, that's all to the good then, because what I have to say is for both pairs of ears.'

Intrigued, Julia let her in. Carol Woods gave her a friendly nod as Julia motioned her towards a seat.

'Come on then, Jane. What is it that's so important?' Julia's voice was kindly and Jane was suddenly at a loss as to where to start.

'I haven't been entirely honest with you,' she began slowly. 'An' I thought it was time as I put the record straight before you reach a final decision about Alice an' me.'

The two women were intrigued and Jane squirmed uncomfortably in her seat as they watched her closely. Eventually she looked up and her eyes locked with Carol Woods's. The children's officer was shocked to see the misery that was in them.

'I'd better start at the beginnin'. I can't remember much about me mam, except that she were gentle an' kind. She died when I was still very young. I think she wanted to die, just to get away from me dad. You see, he weren't what you think – me dad was a bully. Led me mam a hell of a life, he did. Anyway, it were after me mam died that he began to get more severe with me and after that I can never remember him givin' me so much as one kind word. Me dad spoke through his belt, an' I've still got the scars to prove it. He beat me sometimes till I used to wish that I could die an' all.'

She shuddered at the memories and tears sprang to

her eyes, but strangely, now that she had started, she didn't want to stop until the whole sorry story had been told. 'Sometimes if I really upset him,' she went on, 'he would lock me in the cupboard under the stairs. It was so dark, an' sometimes I used to feel spiders crawlin' over me. But I soon learned not to cry – not aloud at any rate, because if I did he'd keep me there all the longer.'

She gulped deep in her throat as the terrible memories that she had kept buried for so long emerged. 'I began to think that he'd done his worst, but then again I was wrong because then I hit me teens and . . .' she took a deep breath '. . . an' one night he come to me room and he . . . he raped me. He told me that this was what all dads did. I didn't have any friends to talk to – he wouldn't allow that – so for a long time I believed him. Anyway, eventually I left school, not that I was there half the time, and it was round about then that me periods stopped. Me dad wouldn't allow me to get a job. He said that there was plenty for me to do around the farm, and it wasn't long after that I started to feel bad. Really bad – sick an' ill all the time. It was me dad that first realised I was pregnant. I was just fifteen years old and so ashamed that I wished I could die. He kept me in all the time, hadn't so much as let me step out of the door for months. I realise now that it was because he was terrified of anybody findin' out about what he'd done. In all that time I'd only ever set eyes on one person other than him and that was Lil – she's me aunty, or at least I thought she were until today, but that's another story. She clocked on straight away to the fact that I was pregnant, but he told her that it was some village lad that had put me in the family way. I thought at the time that she believed him, but it turns out now that she had an inklin' about what was goin' on all along . . .'

For one terrible moment, Jane thought she was going to break down, but with a huge effort, she regained her composure. Nothing would stop her from reaching the end of her story.

'My dad said to Lil that once the baby was born, he planned to have it adopted. I thought then about runnin' away an' I started to think of ways I might do it. Then one night when I was about six months' gone I dropped his dinner carryin' it from the oven to the table. He flew into a rage and give me the worst beatin' of me life. After he'd done I managed to crawl to me bed and it wasn't long after that the pains started. I tried not to cry out, but in the end the pain got so bad that I couldn't help it. He come along the landing just as the baby were bein' born. It was a little girl. I can remember liftin' her an' holdin' her in me arms.' Tears were pouring down Jane's cheeks as she whispered, 'I'd never wanted the baby, but once I saw her it were different. She was so beautiful. She cried for a minute an' then suddenly she stopped and I noticed that her lips were blue. I don't remember much after that, except I knew that she was dead.'

Jane had to pause again. She could feel the tiny body in her arms; saw her daughter die again. She gave a sob of pure grief and forced herself to continue.

'I cried for me dad to help her, but he just picked her

up an' took her away an' I never saw her again. He told me that I mustn't ever breathe a word of what had happened to anyone, and up until this day I never have. After that, I gave up any thought of runnin' away again. I knew that he would have come an' found me an' dragged me back – an' anyhow, I had nowhere to run to. So I just accepted me lot. But I never ever forgot that little girl. I can see her face in me mind's eye now as clear as if it were yesterday.'

Another sob bent her double; the two other women had tears streaming down their faces.

'Then come the mornin' when I got up an' me dad hadn't appeared which was unusual. After a time I made him a cup o' tea an' took it up to his room. He'd been drinkin' steadily all through the night an' he tried to . . . Well, let's just say he followed me across the landin' and fell down the stairs. He broke his neck and as I stared down at him I realised that he was dead, and I cried. Not tears of sadness, but tears of relief. *Now*, I thought, *he can never hurt me again.* But you know, even then I was wrong, 'cos I still have nightmares about him. Sometimes they're so real that I wake up in a cold sweat.'

Jane wiped her eyes and looked at Julia and Carol. For a moment, she had forgotten where she was. Now she plunged on, for her story was not yet told.

'Then I met Alice, an' somethin' about her touched me deep inside. Perhaps I recognised somethin' in her that had been hurt as I had, an' somehow we sort of bonded. Admitted, her dad never raped her – she told me that sometimes he would hit her but I don't think she took the beatin's as I did. But all the same, what he dished out to her resulted in abuse of another sort. What she suffered was emotional abuse, an' I reckon as how one sort is almost as bad as another – they all go hand-in-hand. I know, you see, that she'll never forget what she's been through. I know I never will, because my life ain't been what you thought, has it? You all thought that I'd been a devoted daughter. You thought that I'd never married an' left me dad 'cos I loved him. I never meant to give you that impression. You just assumed it. Natural, I suppose, but now you know different. There ain't nothing that Alice could throw at me as I wouldn't understand an' sympathise with. Because I've suffered just as she has an' I really think that I could help her. That is – if you'll just give me a chance.'

When Jane finished talking a stunned silence descended on the room, which was broken eventually by Carol Woods. Tentatively, she reached out and took Jane's hand. 'Why ever didn't you tell us all this before?' she asked sympathetically.

Jane sniffed. 'It ain't exactly the sort of thing you like to talk about, is it? I suppose I was too ashamed.'

'*You* shouldn't be ashamed, Jane – nothing that happened was *your* fault. You were just a child. I'm glad that you've told me now, though. It must have taken a tremendous amount of courage. Obviously it will affect our decision about Alice, because it seems to me that, if anything, you have suffered even more than she has.'

'That ain't important now,' Jane told her quietly. 'What matters now is Alice. Please remember that when you do decide: *I ain't important.* I only want what's best for her.'

Carol squeezed her hand gently. 'I think I realise just how much now.'

Jane hauled herself out of the chair. Strangely, she felt as if a great weight had been lifted from her shoulders. Perhaps because she would finally no longer have to live a lie? She didn't know what had caused this weird feeling of relief. But she did know that she had done the right thing in being honest with them. Lil had been right.

The members of the panel were gathered around an enormous circular table.

The head of the adoption unit, who had chaired the meeting, glanced around at the sea of tired faces. The meeting had already lasted for two hours, as the numerous dirty teacups strewn across the table testified. But now at last it seemed as if they were coming close to reaching a decision. The reports from Carol Woods, and Julia, the housemother at Henry Street, had been saved until last to be read out. It was Julia's report that swayed the final decision as a lot of emphasis was placed on her opinion.

'So are we all agreed then?' the Chairman asked, and when all heads nodded in agreement he sighed with relief. The decision, right or wrong, had finally been made.

Two days later, Jane received a phone call from Julia telling her that the decision had been reached. *Alice was coming home.*

There were certain conditions: Alice would be placed for between twelve to eighteen months with Jane, and during that time, Jane would be fostering the girl with a view to adoption. There would be frequent visits from Carol to ensure that all was going well, and if at the end of the set period, Alice was happy and thriving, then the adoption process could proceed. Jane readily agreed to the conditions; she would have agreed to walk through fire to have Alice.

'Perhaps you'd like to be present when I tell her?' Julia suggested.

Wild horses couldn't have kept Jane away. 'Could you round Glen up? And Susan should be there too,' she shouted gleefully down the phone. 'I'll bring Lil, an' we'll be at Henry Street within the hour.' Forgetting her manners, Jane slammed the phone down, leaving Julia grinning widely on the other end, as she raced away to find Lil and tell her the good news.

Glen was waiting outside for them as Jane brought the old van to a screeching halt in the car park shortly afterwards. One glance at her face told him all he needed to know and as he followed the two women into the home he was grinning like a Cheshire cat that had got the cream.

Alice was hovering outside Julia's door holding tight to Susan's hand but she had no time to greet Jane, for Julia ushered them all into her office away from prying ears the second they set foot in the building.

'Right.' It was hard to keep the excitement from her voice and she found that she couldn't stop smiling. 'Alice,

I'm delighted to tell you that I have some wonderful news for you. It's finally been decided that you *will* be able to go and live with Miss Reynolds.'

Alice stood as still as a statue for some seconds and then suddenly whooped with delight as she launched herself into Jane's waiting arms.

'Does this mean for ever and ever?' she gasped as she stared into her beloved Banana Jane's eyes. Jane could only nod, for she was too choked with emotion to speak.

It was a joyous occasion; they were all happy and smiling, and Lil and Glen – and even Julia – felt that they were at the birth of what was to be a very special relationship. It was decided between them that Alice's homecoming should coincide with Susan moving to her aunt's, and everyone was happy with the decision. Everyone except one person.

Out in the corridor, Nora listened to the happy group making the arrangements, and her face twisted with malice. Her hands balled into fists of rage, and a cold sweat broke out on her forehead. She could hardly believe that the little slut was really going to Canalside Farm, and the fact that she was going somewhere she wanted to be made it worse. It was unbearable, in fact.

She listened to the joyful voices and knew then that she could not allow it to happen. *Let them all laugh while they may*, she resolved. *Soon their laughter will end in tears.*

Down at the cottage, Lil squinted into the darkness; she was sure that she had seen somebody climbing off the boat, and she hurried on down the garden to investigate.

However, when she reached the barge there was no sign of anyone.

Your old eyes are playin' tricks on you, she scolded herself, yet even so, she felt vaguely uneasy. On numerous occasions of late she'd thought she'd seen someone hovering around the place. She'd heard footsteps in the lane, but when she went outside to look, there was no one there. She hadn't mentioned it to Jane because the lass had enough on her plate at the minute, what with getting everything ready for Alice to come home. The mere thought of that had her smiling again, and she clambered onto the boat, cautiously looking this way and that. *Happen if I think I see anyone again, I'll have a word with Glen,* she promised herself, and comforted with the decision she made her way to bed.

It was the very last night that they would sleep at the home, and Susan and Alice lay side-by-side in Alice's bed, full of plans and dreams and hopes for the future. On the floor their suitcases lay packed all ready to go the next morning.

'Banana Jane told me that I can come an' see yer whenever I want,' Susan informed Alice happily. 'She even said that sometimes I might be able to stay overnight.' She sighed dreamily into the darkness. 'Just think – this is the very last time that either of us will sleep in this room. But I don't mind bettin' it won't be empty fer long. There'll soon be some other poor buggers in our beds, I expect. Still, at least we'll be all right, won't we? I knew things would come right for us in the end.'

Alice grinned; she was so excited that she was sure she would never be able to sleep. She lay back, content to let Susan rattle on, and slowly her eyelids began to grow heavy. The other girl eventually stopped chattering and became silent, and soon her gentle snores echoed from the bare walls.

Alice sighed blissfully, picturing the pretty bedroom that she would be sleeping in tomorrow. And then in no time at all, like Susan, she fell fast asleep.

Someone gently shaking her arm brought her springing awake. It was still dark and she couldn't see who it was that had woken her.

'Come on. It's time to get up,' a voice whispered urgently.

Alice rolled to the edge of the bed. 'W . . . what t . . . time is it?' Her voice was still thick with sleep, but already hands were tugging her pyjama top over her head.

'Never mind what time it is. Just get dressed, and be quiet else you'll waken Susan.'

'D . . . doesn't she n . . . need t . . . to get up too?'

'No. Not yet.' The voice was strangely familiar. 'But you have to. I've got to take you to Banana Jane's.'

Alice struggled into her clothes and a hand gripped her arm. 'Come on then. And remember, you must be very quiet. Everyone else is asleep.'

Alice followed the figure onto the dimly lit landing and when she saw who it was, she started.

'It's all right,' Nora said wheedlingly. 'Don't look so worried. I've already told you – Banana Jane is waiting for you. You don't want to be late and upset her, do you?'

Alice would have walked with the very devil himself to get to Banana Jane, so trustingly she allowed herself to be led away. She was sad that she hadn't had time to say a proper goodbye to Susan and Julia. But still, she consoled herself, they would be seeing each other again very soon anyway.

Once outside she was bundled none too gently into a car, and soon the Henry Street Children's Home was far behind her.

The sound of footsteps clattering along the landing woke Susan. She yawned and stretched lazily. Then as she realised what day it was, she smiled dreamily.

'This is it then. The big day, eh!' She pulled herself up onto one elbow and looked across at Alice's bed, surprised when she saw that it was empty. She could vaguely remember staggering across to her own bed during the night. Alice had been fast asleep then, her thumb jammed firmly into her mouth and her doll tucked into the crook of her arm. But now the doll lay discarded on the unmade bed.

Susan shrugged. Her friend had probably nipped to the lav, she thought to herself, and wide awake now, she clambered out of bed and began to get dressed. Five minutes later she walked along the landing to the toilets. 'Alice!' she called softly, pushing the doors. They swung open. Empty. It was then that she heard Julia behind her.

'Good morning,' Julia greeted her cheerfully. 'What are you up to?'

'I was just lookin' fer Alice. I thought she might be in the lav. She ain't in the bedroom.'

'Ah well, that doesn't surprise me. She was so excited last night that she probably couldn't sleep. I bet she got up early and has gone down to breakfast.'

Susan nodded. Julia was probably right. They had both been so excited last night, she was amazed that either of them had managed to sleep a wink. She grinned at Julia. 'Well, you ain't wrong there. I can hardly believe that I'm really goin'. The only sad thing will be that I'll miss you.'

Julia was deeply touched, and slid her arm around Susan's thin shoulders.

'I'll miss you too, and Alice,' she admitted. 'But you can still come and see me, you know? In fact, I'll expect it. Anyway, come on. This is a special day. Let's not get sad. We'll go and find Alice and then we'll get all your last-minute things into your cases.'

Happy again, Susan smiled, and hand-in-hand she and the housemother descended the stairs. In the corridor they parted; Julia went into the kitchen and Susan headed for the day room, which doubled as the dining room. Being a Saturday it was full. Quickly her eyes scanned the tables, but there was no sign of Alice.

Steven and Lisa, who were seated at the table nearest to the door, leered at her.

'What's up then? Lost your little bum chum, have yer?' Steven said rudely.

Susan ignored him and retraced her steps into the corridor.

'I bet she's gone back to the bedroom,' she muttered to herself, and running now she took the stairs two at a time. But the bedroom was just as she had left it. Her eyes fell on Alice's discarded pyjamas lying in an untidy heap at the side of the bed, and it was then that alarm bells began to ring in her mind. Alice always folded her pyjamas and put them underneath her pillow. She had never known her to simply throw them off before, and then there was her doll, Susan. She never went anywhere without it and yet it was now lying abandoned on the bed. She crossed to the window and looked out across the car park and the garden. It was deserted except for Glen who was heading towards his outhouse. Struggling with the sash-cord window, she managed to push it partway open. Then she poked her head out. 'Hey, Glen,' she called. 'Have you seen Alice this mornin'?'

He stopped and looked up at her. 'No, love, I can't say that I have. But you'll probably find her having a bit of breakfast in the dining room.'

'I've already looked there, an' I've checked the toilets, but I can't see no sign of her.'

He frowned. 'I'll tell you what then. You come down here and we'll have a scout round for her together. She can't be far away.'

Nodding, she snapped the window shut and seconds later she met Glen in the corridor.

Ten minutes later they were back at the same spot. Glen scratched his head. 'I can't understand it.' A note of concern had crept into his voice. 'It isn't like Alice to disappear, especially today of all days. I've looked everywhere and there's no sign of her. I reckon you'd better go and fetch Julia, love.'

Susan sped away and returned in no time at all with Julia close on her heels.

'Right, now we need to do this methodically,' the housemother said authoritatively. 'Glen, you check all the downstairs again. Susan, you go and have a good look around outside, and I'll go and check all the bedrooms. That's probably where she is, saying goodbye to someone.'

Susan hurried away to do as she was told. Meanwhile Margaret, who was also on duty with Julia, joined in the hunt, and between them they searched every inch of the house and grounds. But it was as if Alice had vanished into thin air. There was not so much as a glimpse of her. Assembled back in the office now, Julia began to feel genuine concern. The old gut feeling was back and it was telling her that something was seriously amiss. By now, Susan was crying softly.

'Calm down,' Julia soothed her. 'There must be some logical explanation for this.' She looked to Glen for support, unsure of what to do next.

'You don't think she would have set off for Banana Jane's, do you?' he suggested.

Even as he said it they all knew that it was highly unlikely, but Julia decided that it was worth checking out. There seemed to be no other explanation as to where she could have gone at present.

'I'll ring her,' she told them. 'Meanwhile, you all go into the dining room. Breakfast should be just about over now. Ask the other children if any of them have seen her, before they all start to drift away.'

Glen strode purposefully towards the door with Susan right behind him while, with a feeling of dread, Julia began to dial Jane's number.

Chapter Twenty-Five

The children huddled in hushed little groups as the police walked through them and disappeared into the office. The children's home was normally alive on Saturday morning with the sound of voices and laughter. But today it was unnaturally quiet. Even Steven and Lisa were unusually subdued as they reflected on how badly they had treated Alice.

Inside Julia's office the investigation into Alice's disappearance was about to begin. DI Spooner, the detective in charge, was a large, well-built, slightly balding man. As well as being a policeman he was also the father of three small daughters, and so he was taking the report of Alice's disappearance very seriously indeed. He nodded at Julia, and then looked past her to where Jane was sitting quietly in a corner. Lil's hand was resting protectively on her shoulder, and he guessed immediately that she was somehow connected to Alice. Jane was desperately pale and trying hard to come to terms with this latest setback. Susan, whose eyes looked enormous in her small white face, was standing at the other side of her, gripping her hand as if her very life depended on it. Her aunt was due to arrive at any minute; but for now she was forgotten. A young policewoman opened a notebook and stood waiting silently for the Inspector to begin his questioning.

'This really is a most unfortunate incident.' He looked around at the concerned faces. 'Even so, it could all turn out to be very innocent. It may be that Alice has simply gone off for a walk and lost track of time.'

'No!' Jane snapped. 'Alice would never do that. She ain't even eight years old yet, and she wasn't allowed out of the home on her own. She knew that.'

'I see.' He scratched his head. 'Well, perhaps it would help if we started at the beginning. I need to know everything you can tell me about Alice. How long she's been here. Where she came from. Everything from when she first arrived.'

Julia swallowed, and then slowly related Alice's history whilst the young policewoman scribbled furiously away in her notebook. When she'd finished Inspector Spooner nodded thoughtfully.

'Do you think it's possible that her father may have had a change of heart? That *he* could have come and taken her?'

'Absolutely not!' Julia's head wagged fervently from side to side. 'Alice's father showed no interest in her whatsoever from the day she was placed here. That was before . . . well, before he was killed some months ago in Leeds. He was stabbed to death apparently and the police are still trying to find his killer.'

'I see.' The frown lines in the Inspector's forehead deepened. 'In that case I shall need to liaise with the force in Leeds.' He glanced at the young policewoman who was taking the notes. 'I need to know who is handling the murder investigation there and I'd like them to get in touch with me as soon as possible. Could you see that this is followed up?'

She nodded. 'Yes, of course, sir.'

Satisfied, he turned his attention back to Julia. 'Who was the last person to see the child, and when was this?'

Julia looked at Susan, and colour flooded into the girl's thin cheeks, highlighting her freckles.

Gently he began to question her, and stumbling on her words she told him all that she could.

'Last night we was really excited an' neither of us could get to sleep, so in the end I went and climbed in Alice's bed fer a bit, an' we had a natter. I don't know what time it was when I went an' got back in me own bed. I just know it was dark, an' Alice was fast asleep. Then, when I woke up this mornin' . . . she weren't there,' she finished haltingly.

He smiled at her kindly. 'Are you quite sure, Susan, that you didn't hear anyone enter your room? That you didn't see anyone at all?'

She sniffed. 'No, I swear I never seen or heard a thing. Me aunty always says as when I'm asleep it would take an earthquake to wake me. I sleep like the dead, I do.'

He coughed to hide his amusement. 'Thank you, dear.'

A tap at the door interrupted him. Susan's aunt was standing there, fidgeting nervously. 'What the hell's goin' on then? The car park's full o' police cars an' there's coppers swarmin' everywhere.'

Julia looked back at the policeman. 'It's Susan's aunt come to collect her. Have you finished with her yet?'

He nodded. 'Yes, I think so, for now at least. But I will need her address in case I need to speak to her again.'

'Of course.' Julia beckoned to Susan. 'Will you just excuse me while I go and see her off? I'll be back as soon as I can.'

Pushing Susan gently in front of her, she led her out of the office and up the stairs to her room. 'I'm so sorry that this has happened, today of all days. I so wanted it to be special for both you and Alice.' Susan's Aunt Betty was labouring breathlessly up the stairs behind them. 'Alice has gone missing,' she informed her.

The woman looked horrified. 'What! Yer mean someone's snatched her?'

'We don't know yet.' Susan's voice was tearful. 'Last night she was in our room an' then when I woke up this mornin' she were gone.'

As they walked into the bedroom the sight of Alice's suitcase lying on the floor temporarily silenced them.

Susan looked away and her eyes came to rest on Alice's treasured doll, discarded on the bed. It was then that she began to sob as if her heart would break.

'Somethin's happened to her, I *know* it has,' she wailed. 'She were so happy last night, Alice would *never* have gone off on her own. She were scared o' the dark. An' she'd never go anywhere wi'out her doll anyway. I know she wouldn't.'

Julia secretly agreed with her. But now she was keen to get back to the police and get to the bottom of this mess, so she hugged Susan reassuringly, while her aunt closed the catch on her suitcase.

Kissing Susan soundly, Julia nudged her towards the door. 'You get off with your aunt now, love, and try not to let this spoil your special day for you. Alice will turn up safe and sound, you'll see, and we'll all be wondering what we were panicking about. I promise that I'll let you know the second I have any news.'

She spoke with a confidence that she wasn't feeling, but her words seemed to have the desired effect on Susan, because her sobs subsided to loud sniffs. Julia led them back down the stairs and then followed them out to the car park and watched as Susan's uncle loaded her case into the back of a dilapidated old Ford Corsair. She waved as they pulled away, noting with satisfaction that Susan's aunt, who was in the back of the car with her, had her arm protectively around the girl's shoulders. It was a good sign.

'Be happy,' she whispered as the car disappeared around a bend in the road. Then she turned and hurried back into the home.

'So – let me just make sure that I have this right then, Miss Reynolds. You're telling me that Alice Lawrence was due to come and live with you today?'

As Jane nodded, the Inspector stroked his chin thoughtfully. 'How did Alice feel about this move?'

'She was thrilled about it,' Julia answered for her. 'It's

all she's wanted for a long time, and last night she was so excited that she could hardly get to sleep. She and Susan were still wide-awake when I came up to bed at about twelve-thirty. I could hear them whispering and giggling through the door. She could hardly wait for the morning.'

'I see. It's highly unlikely then, that she might have run away?'

'Absolutely not,' Julia said adamantly. 'Alice adores Jane, and vice versa. Someone must have taken her, that's the only logical explanation. Otherwise Alice would still be here now. Waiting for Jane.'

Just then the young policewoman, who had been using the phone in the kitchen, entered the office. 'I've managed to make contact with the Inspector handling the murder investigation in Leeds, sir. He will be more than happy to speak to you as soon as it's convenient.'

'Very well.' He nodded. 'But first I think it's time we got a description of Alice out to all the police cars in the area.'

'I'll help you with that.' Margaret volunteered, and rising, she and the policewoman left the room.

The Inspector sat for some minutes, thoughtfully strumming the desktop with his fingers. Then he looked up. 'It seems strange that neither Susan nor anyone else in the home heard anything. Do you keep the doors locked at night?'

Julia sighed, her nerves at breaking point. 'Yes, we do, and all the downstairs windows.'

'Mm. That, added to the fact that there seems to be

no sign of a forced entry, is puzzling. Who else besides yourself was on duty last night?'

'Just Margaret.'

'And are you the only two that have access to the keys?'

'No, we're not.' Julia's eyes never left his face. 'Most of the staff who work here have their own set of keys.'

'Was Alice popular with the rest of the staff?' he probed.

Julia nodded. 'Oh yes. Alice was popular with everyone really. A couple of the older children used to pick on her a bit, because of her stammer, but it was nothing too serious. Susan usually sorted them out. But apart from that . . .' Her voice tailed off as a thought suddenly occurred to her, and her face clouded. No, she told herself, I must be wrong. But even so she knew that she must mention it.

'There is just *one* person who isn't at all fond of Alice,' she confided hesitantly. 'But I'm sure that she would have had nothing to do with her disappearance.'

'Nevertheless I need to know who it is.' The Inspector's voice was firm.

'Well, it's Nora Fitton. She's one of the staff here. For some reason she has never taken to Alice. I don't know why, but as I said, I'm sure that she would have had nothing to do with this. She hasn't even been on duty for the last two days as she's taken two weeks' leave.'

'We'll pay her a visit and check her out just the same. Give her name and address to my colleague, please, and I'll get someone round there right away.'

'Very well.' Julia immediately went to the staff file, searching for Nora's home address, as the Inspector turned his attention back to Jane. He noticed her pallor and felt a pang of sympathy for her.

'This really is most unfortunate, Miss Reynolds, but try not to worry too much. I'm sure that we'll find her safe and sound. The majority of children who go missing usually turn up within the first few hours. In the meantime, do you have any idea at all where she might have gone?'

'Well, of course I bloody don't. I wouldn't be sittin' here worryin' meself sick if I did, would I?' Jane snapped.

'Hmm . . . No, quite.' He coughed, aware that Jane's nerves were being stretched to the limit. 'Why don't you get yourself off home, Miss Reynolds?' he suggested. 'There's nothing more that you can do here for now. I promise you that we'll do our utmost to find her, and as soon as we have any news at all we will contact you immediately.'

Glen, who had just entered the room, walked over and helped her from the chair. 'Come on, love, he's right. There's no point you sitting here. I'll take you home,' he offered kindly. 'You're in no fit state to drive yourself, are you? And what's more, once we get back I'll not be leaving you again until Alice is found.'

Unresisting, she allowed him to steer her towards the door. Her legs seemed to have developed a mind of their own, and she was sure that they would let her down at any moment. In the doorway she paused and looked back at the Inspector.

'You promise that you'll phone straight away if you've news?'

'Straight away.'

As soon as they'd gone the Inspector turned to Julia. 'Nora Fitton. How much do you know about her?'

'Not an awful lot, to be honest,' she admitted. 'Nora is a very private person. She seldom talks about anything outside of the home. I think she still lives with her elderly parents. But why do you ask?'

The Inspector scratched his nose. 'Well, I could be totally wrong, of course, but there's something fishy here to my mind. Certain things don't add up. For instance, the fact that no one heard Alice indicates to me that she knew the person who took her – if anyone *did* take her, of course. Otherwise, surely she would have cried out? It seems that she went willingly. She even got dressed first. Furthermore, my officers inform me that there is no sign of a forced entry anywhere around the building, which again indicates that the person who took Alice had access to the home, possibly their own key. Are you absolutely positive that the door was still locked when you checked it this morning?'

'Yes, it definitely was,' Julia replied without hesitation.

'Right then, I think it's time we paid this Miss Nora Fitton a little visit, don't you?'

Julia's stomach twisted into a knot as she slowly nodded. This was to have been one of the happiest days of Alice's young life. Instead it was turning into a nightmare.

* * *

Back at Canalside again, Glen settled Jane into a chair and filled the kettle. He made a very strong pot of tea then poured them all a cup out, adding lots of sugar to Jane's. He'd heard somewhere that hot sweet tea was good for shock, and he needed no doctor to tell him that Jane was deeply in shock. She looked awful and was trembling like a leaf.

'Here, love, drink this,' he urged, pressing the cup into her hand. But she seemed not to hear him and stared blankly off into space.

He and Lil exchanged a worried glance.

Lil took a long swig of her own drink and shook her head sadly. 'What a thing to happen, today of all days! I just can't take it in. Alice is such a lovely little girl. Who would want to hurt her?'

'I don't know, Lil. But the police are doing all they can, never you fear. They'll find her soon and then we'll all be able to fetch her home where she belongs.'

'Oh, no, we won't.' Jane's flat statement made them both look towards her. Glen hadn't even thought that she could hear him; she had seemed so locked in a world of her own. But she obviously had.

'Don't talk so daft, woman.' He struggled to think of words to comfort her.

But she laughed – a soft, bitter laugh. 'I should have known it were too good to last. I was too happy. I never deserved to have Alice, you see. That's why this has happened. It's God's way of punishin' me for bein' bad.'

'*Rubbish!*' The word burst from Glen's outraged lips. 'How can you even think that? Why, you're the most honest, decent person that I've ever met in my whole life.'

'I ain't, Glen. Far from it. In fact, I'm rotten to the core. Me dad always told me so.'

Confused, he looked at Lil, but she lowered her eyes, ignoring the question she saw in his. 'Why on earth would he say that?' he dared to ask, turning his eyes back to Jane. 'I thought you and your dad loved each other.'

'Huh! That's what everyone thought, ain't it, Lil? But you knew better, didn't you. So now you may as well know an' all, Glen. But be prepared for a shock. You might not think quite so highly of me once you know what I'm really like. You see – I ain't quite what I seem.'

'Leave it, Jane,' Lil implored her. 'There's no need to put yourself all through this again.'

'Oh, but there is, Lil. Glen's been good to me these last months. He deserves to know the truth.'

She motioned Glen to the chair opposite her, and once he was seated she began to tell him of her life. All the time she was talking she avoided his eyes, unable to bear the disgust she would surely see in them. For the second time she recounted it all. The abuse, the pain, the recurring nightmares, and the shame she had suffered. And by the time the sorry tale was told, Glen sat rigid with shock as tears coursed unashamedly down his cheeks.

'So you see,' she finished softly, '*that's* why this has happened. I'm dirty, soiled. That's why I've always kept meself to meself. Marriage an' a family of me own were never on the cards for me. Who would have wanted *me*, eh? But with Alice I thought it could be different. I thought I could help her. I thought she would be the child I lost an' loved an' pined for. But it weren't meant to be, were it?'

'Oh Jane.' Glen's voice was strangled with emotion. 'How can you even *think* that? None of what happened was your fault. How can you blame yourself like this? You are neither soiled nor dirty. It was your father who was perverted, not you.'

'I've lived a lie all these years,' she murmured. 'And that in itself is a sin, ain't it?'

'Then I'm as big a sinner as you are. Because I've done exactly the same thing.'

It was Jane's turn now to stare at him in surprise. 'What do you mean?'

Distractedly he ran a hand through his slightly greying hair. 'Well, you've been honest with me, so I suppose I should come clean with you. You see – I'm not exactly what you think I am either.'

Both Jane and Lil were intrigued. Glen had led such a simple life. What could there be not to know about him? He smiled sadly at their startled expressions, and it was then that Lil made to rise.

'Happen it's time I were makin' meself scarce,' she muttered, but he waved her back into her seat.

'No, Lil. There's no need for you to leave. We've all grown close over the last months so I'd like you to hear what I have to say as well.'

She sank back down, and slowly he began.

'When I was young, very young, I lost my mother. My father had left us years before – I can't even remember him. But anyway, to cut a long story short I was put into care in a children's home in Birmingham, much like the one in Henry Street. I got in with a bad crowd and started to get myself into all sorts of bother. By the time I was eleven years old I was a right little devil. They tried fostering me out, but I was too much for anyone to handle by then, you see?'

He met Jane's eyes and smiled ruefully.

'Anyway, one day a family comes along and takes a shine to me. They were very well-to-do – in fact, the Webbs put me in mind of them – and eventually I went to live with them. They had one daughter, two years younger than me, she was. And from the very first minute I set eyes on her I was besotted, even though I was only a kid. She was spoiled rotten, but she was so beautiful even then that she took my breath away. Her mother was much the same, and the biggest snob on two legs. But her dad – well, he was all right. He had a heart as big as a bucket. He spent a lot of time with me, and taught me all I know about do-it-yourself – he was a bit of a fanatic when it came to anything like that. He was a solicitor and not short of a bob or two, and he managed to put me back on the straight and narrow where others had failed.'

Glen took a swig of his tea, now lukewarm.

'They fostered me long-term, and amazingly the placement worked. My schoolwork improved to the point where, when I left school, my foster-dad talked me into going on to university. He wanted me to get a Law degree so that I could join him in his firm. To be honest, by then I'd calmed down a lot, and I knew I owed him a great deal. I would have preferred to qualify as a teacher as I've always loved kids, but to please him I studied Law. Anyway, it was while I was away at university that my foster-mum died. So I started to spend as much time as I could at home. Then things began to develop romantically between Lorna, the daughter, and myself. By this time she was a stunner and she knew it. I could hardly believe my luck. By God, I worshipped the very ground she walked on, I did. Strangely, my foster-dad encouraged the relationship, and when I finally graduated we got engaged. I went to work with Dad in his firm, and for a time all was well. But then he took ill and around about the same time, I sensed that Lorna was losing interest in me. Not long after, her father died.'

Glen gazed at the two women as he recalled: 'All hell broke loose then, because it turned out that he was in debt everywhere, and in no time at all I had the bank breathing down my neck. Lorna and I had to sell the house, the firm and everything he owned to settle up the debts. The only good thing was that suddenly Lorna wanted me again and so we got married and I saw to everything for her. We were left with very little, but I found I could still be optimistic. I was young, I was happy, I had a beautiful wife and my whole life was in front of me. But Lorna was devastated. She was so ashamed that she demanded we move away to somewhere where no one would know us. I was only too happy to oblige – in those days, I would have gone to the ends of the earth for her. So that's when we moved to Nuneaton.'

As he paused, Lil poured him out a fresh cup of tea. He took a swig, refreshed.

'I settled straight away, but Lorna hated it. We had got just enough money left to put a deposit down on a little house. It was nothing like as grand as the one she'd been brought up in, of course, and that was when the trouble started. Lorna wanted me to get a job at another solicitor's, so as usual I bowed to her wishes and went to work for one in the town. I told my wife that I wanted us to start a family, and although she didn't seem as keen on the idea as I was, she agreed. I was desperate to have children by then. I suppose I wanted to give them everything that I'd never had, and so I sat back and waited. But when two years had passed and nothing happened, I started to get a little worried, but Lorna told me not to be so stupid, and so I supposed that I was just being too impatient. Anyway, one particular morning I woke up with a throbbing headache. Lorna was downstairs and so I decided to get myself a couple of aspirins out of her bedside table. It was then that I found an old letter from a hospital in Scotland. She'd gone there to have her tubes tied, on the pretence, I realised, of visiting an aunt. I don't mind telling you, I was totally distraught.'

The big man massaged the back of his head, and then went on, as if to himself, 'I could hardly believe it, but when I confronted her with it she just laughed in my face. She told me that she'd never had any intentions of having a family, because she was afraid that it might spoil her figure. Can you believe that? I mean – that must be the height of vanity. I'd adored her for years and would have carried on loving her, even if she'd grown to the size of a house. All I'd ever wanted was a family of my own to love and care for, and it was then that our relationship changed. Not long after, I saw the job as handyman at Henry Street advertised. The thought of working near children who had gone through difficulties like mine appealed to me – particularly as it looked now as if I would never have any of my own.'

As the painful memories assailed him he gave a little cry; Jane put her hand out to him, feeling his pain.

'Lorna was appalled,' he went on, 'but even so, for the first time I stood my ground. After that, things went from bad to worse. I suddenly began to see her as she really was. Oh! She was beautiful on the outside, all right. But inside she was as hard as stone, with no feelings for anyone except herself. She was shallow, and fickle, and ugly. To the outside world we were the perfect couple, but in truth, our marriage was a sham. The only person Lorna ever *really* loved was herself. Sometimes I admit, I thought of leaving her. But then she became ill and I hadn't got the heart to do it, and so from then on until the day she died, just like you, Jane, I lived a lie.'

Jane stared at him appalled, hardly able to take in what he had just told her. 'Oh, Glen, I had no idea,' she whispered brokenly.

'Well, neither did I,' he laughed bitterly. 'It seems that this is the day for revelations, doesn't it?'

Behind them, Lil lowered her chin to her chest. *Oh yes,* she thought to herself, *it's a day for revelations, all right. Revelations, and more heartbreak than should ever be allowed.*

Chapter Twenty-Six

'Good afternoon, madam.' PC Eric Tilbrook flashed his identity card. 'I was wondering, could we have a word with Miss Nora Fitton, please?'

The old woman glared at him suspiciously. 'You'll have a job,' she muttered. 'She ain't here.'

'Oh, I see. Do you mind me asking where she is?'

'I ain't got the foggiest idea, son. She just upped and took off, she did. Said she was in need of a holiday. Not so much as a thought for me, nor her old dad if it comes to that! Who's goin' to get the coal in for us now, eh?'

The policeman exchanged a glance with his colleague, an equally young WPC called Brenda Sillitoe. 'Well, in that case, would you mind if we came in and had a quick word with you? It's a little public standing here on the doorstep, isn't it? And you wouldn't want the neighbours gossiping, would you?'

Her lip curled in contempt. 'I don't much care what folks say about me, son,' she informed him. 'The way I look at it, while they're talkin' about me they're leavin' some other poor sod alone. But you can come in by all means.' A thought suddenly occurred to her, and her expression became troubled. 'Our Nora ain't in any trouble, is she?' she asked anxiously.

'No, no, of course not,' he reassured her, and the old lady let them in. He and WPC Sillitoe squeezed past her into a dim hallway.

They followed her as she shuffled away into a small cluttered lounge. An enormous coal fire was roaring in the grate despite the heat of the day, and the two police officers felt sweat break out on their foreheads. At the side of the fire in an ancient armchair an old man was dozing, his slippered feet stretched out to the flames, his false teeth resting on his lower lip.

The old woman saw them looking at him and said, 'Pay no heed to him. The silly old sod's senile. He just sleeps for most of the time.'

The words were harsh but were said with a wealth of affection. She motioned them to two hard-backed chairs that were stood against one wall and obediently they sat down, careful not to disturb the photographs that were displayed behind them. It seemed that almost every inch of wall space was covered in them – pictures of children of all ages, shapes and sizes.

The old woman laughed, seeing their surprise. 'They're all me grandchildren an' great-grandchildren,' she informed them proudly. 'Twenty-six of 'em altogether, there is – six of me own I had. Our Nora was the only one out of the lot of 'em as never wed.'

The constable tugged uncomfortably at his shirt collar as he felt a trickle of sweat run down his neck. 'It's perhaps as well, else you might have had a few more photos to add to your collection,' he joked.

She liked his sense of humour and grinned. 'Happen you're right there, lad. I just don't know where I would have put 'em. I'm fast runnin' out o' room, and buyin' Christmas presents for 'em all is a nightmare. Still, that's another story. You ain't come here to talk about me grandkids, have yer? So, how can I help yer?'

Just then the old man stirred. 'Mother, Mother, where are you? And where's me bloody tea?'

She prodded him gently in the arm. 'It's comin', yer silly old bugger. Now go back to sleep an' I'll wake yer when it's ready.'

He sucked in his false teeth and contented, let his chin fall back onto his chest.

Trying hard to hide his amusement, Eric Tilbrook fished a photograph out of his top pocket. 'Have you ever seen this child before?' He handed her a recent photograph of Alice, and she immediately bent her head over it, studying it closely.

'I can't say as I have,' she eventually replied. 'She's a pretty little thing though, ain't she? Why do yer want to know?'

'I'm afraid she's gone missing from Henry Street Children's Home. So we're questioning all the staff that work there, to see if they've seen her.'

'The poor little soul – that's terrible. But I'm afraid I can't help yer at the minute, lad. As I said, our Nora's cleared off on holiday. As soon as I hear from her though, I'll tell her that yer need to talk to her. In the meantime I hope that the little lass turns up.'

'So do we, Mrs Fitton.' The two police officers rose and smiled at her. 'Thank you very much for your time,' Eric said. Relieved to be escaping from the stifling atmosphere, he headed speedily towards the front door.

'It's no trouble at all, my dears. And good luck with your search.'

Lil scraped the untouched meal into the bin and looked across to where Jane sat staring blankly into the empty fire-grate. She was dressed in the same clothes that she had been wearing two days ago when Alice had gone missing. Since then she had neither eaten, nor drunk so much as a cup of tea. Nor had she slept, which was apparent from her red-rimmed eyes. Lil had given up trying to reason with her. There was nothing that she could say to comfort her, so the majority of the time had been passed in silence. All she could do was be there for her. She gazed wistfully out of the window to where her barge bobbed gently on the canal. It was over a week since she had so much as set foot on it, and the urge came on her now to just climb aboard and sail away. But she knew that she wouldn't. For as long as Jane needed her she would be by her side, and to her mind, Jane had never needed her quite as much as she did right now.

The shiny new twin-tub washing machine that Jane had bought especially to wash Alice's clothes in and the new television set that took pride of place in the corner seemed to mock her. She glanced at the kitchen clock and sighed with relief. Glen should be finished with the outside chores soon and then he would be back in. Jane hardly seemed to know that he was there, but even so his presence was comforting. He had been keeping the farm going single-handed, seeing to the animals and anything else that needed doing, and this had only re-affirmed Lil's first impression of him. Glen was a truly genuine, lovely man. Until recently Lil had held high hopes that he, Jane and Alice would become a family. It was what she had always dreamed of for Jane. But now as each long hour ticked away, with still no word of Alice, the dream slipped further and further away.

The Inspector thumped the desk in frustration. 'This is ridiculous,' he spat. 'A child *cannot* simply just vanish into thin air. Are you *quite* sure that you've questioned everyone who works at the home?'

'Yes, sir, every single person. Except Nora Fitton, of course, and we still haven't managed to trace her as yet.' The young policeman swallowed nervously.

'Right, well – visit her parents again and get a recent picture of her. We have to find her! Do you understand?'

'Yes, sir. I'll go round there right away.'

'Good, see as you do. Then get her description circulated to all areas. We'll go on the news to find her, if need be. Right – get moving, every second counts.'

Needing no second bidding, PC Tilbrook fled from the incident room. 'Is there a Panda car available?' he asked in the outer office.

The young WPC nodded. 'Yes, there is. There's one just come back into the yard.'

'Good. Well, grab your coat then, Bren, and come

with me. We've got to pay another visit to Mr and Mrs Fitton.'

She took the car keys from the hook-board, informed the desk sergeant of their intentions and, snatching up her jacket, she followed the young constable out of the station. Soon the police car was cruising through Hill Top and when they arrived at Nora's house the old lady once again admitted them. It was as if they had never been away. The old man was in exactly the same position by the fire. The room was still stiflingly hot, and the old lady was dressed in the same shapeless cardigan.

'If it's our Nora you've come for then I'm afraid you're still out of luck,' she informed them, as she ushered them onto the same hard chairs. 'We ain't heard so much as a whisper from her. I can't understand it. She's never done nothin' like this before, never. It's as if she's dropped off the face o' the earth. An' me, well, I've been rackin' me brains to try an' remember if I've ever seen that little girl before. Here – let me have another look at that picture, would yer?'

'Of course.' PC Tilbrook fished in his pocket again and handed her the now slightly dog-eared photograph.

Once more she studied it closely, but again she shook her head. 'No, it's no good. I'd help yer both if I could, but to my knowledge I don't think I've ever so much as set eyes on the child. What did yer say her name was again?'

'Alice,' Eric told her, disappointed that she had not been able to help them. 'Alice Lawrence.'

To his horror, the colour suddenly drained from her face, and she pressed her clenched fist to her heart. He sprang from his seat and would have gone to her assistance, but she held him at arm's length, obviously struggling to compose herself.

'Lawrence, did yer say?' she gasped eventually, and when he nodded, she sank down heavily onto the nearest chair.

'Dear God. That's a name I hoped never to hear in this house again. It caused enough heartache the first time around, it did.'

'What do you mean?' Curious now, he watched as she slowly raised her eyes to look at him.

'It were a Lawrence as ruined our Nora's life,' she whispered brokenly, and he had to lean forward to hear her. Sensing that she was about to say something significant, PC Tilbrook glanced at his colleague.

'Get your arse out to the car and radio through to the guv, Bren,' he said out of the side of his mouth. 'Tell him to get here as fast as he knows how. I think we may be on to something at last.'

Without even stopping to close the doors behind her, the WPC sped away to do as she was told.

The Inspector arrived within minutes. Loosening his tie as the heat of the room met him he scowled. 'All right then. What have you got?'

The young officer nodded towards Mrs Fitton, who was sitting staring into the blazing fire.

'It seems that someone called Lawrence was once associated with Nora, sir. They might have no connection with Alice Lawrence, of course. But even so, I thought you ought to be here.'

A spark of interest flared in the Inspector's eyes. 'Good work, Officer. You were quite right to call me in.' He turned his attention to the old woman, who didn't even seem to be aware of his presence.

'Perhaps you'd care to explain then, Mrs Fitton,' he addressed her.

Dragging her eyes away from the flames, she stared at him. 'It all happened about seven or eight years ago now,' she said softly, and the memory was obviously painful to her. 'Our Nora had never been much of a one fer boyfriends an' what not. She weren't on the front row when looks were dished out, admittedly. But all the same, back then she were presentable, and she were clever an' all – the brightest of all me brood in the brains department. Me an' her dad had high hopes for her, I don't mind admittin'. We did also expect that one day she'd meet a nice lad an' get married, but time moved on an' we began to think as she'd stay on the shelf. Anyway, she suddenly starts to take an interest in herself an' tells us that she's met this bloke. She was totally besotted with him, she was. He'd been to university and was a teacher at some school in Hartshill, by all accounts. We were thrilled to bits fer her, till it turned out that he was married. "Give him his marchin' orders," I told her, but she'd have none of it. She'd convinced herself that he'd leave his wife, but if yer want my opinion, I don't think he ever intended to. Next thing we know, he tells our Nora that his missus is pregnant an' dumps her like a ton of hot bricks. Our Nora was completely devastated, an' I thought her heart would break'.

The old lady gave a deep sigh of distress before saying the words she'd never thought to share with a stranger. The words that spoke of her daughter's secret. 'Things went from bad to worse, when she discovered that she was pregnant too. I was mortified, as yer can imagine, but our Nora was delighted. She saw the baby as a way of getting Robert back, an' started to hound him wi' letters. But they all came back unopened an' she got more an' more desperate. By this time she was almost five months' pregnant. And then one night when we were all in bed I heard her cryin' out. I was along that landin' like a shot, I can tell yer. And when I opened her door there she was, lyin' in a pool o' blood. By the time the ambulance arrived it were all over bar the shoutin'. Nora had delivered a stillborn baby girl.'

She shuddered as tears spurted from her eyes to run in furrows down her wrinkled face. In his chair beside her, the old man stirred for a second, then went back to sleep. 'I'll never forget it till the day I go to me grave. She wailed like a banshee, she did. It were terrible, an' it took the ambulanceman all his time to get the poor little soul out of her arms. After that she changed an' went from one extreme to another. She grew all bitter an' twisted. Not with me an' her dad, mind. I have to say she's allus been a good girl to us, took care of us, like. She just changed towards men, an' in all the years since, she's never so much as looked at another one to my knowledge. That's about it really. Though I can't see as how any of what I've told you can tie in with the little girl that's gone missin'.'

'I'm afraid it may tie in very well,' the Inspector replied ominously. 'You see, Mrs Fitton, Robert Lawrence was stabbed to death in Leeds some months ago. Alice is Robert Lawrence's child and it appears that Nora knew it.'

The old woman's hand flew to her trembling lips. 'Oh my God! You surely don't think our Nora would have had anything to do with the stabbin' or the child's disappearance, do yer? She ain't a bad girl, yer know.'

'Let's not jump to any conclusions just yet.' His face was solemn. 'We'll find Nora and talk to her, and then we'll take it from there.'

Inspector Spooner beckoned to PC Tilbrook to follow him. Once they were out of earshot of the old lady, his voice took on a note of urgency. 'I want you to get the most recent picture of Nora that Mrs Fitton has to hand. Then get it out to all units. I don't like the way this is going. It sounds to me as if Nora could be the murderer of Robert Lawrence, and if she is, she's capable of harming Alice if she does have her. Now get to it as fast as you can. I have an awful feeling that from now on, every second will count.'

The officer nodded and disappeared back into the house.

The Inspector meantime threw himself into the waiting patrol car.

'Take me back to Headquarters – and put your foot down,' he barked. 'By tonight I want a picture of both

Alice *and* Nora on the front of every newspaper in the UK, and I also want a bulletin on the news, so step on it.'

The car screeched away from the kerb, leaving the net curtains in the street windows twitching uncontrollably.

Twenty-four hours later, the Inspector sat at his desk and knuckled the sleep from his eyes. The public had reacted immediately to the press releases telling of the little girl's disappearance. Almost every available car in the area was following up leads with people who thought that they might have seen her, or Nora. But as yet, neither of them had been found. He yawned and stretched wearily, knowing that soon he would have to give in and get some sleep. Now even the numerous mugs of black coffee he was consuming were failing to keep him awake, and yet still he was loath to go home, convinced that as soon as he did, there would be some news.

Through the glass-plated windows of the office he could see rows of police officers, all especially drafted in to help deal with the case, answering the phones and taking notes. Many of them were hoax calls, or people who just wanted to get their names in the paper, and he cursed every last one of them. He was only too aware now, that with every hour that passed, the chances of finding Alice alive were more and more remote. As a parent himself, he could only guess at the anguish that Jane Reynolds must be suffering. A picture of her deathly pale face floated before his eyes and his hands balled into fists of frustration. But still he stayed on, hoping and praying for the safe return of a little girl whom he had never even met.

At ten o'clock that evening, one of the policemen manning the phones took a call from a police station in Coventry. He flapped his hands urgently, demanding silence, and an expectant hush fell on the room. After listening intently he slammed the phone down and let out a whoop of delight that brought the Inspector running from the adjacent room.

'They've got her, Guv. They've got Nora Fitton. They're holding her at Little Parks Street in Coventry. What do you want me to tell them to do?'

The Inspector was already struggling into his coat as he headed towards the door. 'Tell them to keep her there. I'm on my way. And . . .' He paused, hardly daring to ask. 'Did they say if she had Alice with her?'

'No, Guv. She didn't. Apparently she was alone when they picked her up.'

Spooner's forehead creased into a frown as he hurried from the room. Luckily the roads were quiet, and twenty minutes later the police car, with its blue lights flashing, screeched to a halt outside Little Parks Street station. The Inspector ran up the stone steps, barrelling through the glass swing doors. Within seconds he was at the counter and flashing his ID card impatiently.

'Where are you holding Nora Fitton?' he demanded of the Sergeant at the desk.

'She's in the interview room, sir.'

Inspector Spooner was appalled. 'In the *interview* room? Surely she would have been better kept in a cell?'

'I doubt it, sir. And you'll see why in a minute. I'm afraid she's gone a bit mental, if you ask me. We've already sent for a doctor, and the duty solicitor is on his way as well.' Hastily he came from behind the desk and led Inspector Spooner and his two colleagues along a short corridor.

'She's in there,' he informed them, nodding towards a door. 'Everything's ready for you to begin questioning. But to be honest, I doubt you'll be able to get much sense out of her. We certainly haven't been able to.'

'As a matter of interest, where was she found?' The Inspector's hand was already on the door handle as he asked the question.

'We received a phone call from a person saying that they had seen someone matching Nora Fitton's description wandering around outside the ruins of Coventry Cathedral. We expected it to be another crank call, but we sent a car out to follow it up, just in case, and bingo, there she was, as large as life.'

'Have you got anyone looking for the child?' the inspector asked.

Again the Sergeant's head bobbed. 'Yes, sir. We have officers searching every inch of the ruins with torches even as we speak. They won't leave a stone unturned, I can assure you. If the child is there they'll find her.'

'Well done.' Spooner squared his shoulders and took a deep breath. 'Let's see if we can't get to the bottom of all this mess then, hey?' So saying, he strode purpose-fully into the interview room.

'Anythin' there then, Bill?' The policeman's voice echoed hollowly in the ruins as he called to his colleague. He wiped his forehead wearily as he straightened his back and stretched. It was almost one o'clock in the morning and he felt as if he hadn't been to bed for days. The atmosphere was strained and urgent, as all of the officers involved in the search realised that the chances of finding the missing child alive were slipping away with each hour that passed. Bill moved towards him, shaking his head, seeming to float through the eerie mist that drifted across the floor of the old cathedral. The cold clinging mist gave everything a ghostly appearance and did nothing to lift the spirits of the men. It was dark and deserted, and despite their best efforts they were no nearer to locating the whereabouts of the child. An hour later, the officer in charge of the search blew a whistle that pierced the silence of the old ruins and the dejected men all assem-bled back where they had started, their torches slicing through the darkness.

'That's it then, men. There's nothing here. We may as well admit defeat. She isn't here or we'd have found her by now.'

The men filed silently past him and at last he was alone with the cold statues that loomed out of the mist like spectres and stared down at him from blank stone eyes. He cast one last look at the impressive spire that stood as testimony to the once magnificent cathedral, offering up a silent prayer that Alice Lawrence might be found alive. Then with shoulders hunched he slowly passed the old stone altar and turned to follow his colleagues.

Nora sat quietly humming to herself at a table in the centre of the room. She seemed completely oblivious as to where she was or the people all around her. Across the table from her were two chairs, one already occupied by an experienced policewoman who would take notes, and one placed ready for DI Spooner.

The Inspector sat down heavily and glanced with concern at the WPC. 'Has she been like this ever since you brought her in?'

She nodded. 'Yes, sir. She hasn't said so much as a single word. Just sat there humming to herself.'

'Mm, I see.' He stroked his chin and shrugged. 'Ah, well. We may as well get started. Did someone say the doctor was on his way?'

'Yes, sir. He should be here any minute.'

'Good, then we'll begin. Could you take this down, please? Interview commencing at . . .'

Her fingers began to fly across the page, and thus commenced what was to become one of the longest nights of Bob Spooner's life.

'I'm sorry, but I'm afraid I'm going to have to halt the interview.' The doctor looked towards the Inspector, who wearily brushed the hair from his forehead.

'I suppose we may as well,' he agreed dejectedly. 'We

must have been questioning her for twenty minutes now, and she hasn't said so much as a word.'

'It appears that Miss Fitton has suffered some form of a mental breakdown,' the doctor informed him in hushed tones. 'Perhaps we should let her get some rest, and then start again in the morning?'

Seeing no alternative, the Inspector agreed. 'Has Miss Reynolds arrived yet?' He directed his question at an officer standing by the door.

'Yes, sir, she has. She's out there.' He inclined his head towards the corridor.

At that moment, Inspector Spooner wished that he could be a million miles away, for how could he go out there and tell Jane that the nightmare must continue? That they still had absolutely no idea where Alice was? Squaring his shoulders, he resolutely went to face her.

She was sitting on a hard bench in the corridor, with Glen and Lil on either side of her. In her arms she was clutching Alice's beloved doll, and the sight brought a lump to his throat. She looked up at him and for the first time since he had met her he saw that her eyes were alight with hope, a hope that he was about to quash.

'Has she told you where Alice is?' She flung the question at him before he even had time to span the distance between them.

'I'm afraid not,' he admitted, as gently as he could. 'It seems that Nora has had some sort of a mental breakdown. She doesn't even appear to know where she is herself, let alone where Alice is. But the doctor is in with her now, and by morning I'm hoping that she'll be able to talk to us.'

'*That's* no good!' Jane shouted at him. 'How can you stand there so calmly? Alice could be anywhere – she could be in danger. You've got to *make* her talk.'

Inspector Spooner was saved from having to answer, for just then the door to the interview room opened and Nora appeared, flanked on either side by the doctor and a WPC. Jane's eyes blazed with hatred. She sprang to her feet and before either Glen or Lil could stop her, she had covered the distance between them.

'Where is she? What have you done with her?' she screamed.

Nora didn't even flinch. In fact, she showed no sign of even having heard her. Shock and fear registered on Jane's face as she realised the state that Nora was in, and she stood staring. So rigid that she might have been set in stone.

The doctor glanced at her sympathetically, and then gently gripping Nora's arm he turned to lead her away to the cells. It was as he turned her that Nora's eyes fell on the doll in Jane's arms. Unexpectedly, she pulled away from him, causing him to stumble and fall back against the wall, then before anyone was even aware of what she was about to do, she snatched the doll from Jane's arms and cradled it tenderly against her chest. Once over her initial surprise, Jane made to snatch it back.

But the doctor held up his hand. 'No – leave her!' The urgency in his voice stayed Jane's hand in mid-air.

'So there you are, my darling,' Nora crooned, dropping a gentle kiss onto the plastic forehead. She rocked the doll to and fro and then she smiled and glanced up at Jane. 'This is my baby, you know? Robert's and mine. I lost her somewhere, but now I've found her again. Robert won't be able to take her away from me again because he's dead now. *I killed him* – because he made me lose our baby.'

Horrified, Jane looked into Nora's demented eyes. But Nora was oblivious to her distress and continued to gently rock her long-lost baby.

When Jane could stand the sight no longer she grabbed Nora's arm and shook it in desperation. 'Where is Alice, Nora? Tell me what you've done with her, I *beg* you.'

A sly smile curled the corners of Nora's lips. 'Alice was a bad girl. Evil – like her father. But it's all right. She's gone now, and my baby has come back. Look at her. Isn't she beautiful?'

Even as tears coursed down Jane's cheeks, a plan born of desperation sprang into her mind.

Gently now she again addressed Nora. 'Yes, Nora. She is a beautiful baby. And yes, you're right. Alice *is* bad . . .' The words threatened to stick in her throat and choke her, but she forced herself to go on. 'I need to find Alice, Nora, so that I can punish her for being so bad. She deserves to be punished, doesn't she? But the trouble is, I can't find her, because only you know where she is. If you were to tell me where she is, I would go away then, and I'd let you keep your baby forever this time. I'd make sure that Alice didn't disturb you, ever again. You do know where she is, don't you, Nora?'

Nora stared at her suspiciously, her tormented mind trying to decide if she could trust her. Then she cackled. A mad insane sound that made the hairs on the back of their necks stand up on end.

Nora leaned towards her. 'Do you promise that you'll let me keep my baby this time if I tell you? You won't try and take her away again?'

Jane nodded as she tried to still the trembling of her body.

'It's dark where Alice is,' Nora whispered. 'And it's cold. Alice was bad. But now she's gone, everything will be all right again, won't it? Robert won't be able to take my baby away from me again, will he?'

'Of course he won't,' Jane said shakily. 'You just tell me where that bad girl is and I'll make sure that she never disturbs you again either. Then you can be happy with your baby daughter.'

Nora came so close that Jane could feel her breath on her cheek. 'They'll think that Lil killed her.' She sniggered crazily. 'It's cold in the water, isn't it? She didn't want to go on the water. But she's quiet now.'

Suddenly, her ramblings ceased as abruptly as they had started, and she focused her attention on the doll, lost once more in her own private world.

Terrified, Jane turned to Inspector Spooner. 'What did she mean? Alice is somewhere cold. That could be anywhere, and how could she think that we'd think Lil had taken her?'

As the doctor led Nora away again, Glen suddenly leaped to his feet.

'I've got it!' he shouted triumphantly. 'Think about it. She said that we'd think that Lil had killed her and that Alice didn't want to go *on* the water. I don't mind betting Alice is on Lil's boat somewhere. That way, when she was found it would look like Lil had taken her.'

'My God. You could be right.' Inspector Spooner thumped Glen on the back, but his stomach was churning. After speaking to the police in Leeds he knew that Robert Lawrence had died from a frenzied knife attack. If Nora was capable of doing that to a full grown man, what might she have done to a defenceless child? Without wasting another second he turned to the Desk Sergeant and briskly gave Jane's address.

'I want an ambulance waiting for us when we get there,' he instructed. And then as one the group turned and hurried towards the door.

All the way home Jane prayed as she had never prayed before. Glen drove with his foot pressed tight to the floor, oblivious to the speed limit, with the police car close on his tail. The journey seemed endless but at last they tore into the drive of the farm to find an ambulance with its lights flashing, already waiting for them. Within seconds they had rounded the farmhouse and were speeding down the lawn. Breathlessly Lil fumbled in her bag for the boat keys. But immediately they set foot on board it was obvious that they would not be needed. The cabin door had been forced.

Inspector Spooner was the first to enter, as Lil, who was close on his heels, clicked on the overhead light. The small lounge with galley attached was neat and orderly just as Lil had left it, and Jane's heart sank. They moved on into the compact bedroom, and then into the tiny toilet and shower area. But again there was no sign of Alice. Glen's heart was bleeding as he looked at Jane's stricken face. He had been so sure that he was right.

A defeated silence settled on the group.

And it was then that Jane heard it. She pricked up her ears. 'Did you hear somethin'?' She looked at Glen but he shook his head.

'Ssh!' she commanded, and once again the silence descended. This time they all heard something and deeply shocked, they stared at each other. The Inspector began to fling open cupboard doors like a man possessed. Meanwhile Lil nodded towards the two long padded seats that ran down either side of the cabin.

'Help me lift these,' she ordered Glen. 'I keep me bits an' bobs underneath them. But I could have swore that's where the noise come from.'

Feverishly Glen heaved up the first one to reveal a selection of pots, pans, buckets and bowls. Then without pausing he turned to the opposite one. As he flung it aside, a strangled sob escaped Jane's lips.

Alice was lying with her hands and feet securely bound, and a length of sticky tape across her mouth. She blinked in the sudden light, and squinted up at them beseechingly from terrified eyes. Glen hoisted her from her prison and within seconds he had ripped the tape from her dry lips, causing her to cry out with pain and relief. Then he passed her to Jane and as she held the tiny figure close, crooning words of comfort, he fumbled with the ropes that bound her hands and feet. At last she was freed, and she clung to Jane as if she would never let her go. Someone brought a dressing gown they had found to wrap around the shivering child, who was cold, wet and in agony from cramp. Old Lil added a teaspoon of brandy to a tumbler of water and the child took a tiny sip. Tears like rain fell from every eye, not least of all Inspector Spooner's as Jane held close the child that she loved as her own.

'It's all right, me darlin',' she sobbed. 'You're safe now, and as God's me witness, I swear that no one will ever hurt you again.'

Contentedly Alice nestled further into Jane's arms and for a time Glen looked on, all the love he felt for them shining in his eyes. At last he leaned over and hoisted Alice protectively into his strong arms. 'Come on, my girls,' he whispered. 'It's time we were going home.'

Epilogue

> *'Happy birthday to you.*
> *Happy birthday to you.*
> *Happy birthday, dear Alice.*
> *Happy birthday to you!'*

Glen and Jane exchanged a smile, as Alice made a great show of blowing out the ten candles on her cake. Then everyone laughed, as Lil swiped at Susan's hand as it slyly reached out towards the cream on the top of a strawberry trifle.

'You little sod, you. Just wait yer turn, will yer, like everyone else.' Despite her harsh words the old woman's eyes were twinkling, as unconcerned, Susan licked her finger.

'There ain't nobody as can make a trifle like you, Grandma Lil,' she grinned cheekily, holding out her dish.

Lil waved a spoon at her. 'Well, you should know, madam. I've bloody made enough for yer, that's fer sure. I can't decide if yer come to see me or just come to fill up on me puddin's.'

463

'I'll let yer know when I decide which it is,' Susan chuckled, and Alice giggled as her friend ducked, just in time to avoid a clip round the ear.

Jane sighed contentedly as she watched Alice enjoying herself. She was surrounded by the new friends she had made at the village school – but Susan still remained special to her, and Jane felt that this was just as it should be. She flinched suddenly as the unborn child inside her kicked lustily, and Glen, who had noticed her expression, grinned.

'You needn't laugh,' she scolded as she waggled her finger at him. 'You wouldn't laugh if the little devil were playin' football inside you. I'll lay odds this is a lad makin' hisself felt.'

'I don't much care what it is,' he smiled, 'just as long as you're both all right. What do you say, Alice?'

'I don't mind either,' she admitted happily. 'But it would be nice if it could be one of each, then I'd get to have a brother *and* a sister all in one go.'

Glen looked at her with pride. She had changed almost beyond recognition from the timid little girl that she used to be. It had taken her a long time and a lot of professional help to get over the ordeal that she had suffered at Nora's hands. But now they knew that Nora was never likely to walk free again. Strangely, the resentment and hatred that they had initially felt towards her had turned to pity of a kind. Nora was so disturbed that she had never even stood trial for what she had done to Alice or Robert. Instead, she had been committed to Burntwood, a secure mental unit from which her chances of ever being released were slim.

Julia had informed them that all Nora did all day long was nurse the doll that had once belonged to Alice, believing it to be her long-lost baby daughter. Somehow her twisted mind had blamed Alice for keeping her father from her. But that was all in the past now, and Alice had a whole lifetime of love to look forward to – not to mention a new brother or sister.

The children scuttled away from the table, intent on a game of Pass the Parcel, and Glen organised them as best he could. Then once it was started he turned his attention to his wife. The bloom of pregnancy suited her and he thought he had never seen her look so lovely. Her cheeks had a glow to them and her red hair shone in the sunlight that streamed into the cosy room.

'Right then, madam,' he ordered. 'Get yourself up those stairs right now and put your feet up for an hour. There's nothing here that Lil and I can't see to, is there, Lil?'

'Absolutely not,' she agreed. 'You go an' do as yer husband tells yer. Otherwise it will be you as I'm takin' the spoon to.'

Laughing, Jane heaved herself unsteadily to her feet. 'You're nothin' but a pair of bullies, you are,' she complained, and for one precious moment her eyes locked with Glen's. A feeling of well-being swept over her as she saw the love she felt for him reflected in his eyes, and without further argument she waddled towards the stairs door.

'I'll just have half an hour,' she promised, and Alice looked up from her game and beamed at her. Then she looked back at her new friends and sighed contentedly. She had been at Michael Drayton, her new school, for over eighteen months now, and had loved every minute of it. Her school reports, she knew, were impressive to say the least, and she also knew that both her mam and her dad were very proud of her.

Their wedding had been one of the highlights of her life and when, soon after, they had informed her that she was to have a new baby brother or sister, she had thought that nothing could get any better. But she had been wrong again, for soon after *that*, Grandma Lil had moved in with them permanently, making everything just perfect. Or at least it would be when the baby was born. Alice herself had picked almost every single thing for the nursery, and now as the birth grew nearer her excitement was almost at fever pitch.

But for now she was not allowed to think of things to come, for her friends were impatient to be shown around the farm, so importantly, she rose and beckoned them all to follow her.

'I'm just going to show my friends around,' she told Glen and Lil, and they smiled as she led the stream of children towards the door, with Holly as usual, close on her heels.

Lil scratched her head and looked around at the mess. 'Bloody hell, it looks like a bomb's dropped, don't it?'

Glen began to scrape a flattened fairy cake off the carpet. 'It's nothing that can't be put right between us in no time.'

She nodded in agreement. 'Happen yer right, lad. But

before I even *think* about putting anythin' to rights, I want a nice, peaceful cup o' tea.'

The room next to Alice's had been decorated yet again – this time as a nursery. Unable to resist, Jane peeped in as she passed on the way to her own room. The sight never failed to bring a smile to her face. Alice had chosen all the colours, as well as the cot and most of the other things that the baby would need. Still, she had to pinch herself sometimes to believe that all this was really happening. It was like a dream come true. Gently, she closed the door, and paused as she heard Alice and her friends rampaging around happily outside.

'Do yer know what?' Jane heard Susan say, but before she could go on, Alice piped in.

'Yes, I know what,' she giggled. 'You're going to say – you've had the best time you've ever had!'

The place now rang with laughter, and at last Jane felt that her father's ghost had finally been laid to rest. He could never hurt her again.

She moved on and sank gratefully onto the king-sized bed that Glen had bought for their room. Her pregnancy had both troubled and delighted her for a start. She had been convinced that she was too old to have a baby. But thankfully, the pregnancy had been surprisingly trouble free, and now there were only three weeks left to go. Stroking her swollen stomach lovingly, she fell into a contented doze with the sound of laughter floating through the open window.

* * *

She felt rather than saw the presence at first, and turning on her side she blinked sleepily at a gentle-faced, red-haired woman who was standing by the bed.

'Hello, Mam.' She knew at once who the woman was, and the woman smiled, her beautiful smile that this time held a wealth of love and regret.

'I'm sorry I left you when I did, pet,' Joan Reynolds whispered. 'Your dad was such a bad man, but I should have tried harder to stay and keep you safe.'

'It's all right, Mam. I managed somehow. You don't need to worry any more now. You can go on and rest. This will be a happy house from now on, just as you always wanted it to be.'

The woman's eyes filled with tears that trembled on her dark lashes. 'I never really left you. Through it all I was there, looking out for you.'

'I know you were, Mam,' Jane whispered. 'When things got really bad, I could feel you near me. But like I said, you've no need to worry any more, it's time you went on.'

The presence began to fade.

'Goodbye, my love.' The gentle voice floated on the air as a solitary tear slid down Jane's cheek. Only the soft sweet smell of lavender remained.

Her unborn child kicked her sharply, bringing a smile back to her face. 'You just behave, me lad.' She ran her hands across her swollen belly. 'Else I'll have to fetch your big sister, an' your dad to sort you out.'

She relaxed into a deep and easy sleep.